Seasons

Volume Three

Shift of Power

a novel by

Jim Hicks

Righter Publishing Company
410 River Oaks Parkway
Timberlake, NC 27583

www.righterbooks.com

First Edition
April 2014

Printed and bound in the United States of America

ISBN 978-1-938527-25-8
Shift of Power
By James P. Hicks

Introduction

"All mankind is divided into three classes: those that are immovable, those that are movable, and those that move."

Benjamin Franklin

This series is dedicated to the people of the United States that sacrifice their lives, fortunes, and sacred honor to the preservation of liberty and self-determination found in the great American experiment. Our founding fathers warned us to guard against an overpowering central government establishing itself master-of-destiny over the fates of diminishing individual freedoms. If gone unchecked, the avarice nature of mankind to dominate his brother, would wield a power through the federal government too formidable for the individual to resist. The U.S. Constitution provides limited governmental authority by adhering to the rule of law in opposition to the rule of an aristocracy or a dictator. Even well-intentioned authoritarian power wielded through legislative or judicial means, directly conflicts with individual liberty. Freedom is embedded in the words of our Constitution.

Prologue

The United States no longer exists as a sovereign nation comprised of free people able to determine their own destiny. After a brutal financial collapse, the People's Planetary Revolution took the opportunity of a nuclear strike on Washington D.C., to usher in a communist form of authority over the United States.

The war has been raging for a year and a half as the militia attempts to unseat the green shirts and wrestle control of North Carolina from their grasp. This book chronicles the second fall and winter of the conflict from the point of view of the Colonel who ran 3rd militia. He is most widely known as the militia sniper, Huck.

The green shirts pull back to the major cities while the Sandys expand their foothold on the south. The militia is forced to decide the bigger threat to freedom, the green shirts, or the prospect of a foreign force poised for invasion.

While the next round of fighting looms, Huck faces a mercenary sniper determined to make his mark in the war. No area is safe; there is no refuge for the weary.

Defeat means tyranny; resolve and fortitude are the only steadfast companions of the militia.

Fall

"Momentum"

Chapter 1
Tank

My grandson, Jake, asked me to tell him my stories of resisting the green shirts back in the Second American Civil War. When he found out that I was the militia sniper known as Huck, he insisted we write a book of everything I can remember. Our last book was called, "Will to Resist," where we chronicled the second spring and summer under communist rule. This book covers the second fall and winter of the war. As I always say, "Let's begin where we left off the last time."

My stomach was telling me that I had missed supper. Whether it was the gnawing at my ribs, or the debris scattered on the floor, my stomach hurt. I was hungry, but this was no time for a meal. I lay on the floor behind the Remington sniper rifle with my eye behind the scope. My usual sniper rifle was wounded. A few weeks ago, an enemy sniper nearly punched my ticket. If my rifle and scope had not sucked up the bullet, I would have been dead. Replacement parts were scarce to say the least, back then. There was nothing in our inventory close to the quality of the Kreiger barrel my sniper rifle had before. Maybe someday I would find a new barrel and a good scope in my travels. That was a glass half-full kind of hope anyway.

However, targets out there needed my full attention. I lay in the back of an office some three floors off the ground in what used to be an office building, or perhaps a bank. Most of the windows were completely broken out on this side of the building. I think tank shells had been used to flush out the previous occupants. My camouflaged net was secured in front of me with all four corners tied off to desks and whatever else I could find at the moment. Wind whipped slightly, but the net that kept my image obscured did not move.

My spotter huddled beside me with his spotting scope and AR15 just to the outside of my left elbow. There was no room on my right. The sun was setting and it looked like we were going to lose the light in an hour or so. At least the weather was good. The days were clear and sunny with incredible 72 degree temperatures.

Low humidity and cool nights made you dream of bygone years playing golf with friends and having late summer barbeques. That was before the war, before the communist takeover of our nation, and before our resistance.

I scanned the machinegun nest I had been watching for the past three hours. There were still two occupants manning what looked to be a Russian RPK belt-fed gun behind a wall of sandbags. Their rooftop was only two stories tall, but it commanded a view over the surrounding one-story buildings lining the streets. We were sitting on the outskirts of Gastonia, a community to the west of Charlotte. Most of Gastonia and Charlotte were under control of the "Sandys," as we called them. That was what we called the Muslims coming in from various parts of the Middle East to be resettled in the western part of our state. The People's Planetary Revolution had convened a "Council of Equalization and Resources" that determined parts of the so-called Republic of America to be proportioned for immigration. Basically, the PPR and their communist green shirts thugs were redistributing parts of the United States to foreign powers. If you did not work for the PPR, or the Sandys, you were moved out. We had been fighting the green shirts for a little over a year now. The Sandys had only been in town for a few months and it was the militia's job to keep them contained.

I heard the radio crackle from the spotter's earpiece. Hushed chatter could be heard as the voices over the radio passed out codes and instructions.

My spotter whispered into the microphone, "Roger that. Out." He looked over at me as I lay motionless behind the rifle. "Colonel Huck, Sir, that's like the fourth time headquarters has called us. Maybe we should pull back and get you over there as requested."

"We can't pull out until dark," I told him. "This building is a perfect sniper hide and I bet these guys know it. They are waiting for us to make a move."

The spotter looked through his scope. "All I see are these two guys in the machinegun nest. Everyone else has pulled back. I think the shots we heard a little bit ago were off to the east."

"Take a look at the men in the nest again and tell me what you see," I told him without taking my eyes off the enemy position.

The spotter looked through the scope once again. "I see two Sandys in their standard tan uniform with the green splotches. I can't make out the unit patch from here." He paused and then began to speak again. "They have a Russian RPK, maybe a can or two of ammo, an AK-47, but I don't see anything else, Colonel."

"What do you see in the background?" I asked, leading the young spotter to search harder.

"Sir, I can't see into the bunker 'cause it's all dark under the cover they have," he said, a little exasperated.

I calmly responded, "Look at the guy on the left and tell me anything you can about him."

The spotter adjusted his scope a little and watched for a minute. "Sir, he has a pair of binoculars, he's been on the phone about a dozen times in the last hour, I don't know, maybe he's in charge?"

"You're getting warmer," I told him. "See his uniform? His insignia is on his shoulders. He's an officer. That guy hasn't picked up a weapon since he's been in the nest. Watch him look through the binoculars, and then write something out of sight. He keeps looking down because he is updating his map. That is a laser rangefinder, not just binoculars. He is a spotter for something else But for whom, or what, is he spotting?"

My spotter was quiet for a minute as he watched. "Colonel, what do you think he is doing?"

"I don't know. That is why we are not leaving until we have something useful to report. Besides, I don't want to break cover and risk finding out he has a battery of mortars waiting for us," I told him quietly.

We waited patiently for another half hour in silence. Shadows stretched to the east as the sun set in the west. Things that were visible before were obscured by shadow. I double checked to make sure my scope lens was covered properly and could not reflect what was left of the day's sunlight. We painstakingly waited.

Islamic call to prayers sounded from the mosque in the distance. It was common for this region nowadays. The Sandys controlled this whole freakin' city. The sing-song foreign language echoed off the walls of the deserted streets sending chills down my spine. Oddly enough, I didn't actually dislike the musical sounds of the prayer. But I knew that the people listening to the prayers were absolutely dedicated to conquering what was left of free North Carolina. I felt like I was in Turkey or Syria, not a mile outside Charlotte city limits.

"Sir, I have a target. Tank, M1 Abrams. Look down this street two blocks south of the machinegun nest, right side of the intersection. It's sitting at the gas station with the turret facing our direction. I couldn't see it until the sun bounced off the building's glass on the left," my spotter informed me in a rush.

I pulled the bipod of my Remington Police Sniper Rifle to the left and adjusted my natural point of aim. The gas station was visible from the reflected sunlight of the setting sun. Both garage doors were open, but the interiors contrasted black in the waning light. A metal roof covered the gas pumps and blocked almost all view of the bays. After several seconds, a cloud passed and sunlight once again shown off the windows from the opposite side of the street. The front of the tracks and the barrel of the Abrams tank were visible once again.

"Do we engage the crew then, sir?" my spotter asked still looking through his spotting scope.

"No, we just report this one. We couldn't get enough of the crew from this far out to make that much difference. We would be eating 105mm shells within seconds of dropping the first man," I told him in whispers. We were alone in the building, except for our base floor security squad.

"Let's pack it up and head for base," I ordered.

The spotter said, "yes, sir" and jumped to his feet to grab the 550 cord that held our camo netting in position.

I swiped at him with my free left hand and yanked on his trousers to get him back under cover. He had really screwed up. My spotter hesitated as he stood there completely exposed and let go of the net. As he dropped back to his belly a flurry of machinegun fire raked our office. The remaining window glass disintegrated. Chunks of glass flew around the room as bullet fragments ricocheted off of broken office furniture. Papers flew in all directions.

"Get to the hall!" I yelled over the din.

The spotter crawled to the doorway with me right behind him. I could hear the young man curse under his breath with each splattering of copper jacketed lead hitting the walls. We were in the hallway when the tank shell hit. It actually went through the wall of the office we had been in. Luckily for us, it detonated in the adjacent space and did not kill us outright. The whole world seemed to hum while chunks of wall fell away. Burned carpet smell and black smoke made us cough as we continued to crawl. The building shook at the thunderous explosion, and for a minute, I was not sure how much of the structure was intact or how long this building would stand. We made our way down the stairs only to see a couple of our security guys making their way up.

"You guys alright?" one of them asked.

"Yeah, but we are making a pit stop. We'll be down there in a bit," I shouted. "Be ready to move out!"

When we got to the second floor landing, I directed the spotter to the door.

"We have got to neutralize that spotter team," I commanded.

Machinegun fire still pounded the floor above. We worked our way as best we could to the nearest corner of the building towards the spotter team. This side of the building was not much better than where we had set up. The place was a deserted mess. I pointed the spotter to a position in the hallway where we could see through an open office door. The window of the office was partially broken, but allowed us a direct view of the machinegun nest.

"Shoot from here," I commanded over the din as I pulled the bipod legs open.

"From here, sir?" the spotter looked taken aback.

"Yes, now get down here and we will take both of those guys at the same time. Otherwise, one of them will get another shot at us," I ordered him.

My spotter quickly got into position and readied his rifle.

"Range it," I called out.

"Uh, let me see, sir. About 300 give or take a couple?"

"What are you talking about there, Sparky?" I asked, a bit miffed at the grossly underestimated distance. "The nest? It's closer to 375. Set for 400 and hold under just barely," I told him.

"You get the guy in the left and I will get the guy on the right. Ready?" I commanded.

"Ready, sir" he responded, trying to concentrate.

The machinegun stopped firing as the spotter and gunner tried to see if they had taken us out.

I called out, "One, Two,…" Blam! Blam!, we fired, not quite together.

Through the scope, I saw my target slump and fall to the side. My spotter's round hit the sandbag emplacement low of the intended target. I cycled my bolt and looked through my scope to see where the officer with the radio had ducked. We were on the same plane and the sandbags provided for his cover. I had seconds before he called in another 105mm shell to take us out.

"Shoot the left side of the bunker with about ten rounds and see if you can skip a few off the walls to wound him," I instructed.

I held the rifle steady as my spotter wailed away at the emplacement, sending hot 5.56 brass all over my left shoulder and neck. Somewhere around the eighth round, I saw the officer crawl to the opposite side of the bunker and grab the field phone off the sandbagged wall. I knew time was running out for one of us. Just as I was about to call it a day and leave, I saw my opportunity. The officer thought his position was pretty secure so he sat upright with his back against the sandbags. I couldn't see inside the bunker due to the darkness, but I could see the lights of the radio through my scope. It was then that I realized the man's head was the cause of the momentary shadows. So I trained on the radios lights and waited for them to go out. When they did, I fired.

"Sir, you got him. Holy Cow, you got him!" my spotter yelled aloud in sheer disbelief.

"Time to go, Son," I responded in a whisper. We crawled out of the hallway and met up with our security detail downstairs a minute or so later. After a few minutes of running through the dark streets, we made our way back to more secure lines. We were unhurt, but still shaken after the shots from a tank. I was just glad to have everyone in one piece.

"Good to work with you, sir," the spotter told me as I jumped into the waiting Suburban sent to pick me up. I handed off the Remington sniper rifle I had borrowed from the local sniper sergeant. The rifle's owner examined it to make sure I had given him his rifle back in one piece. Snipers are particular about their weapons. He wanted to know if his prized weapon, his baby, had been hurt in any way.

"Did you learn anything?" I asked my young spotter rather sternly.

"Yes, Sir," he responded with a deer in the headlights kind of look. He knew he had really messed up. He knew that his time in the 4th's sniper ranks was limited to say the least. I just hoped he would live long enough to learn enough to be an asset to our teams. I slapped him on the arm and told the team to be safe and we drove away.

Chapter Two
Politics

Fred, my best friend and fellow 3rd militia leader, looked around from the passenger seat of the Suburban, "I see you made it once again, Huck." He snickered the words as he looked at my uniform. I was covered in gunk from the dilapidated building. Bits of carpet, pulverized glass, and dust clung to me from crawling on the floor to get away from the machinegun.

"Next time I'm taking you with me, Fred. That kid nearly got us both killed," I told him. "He broke cover in the hide, miss-timed his shot and then missed his target. You can tell he is not one of our graduates."

Fred looked around again, "How did you get paired with him anyway? The kid looked to be around 18. I'm sure his momma would like to know the famous militia sniper, Huck, was protecting her precious son on his first operation." I threw a dirty glove at Fred's head as he chuckled at my expense. He knew the bounty on my head was pretty high during that time. I think the green shirts offered a year's supply of food rations or 1,000 state credits leading to my arrest.

"He was the only scout sniper with a radio when we got there," I told Fred. "When my truck picked up the call for sniper support, we were only a half mile away. So, I told them to stop and I went to go find out how I could help. The kid volunteered to spot for me, so I let him. Write a note to his team leader and have him re-assigned."

Fred threw the glove back to me, "So, let me get this straight. We are here for a high-level meeting, with all the top-brass, and you go out hunting on the way to the conference? Good gravy, Huck. No wonder they called you on the radio a hundred times. I wondered why Bull sent me to get you. Geez, Huck."

I hated it when Fred was right. I should have reported straight to headquarters, but when a unit is in trouble, I had a hard time sending someone else. Maybe that was a bad leadership trait. Maybe it was my natural hatred of long, drawn-out, boring meetings. I could hardly argue with Fred though. So, I didn't. We drove for quite some time and I tried to rest a little while I had time.

We arrived in the town of Bessemer City, or as they called it then, New Bessemer. This had been under green shirt control for the better part of a year, until the past summer. When the 4th militia attacked, Bessemer was purged of green shirts in order to support the containment of Gastonia. This town was the key to holding the rail lines coming from the south. Whoever controlled Bessemer controlled the southern routes of all railroads. Now, it served as 4th militia's headquarters.

My friend, the man they code-named Bull, was the 4th's Colonel. As strange fates determined our destiny, I was Colonel of the 3rd militia. However, Colonel for us was a little different. We only had around 100 volunteers and ran the training programs out of North Wilkesboro. My people were from the central part of the state, but had been displaced by the green shirts. The 4th had nearly 2,000 volunteers by this time and was growing fast. 1st militia had been wiped out during the first few months of the war last year. The 2nd operated in the eastern part of the state from Raleigh to the coast. The 5th militia was based around the central part of the state along the southern border with South Carolina. The militias, loyal to the United States, controlled the western regions of the state past highway 77. East of Raleigh was a toss-up. All major cities were controlled by the green shirts. The rural areas were more often than not, free of green shirt control.

Our operations over the last year had been successful enough to force the green shirts into a defensive posture around the major cities. The Sandys were something new this year. They were people brought in from the Middle East to re-settle the southern part of the US. The P.P.R. had such influence over the international community that they were able to shift people from country to country. It was all we could do to contain them for now.

The purpose of the conference was to get all our commands into some kind of cooperative coalition. My Suburban pulled into the parking lot of the 4th's headquarters. The facility was off the road a bit, offering a bit of seclusion from the main roads. We passed tent cities, containers that had been converted to field kitchens, and portable toilets. When we reached the building itself, it was huge. The parking lot was nearly full of cars. Trucks of all kinds, cars, minivans, and motorcycles ferried people in and out. The place was a hum of activity. We passed the security checkpoints and were ushered into the building by uniformed guards. Lights were subtle, but correctly placed for a defensive stance. The place was really in order.

A couple of security men escorted Fred and I through the building, leading us to an office that had been prepared for 3rd militia. Along the way, I saw dozens of volunteers working at desks and maps. It was close to 9p.m. and it looked like 9a.m. in a standard office in a major corporation. As we passed, I noticed an office for the 4th's intelligence group.

"Hey guys, I have to go in here for a minute," I told our escort.

I knocked on the door and introduced myself, to the surprise of the intelligence staff inside. I passed along my notes from the operation and indicated the intersection where we last saw the M1 Abrams tank.

A staff officer on watch said, "Thanks Colonel. We will update the maps and include your report in tomorrow's field report."

Then he stuck his hand out, smiling. "It's a pleasure to meet you, sir." I shook his hand feeling a little weird. A lot of that building was still stuck to my uniform. This guy had coffee on his desk and was as clean as a new penny. He smiled and thanked us for the update as I left with Fred.

Fred and I walked down the hallway as deadpan as usual. "Here's a pen, Huck." I took it from Fred, then looked a little confused. "Now you can sign the photographs on their desks."

I smiled and pushed him into some chairs lining the hall. My security escort turned around to see what was going on.

I pointed forward and joked, "Fred's tired. It's close to his bedtime." The two men shook their heads and pointed us to the first door on the right. The door read "3rd Militia Colonel". Fred caught up to us and followed me inside.

"If you need anything, sir, just dial two. Your staff is through that door. The bathroom is that door on the right. If you want something to eat, the cafeteria should be open for a few more minutes." Fred's eyebrows raised in surprise. "The couch folds out into a bed. The linens are underneath." We stood there in a little bit of a stupor. There was too much to take in. The office was really nice. A dark oak desk with a black leather chair sat in the middle of the room. Maps of North Carolina lined the wall. Book cases were filled with all sorts of manuals and reference material. Reports were already on my desk.

"Huck, I'm going to check out the cafeteria. I'll bring you something," Fred said, as he followed the security guys outside.

I looked around trying to figure out what to do first. Out of curiosity, I walked to the door where my staff was supposed to be. The door opened slowly and I looked through the crack to see three people at desks in the adjacent room.

A woman rose to her feet and looked at me from top to bottom. "Colonel, you've arrived. Your meeting has been postponed until 09:00 tomorrow. Your intelligence reports are on your desk. Messages from your wife and 3rd militia are there as well."

"Thanks," I said, not quite sure what to think. I never really had a staff before."You guys go home. Be back around 08:00 for crying out loud. It's late."

The lady smiled. "Sir, we are just your evening staff. The night shift will take over at midnight. Your day staff will be here at 07:00."

"Oh, carry on then." I couldn't think of anything else to say. I was tired and still hurting a bit from the operation.

I went back to my office and found the bathroom where I stripped down to my field pants. My scars were still red from my wounds received in the mission to retake the capitol back in the spring. The wounds dotted across my stomach and elbows were fresh glass cuts. There was not much bleeding, but nowadays it was just one more future scar. I wondered if my wife, Seven, would give me any grief for going on another sniper mission. She told me several times, "Colonels should not go on sniper missions. Train others and lead them. You don't have to fight every battle yourself."

I stood there looking in the mirror, wondering what to do next. Just then, a quick set of knocks announced a group of people barging into my office. It was Colonel Bull followed by what looked like a half dozen staffers and paparazzi.

In his booming voice Colonel Bull announced to the crowd, "This is the famous sniper, Huck, Colonel of the 3rd militia."

I leaned out of the open bathroom door still half dirty, shirtless, and, thankfully, in my pants, trying to clean up.

I saw eyes go from my head to my scarred shoulders and side. Several people quickly looked away ashamed. Everyone went silent.

Colonel Bull looked around at his followers as we stared at each other. "Let's let the good Colonel have some privacy." He ushered them outside and closed the door.

"Sorry, Huck. I heard you were in and thought I would introduce you to the local free-press."

I walked over to a clean T-shirt waiting for me. There was a Colonel's eagle imprinted on the shoulders with a large "3rd" printed on the front over the pocket. I dressed and walked over to Bull in sock feet and shook his hand, "No problem, Bull. The press?" I asked a bit curious.

"Yes, well, a lot has changed in the last couple of months." Bull told me. "After we took the green shirts and Sandys head-on, people have hope for the first time in over a year. You're a big part of that, Huck. Your raiders really made a name for yourselves. They have been talking about you all over the South."

"Well, great. That just means more people will recognize my face. I guess no more covert work."

Bull laughed and sat in one of the chairs around my desk, "How is Rocket?"

"Your son is fine, last I heard," I told him, smiling. He is back up in North Wilkesboro training motorcycle scouts. He really did a good job with the Raiders."

"Good," Bull responded. "Don't cut him any slack just because he's *my* boy. I don't want anybody promoted just because they are somebody's brother, or son, or whatever."

"He's earned his way, Bull. So, what is all this about?" I asked and pointed to the lavish office.

Bull looked around, choosing his words carefully, thinking how to respond. "Huck, things are going well. Really well."He stood up and paced while I sat down behind the desk."We are entering a new phase that none of us ever really considered until now. The green shirts have retreated to the major cities. They are on a defensive posture for the first time since the takeover. The Sandys are more of a military threat than the green shirts now. We are almost as strong as they are. I hope to surpass them by Spring."

I looked at Bull, "Uh, huh. What's coming Bull?"

Bull looked at me, "How many volunteers and staff do you have right now in 3rd militia?

I thought for a second, "Right before I left, our rosters were close to 100.Why?"

"Huck, thanks to the 3rd's efforts in training recruits, we have close to three thousand fighters in the field right now. We are growing so fast we don't know what to do with all the people coming in. It takes a lot of time to train new people in all the jobs we need filled. I've got to have cooks, mechanics, plumbers, and God knows what else or we will not function as effective as we could. Ex-military guys, Army and Marines, are coming our way for the first time. They heard of your exploits and are taking the revolution and the militia seriously now. They need to be used to their full talents. People are looking at us as the new government, not just a fighting force."

"What does that have to do with me and the 3rd? " I asked a bit warily.

"The meeting tomorrow is going to decide the direction of our state. They are going to elect me as the first militia general. We are going to create a general staff and head up all militia groups throughout the state. I want to fold the 3rd into one of the other commands or make you guys the training and standards unit."

I thought hard for a solid minute, not saying a word.

Bull continued before I could speak. "Of course, you will retain your rank either way. We will want to get you out there promoting the war effort, banging the war drum. Your people can handle training on a day to day basis. You will have resources, we will get you land for ranges, weapons, ammo, whatever you need. And, when this is all over you will be a famous war hero. They may want you as Governor or maybe Senator when this is all over."

It was too hard to grasp the whole vision of a time after the green shirts. After the war was too far away to comprehend. We were still fighting, not thinking about who was going to be Governor, for crying out loud.

I spoke a little harshly. "Bull, I have zero time for politics. I lead a highly motivated group of individuals that will not be content to run schools forever. Our intelligence group is top shelf in anybody's book. We need to be fighting. I, need to keep fighting."

Bull looked down at me. "I see what you mean." He looked at the little wet splotches of blood that had not been bandaged yet. "We have to train new troops, though. The people coming out of your basic training and sniper programs are essential to winning the war. It's your duty to get our people qualified to fight properly. The majority of our recruits are civilians that are not happy working on the farms."

"I know, Bull," I responded flatly. Training or lack thereof is what cost the Japanese the air war in WWII. They never rotated their experienced pilots back home to train the new guys. When they lost their front line, only pilots barely qualified to fly, were up against our fully trained flyers. I see that in some of your people from the 4th I worked with today."

Bull was a bit surprised. "So, you'll do it then?"

"Yes, I will set up your schools and get them going. The schools themselves can be their own command for all I care. But I want the 3rd to remain a fighting force. We can be a special forces unit or intelligence group. I don't care what we call it, but we have to stay in the fight."

Bull took in my request and thought hard. I knew he wanted me to lead the schools, not just get them running. He also wanted my name in front of the press and new recruits to give them motivation. He was getting a little too concerned with politics for my taste. The last thing I wanted to be was somebody's poster boy.

We sat there and stared at each other for minutes, waiting for the other to speak first.

The door opened and Fred walked in with plates in his hand. "Huck, they have pot roast and cornbread!" He looked over and saw Bull in the chair and did not bat an eye." Hey Bull, good to see ya," Fred tried to shake his hand or salute, but the plates were in the way. After some shuffling and mess, he did both. Fred was not the military drill and ceremony type. Somehow, nobody expected it of him.

Bull got up and went to the door. "Alright, Huck. I'll send some staffers your way after the meeting tomorrow. We can start to hammer out the details later this week. Why don't you call Seven to come down here and we will find you a nice little house."

"See you later, Bull," I waved to him as he left. He and I both knew our conversation was far from over. He wanted his training commander and war hero all wrapped into one little package. I wanted to keep in the fight.

I told Fred about Bull's intentions for the 3rd and the request for us to be the trainers for the entire militia. Between bites of pot-roast, Fred used some choice words about Bull's mother. In all honesty it could have been a plate of dead sea-monkeys for all I cared. This was a feast on a Styrofoam plate. After a while, Fred and I sacked out on each of the two fold-out couches. To us, this place was the lap of luxury.

By 07:00 the offices were a buzz of activity. Fred and I woke to staffers coming in to get us ready for the big meeting. Our new uniforms had all our names and rank. We were just as shiny as everybody else in that building. It felt weird really, almost surreal. We had been living so meagerly over the last year, it almost seemed rude somehow to be so dressed up and well cared for by staff. There were still hungry people in the state without electricity or running water. It would be different if the war were over.

Fred and I left the office among a throng of reporters who were only allowed to ask questions in the hallway. Our offices were, thankfully, off-limits. We tried to make our way to the conference room, but were hounded with questions along the way as cameras flashed and microphones were shoved in our faces.

"Colonel, what is your opinion of the war with the green shirts?"

"Colonel, Huck. Are you aware of the bounty set on your head? Reports claim the green shirts are offering 1,000 state credits."

"Colonel, can you tell us anything about your raid and Huck's Raiders?"

"What can you tell us about the 3rd militia?"

Thankfully, the reporters talked so quickly over each other that Fred and I were not able to answer. Security forces stopped them short of the rooms designated for the conference. At least some of the other commanders were able to attend without the press hounding them. I was more than a little upset that my picture was all over the place now. In my opinion it was a major security breach because the green shirts didn't need to know my whereabouts. Just how secure did Bull think his little fortress was here?

The conference room was already half full of leaders and subordinates. Several faces turned to Fred and me as we entered. I recognized a few of them, although most of the other militia commands had new people in charge since our failed attempt to retake the capital back in the March Madness operation. In the last six months, everyone had to regroup. I made my way around the room and shook hands with just about everybody. I caught Fred watching me several times as he sat back and shook his head slowly. Fred never resented my fame; he just couldn't believe I was famous. Several people in suits introduced themselves as politicians hoping for seats in a new state senate. That seemed pretty far off to me. There was still too much fighting to think about any of that stuff right now.

The conference started promptly at 0:900 with introductions around the table. All the commands were represented. I thumbed through the agenda and immediately looked for a coffee pot. This was going to take forever. These things never got to me before, but this meeting was getting under my nerves.

The first few hours were boring introductions, who was doing what, problems with supply, and so forth. To Bull's credit, he orchestrated the meeting with several breaks. He realized that deals were really negotiated over doughnuts and coffee. The first two hours were like the opening rounds of a heavyweight boxing match. Nobody got too heated, big subjects were avoided, and more information was passed from group to group.

Then, Bull asked me to outline the basic training program the 3rd was operating in North Wilkesboro. I knew he wanted to broach the subject off and on during the conference until he got other commands to buy into the concept of a single training effort. I gave a lecture using the dry erase board. I spoke for 20 minutes with several of the leaders commenting on how their training efforts differed. Some commands had never standardized on equipment and as a result, were not able to handle complex operations. They simply could not support men in the field with the appropriate supplies. Another command was getting ex-military who resented the concept of basic training from the mostly-civilian militia.

Right before lunch, Bull took the podium and presented the idea of a single training effort.

"That is *if* the famous sniper, Huck, would lead it."

I looked over at Bull as the leaders considered his proposal. He looked at me, but briefly. He was lucky I didn't have a gun. I was fuming, too angry to speak. For several minutes, the delegates talked about how they could incorporate a common equipment standard along with a doctrine of how to fight using non-standard soldiers. They were buying into the concept.

We broke for lunch as the cafeteria brought in food. I marched out of the room into the quiet hallway. Bull followed me after a few minutes when he could get away.

I ambushed him as he came out of the room. "Just where do you come off setting me up like that? I told you I have no time for politics! I meant it."

Bull answered back quickly. "Huck, you need to do this. You're fame will bring in a lot of volunteers. The civilians know you and will come into the ranks by the droves. The ex-military will look up to you. It's your duty to do this."

I got in Bull's face. "Don't you ever forget that every one of these men is volunteers. They are here on their own. None of us are bound by anything other than our will to participate!"

Bull responded while I spoke. "So, what is it then? Will you quit if I assign this command to you?"

"What I am trying to tell you, Bull, is that you don't have the authority to order other commands around. Don't assume you have more power than the *will* of your people that follow you. We have been fighting that mentality for a year already!" We were both red-faced.

About that time Fred poked his head out of the door. "You guys want to take it out to the playground? I can sell tickets," he gestured towards the conference room with his thumb.

Bull and I looked at him, realizing that our voices had carried far beyond our intention.

"Alright, let's clear this up right now," I said as I marched back into the room.

Bull followed, "Huck, now hang on a second…"

The delegates sat around the tables with sandwiches and so forth and stared as I marched into the room.

I got to the podium. "Gentlemen, I have no time for politics or games. I need to make my position clear. We do need a standard training program. We need clear standards across all commands. I will be glad to help start your training courses, if you think it will help your organizations. But, I am not the person to lead this effort for the rest of the war. Bull seems to think so. However, the 3rd militia will support you by providing cadre that will get your people up to speed. But, we are going to be a fighting force again. We have not yet begun to fight."

Eyebrows rose throughout the room, followed by chuckles and one Colonel who said aloud, "Damn." The room was as silent as a tomb as the delegates stared at each other.

I walked over to the buffet and slapped some food on my plate while the rest of the room tried to get a handle on what I had just said. A round of laughter broke out as I sat and ate. By the time they stopped, grown men were wiping tears off their face.

"That's *some* politics, Huck."

The meeting resumed after a while. Bull seemed to understand how passionate I was about the subject, and didn't bring it up again. A couple of hours later, we took a break before the vote to make Bull the general of the 1st militia army group.

The 5th's Colonel got me to the side and away from people that could overhear. "Colonel, Huck? Can I have word with you?"

"Yeah, sure. What is it?" I asked him.

He continued with his head down, speaking quietly. "I was just wondering if we are voting on the right person."

I took a second. "I don't want to run a school. Do you really think I want to run an entire army?"

The Colonel looked at me. "You could, you know. We need people like you. No nonsense, get it out in the open, no matter the consequences, get it done."

"Not me, Colonel. I agree, but you gotta find someone else," I told him. "As for me, Bull is the right man for the job."

The 5th's Colonel looked at me a little surprised.

When we returned to the conference, I volunteered to vote first, "Aye."

When it was said and done, Bull won the vote. We now had a consolidated army. The 1st North Carolina Militia Army was a reality. Each militia command became a battalion. As such, I was referred to as the Colonel of 3rd battalion, 1stNC Army. As I look back, I think that is when the war turned for us.

When the day's meetings were over, I went back to my office and made a few calls. It had been a couple of weeks since the Sandys infiltrated North Wilkesboro. Our phone system was up and running again. Data, our PC geek, had found ways to make the network more secure since we were getting more support from outlying telephone systems in other towns. He was even getting a satellite up-link so we could communicate with other states outside of our geographic region. It would be the first real contact with places like free Texas. Our hopes were high.

I called the Wooten Valley convenience store where I knew Seven waited to hear from me. She answered the phone with the sounds of a crowd behind her. Everyone was waiting to hear the results of the conference. I relayed the large-picture details in terms that were easy to repeat out loud or on the speaker phone. Our folks liked the idea of being the training arm until I told them the intention was for us to do nothing else. Upon that tidbit, I heard a blast of feedback. Nobody was signing off to be an instructor forever. My folks had a lot of fighting spirit for people that were displaced one time already. After a while, Seven took the phone off speaker and we spoke privately.

"So, I hear you had an interesting time getting to the conference," Seven told me.

Good gravy, there were times I hated her being in the intelligence group. She had likely seen the sniper report I submitted since the tank was involved.

"Yes, dear," I responded hesitantly. "The unit needed some support and we were close by. No big deal."

"Oh, yeah, a tank is no big deal. Maybe I can tell that to our baby when his dad doesn't come home. Or, I can show him the green shirt report that it was likely the militia sniper known as Huck in the building."

"Wait, what?" I asked."You said him? You think the baby is a him?"

Seven scolded back at me, "Don't you try to change the subject. But, yes I think it's a him. He has been kicking a lot today. Annoying after a while, just like his dad."

"Seven, I've got to go. Try not to have the baby till I get back," I told her.

"Take care, Huck. Please don't go out unless you have to. You are the Colonel and you have to make it back before the baby comes."

"I will. Bye." and we hung up. Fred called his wife and after a while we sacked out in the office again. It still felt weird to have a staff. Every few hours, people would come into the office and give us updated reports on the battle for Charlotte.

Around 04:00 the staff came in and turned on the lights in my office.

"Sir, we need to get you and Mr. Fred to the conference location."

"The wha...? I asked blearily, trying to wake up.

"Sir, the general has called all the senior staff to a new location for the remainder of the conference."

Fred was still snoring as the staffer-lady left. With more than a little effort, we both got dressed and gathered our gear. Security details ushered us and our staff to waiting vehicles by 04:30. An entire column of vehicles sped us off to the west and drove a series of back roads. An hour passed before we finally arrived at our new location in the town of Rutherfordton. It was still dark when we pulled up to a remote office building that looked deserted from the outside. The place may have been a medical facility before the war. We parked in the adjacent parking deck and walked inside among armed security and covered walkways. I must admit that I felt better being an hour from Charlotte and all the fighting. This was far more secure for so many of our leadership to gather.

Once inside, the scene changed. The cool night air gave way to lights and central heating. The place was also a hum of activity. I could see surprise on everyone's faces as we entered.

"Welcome to the 1stNC Army headquarters ladies and gentlemen. Please proceed to the second floor for your offices and conference room," one of the local security people greeted us. "Your staff will be arriving in the next few hours with all your office gear."

This place was just as nice as the one we had left an hour ago. We settled into new offices, again, with our names on the doors. The rooms were mainly bare as I imagined the people I met the day before loading old Xerox boxes with all the office stuff. A very large conference room waited for us with maps, pads of paper, and pitchers of water. Bull had really gone to a lot of trouble to prepare this place.

After a bit of rest and some breakfast, the conference was re-convened.

Bull's people ushered us into the room as dawn broke. "Everybody come on in. We have a lot to discuss and there is information we need to pass to your commands."

We all sat around the table and noticed that there were no politicians among us this time. This was all senior militia staff with very few aids.

Bull stood at the podium as the last of our group sat. "Good morning everyone. Thank you all for bearing with me. The facility where you came from is a fake. All the activity you saw there was a complete farce for the local press. All the troops you saw on the grounds have been moved and by lunch you will never know we were ever there. We wanted to draw the Sandys into a trap. We suspect some of the local press to be passing along information to either green shirt operatives or the Sandys directly. We also wanted to see how plugged-in they are to our operations."

Murmuring spread through the leaders. I, for one, was relieved to hear it. That place was way too close to the fighting for my taste, way too open.

Fred leaned over and whispered in my ear, "I hope they brought that cafeteria and some of that pot roast." He said it so deadpan that I almost cackled out loud. Luckily, my snort was camouflaged as a sneeze and one guy on the other side of the table actually said, "Bless you." I nearly died trying to stifle the intense urge to laugh. Fred tried to hand me a tissue looking all concerned. That surely didn't help things. The meeting continued as tears ran down my face.

After a few briefings from local commanders, the projectors showed the real progress of our Charlotte operation. The Sandys were contained at the moment. Our largest problems were the rail-lines leading to the east and the port city of Wilmington. Our men had to watch out for the green shirts around Fayetteville, Fort Bragg, and Pope Air Force base while trying to stop the trains. It was a daunting task to cover a 200 mile stretch of track. What few green shirt air assets remained, patrolled when trains came in from the coast. We had to stop the import of supplies if we were going to kick the Sandys out.

It seemed the green shirts had stopped their efforts to keep highway 77 open to the north. The loss of their armored task force really changed their plans. Most reports showed that the green shirts were consolidating into the major cities leaving only token forces in key rural areas. Presumably, the green shirts wanted to maintain control over crop production. Green shirt offices were closing in smaller communities and their personnel were sent to Raleigh, Durham, Greensboro, and the like.

Overall it was looking good for us and our movement. We had recovered a good portion of our strength even after our failed coup attempt in Raleigh back in the spring.

The Colonel from 2nd Battalion, who oversaw Wilmington, chimed in. "We cannot allow the Sandys to keep bringing in troops and supplies through Wilmington. I need heavier weapons and more men if we are going to close the ports. The Sandys brought in some serious firepower and there is no way we can cover the whole eastern part of the state *AND* close down a place the size of Wilmington."

Bull was silent for a moment pondering the situation. Then he looked over to the 5th battalion Colonel. "What does it look like around Fayetteville? Can we count on disbanded Army personnel to help us?"

The 5th's Colonel looked at him and passed a report that had been prepared. "General Bull, we are getting more and more volunteers from disbanded Army personnel every day. But we are having a devil of a time trying to get them equipped. The green shirts realized early on that ex-military could cause them problems. The green shirts went around and destroyed almost all the weapons in the depots. You have more firepower here in this county than our entire area of operations."

General Bull looked back to the 2nd battalion Colonel. "What about Marines out of Lejune? Are we getting volunteers from there?"

The Colonel looked back with hesitation. "Sir, we have been getting a few, but we are having a hard time getting them to join the militia. Those that have avoided arrest have kept to themselves or formed small cliques. They are not team players."

That got my attention. "Marines not team players?" I asked out loud in disbelief.

Fred sat back in his chair and covered his mouth. "Oh Lordy, Huck."

The room fell silent at my question.

I continued, "You've got to reach out to all our ex-military and teach them what we are all about. Appeal to their sense of patriotism. You have to take into account the command structure they are used to, and let them form their opinions by working with your teams."

The 2nd's Colonel looked back at me with contempt. "We have been trying to get them to conform, but they will not listen. They think we are a joke, inferior compared to their so-called skills. Every time we try to integrate them, it fails and we lose volunteers."

I retorted, "Marines are all about the challenge of the fight. If you try to have a pissing contest to see who is better, you will never gain their respect."

The 2nd's Colonel looked away from me and stared forward. "Yeah, and just how many Marines do you have in your command, Huck?"

"Captain Gunny has been with my unit for more than a year," I told him flatly.

One of the other men from the 5th's command asked incredulously, "You mean you turned an ex-gunnery sergeant into a *Captain* in 3rd militia?

"Yes, Gunny didn't like it at first, but he really gets the job done. He's the one that runs our sniper training program."

General Bull chimed in as the others sat back and grinned. "That is why Huck would be so affective in recruiting."

I looked over at Bull and smirked. The 2nd's Colonel was upset to say the least, but had nothing left to argue about. His background was not military and he was evidently having a hard time getting into the right mindset to pull in ex-soldiers. He may have been a councilman or banker before the green shirt takeover, I don't recall. Either way, I was concerned that his leadership would be a problem if we were to really take the fight to Wilmington to close the ports.

During breaks in the conference, Fred and I worked from our new office and looked at the local maps.

"Fred, move that marker out to this street," I said.

"Huck, we need to get an update from Bravo company. They were supposed to attack that sector yesterday. I haven't seen how far they got."

"Let's get an update from that guy in there," I stammered, not knowing what to call the staffer.

Fred looked at me. "Just call him in here."

"What's his name then?" I asked Fred.

"I don't know," Fred admitted as he walked to the door and stuck his head through. I could hear Fred say, "Hey! You in the shirt there, bring us the Bravo company report from yesterday's battle, or raid, or whatever."

I looked over at Fred who sat back at the desk beside me. "You are hard-core militia Fred."

He stuck his chin out like he was sitting for a portrait, "Ain't I?"We went back to work as best we could between laughter.

The third day of the conference was of particular interest to me. We met in the conference room as usual, while some of the intelligence squirrels gave their briefing.

"Gentlemen we have been compiling these reports from sources all over the US. Ham radio operators, green shirt news, limited internet, and captured documents have been compiled for this one report. We are sharing it with some of the other resistance groups in other parts of the country."

The lights went dim and the projector screen flashed the first shot of the Southern states. The states were outlined in white against a black background. The zones colored in green were green shirt controlled areas while tan blotches showed the imports from the Middle East. Red zones were militia strong holds. There was a little legend on the side to remind you what color stood for what group. I was surprised to see a lot of black areas indicating no one group dominated the area.

"Gentlemen, we don't have many reports from areas south of Tampa. We expect that the Central American countries still hold a major part of Florida south of Jacksonville. We show that area light green since the PPR orchestrated their invasion. As you will see, the PPR has tried to make Georgia their gateway entry point for the South."

He took a laser pointer and followed a line from Savanna, through Macon, and on to Atlanta. They were all tan. The routes leading to Columbia South Carolina from Atlanta were tan. Relatively little pockets of green shirt influence dotted the larger cities not occupied by the Sandys. Most of the south was the same. The majority of the states were uncontrolled from a geographical point of view. Yet in almost every instance, the Sandys had taken over a port city and charged inland from there. They kept the ports open and the lines between them open. South Carolina was mostly uncontrolled. There was little green shirt activity anywhere in their state, other than the capitol.

"Gentlemen if you look at Alabama, old Miss, and Louisiana, you will see pretty much the same picture. The green shirts hold the major cities while the Sandys control Montgomery and Jackson. Reports suggest that the defense contractors have been moved north by the green shirts. Pretty much all of the Lockheed, General Dynamics, and so forth have moved a large portion of their facilities into green shirt territory."

"What does it look like up north?" another Colonel asked.

The presenter said, "Well sir, the picture up there is incomplete. It looks like Virginia is pretty wide open when you get away from DC or anywhere west of I-95.West Virginia has spots of green shirts along the major roadways. Kentucky is the same way. But most of the northeast is under the very firm grip of the green shirts. It looks like there are no foreigners coming in north of us. Charlotte is the northern-most outpost."

Fred chimed in with the usual hushed tones he had learned in a saw mill. "That makes sense, if you think about it."

The whole room looked over at him with question in their faces.

Before I could think, he spoke again as he walked to the screen. "If you are the PPR, or the green shirts, you know the South is going to give you the most trouble. The green shirts don't have the people to pacify us all. They just want the major cities so they can control what's left of our economy and whatever resources they need." He pointed to all the cities with green splotches. "Then they tell all their Arab buddies to go settle in areas that will keep us native troublemakers busy for a while. What do they care if the Arabs take over the South? They have their little Carl Marx utopia up there in the Northeast."

We all shared glances around the room. Fred was right. I was surprised he knew who Carl Marx was.I'm sure he couldn't spell utopia, but I sure was proud of him at that moment. Fred had made everything come into to focus for us. He was right.

General Bull said rather stoically, "Fred, you might be right. We will have to see what we can do to confirm what you said. Good thinking. Now gentlemen, let's get to the next topic. What do we estimate for population losses to date?"

The room fell silent as the Intel presenter passed off to another person in the room.

He started, "Well sir, as you will see in a couple of slides….we cannot be for certain, but it looks like 22% of our state is either displaced or feared deceased."

The room filled with gasps and whispers.

"How did you come by that number?" one of the Colonels asked.

"Well sir, we used the census from a few years ago as our starting point. We estimated the number of military that were stationed here, but were let go while deployed. "Blah, blah, blah... This techno-speak was what I hated about these meetings. We got through it, but I was ready leave by the time they called for lunch.

After lunch, General Bull introduced a man that had just come in from free Texas. Our delegates murmured as the man approached the podium. He was tall, 6'-4", with a chiseled chin. He could have been a tight-end or a state trooper by the looks of him. We had not met anyone from Texas since the green shirt takeover.

Colonel Bull tried to quiet the meeting. "This is a representative from the Texas Rangers. He has come here to give us a briefing on how things are going in his neck of the woods. He has information on the western states and is here to form an alliance with our efforts here in the South."

The murmuring continued with several men blurting out questions all at once.

"Will you be able to get us more gasoline?"

"What is the status of the Mexican border?"

"What happened in California?"

Those and a million other things were blurted out. We wanted information really badly. I sat quietly, trying to listen to the flurry of questions. Fred leaned over to me and whispered, "So, do we call him the Lone Ranger then? I mean, we already had Tonto for Pete's sake. I thought they all wore cowboy hats down there."

I cracked out loud at Fred's observation. The momentary distraction allowed Bull to get back in control of the meeting. The Ranger reported that Texas' border was contested militarily on a weekly basis. All along the Southern border drug cartels and Federalis tried to poke holes in the Texan defensive lines. The northern and eastern borders along Oklahoma, Arkansas, and Louisiana were contested by green shirt forces. The western border of Texas with New Mexico was hardest to identify and draw. The vastness of the desert contributed to the difficulty of identifying actual borders. Overall, Texas' size kept almost all their units on border defense. In essence, an offensive strike from Texas was not coming any time soon.

The Ranger told us that what was left of California, Oregon, Washington, and Colorado was under green shirt control. From Idaho to western Minnesota was free territory, although the green shirts claimed that those states were under their control officially. Arizona, New Mexico, some parts of southern California, and southern Nevada were controlled by a mixture of Mexican nationals and drug cartels. The northeast was under strict green shirt military rule. Only a few rural areas from western Pennsylvania to southern Illinois had pockets of freedom. Otherwise, the green shirts were in complete control of the north.

The south, as we knew first hand, was ham-strung in the major cities by the green shirts. Every month that followed, saw an increase in the number of foreigners coming in through the ports. We were being displaced while just enough pressure was applied to Texas to keep them on a defensive posture.

The Ranger concluded his presentation and allowed the rest of us to discuss what he presented. Our men gathered around in groups and talked among themselves.

"Hey there,....Silver," Fred called out to the Ranger. I don't know what got into Fred that day.He was nothing short of being a class-A goof.

"What'd you call me, son?" the Ranger asked as if he didn't hear it. He and General Bull looked at each other as if to question what they both heard was correct. I clapped Fred on the shoulder. He didn't seem to care that the guy was about twice his size and was someone you didn't want to piss off.

Fred continued, "I said, Silver. You know, like the Lone Ranger's horse. I think that's what we should call you. We all use code names around here." Fred continued as deadpan as only he could do.

"You are calling me the horse?" the Ranger asked incredulously. He stepped over to Fred and me, until we were looking up at his chin.

Fred looked up at him. "Well, I thought Spurs was a bit much." I had to chuckle at that. Until then, there was a bit of tension.

The Ranger looked down at us and smiled as he grabbed us both by the shoulders and squeezed us in a giant bear hug. He and the rest of the room busted out in laughter at Fred's suggestion. I was just glad I didn't have to clean Fred off the floor. You could feel Silver's strength in his grasp. If he wanted, he could have squashed us until our eyes popped out. And yes, the codename stuck.

After Silver caught his breath, he asked, "So what do they call you?"

Fred looked at him as deadpan as usual, "Fred."

Silver looked taken back for a second. "Why?"

Fred responded as if everyone knew. "That's my name."

Silver looked around as everyone else in the room considered it for the first time. Fred had always been Fred. Nobody ever questioned it before now.

Once the laughter died down, Fred asked, "So, what do you have in the case?" He pointed to a black Pelican case by the door.

"Oh, that's a present for one of your snipers from 3rd militia. He's the one we read about on the free internet. They call him Huck. Do you know anyone from the 3rd that can get it to him?"

Fred looked back at him in amazement. "You've heard of Huck all the way in Texas?"

Silver grabbed the case and brought it to the table where he unlocked it. "Oh yeah, we hear Huck stories on free-radio and on the web when we can get through to your area. Some Star Trek fan keeps everybody posted on what Huck does. Fella calls himself Data."

Fred chuckled at that one and I made a mental note to have a word with Data about operational security. I never gave him permission to spread stories about me.

Silver looked to Fred. "So, Fred, do you think you could point me in his direction?"

I raised my hand as if in school.

"Can you get it to him?" Silver asked me.

"I'm Huck." I told him flatly.

"You?" Silver looked at me closer from top to bottom. He couldn't believe I was the guy behind all the stories and was not sure if I was kidding. "There's not two of you, is there? "Silver turned to Bull for confirmation. Bull loved this exchange and smiled as he shook his head.

"It's just me." I told him. "I'm Colonel Huck now, of 3rdbattalion. We've consolidated into the 1st North Carolina Army group."

Silver said, "Well, this is for you then. My boss, the man that runs the Rangers, heard you needed a new rifle after yours was *wounded.*" Fred rolled his eyes in disbelief.

Silver raised the lid of a black plastic pelican case that was simply marked "for Huck" .Inside lay a brand new, never fired, IRA-X, *Thor.* To most people that sounds like a comic book hero that carried a big hammer. To me, it was the rifle equivalent of a sports car on par with Ferrari. The Thor was a custom AR15 chambered in 7.62x51. A long range craftsman out of Colorado made only a few dozen of these rifles every year. Most of these rifles were in the hands of police and military units where a precision semi-automatic was highly coveted.

Fred looked on with nothing short of envy. I loved it when Fred asked, looking into the case, "Is there another one in there for me?"

I had never seen an IRA rifle before and was thrilled as I pulled it from its foam bed. I read about them in magazines, but I had never actually held one. You could tell that the builder was a craftsman in an instant. The receivers were fitted together without a hint of pin wiggle. Each part was fitted as if it were made just for this rifle. The billet-style receiver was ground smooth to the touch, as if the 7075 aircraft-grade aluminum was coated in silk. I pulled back on the charging handle to cycle to bolt. There was no harsh metal on metal scraping like you get in high-production rifles. The bolt flowed through the receiver leaving only a slight ring from the high-quality bolt face as it locked into battery. My finger felt for the trigger as I shouldered the Magpul PRS stock. The trigger snapped the back of the hammer around two pounds with no creep or any amount of snag. The hammer gave a solid, yet crisp, slap to the back of the firing pin with a single click. My eyes envied the Night Force scope on the angled upper receiver. This receiver must have had 20+ degrees of angle to allow for extreme drops over long ranges. It was love at first sight.

Silver pointed out, "I saw you look at the rail. It has 23 degrees of angle built in for long range shots. See the custom target knobs?

They are set up for Federal 175 grain match ammo. You were using a Leupold before, right? These knobs are closer to what you were using. These are marked for long range dope out to a thousand yards. They say this rifle will reach out just a bit further in the right conditions."

Fred asked, again in disbelief, "You guys even know his previous rifle had a Leupold scope?"

Silver looked at him. "All the free people have heard about the famous Huck. We wait around the radio every week to hear about what Huck did lately." Silver said it in such as way that irritated Fred to no end.

"You're kidding?" Fred asked. "What about his good looking best friend? Does anybody know about me? I should be just as famous."

"You are, Fred. You're the cornbread slayer," I reassured him. Fred looked a bit left out. After I saw this, I included to Silver, "Fred did save me a couple of times. He was the one that got me to the hospital when things turned out badly in our fight to retake Raleigh."

"Yeah, I threw Huck over my shoulder and carried him fifteen miles through the green shirt armored attack," Fred bragged as he stuck out his chest and hitched up his pants.

I looked over at Fred."Over your shoulder? You walked with me maybe a half a mile before you chucked me in the hospital wing of the loony bin."

Silver got a big kick out of that one.

I looked to Silver with sincerity. "Tell your boss and everyone that contributed, thank you. I really mean it .I will put this rifle to good use." By then, almost the entire room was coming over to visit my new rifle. Everybody wanted to pick it up and try the trigger.

We talked with Silver until the conference re-convened. He absolutely ate up every story we told him. I kept Fred from embellishing too much on the details. Silver nearly passed out when I recounted the incident in South Boston where I used the Barret on the helicopters. He must have been a sniper or a long range enthusiast at least. The Texas long range shooters were used to high winds and long distance shots not common in North

Carolina. I wondered if some of those guys considered the accounts of my engagements a bit amateurish in comparison. Heck, the hard part was always getting close enough to make the shots.

It already seemed like a long time back, but it had been only a few weeks ago. At least, I think a few weeks. Maybe it was closer to a month or more since we got back from the Huck's Raiders mission. When you lose that many people, you try to shut out the details and you don't allow yourself to dwell on them.

Silver stayed with us for the next couple of days until the conference came to an end. He was due to leave earlier, but chose to stick around for a while to hear more stories. Before he left we traded promises to come to each other's home town when the war was over. I only hoped there would be a home to town to visit after all was said and done.

Chapter Three
Baby Time

Fred and I were scheduled to leave for home the next day as we sat in the general's office finishing our plans. We had files for our Intel team that would keep them busy for months. Bull's Intel teams were gathering a lot of details on the Middle Eastern units occupying Charlotte.

The general sat behind a desk of papers. "Huck, I will cut you some orders for the training command. Start getting your cadre going on training more instructors. Fred, I want your plans for you and Huck to visit all the other commands. While you are there, coordinate how to get their troops to your camps up in North Wilkesboro. We will work out the details later, but I want to send you trainees in a month."

Fred was writing ideas and directives on a pad. "Yeah okay. We will get you a supply list in a few days. We will need bullets, beans, and so forth."

The General watched him write. "I have a couple of Suburbans lined up to take you home tomorrow. See that Huck gets back in one piece, please. "Just as Bull finished, the phone on his desk rang. He picked it up and answered, "Yes? He's here."Bull looked at me then slid the phone around. He pushed the speaker button.

"This is Huck," I spoke to the unknown person on the other side.

"Yes, this is your midwife. It's baby time."

I was stunned and an instant lump formed in my throat. Fred looked worried. Bull grinned broadly, but the lump in my throat grew to the size of a water melon.

"How much time do we have?" I asked with half a breath.

She responded hesitantly, "Well, this is her first. It could be a few hours, or it could be tomorrow."

"Is she alright?" I asked.

"She's fine," the midwife responded. "I will tell her you are on the way. Do you have someone to drive you?"

Fred chimed in as we rose to our feet, "I'll get him there if I have to get out of the truck and push."

We clumsily hung up the phone and wished Bull well as Fred and I raced out of the office.

Bull hollered out as we ran to the stairwell, "I'll send your orders in a week or so." I could hear him chuckle as the doors closed behind us. Fred and I took three steps at once and ran to our office on the floor below. As we barged through the door the office staff was busily stuffing papers into briefcases. Bull had warned them of our pending departure.

"Sir, we have your suburban waiting out front. The desk sergeant has packed your deployment bags. Leave those reports for us and we will get them to you in a couple of days."The staff was all smiling as Fred and I were fumbling with our gear, trying to figure out if the desk clock was really worth packing. Minutes later we headed for the front door with well wishes from our office staff.

Out front, we loaded into the Suburban and headed for the open road. If all went well, we could make it back to North Wilkesboro by nightfall.

"Fred, take the next right. That should get us on 64. Fred, this right. RIGHT HERE, FRED." We veered from road to road as Fred tried to get us onto 64. It's hard to read road signs at 90 miles an hour. We finally reached 64 and sped north as fast as we dared. During this era, road traffic was fairly limited. Gasoline was in such short supply in the free territories. Highway 64 was rural enough that I worried about local traffic. I didn't want to hit some poor guy in a horse buggy or blast some farmer off his tractor as we raced north.

A couple of hours passed as the sun began to set in the foothills. We were passing through more populated areas as we neared Morganton, our halfway point. Normally we didn't like to run that fast through towns. Even as militia, we didn't want to pick a fight with local law enforcement.

I looked over at Fred. "Fred, back it down a notch or two. The Sheriff of Morganton is friendly to the militia, but I don't want to push it by running over some jerk on a bicycle."

Fred slowed to sub-light speed as we passed markets that were set up in the parking lots of home improvement stores. Highway 40, and its overpass, loomed ahead. The green shirts had never come this far west with any real force. The green shirt office in Morganton was one of the first targets hit back in the spring when we tried to retake the capital. They never tried to re-establish the office as far as I knew.

Fred looked ahead and strained to see. "Just what is this all about?" He and I could see multiple police cars with their lights flashing. I-40 was closed as well as Highway 64. Fred slowed the Suburban as we approached. We were always careful when approaching something like this. It might be green shirt activity, or a lockdown by locals, or more gang raids.

We came to a stop as Fred rolled down his window. "What's going on deputy?"

"You boys turn this truck around. The road is closed," the deputy ordered as he gestured us to move.

I leaned over and looked at him. "Deputy, I'm Colonel Huck of 3rd militia. Can we be of assistance?"

My codename impressed the man. His expression was one of relief, "Colonel, somebody just hit the jail where we keep the *gentlemen from out of town*. You know what I mean. They shot the place up and we are trying to block their means of escape."

I knew the out-of-towners to mean the Sandys we captured up in North Wilkesboro and Charlotte. The detention center was kept a secret to protect this very thing from happening. Our borders were not that secure if you really thought about it. It's not like we had a wall around free territory or roadblocks at every intersection.

"Can I talk to your Captain?" I asked.

"Well, our radio has been out since the raid. I haven't heard from anyone other than my sergeant who is up on I-40 right now. We were supposed to lock this intersection down until relieved."

Fred and I looked at each other, knowing I was going to be late getting back to North Wilkesboro and Seven. We pulled over and got out of the Suburban. Fred pulled out his customary map while I looked over his shoulder.

Fred asked the deputy, "What all did they hit and when did they do it?"

The deputy pointed to the map. "The first hit was here at the police station. They had machine guns and all sorts of firepower. They blasted the whole place. Our guys are still trying to get a handle on what all happened. It's a mess up there. That smoke over there is our police headquarters and jail. West McDowell Street and South College Street on your map," he concluded.

Fred asked, "Has there been any trouble today? Any shootings or any trouble out here?"

The deputy looked at the map, "Well, they had some problems in Hickory this morning." He pointed, "Somebody had a firefight near the airport this morning. I don't think anybody got hurt, though. It was a bomb or something."

Fred looked at the deputy. "Did you guys send some people over there to help them investigate?"

The deputy looked a little hesitant, "Our Sheriff has an agreement with the Hickory Sheriff. We help them when they need it. They help us sometimes, too."

Fred thought for a second while I told the deputy, "We do this to the green shirts. We create a diversion to draw units away from our main objective. Then we hit the place with full force and get out before anybody is the wiser. The question is where did they go?"

"I have a theory on that," Fred spoke up. The deputy looked skeptical to say the least. All said, this guy was still a cop, and may not have too much respect for us "untrained" militia types.

"I will bet that the raiding party is somewhere about here." Fred pointed to a town West of Morgantown called Nebo.

"And just how do you figure that?" the Deputy scoffed.

"Well, the raiders drew you to the east with their diversion. They came from the east, so they won't want to go back the same way. If I were them, I would steer clear of north because I might not be able to get over the few bridges crossing Rhodhiss Lake. Highway 64 south would be the fastest way to get back to Charlotte; I guess that's their ultimate goal. But it's too big and they know militia use it regularly. I-40 is too open and they know you guys would have them pinned pretty quickly."

Fred continued, "That leaves west. They know its rural, isolated, and the most open back roads. They most likely want to turn south somewhere." He thumbed around for a few seconds looking. "There is no good way south. They would never try to get through 221 and come in through Rutherfordton. They know the militia holds the western flank strongest of all."

Fred went silent for another few seconds. "Unless they don't intend to drive out."

"What do you mean Fred?" I asked, puzzled. The cop stood there looking down at the map. He may have zoned out for a second, I couldn't tell.

Fred pointed, "What is this airfield here? Shiflet Field? Is it still operational?"

The deputy looked down. "It's just a grass field. My dad used to have a cabin over there on Lake James. Nobody flies in there anymore as far as I know."

Fred looked at me. "If I were planning this raid, I would have a small plane parked over there to get my team out. It's the quickest way to get the job done."

"Thanks for your help deputy. We are heading to that field. Send the cavalry as soon as you can. Reach us on GMRS radio channel 16 with 00 as the security code. We will see if we can stop them or at least slow them down long enough for you to get there."

Fred and I were already loaded back into the suburban as the deputy tried to dissuade us.

I rolled the window down and hollered, "Tell your people what truck we are in. I don't want to get shot today." The guy just stood there and watched us as Fred drove up the off ramp. I only hoped he took us serious enough to tell his superiors where we were going.

Fred drove us down deserted I-40 with the sun getting to the point where the mountain shadows covered the surrounding valleys. What remained of the fall leaves were a beautiful mixture of reds and oranges The drive would have been nice in other circumstances. We were actually searching for people that had the firepower to blast open a police department and get away with it. Fred and I were hardly an entire army.

After a mile or so, I told Fred to get on the right side of the road. It was just too freaky to drive on the wrong side even if there was very little traffic. While Fred drove, I climbed into the back of the truck where we had thrown our gear.

"What's our e.t.a., Fred?"

"We should be there in twenty minutes if we don't run into any problems," Fred hollered back over the engine noise.

I chucked bags here and there, trying to find the gear we needed. We were not loaded for a combat mission. The Suburban had an MP-5 with a telescoping stock. I could only find three magazines for it though. Fred had his sidearm and I had mine. My deployment bag was filled with odds and ends for sniper work, along with a few rations. All I had for a rifle was the IRA-X Thor that Silver brought me, but I had never shot the thing. I had no idea if the zero was good. It usually takes hours to thoroughly test out a rifle at the range and tweak it to the way you shoot. An unfamiliar rifle in your hands is not a motivator to say the least. I hoped I could hit the broad side of a barn with it.

A few minutes of searching revealed a few boxes of 175 grain match ammo and four 20-round magazines. Fred and I were not equipped for much of a firefight. I dressed in as many layers as I had shirts while passing things to Fred as he drove. We were literally cramming bullets in our pockets and loading magazines. We had no load bearing vests or web gear of any kind. I climbed back into the front seat as Fred exited I-40 and we turned north for the airfield. Fred drove with an MP5 magazine between his legs and shoved bullets into the top.

I was busy loading mine when Fred said, "We most likely already missed them, Huck. We don't have to do this you know. We can still make it back to Seven tonight." He drove without looking at me; he didn't want to wreck or miss our turn.

"You're right, Fred," I admitted quietly. "But these guys are the ones we arrested back in North Wilkesboro. These are the same guys that tried to hit our families."

"I know, Huck. But these guys might be with some real special forces types, professional soldiers I mean. We might be getting in over our heads here." He held up the magazine with the little 9mm bullets.

"Fred, we have to try. If nothing else I might take a few pot shots at them with the Thor. We will stay far enough away so we don't get too deep in a firefight. I know we aren't equipped for it."

Fred looked over at me, "That would be a first, Huck." He smiled. I knew Fred would follow me wherever I went, but I didn't want to get us killed trying to do more than we ought to.

We drove another ten minutes towards the airport trying to navigate the back roads. Darkness was falling around us as the sun set below the horizon of the nearby hills. The lights of the Suburban illuminated pavement that was riddled with pot holes and cracks. We were in farm country where tractors plowed the nearby fields when gas was available.

I saw a sign for the airport as we passed. "Fred, that's our turn!"

Fred didn't budge as he flew past. "I'm taking us in the back way. Maybe we still have a shot at these guys. We can't go up there right down the main road."

He sped us down Yancey Road until the left side of the roadway cleared and the end of the runway lay just a hundred yards on the other side of the ditch. Fred killed the lights and took us down a trail until the truck was well hidden in a grove of what looked like Christmas trees. We quickly got out and grabbed our weapons, trying not to make any more noise than necessary. Fred pointed a direction and I chambered a round in the Thor. I heard Fred's MP5 drive home a round and we marched off in the near darkness through some tall grass. It was about then that I realized how cool it was getting at night. Fall had taken most of the leaves with the recent rain. Tonight's sky was clear with some of the brighter stars already twinkling. We only had another 15 minutes of light before total blackness.

Fred hustled us along the northern edge of the field which was surprisingly well kept. Opposite us, and slightly further west, were several rows of steel hangers only large enough to house a single engine Cessna 172 or other small plane. A control shack, you couldn't call it a tower, sat next to a maintenance shop at the other side of the tarmac. I imagined fuel tanks nearby, but I couldn't see them. There were only a couple of lights on between the rows of hangers. The place looked empty, deserted.

I pointed silently to a spot well off the runway on a slight ridge that separated the river from the field. A stand of small evergreens stood between fields with withering corn stalks. I took up a position and covered the rifle with my sniper's veil. My hope was that we looked like a blob under one of the smaller trees. Fred lay beside me and off to my right in the classic spotter position. The place was dead silent. Cold was already creeping through my clothes. I pulled quietly at some underbrush to conceal my position as the first vehicle passed by on Yancey Road. The SUV was going maybe 10 miles an hour, obviously looking at the airfield.

Fred looked through his binoculars and said in a low hushed tone, "I hate being right all the time."

We watched quietly as the SUV turned onto the airport road and shut off its lights. It approached cautiously, carefully, just like we operated. For all we knew, this could be our local militia here to back us up. However, I seriously doubted the deputy we talked to would be able to coordinate so quickly without his radio. Fred and I watched and listened until our ears nearly popped from the silence. Just about then the sounds of a deer came crashing through the edge of our little thicket. Something had pushed him out of the field or from the edge of the adjacent corn field. Within a minute, the sounds of human footsteps could be heard.

Fred eased his head to the right as I, too, tried to peer around Fred's body. These footfalls were no deer. This was a man walking through the leaves. We sound way different than deer. Our big old boots squash leaves, while deer prance through leaves clipping along as if gravity doesn't really have a hold on them. The sounds got closer and closer as a man appeared from the western side of the cornfield. He was carrying an SVD sniper rifle which was backlit by the light colored weeds next to him. He was definitely not one of ours. The SVD is a Russian rifle used by the Sandys marksmen.

The man paused for a second and looked around at his surroundings. He then proceeded to walk right up the small rise where Fred and I lay under the tree. The man was evidently a sniper and had picked the same vantage point to cover the field. Fred and I became stones; we didn't dare breathe. By the time the sniper stopped, he was within 20 feet of Fred's right arm. We had gotten to that position only eight minutes before the man sat in front of us.

As the enemy sniper looked through his binoculars, we lay behind him not able to move a muscle. Any sound would alert him to our presence. My mind raced. Would we be able to stay concealed? Are more coming? Could we kill this guy and get a shot at the primary targets? I know Fred was thinking the same as me. I could just see his outline as he moved his hands ever so slowly to grasp the MP5 into a shooting position. Over the next ten minutes, Fred pointed the MP5 in the man's direction. I watched the SUV take up a position next to the maintenance shack then stop. The lights around the hangers suddenly went dark.

I could barely make out the sniper, even knowing he was only 20 feet away. I watched the little airfield for any signs of activity. The interior lights of the SUV came on a couple of times, but briefly. The occupants were betting on this place being empty.

After 20 minutes of silence, I heard the sniper's radio crackle even though he was wearing an earpiece. A second later he responded with something from his own language that must have been some sort of acknowledgement. I couldn't understand what it meant, but I didn't have to wonder for long. A figure darted along the airfield runway with a road flare burning bright red. A second and third flare marked the southern edge of the field as the sound of an airplane's engine droned in the dark sky above. The sound grew louder and louder as it approached the field.

In a few more seconds, the plane raced low over the field and directly over our heads. The sniper watched it closely as it circled. He went back to scanning the opposite tree line as my heart started to beat once again. All this adrenaline rush would play hell with my shooting skills. I knew our opportunity to do anything would be short to say the least. I just hoped I could see a target from what I estimated to be around 400 yards. Fred and I didn't have time range or anything. I couldn't ask Fred's opinion with this sniper sitting right in front of us. To boot, the lights were off and I couldn't see much at all, other than the flares.

The airplane circled once more and came on to final approach. A second SUV drove up to the field and parked beside the first one. However, this driver kept the lights burning as the plane touched down. I watched through the scope as I saw four men sitting in the second SUV. Three of the men wore prison uniforms while the driver wore the dull tan and green uniform of the Sandys. I still couldn't see the occupants of the first SUV. I imagined them to be security, or the raiders, as if there was a difference.

I felt for the selector switch on my rifle and started to press downward to the fire position. Normally, this would make a small click sound which was no big deal. I couldn't afford even that level of sound. I painstakingly tried to muscle that lever without any sound. After a few seconds, the sniper suddenly stood up as the airplane taxied back up the runway. As the sniper walked towards the field, I clicked the selector to fire. I knew I had only seconds before the man was out of Fred's range. I had to take a shot almost immediately.

I looked at the SUVs again. Four or five men stood around the vehicles, but the primary targets still had their doors closed. I cursed under my breath at the opportunity being lost. The plane wound its way over to the waiting raiders and slowed to a stop. Only then did the freed prisoners open their doors. I watched as the men made their way to the plane. There were few lights; this was going to be difficult to say the least.

I looked back to the sniper who was walking across the airfield 50-60 yards away. I had to take a shot now!

The only light was from the interior of the airplane. I trained my crosshairs on the upper steps of the foldout doorway. The plane was a twin engine 10-seater with one of those side doors that make its own ladder. When the first prisoner touched the railing, I whispered to Fred, "Shot coming in three, two, Bang!"

Fred ripped loose with the MP5 a moment later with a burst of 9mm. The muzzle flash from his weapon was more than I anticipated. I recovered to see a mad scramble to the aircraft as men ran to the ladder. I sent three more shots into the crowd as man after man loaded onto the plane. My adrenaline, coupled with the rifle's smooth action, barely allowed me to comprehend the recoil. In fact, the action was so precise, I watched for brass to eject to make sure the rifle was operating properly.

In the confusion, the security men covering the plane were on us like flies on a cake. One of them set up a machinegun, like an RPK, on the hood of the SUV and wailed away at us. He was an experienced gunner at that. If he had been a little lower, Fred and I would not be here today. Tree branches fell all around us as the bullets ripped the shrubbery. Bits of bark and limbs fell as we crawled for cover. The plane revved up and turned to taxi back onto the runway.

Fred and I managed to make it a few yards away from our position and turned to set up another shot. Using the nearest tree for support, I looked through the scope for the source of the firing. The muzzle blast of the machine-gunner gave his position away like a blaze orange beacon. I guessed again at the distance and held the crosshairs over the muzzle flashes. Boom, I cranked off the round, surprised at the crispness of the trigger. With such little recoil, I watched the round bounce off the hood low, somewhere under the gun. Some fragments may have hit the man because the firing stopped immediately.

More rifle fire erupted from two or three more locations. AK-47s have a distinct sound. Thankfully, they are not so accurate at such distances. The plane sped off to the end of the runway and turned to take off. I moved over to get a better view of the plane. My finger felt the trigger as rounds bounced around Fred and me with unnerving precision. As the plane rolled forward, I fired again and again. I was aiming at the cockpit, but would settle for hitting the port side engine. Blam, Blam, I fired as the plane roared past. When my magazine was empty and the bolt locked back, I watched the plane leave the ground and take off. His port engine was smoking, but he was airborne.

Rounds were walking in closer as Fred and I climbed over the little hill for cover.

"Don't shoot that thing again, Fred. They can see that muzzle flash a mile away."

"No kidding," Fred replied as he changed magazines.

"Did you get the sniper?" I asked him.

"Maybe. I know I hit him, but he was still moving last I saw."

I pointed further west. "Let's change position and see what is left of their security element." Fred and I crouched low and moved 100 yards or so along the ridge. By the time we reached our new perch, the AK47 fire was silent and I had time to reload. Fred looked down the field with his binoculars to see if the sniper lay where he fell. I looked across the field to where the two SUVs were parked. I watched as two men climbed aboard and started the engines. They sped off down the road from which they came kicking up dust and rocks.

"I don't see him, Huck. It's just too dark." Fred reported.

I was just about to respond, when a couple of things happened all at once. Two more men headed for the second SUV. One was obviously wounded and the other was helping him to the passenger door. By the time they reached the truck, gunfire erupted again. This time, the fire was distant, somewhere down the road a little way. The first SUV had run into what I hoped was our backup. I trained the crosshairs on the door of the second SUV by moonlight and estimated the distance to be just under 250 yards. It was so hard to tell for sure in the dark like that. When the door opened I fired at the figures with two shots in rapid succession. For all you non-shooters, that's a double tap.

Weird thing to note here; I remember the brass ejecting out of the rifle, still glowing as it spun through the air. It's weird what you remember sometimes. In some cases, there are smells that trigger a time and place. For me, the smell of broken concrete and smoke from the destroyed buildings in Raleigh will never leave me. Why I thought of that right then and there, I will never know.

Both figures by the SUV fell out of sight into darkness. I couldn't tell if I had hit them or not. The airfield was still quiet, but the firefight down the road was really heating up. I could hear the rata-tat-tat of a machinegun again. Fred started to move and I grabbed him by the shirt to stay still.

"Let's go see if you hit anything, Huck."

"Fred, that sniper might still be out there," I told him. "We can't go traipsing across the open runway like that."

"Let's go around," Fred suggested. I followed him as we made our way around the airfield. It took several minutes, but we ended up on the back side of the maintenance shack. From there we saw at least two or three figures lying on the grassy taxiway. The SUV covered one or two men lying behind the front tires. Both appeared wounded. I swapped out magazines for a full one in case we met someone we didn't expect. Fred was still loaded as we sat and watched for another minute.

Just about the time we decided to charge the SUV, a truck came zooming up the road towards us. It was the first SUV that had left a few minutes prior. They had returned. The rear window was gone and the machine gunner blasted down the gravel road with a few shorts bursts as the SUV skidded to a stop. With his headlights shining on the second SUV, the passenger got out and ran to the wounded men. The driver stood by the door as the machine gunner covered the road. Fred and I were crouched 20 yards away trying to become the darkness.

I looked over to give Fred a hand signal and he wasn't there. I was shocked. Fred was not the type to bug out and leave me there. I was instantly worried and curious.

Then the lights came on with a great metallic ka-chunk. Fred had thrown the switch on the field lights. The men dashed around as I took a hasty aim at the figure manning the machine gun. I double tapped him as he tried to pull the gun around. The other men sprayed AK fire in our general direction. I pulled back behind the maintenance shed as rounds punched through the sheet metal. A grenade from nowhere exploded near the vehicles with a thunderous boom!

I heard Fred on the left side of the building blast away with the MP5. I could see the muzzle flash light up his little alley between steel buildings as I crawled to his position. Then a distinctive single shot pierced the air from way off the other side of the runway. Fred's gun went silent.

I cursed myself for not being more careful. I crawled around the building as all the rifle fire fell silent.

From the rear of the alley, I peeked to see Fred lying on his back. He was moving. The opposite side of the building was bathed in light from the burning SUV and the overhead street-lamps. Crawling on my belly, I made my way to Fred.

"Fred, where are you hit?" I asked.

"Huck, they got lucky this time," he groaned. "I caught one under my arm."

I grabbed him by the collar and dragged him back to the darkness. As I did so, another shot rang out from a spot just on the other side of the runway. I saw the muzzle flash briefly as the sniper's round passed over us by no more than a few inches. The bullet struck the metal building with a distinct twang followed immediately by the report. He was close. I got Fred to cover and opened up his shirt. He was bleeding from a gash that stretched from his chest to a spot under his arm. Luckily for him the round had only pierced his flesh and ripped open his skin. Perhaps it was the odd angle his silhouette presented to the shooter that saved him. He was bleeding pretty badly though, so I pulled out a field dressing and covered his wound while applying pressure with my hand. I scrounged around for a second bandage from my pack and tied him up with as much care as possible.

"Fred, I have to go take care of this guy," I told him. I put his pistol in his left hand and made sure it was loaded. My rifle had performed well so far. Now, it had to issue some payback.

I crawled around to the left side of the building in the darkest part of a shadow. There, I set the rifle on a brick and scanned the area where I saw the muzzle flash earlier. There was nothing more than inky blackness. I don't know how I knew, but I knew the sniper had pulled back. As I sat there watching, three pickup trucks pulled in behind the SUVs. One of the SUVs was fully engulfed in flames. Bodies were scattered around the scene as if we were in some low budget zombie movie. I rushed back over to Fred's side just in case these were more raiders.

Luckily for us, it was the local militia and a squad car of deputies. I identified myself from cover and asked if they had a medic.

"You're Colonel Huck?" one of the younger militia volunteers asked.

"Yes, do you have a medic in your unit?" I looked from man to man. These were all young men with little experience. They were most likely farm workers that lived in the area.

"Well sir, we don't have a medic, but we can call Doc Johnson this time of night. He takes care of us if anybody gets hurt."

"Let's get him on the radio then," I ordered.

"Well, you see, the doc don't have a radio. We have to take your partner over there to his place."

"Alright son, whatever it takes. Let's just get going," I motioned to him. In seconds, I had several people hoisting Fred into the back of a dusty pickup truck. Fred was in a lot of pain and

I didn't want him to go into shock so I covered him with my jacket.

Fred looked at me. "Huck, don't let that guy get away. He's still out there."

"Who is your team leader?" I asked abruptly to the volunteers.

"Denver over there," the young man pointed.

I walked over to where he and the deputy from earlier stood. "Denver, the plane got away with at least one of the prisoners and some of the security detail. You also have one sniper that is in the area on foot and wounded. He is very dangerous and has some talent with a rifle. My truck is over there off Yancey road in the bushes. Can you have someone go get it and meet me at Doc Johnson's place?

Denver looked at me, puzzled. "Doc Johnson, you say?"

"Yeah, what?" I asked, a bit curious as to his tone.

"Well, it's just that he is the local vet. He's good 'n'all, how bad is your man hit?

"He is going to need a bunch of stitches, but I think he will be okay if we can get the bleeding stopped," I told him. "How far away is a hospital?" I asked, hoping for a better answer.

"30 minutes, maybe an hour with all the fuss in town," the deputy informed me.

"I better go ahead and get him to the vet," I told them.

I passed along as much detail about the sniper as I could, given how badly Fred was hurt. Besides, if Fred ever gave me any lip, I would just do a horse impersonation and get all sorts of mileage out of that joke. Oh, there would be no end to the ribbing after being stitched up by a vet.

As I walked away, I told Denver to give me a full intelligence report on the people scattered on the ground. He eyed the bodies and mayhem I left behind and gave me a thumbs-up. I promised to return as soon as I could.

The local militia guys came through in fine fashion on the vet. Within 15 minutes of getting wounded, Fred was being rushed into his office behind a single story ranch house. The doc was already awake due to the noise of the firefight.

"You're lucky son, the bullet just gave you a good stiff kiss," the doc assured him after a quick exam under the bandages. He injected Fred with a hypodermic to ease the pain. Fred's eyes went blurry and he dazed off into la-la land. The doc worked on him for an hour or more and used a bunch of stitches to close his wound. The doc wouldn't draw a picture with the thread and needle like I requested, but it looked like Fred was going to be okay.

"Don't let him do much to bust them stitches," the doc instructed me. "He is gonna hurt for a while. Watch for signs of infection over the next few days. If you see any swelling or redness, we can give him some antibiotics."

"I'll watch over him, doc. Thanks," I shook his hand. "When can I move him?"

"He needs to stay here till tomorrow or the next day at least. He was shot, for crying out loud." The doc looked at me like I was a nut or something. "What are you in such a big hurry for, anyhow?"

It just then dawned on me. "We were on our way home. I was supposed to get back to my wife who is having our first baby."

The doc's face reflected his instant understanding. "Oh, well, you can go, but Fred here needs to stay. Come back in a day or two." This felt like the doctor was treating our case like the sale of a cow or pig. It was really funny later, now that I look back on those times.

In another hour, the local militia brought me the Suburban and an update on the sniper. He had escaped their dragnet. The guy must have gotten across the river before they could set up a perimeter. They confirmed that he was wounded by a blood trail, but found no other signs of him after the river. Denver also reported that two of the raiders were barely alive and being treated. If they recovered, our men hoped to get some useful information from them. Two of the escaped prisoners were dead; the third must have gotten on the plane.

The sun rose in the east as I sat on the doc's porch. Fatigue gnawed at me as the rush of adrenaline wore off. My nerves were shot. The sniper had escaped. What bothered me most was the skill we were up against. Fred had almost been killed. I was late getting back to Seven. Whew. Everything seemed to be piling up.

"Colonel Huck, sir? Your truck is ready. I can drive you back to the airport, if you want."

"Sure, let's get going. Is Denver still there?" I asked.

The young man wanted to impress me, I think. "Sir, can you tell me how you bested those guys?"

I looked at him. "Maybe later. Let's get going to the airport."

The volunteer rode with me back to the airport and pointed out the best route. It felt weird not having Fred beside me. We pulled back into the field in the daylight among several militia vehicles. The place looked completely different. The bodies had been removed, but the two SUVs still sat where they had been the night before. Several people were gathered around the vehicles, going through every shred of equipment inside.

"Denver, what have you got for me?"

Denver looked at me with bloodshot eyes. "Colonel, we stripped the cars and the bodies for further study. I don't know what I can tell you about it all, though. The papers need a translation. Maybe they are in Arabic or something."

"Where are the weapons and packs?"

"Over here, sir. They had a pretty big machinegun there in the back of the truck. It is like our M240, but uses a more powerful cartridge. That thing ate up a couple of our pickups and wounded some of our people. We were lucky they pulled out when they did."

I bent down to several of the packs and went to the one with a sniper veil strapped to the top. The pack revealed a data book, range finder, and all the typical things you would expect to find in a sniper's kit.

"Have you found the sniper?" I asked without looking up.

Denver watched me go through the pack, "No sir. He got across the river and disappeared. We are trying to use some local hounds, but they aren't trained to track people. They are deer huntin' dogs."

I flipped through the sniper log book and stuck it in my jacket pocket. Another pocket revealed a few short 10 round magazines full of ammunition.

"What are those short magazines? Those aren't regular AK-47, are they?"

I passed Denver a magazine. "These are for the Dragunov sniper rifle. It uses a 7.62x54 round that is a lot like our .308 or .30-06. These have been customized for his rifle. See the tooling marks? That is the work of a craftsman, not a punk with a scope. His data book is interesting too. It's not written in Arabic, it's something else. His gear is not typical like the others. He has a different type of knife, his mess kit is different than the others, and this spare field shirt is nothing I have seen before."

"You think he might be a hired gun?" Denver asked.

"Could be," I sat and thought. "He doesn't have his gear now. If you hurry, you might still get him," I told Denver. No time now, I thought to myself. I have to get going back up to North Wilkesboro. "Here, use this email address to get in touch with me. Expand your search and concentrate south for that sniper. Catch him if you can."

"We'll try, sir," Denver tried to assure me. I doubted they would find him. This guy seemed to be very crafty. He was like nothing we had come across before. Well, other than the time when my rifle got hit a few weeks ago. Hmm.

Chapter Four
Home

I took the Suburban and headed to North Wilkesboro and my home in Wooten Valley. It was midday before I pulled into the access road that led to our small community. By then my nerves were killing me. Was I too late? Was there a baby at home? Was Seven alright? Security welcomed me as I parked the Suburban and crossed the river. They drove me the rest of the way up the valley in one of those four-seat ATVs.

"Good luck, Colonel," the driver said as he pulled away.

I walked through the front door of our little house and immediately saw Fred's wife. Fear struck me. Had she been told of Fred getting wounded?

She looked at me as I plopped down my rifle and pack. "They are upstairs. She is sleeping; both of them are okay." Her eyes searched me up and down. I was vaguely aware of my appearance. I was covered in dirt, grime, and Fred's blood.

I stared blankly at the ceiling with a lump in my throat. "Okay."

"Where is Fred? Did he go home first?" She didn't know.

I walked over to her. "Fred and I had a run-in last night. He's okay, but it is going to be a day or two before we can bring him home."

"Is he hurt badly?" she asked with tears welling in her eyes.

"The doctor stitched him up. He has a good gash from here to here," I motioned with my hand. "He will be okay in a few weeks, but he will be sore for quite some time. He will be home for Christmas."

"Oh Huck, you two scare me to death. Can't you stay out of the middle of everything? Some day you're not going to be so lucky. How many times have you two been wounded already?"

"I know, I know." I reassured her as much as possible with a hug. I hated bringing her news that Fred was hurt. I felt responsible every time one of us got in the least little scrape. This time was no different. It was my decision to ambush the escaped prisoners.

After a minute or two, she left and I headed upstairs on my tiptoes. The top step creaked as I saw Seven in the bed with a little blanket bundle beside her. The window allowed the sunshine to bathe the small room in light. There was a slight smell of wood smoke from the little potbellied stove. It was peacefully quiet. Seven opened her eyes and saw me. She smiled weakly. I sat on the bed and looked into the blankets. A little face with Seven's nose lay there. I picked up our baby and smiled as he yawned.

"Were you right? A boy?" I asked.

Seven said quietly, "Yes."

We sat there for several minutes without speaking. My heart was beating fast. I couldn't believe I was a dad. This was a crazy time. The country was in shambles. Our state was split into pieces. We had foreign invaders, and I was part of the army fighting them. What a weird time to have a baby.

Seven looked at me and looked to the stairs. "What kept you?"

I stammered slightly, "Fred got hurt last night. He will be home in a day or two. We came across some trouble. A sniper."

I could see the concern in her eyes as she looked at me. "Will he be alright?"

"Yes. He was shot, but it just gave him a scar opportunity. He will be out of it for a while, though."

She touched my field shirt. "This is nasty. Go change before you touch my baby again. You're filthy."

I went and cleaned up while my little family slept. The next day I drove into town where Data had his office set up. I gave Data the sniper data book and had him translate the writing. His software packages could decipher just about anything.

Data looked at the writing. "Hey, I have a guy that I send stuff to that used to work for a university that taught middle-eastern languages."

"Can he be trusted?" I asked.

"Well, I give him pieces and use the software to do the actual translation. I will send him a photo and see what he comes up with."

Data and I also talked about things that were going on. Seven had been working hard over the last few weeks, making sure the intelligence department could run on its own. She knew she would be out with the baby for quite some time, but didn't want her absence to slow the work. They were producing so much information that a daily report to the general's staff was required. We had come a long way in the last few months. Back in the spring, we were nearly wiped out. It was mid-October and we had the green shirts on the defensive, had dismantled the foundation, and had the Sandys contained for the time being. How did we get so far along in so few months?

"And just what the heck are you doing publishing war stories? Do you realize that people in Texas have been following your blogs? Don't you think the green shirts or the Sandys have been working on a profile of me? What were you thinking?"

Data sat back in his chair a little worried that I might take his head off. "Seven said we could use the blogs to pass along some disinformation and do some counter-intelligence."

"Yeah?" I asked warily. "Seven approved?"

"Oh yeah, we have a whole program set up. We only use stories from at least a month back. We add in some bad information, change the story sometimes, and track it when the green shirts report on our stories."

I was surprised to say the least. I didn't expect Seven would have ever approved of such a thing.

As I sat there and tried to think of anything else to scold Data about, the phone rang.

"Hello?" Data answered.

"Yes, that is an interesting page, isn't it?" Data tapped the sniper's book as he listened for a solid minute. "Okay, I will send more if I can. Thanks for the information. Alright, you too. Bye."

Data hung up the phone and talked while he typed. "That was my language man." He was typing in his usual light speed as he spoke to me slowly. I could barely keep up with what he was writing.

"The professor says this is Serbian, written by someone living around Kosovo that has an Egyptian educational background. The professor wants more on this one. He says that this is a real unique individual. He uses Serbian, but makes some notes that suggest he was either educated in Egypt or that his parents were from there."

"Really?" I asked a bit surprised. I knew there were Muslims in Kosovo, but I doubted there were many from Egypt.

Data tapped the return key and sat back. "I scanned each page and now that I know what language to use as the basis, I can take into account the sub-dialects, and then convert the text into English."

We watched the screens translate the writing one page at a time. I was trying to read it as fast as the computer flipped from page to page.

"Go back to that one," I pointed at the screen.

Data backed it up to the page and stopped. We sat there and read the sniper's note.

"What is it?"Data asked.

"The date. This is the date we ran into the Sandy's special forces group that was trying to take over North Wilkesboro. This is the date we got back from operation Game Warden."

"I thought we got that sniper?" Data commented with a question in his eyes. "Didn't you guys blast the guy right out of the window?"

"We thought it was him. But from the looks of things, that was not our man."

Data looked at the screen. "So, we have a Serbian sniper working for the Sandys? I will see if I can find something on the guy. Maybe he was trained by the Russians or is a mercenary of some sort."

While Data typed away, I read through the pages on another screen. This sniper was classically trained. He recorded every aspect of weather conditions when he pulled the trigger. There was a record of the number of rounds the barrels had on it. The last time the barrel was changed was a custom job. I read the sniper's notes about the day he shot at me. He listed the encounter as a counter-sniper shot where he noted a corrected bullet drop based on the shot result.

The page read, "Sniper engaged. 950 meters estimated. Impact low +2 minutes elevation from 3rd floor window."

It felt weird seeing this guy's account. Until now, I had never known where he shot from. It was spooky to read how he noted the need for more elevation at that distance. I remembered how his round hit my rifle, damaging my scope and bending the barrel. I was incredibly lucky to be reading this account. He was just a bit off that day. It was surprising that his Dragunov was that accurate. Most of those rifles were only good out to 600 meters. His notes continued about the ammunition used. It too was custom beyond the normal 7N14. No wonder he was so hard to catch; he was most likely trained in a war zone. Fred and I were really lucky to be alive. This was my second time being shot by this guy and I was still alive. I betted that few people could say that.

I took the original sniper's log book along with the translated version back home with me. Over the next few days, Seven and I got used to having a baby in the house. We got excited about poopy diapers and so forth. We were a bit giddy.

Each night, I met with the volunteers from 3rd battalion. We had to augment our programs to start teaching instructors. We would be training volunteers from other commands as well as create a cadre of new instructors. Bull had been sending proposed schedules for me to visit the other commands. He really wanted me out there as soon as possible.

I sat in the convenience store which was our unofficial headquarters for 3rd battalion. We trained our sniper volunteers there in Wooten Valley. Everyone else was spread throughout the county on several remote farms where we did basic training for militia volunteers. We had converted the convenience store into a community gathering place where you could eat, talk, play darts, and relax. A lot of decisions were made around those tables. The place was recently equipped with electricity. It looked weird not being bathed in oil lamp light.

"How ya doing, Huck?" Captain Gunny shook my hand. He was sitting with a stiff-backed Fred who smiled blandly at me.

"You alright, Fred?" I asked him as I sat down at their table.

"I'm hurtin' a bit, Huck," Fred admitted through gritted teeth.

I lifted up his glass which had a clear liquid in the bottom. When I sniffed it, my nose hairs nearly melted. It was home brew made by someone up there in the hills.

"Take another swig of that and you won't be able to feel your feet," I told him.

Gunny downed what was left of his glass without making a face. "Fred, take your *medicine.*"

Fred did like he was told and sipped the clear liquid and coughed stiffly. He stifled any movement and his eyes watered until tears ran down his face. I hated to see Fred in such pain.

A few minutes later, I toasted Fred and pitched in, taking a little *medicine* as well. Within minutes, my face was numb.

"Gunny, I'm going to need you to come with me on this little road trip that Bull wants us to do."

"Yeah, what do you want from me?"

"We need your help getting ex-military integrated into the militias. The other commands are having problems. We are missing a great opportunity there."

"Alright, alright, I'll go with ya." Gunny slurred. He must have taken too much *medicine*.

Fred's cheeks were rosy. "Huck, give me a couple of weeks and I will be right there."

"Fred, I don't need a horse whisperer," I joked.

Gunny looked confused. He wasn't sure he had heard right through his *medicine* flooded ears.

Fred rebuffed, "Good Lord, don't start that, Huck."

Gunny looked to me for an explanation. "What?"

The guy that stitched up Fred here was not exactly what you call a real doctor."

"Huck, shut your mouth," Fred warned.

Gunny sat there looking between us, waiting to hear the punch line. Fred rolled his eyes knowing his secret was about to come out.

"Fred here was stitched up by the local vet."

Gunny looked at Fred for confirmation. Within two heartbeats, Gunny was rolling on the floor laughing his butt off. Half the place was already watching and listening. Everybody liked Fred, and this was too funny to let go. The place fell out laughing. Half the guys were wiping tears of laughter, the other half were ready to pass out. It was right about then that Fred's wife came and collected him. She helped him to his feet and walked with him to the door as he made a rude hand-gesture behind his back. I was number one in his book. Boy, those were some good times.

The next couple of weeks passed too quickly. Those of us that had escaped to the North Wilkesboro area loved Wooten Valley, but it was not exactly home. We still felt a link to our home back in the central part of the state. If the green shirts had not tried to take over our whole way of life, we would still be there. Wooten Valley felt like a vacation home or something specific to our resistance movement. We kept the place secure; this was not a free and open community. This was our valley where we trained for war. It was comfortable, but we were under constant threat from green shirt or other forces. Winter was on our doorstep and we knew times were going to get a bit harder.

Thanksgiving was special to us there in Wooten Valley that fall. The air had turned cool, the nights were freezing. Our training cycle was complete and our volunteers were traveling back to their home units. We held off on scheduling any new courses till the new year. We knew that the general was going to be working us really hard and we wanted our people rested. We had been working really hard all year and needed a good long break.

Almost 50 of us stayed in Wooten Valley on a regular basis. Some of the younger guys went into town to be with the local ladies, and others took up some temporary jobs. Our family people pretty much lived in the Valley and were content. Thanksgiving meal was something special, spiritual. We gave thanks for being alive. We knew how lucky we were. Fred was getting better, but his was a slow recovery. His wound had been deep. He had been very lucky not to bleed out.

Seven and I spent Thanksgiving with our little one we named Howard, but we normally called him, Punkin, due to his birthday near Halloween. Seven's folks came by almost every day and helped us with the normal running of the house. Seven was not used to being home so much. It was hard for her to stay home day after day. She was so used to being plugged into every report and every mission. She climbed the walls there for a while. I caught her reading reports more than once while nursing Punkin.

Even though the 3rd wasn't running any operations, we kept security tight. The Intelligence group was busy, and those of us in leadership planned for the upcoming road trip mission. We took in some units from the 4th that needed a break. They stayed at the training facilities we had on the farms nearby. We had to keep people rested and rotated so they would not lose focus on our mission. We were dealing with people that were not professional soldiers and they needed to be with their families from time to time.

Chapter Five
Recruiting Drive

My time off was shortened when General Bull contacted us right before December.

Part of Bull's note read, "The timetable for everything has moved up. I need you and your teams to head out by the end of the week. 2nd and 5th battalions are working on their plans for getting people to your schools in early January."

"We have seen a spike in ex-military coming our way and I want to get them into our ranks and through your basic training course."

Fred and his wife were over for dinner at our house the day the message came through. We sat around our little table with Punkin in his crib beside us. Even though we had power, we still used the lamps on nice quiet nights like this. The night was cool while our wood stove kept the rooms nice and toasty warm. I love the crackle of white oak in the stove; it just feels cozy somehow.

Fred sat in his chair after the meal. "Huck, that was pretty good, but you got the cornbread a little hard."

"Is that right Fred? No *horsing* around? Maybe I can get you some oats next time. It will make your coat shiny and clean."

Seven bit her lip, smiling. Fred's wife covered her grin in her napkin with a stifled snort.

"It still ain't funny, Huck." Fred said before smiling with the rest of us. "You just wait till you get hurt next time. It won't be some nice nuthouse. I'll take you to a dirty outhouse."

The ladies smiled blandly at the thought of us getting hurt again. It bothered them to think of how many times Fred and I had been wounded. I chose a tactical retreat to change the discussion.

"I have to go on a mission soon," I told them aloud.

Fred looked at me with concern. "The big road trip?"

"Yeah, Bull has requested that I get going this week. It will be a recruiting mission, not combat." I'm not sure that my tactical retreat was such a bright idea right then and there. I knew Seven was not fond of me leaving right after the baby was born.

"Combat seems to find you two no matter where you are," Fred's wife jabbed at us. Fred's wife had been more sensitive since he had been hurt. Who could blame her? There were times I felt the same way.

Fred also wanted to change subject, but chose his subject poorly. "Any word on that sniper we ran into?"

I looked at the faces of the ladies around the table. "Yeah, we have some leads on him. They think he made it back to Charlotte." I watched as Fred's wife lost all the color in her face. Fred winced at his stupidity. He was used to talking with Seven and me about such things. His wife, not so much.

"Thanks for having us over guys," Fred thanked us."I'm getting tired. Let's head for home, dear."

They each tickled the baby's nose and we walked them to the door. "Goodnight, Fred. Go hit the *hay*!" I told him through the doorway.

Fred continued down our little gravel road. "Oh you are hilarious, Huck. So funny!"

We all waved goodnight. Seven sat by the stove with Punkin in her arms.

"Fred is going to hear about that one for the rest of the night," I observed.

Seven looked at me. "You both are." I had been expecting this speech, and I didn't want to argue about it. "You didn't make it here in time to see our son born and now you are heading out across the *state* before he is a month old."

I sat beside her and hugged her closely. "You know I have to go. This is really important and could change the whole outcome of the war. If we can bring in the ex-military, we might…"

"Why you?" She interrupted."Why does it always have to be you?"

"Bull thinks that I can use my fame to get the military guys on board. If they focus on me, they might drop their attitude and join us."

 Seven didn't look mollified. She shook her head and tears ran down her cheeks. I hated to see her pretty face so contorted with fear. Then I realized that this was something she just had to get out. She wanted me to listen, not debate her. We talked for quite some time that night. Mostly, I listened. In the end, she knew I had to go on the mission. Seven just wanted to let me know she didn't like me leaving.

The following few days were crammed with preparation. Our units scrounged a bunch of trucks like we had used before. This time, we chose a number of other vehicles commonly used by the green shirts to go along. The plan was to split into two groups with plans for a four-way split in case of emergencies. Several of my team from Huck's Raiders volunteered. Rocket, General Bull's son, was chosen to prepare and lead the scouts. His motorcycle scout school was turning out its first batch of recruits about then. They would ride ahead of our convoys and direct us to the safest routes. Our main mission was different than a couple of months ago. The new mission was to meet with each battalion and help in their recruiting. Our secondary mission was to map out specific routes for their volunteers to travel back to our training camps.

If current intelligence reports were correct, the green shirts were keeping inside the large cities. However, we knew first-hand how unpredictable the green shirts could be. I wanted to see the port city of Wilmington and the layout of the terrain if possible. If there was any way to stop the Sandys from coming into the country, I wanted to be a part of it.

Within days, my team of scouts and security forces were packed and armed for a three week tour of the state. If all went well, we were scheduled to return to North Wilkesboro right before Christmas and winter.

Bell sent word that he was sending along a group to help us with the meetings. He wanted there to be sound systems and a portable stage. Maybe even a big tent for times when it rained. It seemed like a bit much to me, but he was the general. If another group was responsible, what did I care?

The day of our departure, my guys and I were at the 3rd battalion headquarters in North Wilkesboro waiting for this group we had never met. My security guys were armed to teeth and dressed for a run and gun conflict. M240s were mounted over hoods as we had done before. Everything was camouflaged. We were not going unprepared. To us this was no picnic, this was war.

Then, a panel truck and a van drove down our street and turned into our parking lot. I was standing beside my truck with my rifle on the hood. Rocket and some of his people milled around as we had been waiting for these goofs for more than 45 minutes without so much as a call on the radio. Some woman with square glasses, clean leather boots, and an eyebrow piercing, jumped out first. Her eyes scanned from man to man without speaking. Two men followed her from the side door of the van. They were all young Hollywood types. Bull had to be kidding. My first impression was that these people were lost. There was no way Bull had sent them for such an operation.

One of the men looked at us staring at them. "Where can we find Colonel Hunk?" The guy looked down at a piece of paper. "I was told to find him and tell him, *Cathleen*. Must be some sort of code, I guess?"

The men around me snickered and coughed, not quite believing what they were seeing or hearing.

"It's Colonel *Huck*," I said slowly and deliberately. I heard the men behind me make some comments as to the sexual orientation of the two men in front of me.

I turned and looked at the offenders in such a way that suggested I was having none of it. If Bull sent them, there must be a reason. I just couldn't imagine what that reason was.

"You people are 45 minutes late. Are you ready to go?" I asked the man in front of me. He looked around as if he didn't know quite what I was talking about.

He looked back at me with exasperation, "We just got here. We've been on the road for six hours. We had to get through all the checkpoints, blocked roads, and we even heard some shooting at one point. Can we hang out here for a couple hours and stretch?"

My guys laughed out loud this time. Two of the scouts started their motorcycle engines without my telling them to. They were still laughing through their helmets as they pulled out of the parking lot.

Rocket boarded his bike and fired it up. "Good luck, Hunk."

I flipped him off as he pulled away. The three Hollywood types looked at me as if in disbelief. They were really hesitant by now. They did not trust a bunch of camouflaged gun-carrying good ole boys. We must have scared the crap out of them. Little did they know what they were getting into.

I looked to my waiting teams. "Drivers, take over these two trucks. Security, spread among the trucks and van. Standard formation, check radios before we get a mile down the road."

My men ran to their stations while the three Hollywood types looked at me blankly. "We already have drivers."

"They don't know how we operate and they don't have our radio frequencies," I informed him.

I grabbed my rifle off the hood. "What are your code names?"

"I...uh....well, my what?" one of the guys asked. The other two looked as clueless as before.

I looked at them, standing there unsure of the situation, and an idea popped into my head. "Okay, you are Spanky. You are Alfalfa, and you are Darla," I named them as I pointed to each.

"Who?" the young woman asked.

"Spanky? How did I get Spanky?" the first man asked.

I opened the door to my truck. "Who has the schedule?"

Spanky raised his hand. Motors fired up in the background.

"Grab it. The rest of you get back in the van. Spanky, you ride with me until the first checkpoint. Let's go! We have miles to go before we sleep."

Spanky ran to his van and rummaged through his bag. The rest of his people jumped onto the back seats as my driver rolled their van forward. Spanky ran back to my truck with a fist full of papers and out of breath. He jumped through the door and opposite me. Our electronics gear and my rifle were stuffed between us. Seconds later we were blazing a path through the back roads leaving town. All the vehicles were in formation and all the drivers checked in. We were underway at last.

Over the next couple of hours, we made our way north then east along a bunch of back roads. Then more back roads. And a few more back roads. These were winding mountain roads that people seldom traveled this late in the year. The goal was to reach a secluded parking area just east of Mount Airy called Brown Mountain. Once there, we were to stop at the Baptist church just off of highway 66.

I thumbed through the schedule in the back of the truck with the night light on. Spanky was trying to hang on to whatever lunch he had eaten hours ago. He periodically hung onto the interior handles for the unexpected lurches of a truck doing 60 miles an hour down dark gravel roads. Night had fallen some time back, yet we were still a good ways off.

Spanky's car-sick face looked over at me. "Aren't you afraid they will hit something or run off the road at this speed?" It was more of a plea than a question.

"Hit something? Like what? Not too many people use these roads at night in the winter," I told him.

"What about deer?" Spanky asked.

"Then we will have supper," I smiled at him. It didn't help his complexion. I wondered how this guy had survived a year and a half without eating deer. "How do you know the general?"

Spanky thought for a second. "Well, I don't know him well. I only met him a few days ago. There was a call for videographers with sound and stage experience."

"Oh yeah? I bet Bull told you guys he wanted a real USO kind of look and feel," I chuckled.

"He did! Those are almost the exact words he used," Spanky laughed. Talking made his car-sick complexion better.

"But really, how did you get involved in the resistance?" I asked.

Spanky didn't look like he really wanted to answer and thought for a second before he answered. He looked at me with a lump in his throat and I could tell that his emotions were strong on this subject.

Spanky looked forward and began his story. "I was in school back when the power went out last year. It was a school of arts where we did all kinds of productions and traveled all over the country. We did theatre in the park, Les Miserable, some Shakespeare, and some web based low budget movies. My partner and I were the biggest hits in South Carolina." His last statement made him look my way to see if I picked up on his use of the word partner.

"Alfalfa?" I asked in as polite a way as I could.

Spanky smiled thinly. "No. He and I are not....well, you know. He likes Darla, been chasing her since we all met. No, my partner is...well....gone. When the green shirts came to power, our school became something different, a *tool* for the green shirts." I could tell by the way he said "tool" that he hated the green shirts. "We were tasked with making political commercials, real propaganda kind of stuff. We did videos on capitalism for the department of education and all sorts of productions for web and television. "

I interjected, "Yeah, I know some of them. I remember the one with the little girl freezing in the cold because of the greedy capitalist that wouldn't share the electricity, or something like that?"

Spanky's eyes lit up. "That was one of ours! We did that one! I can't believe you saw it." He was relaxing even though the story bothered him. "We were never what you would call right-wing kind of people; not too many in that kind of school." He smiled and looked over at me as if I would say something negative. I simply let him know it was okay. "Well, my partner and I needed work, so we were happy when the green shirts made us full producers. Their communications office directed everything. We just made it come together in a way that would keep people's attention. We were popular, the people in charge were happy, and we were happy. The politics aspect of what we were doing never dawned on us."

I listened to Spanky's story with great interest. It was fascinating to hear how someone who had actually produced the propaganda videos, would actually be sitting next to me a nearly a year later.

Spanky continued. "Then we made the video that ended everything. We filmed a video documentary that was not quite flattering to the party. Somehow it didn't get the approval of our local inspector, which was also bad. It was meant to be a spoof, something funny about the new administration. We weren't really making fun of anyone in particular. It was posted on the official web site just like dozens of others. We had no clue they would react so badly."

Spanky teared up. The whole truck was listening to every word. I was anxious for him to finish.

"So, what happened then?" I asked.

Spanky spoke through a choked throat. "I was coming back from a shoot where I was in costume. The regular extra was gone somewhere. I was heading back to the dressing room when I noticed the special police; they were ransacking the place. People lay on the floor with bloodied faces and their hands behind their backs. Everyone was arrested and carted off to some prison. They didn't recognize me or didn't see me, so I ran out of the back door. The girl you named Darla, just happened to be coming in for a smoke as I rushed out. Together we made our way back to my parent's house. They arrested everyone else in the studio that day and nobody has heard from them again. My father found us work and introduced us to some of your people in the resistance a few months later. We spent the better part of this year in Rutherfordton."

"How about Alfalfa?" Was he a part of your production group?" I asked.

"No, he was working locally somewhere. We met him about a month ago. He is a writer, does a lot of our scripts," Spanky told me.

One of the guys up front said, "Everybody has a story like that. Everybody had a point where they had to escape from something the green shirts tried to pull on them. They tried to arrest the Colonel once or twice, didn't they, sir?"

Spanky looked over at me. "You are not what I expected Colonel."

"I bet you heard some pretty wild stories, Spanky."

"Is it true that you were a part of the operation that fought in Raleigh back in the spring?" Spanky asked me as he wiped his remaining tears.

"Yeah, I was there; spent some time in their political prison hospital, too. Not a place I want to see again," I admitted.

If they treated their friends like they did me, then they must have been hard on their enemies," Spanky guessed out loud.

I looked at him. "Those of us that escaped were the lucky ones, that is for sure. You see, they didn't spend a lot of resources trying to keep us alive. They just wanted some people to parade around for TV cameras," I told him flatly, without thinking.

Spanky looked a bit worried. "So someone like me could make a video that would scare the masses into thinking you guys were nothing more than a bunch of crazed killers. I wish things could have turned out differently, Colonel."

"Me too, Spanky. For us all."

It was the middle of the night before we reached our stop. The place was peaceful and quiet. The night air was cool to say the least. Frost made our footsteps crunch what was left of the grass as we stepped out to stretch. Icy leaves lay all around as Rocket introduced me to the local militia leader.

"Good to meet you, Colonel Huck," the gentleman greeted me. "They call me Big Hoss."

"Glad to meet you Big Hoss. Point us to our park and we will setup camp for the night."

Big Hoss looked at me and pointed with a big smile, "You guys have that house right there. Just pull your vehicles around behind those trees for tonight. The last of our teams will be here by lunch tomorrow.

I liked the idea of a real house to sleep in. "What about security?"

Big Hoss smiled. "The general's staff told me you were like that. We have teams set every few miles watching the roads. We should have a ten minute warning if the green shirts, or anybody else, comes calling. Sleep tight, Colonel."

We got all our people sacked out for the night. I was really glad not to be under some tarp beside the truck. In the morning, the Little Rascals started to work on a portable stage they brought with them. They set it up in the edge of a field where several tents already stood. One of the tents was a field kitchen where breakfast was served. This was like being on a Boy Scout camping trip so far. It was relaxed, the people were friendly. Everybody wanted to shake hands and meet us.

"Colonel Huck, good to meet you. Can I get a picture with you?"

"Uh, yeah, sure," I told the young man with his friends. It was weird too. How could all these people know me? I felt like Patrick Stewart at a Star Trek convention. Person after person showed up in various uniforms. Well, mostly it was camo jackets over jeans and boots. Everybody had a rifle and it looked like no two were the same. In the back of my mind, I worried about a green shirt aircraft spotting this gathering. I didn't want to eat a 500 pound bomb while meeting and greeting. That would spoil everybody's day.

Twenty minutes before my speech, Spanky and Alfalfa pulled me to one side. "Colonel, we need to prep you for your speech."

"Okay, what for?" I asked."These are my people, I will give them the good ole one two and we will get out of here."

Alfalfa handed me a couple of pages and began to instruct me. "Here are the unit names here today. Here are the bullet items you need to touch on. They came from the general's staff. Try to get them to come to militia basic training. Touch on unity and get them to sign up for the militia army group. Oh, and here are some one- liners."

"Guys, I'm not Bob Hope or a politician. I can't script what I am going to say. "I handed the papers back to them. They refused. Instead, the guys kept handing me more pages. "Alright, alright, Leave me alone for a minute so I can read through all this stuff," I relented.

I hadn't crammed like that since I was in college. By the time of my speech, my brain was fuzzy. I was nervous to the point of hoping for a plane to come blow us up, but it didn't.

Big Hoss introduced me and I made my way to the stage. I felt like a 4th grader having to do a speech on homework I had forgotten to do. But then I saw the men who watched me walk to the microphone. They were like me. They had seen the same destruction of their country. If they were brave enough to carry a rifle, I was brave enough to talk to them.

"Good morning free North Carolina!" The audience cheered heartily. "I could tell when we crossed over into the 12th Mountaineer's territory last night. The green shirts were nowhere to be found, and all that was left was their soiled underwear and the cat was pregnant. "The place erupted with laughter. "Y'all have heard the stories of the capitalist renegade sniper, known as Huck, I take it?"

The crowd shouted, "Yeah."

"Well, they report my death about every other day, don't they? They tried a bunch of times, I can testify to that. But if you believe everything they say, I must be ten feet tall and...," I held the microphone to the crowd.

The crowd completed the phrase, "bullet proof."

I don't remember much of anything else I said. It was an adrenaline blur as I just talked and talked until I thought I was finished. When I got off stage, my Rascals congratulated me. They said I almost got every bullet point form the general's key issues. They also said they would work on my delivery and they liked the tie-ins to the local units. Big Hoss said it was a great event and was sure he would have close to a hundred men for our basic training classes. They were also interested in becoming a regular militia unit under the command of our general. Until now, they had been completely on their own. I guess Bull knew what he was talking about.

In two more hours, we were packed and back on the road to our next destination. We had more than a dozen stops like this over the next three days. Sometimes we stayed overnight and other times we spent only a couple of hours. I only hoped we could avoid the green shirts long enough to do some good. The next day we visited Sandy Meadows, Danbury, and Meadows. From there we continued east towards Yanceyville. I was almost sure we would be ambushed by green shirts before long.

Chapter Six
Yanceyville

Each small community was going through the same thing. They were just coming out from under direct green shirt control. They were electing new mayors and rebuilding their police departments. Yanceyville had a pretty good sized green shirt office up until two weeks before our arrival. Former 3rd militia units that didn't escape with us, formed up over the summer. They became strong enough that they were able to overthrow the green shirts in town. It was nothing short of amazing, although I expected the green shirts would make a new effort at the outlying towns in the spring. Spring meant fresh crop planting which the green shirts would one day want to harvest for themselves. Then they would distribute to people that mindlessly obeyed their rule over their lives.

Our scouts ran through town and through the back streets of Yanceyville. It was only a few months back when I rode north of here trying to stay one step ahead of my green shirt pursuers. Now the streets were clear of their filth. After a thorough search, the town was declared clear enough to enter. The scouts reported that a crowd had gathered in the main street courtyard. Surrounding this courtyard was Yanceyville drug store, a bicycle shop, auction house, and the blue-roofed Department of Agriculture building. What my scouts failed to mention, was the attitude of the crowd.

Until now, we had been welcomed as victorious heroes returning home from war. The crowd that had gathered was not that enthusiastic at our arrival. My little convoy stopped in front of the auction house according to the local militia's instructions. My security element kept a perimeter around our vehicles as we met the people gathered around. The look on their faces was nothing short of exasperation. I looked around from person to person as they shouted demands for food, demands for security, return to state jobs, and the like. I could hardly believe what I was hearing. There was anger for driving out the green shirts.

"At least the green shirts cared for us," was one of the cries.

"When are you going to send us food?" another person wanted to know.

"When are you guys going to stop the fighting and the killing? Haven't we had enough?"

I walked over to that person and looked right into his eyes. "What was the population of your town before the war?

The man blinked, trying to think of the answer. My nose to nose confrontation sent him into a cowering position normally reserved for green shirt officials.

"I'll tell you. My reports say that Yanceyville's population before the war was just over 2,000 people. Today, you have a workforce of just over 500 able-bodied citizens. It wasn't us that sent you to the prisons. We didn't force you into labor camps, and we haven't been the ones stealing your food!"

The man looked up at me expecting me to thump him for his words.

I continued, "You cower at my feet because you are so accustomed to someone ruling over you with a billy club in one hand and bread in the other. Stand up a free man and start doing for yourself!" Some in the crowd heard me, while others did not. The crowd as a whole continued to pelt us with demands. These people had been conditioned to eat from the government trough. Thinking on their own was not allowed in the slightest. It was as if these people were on a drug induced stupor; logic and reason had no place among them. They relied on someone else to think for them, to feed them, to make them work and make them obey. It was as if the people would need to go through a detox to learn to think for themselves again.

About that time, I was ushered into the auction house by my security detail. The local militia had set up headquarters in the auction house that smelled of molded corn and dirty floors. I doubted that any amount of scrubbing would ever fully get rid of the odor of raw tobacco that hung in the air. This was prime tobacco farm country before the war. I betted that the green shirts were still using the local population to farm crops of it for sale overseas. It was one of those ironies of the green shirts. They had outlawed cigarettes for health reasons; then used our farms to supply their black market. It must have been a profitable business and I doubted the green shirts would leave it so easily or for very long.

"Colonel, we would like you to meet the local militia group responsible for liberating Yanceyville."

I shook hands with a group of rag tag fighters. Their weapons were old and looked to be in need of oil. Their arms were shotguns mostly, a few rifles among them. Pistols were tucked into belts. They must have surprised the green shirts and blasted their way through the local office was my guess. These fighters reminded me of our own movement from about a year and a half ago. We must have looked just as shabby and ill-equipped to the 1st and 2nd militias when they advised us on organizing the 3rd.

I looked at the two dozen men who gathered around in the cavernous room. The jeers of the crowd outside could still be heard, but muted somehow in the presence of these heroes. I shook hands with everyone I could reach. "You guys did a heck of a job with what you have."

"Thanks, Colonel. We have been waiting a long time for this day. The green shirts have been gone two weeks to the day," a young volunteer announced proudly. He must have been 20 years old perhaps.

Other men came forward and shook my hand. "Colonel, it's good to see a friendly face around here," he gestured to the door and the crowd outside.

"Don't be too hard on them, guys. They have been programmed to respond like this. Remember, they have been spoon fed by the green shirts to be totally dependent for over a year. It will be like dealing with an alcoholic who is quitting cold turkey." The men smiled. A few looked to the doors and listened to the ranting outside with a little hesitation.

I wished Fred could be with me on this trip. Gunny was supposed to meet us in a day or two. But I had to get to work. I stood there and started to spell out how we were recruiting and trying to get good people like them to our basic training programs. They listened intently as others in the background whispered back and forth as messengers came into the room. After a few minutes, I excused myself from the men and walked over to my security detail and two local militia men who were deep in conversation.

I walked over. "What's the problem guys?" I could tell by their body language that there was something going on.

"Sir, we lost contact with our scouts about 5 minutes ago," my chief of security told me. "Their last reports were, all clear, though."

This by itself was not unheard of. We even had a standing order to switch to a backup frequency in cases where we lost contact. Any time now our scouts would report in on the secondary channel. If that didn't work, they would report back to this building. It had happened several times in the past, no big deal. But for some reason, it made the hairs on the back of my neck stand out.

"Gentlemen, where do you have your map of town?" I asked the local leader.

"Oh, it's right in here," he led us to the auction house office. We stepped through the doorway where a large county tax map hung on the wall. I looked over the map quickly and pulled a sticky note off the map with today's date and my name.

"This is not a good idea for security," I scolded him. "Anybody could walk in and take a photo of this map and we would have all kinds of problems."

"This place is guarded night and day, sir," he said defensively. "It's not like everybody didn't know you were coming. If you wanted your visit to be a surprise, you shouldn't have sent us the message three days ago."

I looked at the man square in the face. "Just what do you mean, three days ago? We radioed you yesterday morning."

The man looked back at me more confused than ever. "We got an email about your arrival three days ago. It was from 4th militia headquarters. I didn't think it was worth mentioning before now. After all, we had to deal with some shootings this morning and lost a couple of people." The room fell silent as we sat there and thought.

"What kind of shootings?" I asked, more confused than ever.

"Oh, we had some rogue gang strangler or something. We didn't find him," the local militia leader told me. "What was strange was that each of our guards had a single bullet wound to the head. They were executed mafia style." He gestured with his hand shooting someone in the back of the head.

"How could you tell they were shot with a pistol at close range like that?" I asked, curious.

"Well, how else could you kill two guards but like that? They must have been disarmed and shot. It must have been some real tough guy, too," the local leader offered. "My guys ain't no wimps."

"Were your men stripped bare?" I asked.

"The guy thought for a few seconds. "No. The killer must have scrammed before our people showed up. We recovered their weapons."

I looked around to my security detail. "Any word yet from our scouts?"

He shook his head no. "If they follow SOP they should be here in five minutes or so. All our channels seem to have some weird static. It's as if somebody is broadcasting dead air."

"Show me on the map where we set up our sentries," I instructed my security team leader. Things were adding up to real trouble.

One of the locations was the exact same spot where the men had been killed that morning. The local militia had rightly set up a checkpoint on the southern end of town where highways 86, 62 and 158 all converged. The map showed a small sub-station and a barbecue house in the area. Otherwise, the lonely intersection was the only open space surrounded by thick woods on all sides.

I looked to the local militia leader. "Go tell your men to pack your bags. You need to bug out of here right now. If you have vehicles, get them here now and you can come with us." I turned to my security chief. "Have the guys move the vehicles inside and get some shooters on the roof. I will bet we have a group watching us already. And, let me know when Rocket reports back in!" He was already half out of the room as I yelled my last instructions.

The local militia man grabbed my arm. "Colonel, you don't have to get the men all worked up like this. The green shirts haven't been here in two weeks. We ran them out. We would know if they were back in town." His demeanor surprised me to say the least. The man could not believe he was having a problem, even after losing two men.

I turned on the man and took his hand off my arm. "You have been fed secure information from an unknown source, you lost two men the day we happen to arrive, and I get here and we lose communications? Do you need somebody to send you a freaking post card? Now get out of here and get your men to disperse the crowd outside." The man obliged, but slowly, unsure if he believed me. This is the type of situation that can get out of hand quickly. If we didn't act fast, we may have a bunch of casualties on our hands. I hated to think the green shirts may have caught us in some big trap with our pants around our ankles. They had never used this tactic before, but it sounded like we were being set up for something.

The first of my trucks drove into the auction house as the doors opened. Two of my motorcycle scouts followed. Men quickly pushed tables and chairs to the side to allow more room for all our vehicles. Men yelled instructions to others; it was pandemonium.

"Sir, our radios aren't working," one of the scouts informed me as he sat on the running bike.

"I know. You two park the bikes and report in. We might have a sniper problem." The man hustled up just like they had been taught. I hoped we were a good example for the local guys. About that time, I heard a series of shotgun blasts out front. The local guys were firing their shotguns in the air to scare the crowd. Screams of terror echoed in the streets as people ran all over the place.

I grabbed one of my drivers who stood by the open door of my truck. "Go tell those jerks to stop shooting. They will turn this situation into a full-blown panic if we don't stop them."

I pulled on my Voodoo chest rig and grabbed the Thor. I loaded a 20 round P mag then chambered a match grade 175 grain sniper round. I checked the chamber of my M&P and holstered the pistol back under my multicam field shirt. The whole auction house was full of men scrambling to arrange gear and pull weapons from trucks. I saw our security guys test the side doors to the loading dock to make sure we could use them later. The crowd was gone from the front of the building inside of a minute. Rocket and five of his scouts rode through the front doors as they were closing.

Rocket pulled off his helmet and pulled out the radio earpieces. "Colonel, our radios are having fits," he announced as he surveyed the flurry of activity all around him.

I walked closer to him. "Rocket, any sign of green shirts?"

"No sir. But the radio thing is really weird. It's like someone is transmitting on all the channels and sub channels."

I told him, "We're being jammed. It's most likely a truck with an antenna somewhere nearby. Have all your scouts reported in?"

"It looks like we have everybody except for the guys at the southern crossroads. They should have been back by now, though."

"Alright, get into the office and we will work out a plan," I ordered him. Rocket got his men to fuel up the bikes and prepare for a long run just in case. My, he had come a long way since this summer when he was a punk kid that was fast on a motorcycle.

As I walked back to the shabby office, I ran into Spanky.

He and Darla looked scared as people hustled around. "Colonel, what do you want us to do?"

"Where is Alfalfa?" I asked.

Spanky looked around. "He was out front when we stopped. Darla, have you seen him?"

Darla was nearly in tears. She had never been in a situation like this. The air was filled with tension. You could feel a fight coming.

Darla stammered, "He was with me until the security guys told us to park our van inside. The crowd was going crazy and then there was all the shooting. I haven't seen him since. What is going on Colonel?"

I looked at her. "I am going to find out. You guys load into the van and be ready to move out. I will send you a driver and security escort if I can. If you see us leave, you follow. Alright?"

About that time, the door opened and Rocket sped out of the door followed by one of his scouts.

I marched into the office where there was a hum of activity. "Where is Rocket going?" I demanded of the security detail.

"I sent him to go get the southern team and bring them in," my man shot back at me. Don't get me wrong, he was a good man. But this was a bad move in my opinion. If we did have a sniper in the area, I didn't want him to have two nice motorcycle scout targets to shoot at. If it were me out there, I would try to draw in my enemy one at a time where I could pick them off.

Then it dawned on me; was I being called out? Someone had information that we were to be in the area. There was likely sniper activity and someone was jamming our communications. We had been set up by someone with resources and technical support. The green shirts were not that plugged into our operations. Could it be the sniper Fred and I ran into? This situation felt just like the stories I heard about in Serbia back in the 90s.The UN would get drawn into a small town and chewed to pieces among sniper and mortar fire. If they fired back, there was the media filming the UN shooting up schools. Never mind that the schools housed tanks, the fighting was a political tool for shaping political opinion. We could not afford to get bogged down here and screw up our whole mission. We had to get back on the road as soon as possible.

I walked over to the security chief and got in his ear quietly. "Pack it up and get out of here in ten minutes. Keep an eye out for the guy I call Alfalfa. He's disappeared. He may just be freaked out, or he may be working for the other side. You lead the convoy south through the crossroads and collect Rocket along the way. Don't stop, don't get bogged down. Send my truck back for me at midnight tonight."

He looked at me. "What? Colonel, you know I can't do that. The general assigned my team to you personally. You cannot go by yourself."

"Okay, I'll take your best two men and they can go with me," I told him. "But that is it. This is going to be tricky enough."

"Alright sir, you can have the men on the roof. They are good men and can help you do anything you need," he assured me.

I patted him on the shoulder. "Listen for me on the secondary channel and proceed to the next checkpoint. Park the convoy under cover and stay alert."

"Right, sir. Good luck," he told me as he hurried about coordinating with the local militia.

I went back to the shop where the trucks were parked. I grabbed my pack and slung it over my arm. Spanky and Darla were sitting in their van watching as the local militia collected their stuff. Were my rascals a security threat? I didn't know. Perhaps time would tell.

From there, I made my way to the roof where I informed the men what we were about to do. They took the information in stride and understood what a chance we were taking. We pulled back under the roof top and sat behind the air conditioners as if we had left. In ten minutes the doors of the loading dock swung open and the convoy left the auction house. Vehicle after vehicle rolled down the dock and onto the street.

As the last pickup left the auction house, my team and I sped down the rear fire escape ladder. We ran along the northern end of the auction house property using anything as cover. There was a church with a cemetery just behind the parking lot. Several rows of houses lined each side of the street as we ran by hoping to avoid the occupants. A row of trees blocked unfriendly eyes. At least, that was my hope anyway. There was still a lot of daylight left as it was only two in the afternoon.

We crossed several small streets as the cracks of sporadic gun fire popped in the distance. I hoped I had made the right decision in sending the whole convoy to the southern checkpoint. The green shirts might be parked anywhere just waiting to spring a trap on us. My team and I looked for any spot for us to set up and watch the auction house from a distance. There was a water tower just off the main road as you drove up highway 86. I had seen it many times as I drove this very road before the war. We eased our way to the trees nearby and waited for all foot traffic to pass. There were a few people milling around, wondering what the distant gunfire was all about. After several minutes, we managed to slide under the fence and climb up to the first level of supports. This allowed us a great view of the area in almost every direction, but it was just too open. There was no escape route if we were spotted.

I whispered to the men, "This is no good. We need a place with more cover. We can get caught here and have no place to go."

The men and I looked around. One of the security guys pointed to a building on the other side of 86 and shook his head yes. I didn't like it, but agreed it was the best choice. The only reason I didn't like it was the wide open highway we had to cross to get there. But there was no other choice that offered everything we needed.

We made our way to a tree covered ditch by the roadway and sprinted across when the coast was clear. All that running in broad daylight made me nervous. Somebody would have surely spotted us by now.

While my men stood guard, I climbed the back of the metal structure that may have been a diesel mechanic's shop. With a little effort and some noise, I made my way to the rooftop and looked towards the auction house. All seemed quiet over there. Pops and distant cracks sounded to the south, but with greater periods of silence between shots. It sounded like whatever firefight had taken place was mostly over. There was not enough of it to make me worry that the convoy had been severely damaged.

My security and I hunkered down to let things settle down around us. We might have to be here for quite some time. My team dispersed to a nearby dumpster and an abandoned truck cab that was derelict. They could see around the building where I could only see over the apex of the roof. I watched through the Thor's scope the auction house we left behind. Nothing was moving. The cool air of winter chilled the sweat I had produced running to this hide. I wished for a jacket about right then. Mine still hung on the back of my seat in my truck. My hands shook as I scribbled sniper notes on distances, temperature, estimates of wind conditions, and the like. Crap, it would be cold when the sun went down.

An hour passed before I saw anything move around the auction house. A lone man walked down the street towards the building and paused only a half block from the open doors. I adjusted the scope to its full magnification and identified Alfalfa clearly in his normal grey jacket. In the back of my mind I regretted not making more of an effort to search for him before we left. He could have just gotten scared and run off. He might be looking for us right now and think we had abandoned him. I wondered what Bull would say to me leaving this poor schlub out here by himself. All those things went through my head as I sat there and watched. I doubted every move I had made that day. If had it to do over again I would do everything differently. Turn left, not right, etc.

That is until I saw Alfalfa raise a radio to his head and speak into the microphone. A few seconds later he walked the rest of the way to the auction house slowly and carefully. He kept looking around as if his head were on a swivel. I saw him look through the open doors of the loading dock and disappear for a minute. Then I saw him come back outside and continue to talk on the radio with some unknown person. A minute or so later an SUV drove to his position where four men climbed out. None were in uniform, but I recognized them immediately. Sandys. Alfalfa was a mole.

Through my scope, I watched as Alfalfa gestured to the men from the SUV towards the south. I could not let that dude just go like that. He had been with us for several days and may be able to provide very sensitive information about the militia and the people we had already visited. My hope was that he had not had enough time to tell the Sandys much about us yet.

I double checked my sniper chart where I estimated the front of the building to be just over 625 yards. The nearest doorway was a typical 6'-9" tall, 36" wide door which looked to be about 1.5 mils wide through my scope. Normally I would set for a 600 yard shot (125 inch drop) and use Kentucky windage from there. But these guys kept moving around looking through the doors, trying to gather whatever intelligence they could. I watched and waited for my opportunity with two pounds of my trigger held steady. I no longer felt the cold. I was watching the wind dance and swirl. I watched the grass sway to the breeze as it gave up the wind's secret unseen flow. I waited. There was no time for a trial. No time for debate; I had to kill the traitor that could sell us all down the tubes. Looking back on that shot, I didn't see him as a man. He was simply a target, albeit a strategic target, that had to be taken out to keep others from harm. Some militia volunteer's secret identity was their only security in some cases.

For another five minutes, I watched Alfalfa and his cohorts until they gathered around the SUV over a map. Alfalfa had his finger on the paper when I squeezed off the first round. His back was to me as he stood in front of the truck. To my satisfaction, the round drilled him in the center of his back right between the shoulder blades. His friends scrambled as Alfalfa bounced off the grill and slumped to the ground. As a sniper, I hated to shoot twice because it gave away my position .But this guy was worth the risk. My second and third shots caught him as he lay in front of the truck. I couldn't tell you where I hit him; only that his body flailed as each round impacted. At least one of the Sandys was hit as I covered my withdrawal. In a matter of seconds, my security team and I ran through the woods behind the shop. The cover of the trees was preferable to the relative openness of parking lots and rooftops.

Popping and zinging sounds of incoming bullets ripped through the leafless branches making us hunch over as we ran. The metal building gave a twang after each 7.62mm AK round impacted. We ran for nearly a half mile before stopping to gulp in air. Luckily for us they didn't have anything more potent than AKs to shoot at us. We were well out of their range before I fired the first shot. The Thor was instantly becoming a favorite companion. Any rifle that accurate and dependable is worth its weight in gold.

In the waning hours of the day, my security team and I crept slowly and listened for any approach of the enemy trying to flank our position. But none came. After a while, the wind slowed to a stop and the brightest of stars began to twinkle in the waning light. I pulled my sniper veils from my pack and wrapped them around me for warmth. The adrenaline rush and sweat from the run was turning cold. My muscles shook to keep warm. The cloudless sky meant that this was going to be a frosty night by dawn. What in the world was I thinking when I left my jacket in that stupid truck?

The three of us still had hours to wait on the dark, so we huddled around and talked quietly between shivers.

"You think they bugged out, sir?"

I looked over at the man's face. "Yeah, most likely. I don't think the Sandys were in that tight with the green shirts, or else we would have heard more of a gunfight from the convoy," I told him.

As we talked, I shoved dry pine needles under the sniper veils for insulation. Anything short of a fire, I would have done at that point. But a fire was way too big a risk for a forest with no leaves.

"Colonel, what time is the convoy supposed to come get us?" the second security man asked.

I answered, "If they are okay, they should be back in town at 0:00."

"What if the radios don't work by then?" he asked in return.

"Well, we will have to get back into town and see how close we can get to the auction house," I told them.

"Sir, I'm not liking that plan a whole lot. They are bound to have somebody there by now," the second man said frankly.

I admitted back, "To tell you the truth, I'm not happy with it either. So, if you have a suggestion, we have time to hash it out." I always wanted my people to know that they had a say in the matter. Some would say that was not a good leadership trait, but I was dealing with volunteers, not hard core soldiers mind you.

"Well, what did you say is blocking our radios? A truck maybe?" he asked.

"Yep, a truck with a mast antenna, or radio tower, something like that," I said.

"Like that one over there?" he gestured off through the trees.

I turned around to look. Holy cow! It was a radio tower's red light blinking above the tree line further north and east.

"We have time to check it out; let's go see what we can do," I offered.

We walked in the dark for a solid 20 minutes with only the stars as our light. Unseen branches poked us in our cold faces. Walking in the woods at night can be a real pain in the butt. You fall, you step in creeks or wet spots; it is harder than you think. By 20:00 hours we were on the edge of a field that was home to the local radio tower. The place may have been a gospel station before the war. The guy-wires stretched for hundreds of yards to large concrete blocks set deep into the surrounding field. Someone had taken the opportunity to use the field to plant corn this year I noticed. Pieces of dried stalks littered the ground as we knelt by the edge of the woods.

Through my scope, I could see a small brick building that housed the radio equipment some 50 yards further than the tower on the other side of the field. Another building was adjacent to this lot, but was separated by a hedgerow of trees. This hedge of trees was common between small fields. Usually a ditch ran under the old fence separating the two fields. Those are always good for sneaking right up to a place. Wet soft ground is quieter than dried leaves and sticks any time.

"What do you see, guys?" I asked.

The other two men were looking through their rifle scopes or binoculars. One of the men spoke quietly, "I see a guy down there off to the right. I can't tell if he has a weapon or not. He might be out taking a smoke break."

The second of my team added, "What are those lights on the other side of the road?"

I looked where he indicated. "I think that's a school. I used to come through here from time to time before the war. Don't know if it is still being used. Let's work our way to that side and see what is in the parking lot."

My security man led the way with me in the middle. We worked our way around to the spot where the trees separated the fields and found the ditch as we expected. We crept slowly forward, trying not to make a sound. The cool night air would carry whatever sound we made to the man outside. Every few steps, we stopped to look and listen. The cold was no longer a factor. Movement kept us warm and fear sent the adrenaline through our veins. In a short time we made our way to a spot where we could plop down and see the opposite side of the building perhaps 60 yards away. From below the cover of the ditch, I stripped off the sniper veil and let the pine straw scatter. Once the veils were stowed back in my pack, I scanned the parking lot.

Sure enough, there was a simple looking panel truck with an antenna mast attached to the back. It was my guess that this was a COW .A C.O.W. is a Cell On Wheels. This simply means that this is a portable cell phone tower built into a nice clean enclosed truck. Phone companies use these during emergencies to restore cell phone service to an area damaged by a natural disaster. However, in this case, the COW was being used to block our short range radios. This was a real opportunity here. Whoever manned this station was really plugged in somewhere important. These trucks were not standard issue and would have been highly prized by the green shirts in large cities.

I gave the men hand signals. This position was our rally point. I pointed to the adjacent lot and then my first security guy. I gestured for him to scout the adjacent lot and come back in one hour. The second guy I handed my sniper rifle and motioned for him to sit tight and cover us. I then pointed to myself and the brick building with the truck outside. Each man nodded in agreement. We didn't need to speak; this was all part of our training.

We headed out to our assignments in silence with me armed only with my M&P. For some reason I didn't even think to trade for the security guy's M-4.But hey, it's an imperfect world and I made mistakes like everybody else. I worked my way to the side of the building and listened for anything out of the ordinary. It was quiet. Two or three cars were in the parking lot. I guessed that to be usual. The panel truck was cabled directly to the building with its generator humming in the background. I saw the man from earlier loop around the parking lot only 40 yards away. He was armed with a pistol on his belt. He walked casually and strolled through the lot like a man secure in his surroundings. He must be special security if he was smoking. Cigarettes were outlawed to regular folk. This guy must have been something special.

I crawled to the edge of the building under some thick green bushes, maybe junipers of some sort. About the time I got settled the door swung open and a man walked down the concrete steps into the parking lot.

He was speaking to someone following him out of the room. "I have to get this truck back to Durham tonight. I don't care what kind of operation your people are running up here."

Another man's voice came from the door with a thick middle-eastern accent. "I was told you would be cooperative."

The first man stopped in his tracks as the guard walked over to him, flicking the cigarette to the street. "We are being cooperative. Look, the militia is long gone, not a shot in hours. But my supervisor told me I had to return the truck by midnight. It's an hour drive, so I must leave in the next hour to get back in time."

The guard talked to the man on the steps without taking his eyes off the man in the lot. He spoke in Arabic or some such, but it needed no translation. He was asking if this man needed to be *convinced*. The look in the guard's eyes was fierce, uncaring. It is rare to see someone like that. The guy looked like he would kill you for sheer spite if the need arose.

The man from the steps spoke slowly and clearly. "You will stay until we are finished. You will make the truck run like it is supposed to. If you do otherwise…"

The man in the parking lot was shoved by the guard into the side of the truck with a bang. The threat was clear and nothing else was said. The guard followed the other man back inside the brick building. The telephone man breathed hard in the cool night air, issuing a cloud of warm vapor. He looked like he was about to pass out. After a minute, he walked around to the back of the truck and climbed the rear ladder where he stepped inside the truck body.

I sat there with my mind racing. This could be a great opportunity if only I could talk to this guy. Was he a green shirt or was he simply a worker who was under strict orders from two different supervisors? If he was just a worker, I wanted to shut down the truck, but protect him in the process. I choose the dangerous option. Like a fool, I crept through the parking lot, knowing my sniper overwatch was cursing my name, wondering just what the hell I was doing. I wondered the same thing.

I made my way carefully to the back of the truck and climbed the steps. With my left hand I opened the door and led the way with my M&P. The man sat at a little foldout table at the end of the small aisle flanked by radio equipment. Little green, red, and yellow lights blinked as the equipment did its function.

He heard me close the door. "I told you, I will keep the…." He looked at me finally because I didn't move as he anticipated. He froze as his eyes met mine over the sights of the M&P. The bore of a pistol looks mighty big when you are staring right down the barrel.

He said a bad word and looked like he would stroke out any minute. His breathing was rapid and his eyes looked as big as teacups.

"I'm not here to hurt you," I said slowly. "But if you alert them, I will smoke you. "He believed me.

He managed to squeak out, "Okay."

"You are transmitting in 462 megahertz?" I asked without flinching.

His demeanor relaxed for a split second. His face showed the questions going through his mind; fear was turning to curiosity. "Yes?" His reply was both an answer and question.

"What else are you doing here? I see you are operating a single carrier on the whip antenna as well. What for? Who is using cell phones around here?"

The man looked at me as I moved forward. "They will kill us both if they find you here."

"Not if I get them first. How many of them are inside?" I asked.

The man looked at me, still thinking about what level of cooperation he was about to give.

"Three, I think. But there is an SUV that was here earlier, it had three or four guys in it. All Arabs, or whatever. But there must be one more somewhere. They are supporting some guy in town; they talk to him all the time by cell phone."

I asked, "What do they call him?"

He looked at me and thought for a second, "I heard one of them refer to him as, *teegar snadgper*, whatever that means." His eyes flickered and recognition came as he stared at me. "You are the militia guy they are looking for aren't you? You're that Huck fella, right? Shot the central office supervisor down there close to Durham. That's how you know radio equipment. You were a phone guy before the green shirts took over."

I lowered my gun a bit. "Yeah, well things have been weird for a while now. Will you help me make a call? I will try to keep you safe if I can."

The guy was hesitant. "They know where my family is. I have to cooperate or they will kill them. Half our office has been sent to prison already in the last year. I can't."

"I understand; but I need your help. The resistance needs people like you. You can still make a difference. You can be the one who helps us from the inside. I was just like you until my supervisor tried to kill my wife right there in his office."

He looked back at me after a few seconds, "Okay, but we have to move fast. They will be back in here in a second if they catch any whiff of this."

In a minute I was dialing home on a secure line that hopefully led to free telephone systems. After several tense seconds, an operator picked up. I spoke a series of code words and waited for the line to be connected.

Data answered, "Colonel Huck, where have you been? I have been trying you all day. You missed your report time and I have all sorts of stuff to give you."

"Data, send them to my secure laptop and I will get to them later. I will call you in the next 24 hours. Was there anything on that sniper?"

"I am sending you the report now. We found his profile and have a bit to pass down to you. Watch out for this guy. He is a pro. Mercenary type goes by the name Sniper Tiger or Tiger Sniper."

I interrupted Data's long winded information dump. "Yeah, I've heard of him, I think. Tell Bull he sent me a mole. I will report on that later. We are changing our schedule. Tell Seven to kiss Punkin for me. Huck, out."I hung up the phone.

I could see the question in the phone man's face .It must have sounded gibberish to him. At least, I hoped so. My mind raced as I thought how to proceed.

I looked over to the phone man. "Patch me into the radio channel this *Tigger* is using."

The man looked back at me with real fear. "They have some computer equipment in there that does stuff I have never heard of. They will pick up on it in a matter of minutes, maybe seconds. There is nothing I can do to mask our monitoring."

I lowered my pistol further. "Believe me; I know the risk you are taking. But do this and I will protect you as best I can. Do this for your country. We must bring these guys down."

The man relented and began to pull cords from cross-connect panels. He rapidly plugged into ports and watched lights flicker on from various radio components. In 30 seconds, he handed me a handset and breathed deeply. He hesitated for a second and looked me in the eyes. This was my last chance to back out. I reached over and plugged the handset in as he winced.

The handset speaker crackled for a second and I heard a conversation already in progress.

The first voice was eastern European sounding. His voice was one of a forty something with his English learned second hand. Whoever taught him was from Great Brittan.

"I do not care what the green shirt infidels want. They will have this peasant town after I am through."

The second voice I recognized from the man on the steps earlier. He was from the Middle East, yet his English also reflected a twang from Great Brittan. It was weird to hear two guys using English as a second language with both of them sounding British.

"The green shirt governor has been very cooperative. We must allow them to retake the town soon. The militia pulled out hours ago. We should hunt down their convoy and kill them on the road."

"You hired me to kill the militia sniper, Huck, and that is what I will do. I am not convinced he has left. My security team was attacked *after* the convoy was gone."

The second man began to argue again. "We will....get you the support we can....go ahead and take your time. Let us know how we can support you." His pauses were dead giveaways.

I pulled the plug out of the handset knowing that they were onto me. In the back of my mind, I hated myself for taking so long in that truck. I went to the back door and opened slowly, my M&P at the ready. Cold air rushed into the truck as I peeked around the edge. My security man was halfway to the back of the truck as he saw me open the door. Our eyes locked for a brief second as he froze in position. The door of the brick building swung open as the intense guard from earlier walked through with an AK-47.My man had the drop on him as he demanded the guard drop his weapon. The guard dropped the AK without blinking. He was not intimidated in the least.

Then several things happened so quickly I can hardly remember the order. Before I could speak, I saw my second security man jogging from the field towards us. When I looked back, my first security man had stepped closer to the guard as he walked down the steps. A figure from behind the guard was silhouetted against the internal lights of the office as he approached the doorway with an AK-47. He fired into the parking lot sending rocks in all directions. I was barely out of the door as all this happened. The Sandy guard took the opportunity of the distraction to attack my man. He was like a leopard the way he moved. In the blink of an eye my man was disarmed and off balance. The shine of a sharp blade flashed against the parking lot lights. I fired at the silhouette in the doorway and he backed away out of sight. I jumped over the ladder's steps as the guard released the limp body of my security man. His knife was bloodied and ready for me as I approached. At first, the guard must have thought I was going to attempt to tackle him, and readied himself to take me the same way. That, however, was not my intention.

I raised the M&P while advancing on his position. The pistol cycled round after round as my rage pressed the trigger at lightning speed. I watched as the man stood awkwardly, almost frozen in position, my rounds pummeling his chest. Brass spun from the M&P's ejection port, leaving a trail as I charged forward. He was lifeless as I ran over him on my way to the door. By then, the man with the AK-47 blasted away at the doorframe from somewhere inside as he retreated. My second security man and I pressed up against the bricks on opposite sides of the doorway. He held my sniper rifle with his M-4 across his back. All I had was my pistol. There was no way I could reach the guard's AK or my man's M-4.

I hand gestured pulling the pin on a grenade as full auto AK fire blasted in our direction from only yards away. The sound was deafening. My man dropped my sniper rifle and rummaged around for a second. I reloaded my M&P and reached it around inside and started blasting blindly. My guy threw the grenade in the door and yelled, "Grenade Out!"

We both ducked back and waited for the blast. VaBoom! The little building shook all over. Bits of glass showered outward from the concussion. The door hung sideways as I grabbed the AK off the steps and charged the bolt. My security man was right behind me as we charged the room. I blasted with the AK at both figures lying on the tile floor. Lights dangled from the ceiling in pieces. Equipment sparked in the racks and smoke hung like a fog.

"Clear!" I announced loudly. My ears were once again ringing.

"Clear!" My man repeated.

It had all happened too fast. We breathed for what felt like the first time in an hour. I was sweating and shaking from the adrenaline rush. Both of the occupants of the building were dead. The place was a complete wreck.

After a few seconds, my remaining security man remembered our fallen comrade outside and went to check on him. I followed him out as the phone man met us in the parking lot. He was standing over our wounded man as my security guy rushed toward him with his weapon drawn.

"Stand down!" I yelled to my security man as he stuck his M-4 in the man's face. I grabbed him by the shoulder to calm him down. He reluctantly lowered his rifle and crouched by our wounded man on the ground. He was barely conscious and bleeding.

He mumbled, "Sorry" I think it was, and closed his eyes. We bandaged the small slit under his arm where the knife had penetrated and bound it tightly. If our medic could get here in time he had a pretty good chance for survival in my opinion.

A few minutes later we had our man wrapped up in all the warm things we could find. When I checked his pulse, I was shocked to find him dead. I never thought a stab wound could be so fatal so fast. There must have been more internal damage which did not result in outward bleeding. His killer lay beside us on his back with his chest resembling hamburger. That man must have trained as a professional soldier to use a knife so effectively and efficiently.

A wave of emotions flooded me. It was my fault, if I had taken less time in the truck, if I had set up better orders, if, if, if. Why were these Sandys so determined to come here and rule us? Why did the green shirts want to rule their fellow man with such an iron will? What was it in the hearts of man to dominate his brother? But, in the background of it all, I was mad.

I stood up and looked to the phone man as I re-focused my attention. "You, get back in the truck, we are making a call. I looked around to my remaining escort. "Let's get our gear squared away; we're leaving as soon as our people get here!"

Inside the truck, I had the phone man shut down all the jamming operations which allowed me to call our convoy. It was close to 23:00 hours and my pickup was not far from the edge of town already. I gave them directions to pick us up and instructed the rest of the convoy to leave the staging area and come to the northern end of town. My people were more than a little surprised, but they obeyed quickly.

Rocket and a couple of his scouts met us first about 15 minutes later. By then, I sent the phone truck back to Durham so he could avoid trouble with his local supervisor. The phone man's shirt pocket contained a little note with some code words and instructions on how to use them. He promised to try to help us if he could.

By the time the trucks pulled up, we had gathered several bundles of intelligence items like computers, paperwork from the vehicles, and the contents of the dead Sandy's pockets. Basically, we took everything that wasn't nailed down.

My truck pulled into the parking lot and loaded us and our gear. We wrapped our dead man in a poncho and carefully laid him onto the bed. I finally got my jacket back and we gathered around the radio with Rocket and his scouts listening nearby.

I keyed the handset. "Group, there are some pretty bad Sandys out there and the green shirts are coming. We are going to round up the Sandys and we are going to keep the green shirts out of Yanceyville. This is a free town and they can rot in hell before I let them have it back. Split into our four-element groups and we go street by street. Look out for a white SUV with four Sandys. One of them is wounded."

It was dawn before we found the Sandys in the SUV. One of our groups caught them trying to break our barricade on the south side of town. Later, a small green shirt convoy coming from highway 86 was convinced to go back to wherever they came from. A short but effective firefight left several of their patrol cars and swat vans burning on the side of the road. They were not all that interested in the town without the Sandys there for backup. If the green shirts didn't have air support or heavy weapons, they pulled back. It was a mystery for a while why they were so conservative. We didn't find out why until sometime later.

The sniper they called the Tiger, was nowhere to be found. He must have bugged out before my groups swept over the area. From that time on, I referred to him as Tigger. I doubted that would be the last time we heard from him.

We lost three men in Yanceyville and a few more had minor wounds. As we drove, I found out that our two missing motorcycle scouts had been found. Tigger had killed them at the crossroads along with the local militia sentries. Most of us agreed that he was trying to draw me into a sniper versus sniper duel. My security man was the third casualty. We ended up with a few extra volunteers from Yanceyville from the local group. Instead of trying to get them on the job training, I sent them to North Wilkesboro with our captured information. Data could analyze everything better than we could on the road. I sure appreciated the Sandys donating a couple of nice SUVs for the task.

Chapter Seven
Charlie Mike

When a mission gets interrupted, you have to get it back on track. Continuing mission is referred to as Charlie Mike from the phonetic alphabet code.

We trashed the rest of our scheduled events and completely changed our planned route. Speaking engagements with little groups of militia were put on hold for the time being. We just didn't want to risk leading any Sandy mole or green shirt spy into their ranks. I trusted my men, but the two remaining rascals were suspect. So, we did as always prudent after discovering a spy. You change everything. The convoy sped south as if we were following the green shirts out of Yanceyville. Our scouts directed us for 20 or so anxious miles until our maps indicated a great spot for an overnight park.

Just off of Luck Stone Road was a quarry outside the little town of Haw River. It was the perfect place for us to rest. Haw River used to be one of the major cotton mills and hosiery manufacturers back in the early part of the 20th century. By the 1990s, most of the textile industry had moved to cheaper labor forces overseas. This town was important for us because we needed to cross Interstate I-85 in order to visit the 5th militia headquartered around Fayetteville. I-85 is the central link between Raleigh, Durham, and all major cities west. The green shirts were not about to let the militia cruise down the road unopposed. They were sure to have many patrols in the area making sure no militia tried to sabotage a bridge or the like.

We made camp in the darkest, most remote place we could find and set up our camouflaged nets. As always, we took that opportunity to rest and recover from the Yanceyville operation. Trucks were fueled, scouts rotated, and weapons were cleaned. I sat on my watch on the top of a little hill where I could see over the quarry pond. The sky remained clear the whole day. It was a great winter day all being said. Sometimes the North Carolina climate can throw a horrible ice storm which just stops everything in its tracks. Like last year; it was a horrible winter when Seven I were married. Nobody could move. People from our home town died from the cold and lack of medicine. It was such a strange mixture of sadness and a strange sense of joy all wrapped up in the same memory.

I was tired, but unable to sleep much that day. The war was taking a toll on me that winter. I had been wounded with a concussion twice, scarred from a tank shell, and seemed to always get banged up one way or another. Seven and the baby were getting to know each other at home while I was out playing Captain America. There were times I wondered how much we could actually do here. Were the green shirts in total control and just letting us gather our strength again to wipe us out once and for all? Or, could we take on the green shirts and Sandys all at once? If we won the state, could we take it on the road and go help free South Carolina? Georgia maybe? It all seemed to be so improbable.

When my shift was over, I reported back in to the group that I saw a helicopter fly down I-85. Presumably it was keeping an eye on the road for us or anyone else not authorized to use the interstate. There were checkpoints and authorizations to use the major highways in those days. You needed to have approved green shirt business in order to travel that highway. We hadn't seen a helicopter in months and I wasn't thrilled to see any more. We didn't have a good way to fight off helicopters with just small arms.

I sat among the team as night started to fall. Our wounded were being treated before the light gave out. One man had bullet fragments in his arm. Another man had been grazed in the leg. One driver was bruised severely from a round that destroyed his door handle and window mechanism. Somehow the round pushed the inside of the handle up against his arm leaving him very sore. He was thankful, though. To my great displeasure, we buried our security man in small patch of woods where nobody would stumble upon it. A brief, but heartfelt, ceremony marked his passing. It was somber as we all considered the likelihood that, someday, our friends might bury us the same way.

Spanky and Darla saw me walk back from the burial detail and met me at my truck. Spanky looked remorseful even though he didn't know the man we buried. "Colonel? May we have a word?"

I walked over and sat by the truck. "Yeah, what's on your mind?"

Spanky asked with a stack of small papers in his hand, "Are we going by the schedule, sir? We were supposed to be in Roxboro today and Rocky Mount in the next two days, but we seemed to be heading south."

"Spanky, we had to change our entire schedule. Give me the list and I will have the general's staff contact those groups we are bypassing," I informed him.

Spanky followed up, "So, are we heading south now? Who are we going to see?"

"I looked at him frankly and spoke the same way. "You don't need to know right now."

Spanky looked blankly at me. He didn't know what to say.

Darla addressed Spanky, "He doesn't trust us anymore. Do you, Colonel?

I stared into her emotional eyes. "Nope."

Darla looked back at me with anger. "What happened to John, err, Alfalfa you called him, back there in Yanceyville?"

"I shot him," I informed her in a casual tone.

She looked stunned. Spanky's eyes widened at the news and he gasped.

Darla looked at me as if I was a sticky something under her shoe. "Why? What for?"

"I caught him working for the Sandys. Alfalfa was a plant in the organization or some kind of spy."

Darla questioned me further, like an attorney. "How do you know he was a spy? We have been working with him only a month and there was no indication he ever did anything to betray us."

I leaned forward and explained clearly. "I shot him with his finger on a map pointing out the direction of this convoy and YOU! His dusty bottomed friends were trying to figure out a way to get our convoy to stop long enough to pin you all down. They brought in a mercenary sniper who was waiting at the southern end of town and had green shirt backup already on the way."

Darla and Spanky sat back with this revelation of information. Darla's anger toward me looked at least mollified for the moment. I'm not sure how much she liked Alfalfa or what kind of relationship they really had. She looked distraught, with tears running down her face. "This is all too much to process. I can't handle all this sneaking around. People getting shot, running all over the state in the dark, it's crazy. It's too much."

Spanky hugged her and tried to console her. They left for their van as she sobbed. My men just watched and spoke softly between themselves. How could Bull send these *artsy* kind of people with me on this trip. Not everybody can handle this level of stress.

At nightfall we made our way through the routes our scouts picked out along Jimmie Kerr Road. Just short of the interstate, our scouts had us halt and wait for the interstate traffic to clear. We sat and looked at the lights shining over the six traffic lanes. Those were anxious minutes as we sat on the edge of that darkened side road. We hoped not to be discovered by some fresh green shirt recruit, or mail man, or some jerk walking his dog .Men sat by their guns, quietly watching in all directions. But soon enough, our scouts radioed all units to race across the bridge in single file. We obeyed with all the speed our vehicles would allow. I don't know what was scarier, going over the overpass in the open or waiting by the side of the road. All I know is the cheer of men on the radio as the last of our vehicles made it to the southern end of the overpass and back under the cover of darkness.

We raced south as fast as our scouts could leap ahead. It was our distinct hope that nobody had witnessed our crossing and we could get far enough away to avoid their standard security sweeps. Crucial minutes passed as we blazed along highway 54. After 20 minutes we calmed our pace and felt secure enough to let our scouts reach out several miles ahead. Our goal was to get as far south as possible that night in the hopes that we would be within a reasonable distance of the 5th battalion headquarters near the town of Carthage.

Adrenaline turned to a groggy sleep after a few hours. Good gracious, I missed the good ole days when you could just drive a straight line somewhere, but sadly, those days were long gone. We had to keep changing back roads and turn every few miles to make sure anyone that may have spotted us would be thrown off track if they chose to pursue. It took an hour to go 10 miles, for crying out loud. But it does keep the other side guessing. More than once I heard stories from townspeople how our militia vehicles would get the attention of a squad car and then disappear. It was great for security, but it drove us mad changing routes all the time.

Anyway, we made our way to Carthage, where we got to a secure park off of highway 24.We were only a week early. But I am glad we made the change, because a couple of interesting things were discovered sooner rather than later. But I will get to that in a minute. After we made camp in the dawn of the new day, my scouts headed toward town to make contact with the 5th battalion leadership. I didn't expect them back until later that night, so we made use of the day and set up our little operation.

Gunny's plane had been directed to Southern Pines to meet us. I drove with the men to pick him up at the Moore County airport. The place was much nicer than anything I had used since the green shirt takeover. The runway was paved and had lights surrounding the perimeter. There was an actual control tower, and a car rental was on the premises, but long since closed. This was the largest operating airport in free territory to date. I remember seeing that large tarmac and the adjacent runway with the great big 5 painted on the end. A few Cessnas were parked here and there in the open. All the little steel hangers looked to be intact.

My truck rolled into the parking lot and we watched the place for a little bit. Then we noticed Gunny walking toward us from the main building.

I jumped out of the truck to greet him. "Gunny, good to see you could make it."

He walked by, saluted in his own way, and handed off a duffle bag. "Yeah, yeah, let's get going."

My guys watched Gunny get into the truck and we followed suit. The driver looked back at Gunny and tried to make small talk. "So, Captain, how was your trip?"

I sat back and listened as I opened the duffle as we drove off.

Gunny started in on the guy. "Somebody forgot to tell us you turds had changed plans. My plane didn't get the message until we were an hour outside of Roxboro. Then they took another half hour trying to figure out where you went."

The driver responded a little defensively. "We ran into some trouble in Yanceyville and had to change our plans. Damn, Gunny."

While Gunny gave him a love tap on the back of the head, he said, "We spent the last two hours of the flight trying to get across I-85.They got friggin' helos running up and down the place lookin' for little ole airplanes. Could we fly straight? No. We had to fly just above the trees to keep off the radar. Damn operations people don't have a clue," he finished, with his arms folded. He was grumpier than normal this morning and I guessed he was lacking in sleep and coffee.

We made our way back to camp just north of Carthage and waited for the 5th battalion emissaries to arrive. By late in the afternoon our scouts reported that a group would be coming later that night. 5th battalion was pleased to hear from us, but unprepared to host us properly. Our little camp was quite comfortable there off highway 24. I think it used to be a horse farm because of the large barns around the property. The whole place was surrounded by a large loop of paved driveway that traced the perimeter of the woods. Nice fencing encircled several areas that could have been horse training rings. It was like camping in a country club with the carefully trimmed trees here and there.

I took the time to set up a little table in the tent we had erected. This was one of those large party tents that could house dozens of people at once with room for a wood burning stove. The whole thing had been dyed a greenish brown color. It was definitely feeling like winter outside, so I sat by the stove and one of the lanterns. I handed out packages to my people. Some of it was mail from loved ones. A couple of administrative packages were mine. They included orders from the general, forms to help keep track of volunteers, schedules for the basic training school. The last thing I pulled out of the bag was a small dry box with a lock. Colonel "Huck's Eyes Only" was written on the lid. Just what in the world was this?

"You might need this," Gunny handed me a key from a band on his wrist. "A special courier gave it to me just before I took off."

I looked up at him and took the key. "Thanks Gunny. Feeling better?"

"I'm fine, why?" Gunny looked perplexed.

"Never mind, Gunny," I smiled at him as he grumbled to the other end of the tent.

Seven sent me a note which I read and pocketed. That one was personal and I'm not sharing that in this book. Let's just say, I still have it. I went through the packets of information and did all my administrative work. The black box sat on the table in front of me a complete mystery. But it also contained something that the general or his staff entrusted only to me. That meant it was important and highly classified. We didn't keep too many secrets in the militia. We found it better to share information with volunteers. I don't know if it was my run down state, or what, but I didn't really want to know what was in the box. One more thing to think about was just not something I wanted to deal with.

Before I could think about it too much, I put the key in the lock and opened the box. The insides were crammed with folders and packets labeled 1-5.A small note read: Read in Order.

Folder One: Operation Lynx. This detailed information packet was on the three people I code named the little rascals. Their backgrounds were detailed, their work history for the green shirts, age, weight, etc. I flipped through and saw Alfalfa's file. Yep, Bull's intelligence group identified him as a security threat. They were not sure about Spanky and Darla though. The Intel group gave me a set of ways to root out problems and suggested to proceed according to the second packet.

I sat back. "This would have been good five days ago, damnit!"

The second packet was filled with a small sheet of code phrases to leak into Alfalfa's hands. This was a dis-information file that we could track through the partial internet and so forth. It may still have some uses vetting the rest of the rascals.

Folder Three: Maps and Routes. This folder was filled with suggested routes to send recruits back to North Wilkesboro. There were things to hand out to local militia groups like flyers and so forth. Basically, it was just updated versions of the stuff we already had. Not really secure enough to warrant this box, I thought. A note from Fred read, "Get bent."

Folder Four: Fayetteville. This might actually be useful. The folder had a seal on the back which was quite unusual .I opened the folder and pulled out a hand-written message from Bull. To paraphrase, Bull was concerned that the 5th battalion leadership was not up to the task of running operations in Fayetteville. The green shirts were active in the town of Fayetteville as well as on the strategic bases of Fort Bragg and Pope Air Force Base. My mission to recruit was still primary, but my new secondary task was to study the situation and make a recommendation for the 5th's future. There were maps for me to mark up and instructions for specific recon missions requested by the intelligence groups.

Folder Five: Wilmington. This packet also had a seal, which I opened. This mission was different to say the least. Bull had every confidence in the 2nd's commanders, but the situation in Wilmington was becoming direr by the day. The Sandys were intent on making Wilmington a foothold. It was unclear how many of their ships could dock at any one time, but they were bringing in heavier and heavier weapons. The 2nd could not make much progress on slowing the Sandy's imports, and if things continued that way, they would lose ground. I was ordered to support their special operations program and see what I could do to improve it. Again, my secondary task was to write a series of recommendations.

I sat back feeling like my hair was on fire. The tasks were massive by themselves. I could literally spend six months on each of these last two folders. The men sat in the tent around me trying to relax. Others changed shifts and sentry positions, while more people prepared the evening meal. Sleeping bags were rolled out and fighters sat on mats that lined the perimeter of the tent. None of them had any clue what we had been tasked to do.

"Gunny, I need you. Come here," I called out.

He strolled over, knowing I didn't beckon him for nothing. Yet, in true Gunny fashion, he was not about to show interest. "Yeah?--sir?"

I motioned for him to sit next to me. "Here, take this intelligence package and get the motorcycle scouts and whoever we have sniper training to start immediate recons. The Intel folks need us to update these maps. The 5th battalion guys don't need to know about any of this either. If they ask, we are doing route patrols or something."

Gunny looked surprised in his own way. "The 5th can't provide this stuff?"

I handed him the rest of the folder. "Let's see what our people can find out there. Then let's see what the 5th reports and compare."

Gunny's eyes flicked through the package. I am sure he read through Bull's letter twice to make sure he understood it right. He got up and said, "I'll take care of it." There was no grumbling in his tone. He knew the severity of what we were tasked to do.

I made myself aware of the maps in the area while we waited for our hosts to arrive. By 19:00, two Captains from the 5th pulled in through our security checkpoint. They met me and the rascals at the tent entrance as our people began chow time. Instead of staying inside Darla suggested we take a stroll around the farm. We walked and talked for quite some time in the cool night air.

One of the Captains asked, "Should we bring in potential recruits or our regulars for your dog and pony show?"

I wasn't sure how to take his reference, but I chose tact. "Let's do a rally for your regulars and then we will do another event for potential volunteers along *with* your regulars."

The second Captain asked about our stage and tent area. The rascals told them of our sound system and little stage.

I asked, "How many volunteers do you have right now and how many will be coming to each rally?"

Both Captains hemmed and hawed at my question. If the rest of the staff were like these two, I could see why Bull questioned their leadership abilities. The first thing I noticed was the age of these two men. They were both in their late forties to mid-fifties and not in the best of shape. Young men, ex-soldiers in hiding, would not immediately want to follow their overweight dad into combat.

"So, gentlemen, what is the situation in Fayetteville?" I asked.

One of the Captains responded, "The green shirts have taken a real interest in Fayetteville over the last couple of months. They control almost the whole city. We have identified several units from other states coming down from the north. They seem to have a renewed interest in Fort Bragg and Pope."

I looked over at him. "It's hard to believe somebody could turn their back on Fort Bragg."

The other Captain chimed in, "That is one of the most common misunderstandings we have. People think that we have all sorts of equipment, but we don't. The green shirts dismantled the military almost completely. They let a bunch of the younger soldiers stick around and destroy the weapons while they shipped off the veterans to labor camps or prisons."

I couldn't believe what I was hearing. "How did they get the vets to turn themselves in so easily? Of all the people in the world, how did *they* get imprisoned so easily?"

The first Captain elaborated. "That was one of the most sinister things about all this. They didn't come in with tanks or guns at first. The VA hospital demanded a series of treatments for anyone with PTSD as a requirement before termination of their service. Almost everyone with more than a year of service was labeled PTSD. Before anyone could object, the people were gone, shipped out. That was right after the blackout when there were no news outlets operational. With no public opinion to deal with, it was a master stroke of deception."

I asked, "What did the families have to say about all this?"

"Oh, they were told all sorts of stories. There was a phantom outbreak of swine flu. Then tainted drinking water was blamed for longer term hospitalization. Every step demanded a new excuse. Our men were given tranquilizers in such quantities that they were barely mobile by the time they were transported. It was horrible to watch it happen day after day; nothing but lie after lie. Those of us that raised concern were arrested. People backed off with inquiries because they were charged with rioting. It was always something with the green shirts. The power was off, phones out, internet off, people just didn't know what to think after a while."

I offered them, "Yeah, I understand. It happened for us the same way. I heard from a guy at the capitol when it was overrun. The police were ordered to stand down from within. Then the police were dismissed and replaced.

We talked for quite some time that night. I walked them back to the tent where we worked out the details of new recruits coming to our farm. The Captains left with promises of many people coming our way the following night. They didn't notice our extra motorcycle security escort that followed them to the outskirts of Bragg.

In the morning, our crews started to prepare the small stage tucked into the woods. We were able to create an amphitheater setting against a small rise covered in large oak trees. A bonfire was prepared and netting was set up to block the firelight from unfriendly eyes. It was a great place, almost reminded me of Boy Scout camp from years back.

By night, we had close to a hundred men there. Several of the officers from the 5th showed up. Dozens upon dozens of men and ex-soldiers came from the surrounding area. This event was different from anything we had done so far. Those were ra-ra sessions for the local guys who had been fighting since the outbreak of war. The people that came that night were people that had survived under harsh conditions where the green shirts controlled almost every aspect of the local big city.

Our "show", for lack of a better word, was the venue by which we made our sales pitch to join the militia. We had several speakers from the local group as well as some from our ranks. Gunny was his usual self. He really didn't like Army brats too much, but he recognized an opportunity to square them away if they came to his sniper school. I was designated the keynote speaker. I shared my stories while they listened. My tone was that of someone that had been there and I didn't brag or exaggerate. The price on my head made a difference to the men sitting there. My speech ended with a question and answer session.

"Colonel, a lot of us here have been through basic training. If we join you, why do we have to do it again?"

I answered back, "That's a good question. You will find that our basic training is not what you get from the Army. The Army taught you how to go from a citizen to a soldier. You learned the Army way, the Army doctrine, and their rules. We train you to use a variety of civilian weapons as well as military issue gear. We train you on how guerrilla forces run operations, how we use codes, methods of secret communication, and standards on intelligence gathering. It is more like the Army's Robin Sage training program." They all recognized the Robin Sage reference and understood at least a bit better.

There were several more questions which we answered one by one. Overall, it turned out to be a great success. Many of the men there recognized the seriousness of our movement that night. They promised to go back home and tell their other friends in hiding and bring them to the next rally. I stood around and shook hands for a couple of hours as men left. The 5th battalion men were amazed at the number of recruits that signed up that night.

Chapter Eight
New Friends

While there was a lull, a man came over to me that I recognized from a back row in the amphitheater.

"So, you are the one they call Huck?" he asked. The man's movement suggested that his body was a fine tuned machine. When he moved, it was a fluid exercise, as if it took no effort for him to walk. He commanded respect at the first words he spoke. I wondered for a second if I should fear this guy.

I looked at the man square in the face, wondering about the question. "Yeah, they call me Huck. It was a nickname of mine from a long time ago."

He watched my features, looking for a hint of dishonesty. "Then you must know somebody from 3rd group, surely."

I looked at his face again, trying to figure out if I had competed against him years ago in a shooting competition. I didn't recognize him, but I might know who he was talking about.

"You mean so and so," I guessed. I didn't say so and so, I used the guy's real name. I just don't want to record it in this book. His anonymity is out of respect. "You know him? Did he make it back from Afghanistan before the blackout?" I asked to confirm I knew the man.

The man looked at me for a second. "He made it back alright, but the green shirts got him over the summer. He guessed you were the sniper known by the green shirts as Huck."

I was heartbroken to hear my friend had been killed. I didn't get to see him much. There were shooting competitions all year and he would come compete when he was back in the states. His fellow soldiers said he ought to buy a house in Afghanistan, he was there so often. He survived countless encounters against the Taliban only to be killed at home by communists. It was a disgrace and shame.

The man stuck out his hand to shake mine. "Our friend will be sorely missed. He always said you would be involved in the resistance." I was going through some emotions when the man continued, "You know? I know a few things about Robin Sage and might be able to help you and the cause. We have been waiting for the militia to get better organized. Perhaps it is time for me and my men to come into the ranks."

"You and your men are most welcome," I told him. "Tell me, what groups do you represent?" I asked. For those of you that don't know, a group is a reference for one of the Special Forces detachments that were represented in the Joint Special Operations Command at Bragg. 3rd group had been stationed nearby. Group one, well known by Hollywood movies as Delta, was just down the road. 7th group operated in Central America and so forth. The financial collapse and mass exodus of military personnel made things strange for everyone. Rumors suggested that commands had been changed or shifted in the early months of the green shirt takeover.

"Call me Major Arrow, I ran Robin Sage before the green shirts took over management. I can bring in a mixed bag of men from almost all the groups. Some are nearby, while others have relocated to outlying areas for security."

I couldn't believe what I was hearing as I admitted to him, "Finally, I met a man with a bigger price on his head than me!"

Major Arrow smiled for the first time in our conversation. "When can you come out and meet some of the men?"

Holy cow, this was the opportunity of a lifetime. This might change the war. If I could convince these guys to come on board, we might have a chance to do everything that seemed impossible two days ago. "Give me 15 minutes and I will meet you at the front gate."

Major Arrow looked at me as if slightly surprised. "We may have a few guys around the shack tonight. See you in 15. "He strode off down the path towards the driveway. He didn't stop to talk with anyone in the tent. Nobody from the 5thmilitia took notice of him or our conversation.

I made my way back to the tent where a throng of my people had gathered. New volunteers were signing up at tables. Others handed out flyers and timetables for transport to North Wilkesboro. Everything was under control and going just as we hoped.

"Gunny, come here for a second," I motioned for him. When we were out of earshot I said, "Gunny, I have to go meet some special forces in hiding. These might be the people that will help us win the war. You are in command until I return. If I don't come back by noon tomorrow, pack up and leave. Look in the black box for special orders from Bull. Keep this under your hat, even from the 5th battalion."

"Okay," is all he said and went back to the men he had been standing around with. To his credit, he didn't bat an eye. His demeanor never changed. If anyone watched our conversation, it looked like a simple order that he simply understood. Nobody would have ever known that I had made him the commander of the unit just then.

Outside the tent, a motorcycle scout had come in to refuel. I tapped the guy on the shoulder. "Report to Rocket that I have your bike; I'll be back tomorrow." The man gave me a salute and stood there in a daze, the empty gas can in his hand.

I drove by my truck to pick up my gear. With jacket, pack, and rifle, I rode to the front gate where the Major sat on his own motorcycle. His bike looked like one of those KLR bikes the military used. Once there, I followed Major Arrow on the motorcycle through a series of back roads until we got to the southern end of Fort Bragg. From there we rode tank trails and old land navigation courses long since abandoned. We rode forever it seemed until we neared a small hill on what looked like the business end of an artillery range.

A half a mile from the top of the hill, the major stopped. "Follow my tire tracks exactly. There is a lot of unexploded ordinance around here." He pointed to a sign that showed a stick figure being blown up. He led off again as I stuck as close to his rear tire as possible. From time to time I saw little dark blobs in the ground that could have been dud rounds from years of artillery practice.

The major rounded a small hill and I followed. On the tree covered side, you could plainly see a concrete wall jutting out from the hill. It was old, worn concrete that had been set in the 40s during WWII. Trees overshadowed the long, narrow, concrete walkway and doors. I felt like I was about to enter a James Bond secret hideout. This was way cooler than anything we had ever built back home. The major parked along the walkway and waited for me to park.

"Huck, welcome to the lair." He pulled open a large sliding door on a series of steel tracks. Inside laid a small room with two doors. The major closed the sliding steel door and latched it. The interior room was pitch dark, but I could hear him walk to the door on the left and open it. Light bathed the little room and the Major ushered me in. Lights shined from rows of lamps in the ceiling. The bay was perhaps 30 feet wide and well over a hundred feet long. Computers and communication equipment were housed in a U-shape of tables nearby. Cords connected PC to PC and radio equipment to PC, all over the room. Maps hung on the wall with intelligence pinned to certain positions. A small nautilus center with weight benches and free-weights was adjacent to an area further down that had TVs. A common area was next to a series of bunks with personal gear. The left side of the wall was open lockers like you see in football. However, in these lockers you found weapons, load bearing vests and thigh rigs for pistols. All the way at the end of the bay I saw HUMVEEs and what looked to be the GMVs. The GMV was a truck specially equipped for Special Forces Groups. They had weapon spindles on both sides for M240s or whatever else you wanted. This was like walking into the Bat cave and finding out Batman had a bunch of bad-news brothers. At a glance, this place was amazing.

"Let me introduce you to some of the guys, Colonel." Major Arrow walked me over to where several of the men gathered around the operations tables. Some came from other parts of the complex when they heard I had arrived. I shook hands with men that could rip my arm off and beat me with it. I felt like a shrimp in an ocean of sea-monsters. Their small guys were muscle-ripped and lean. I passed my rifle over for the men to inspect. They had heard stories of the resistance sniper known as Huck from free radio. Now that the internet was back up, they had also been monitoring Data's web page of my exploits.

One of the guys looked at me. "We heard you used a Barret on those helicopters up in Danville. Nice!"

I looked back at him a little perplexed. "Yeah, but how did you know about that? Data didn't post much about that one because I was on my own."

The Major said, "We've been monitoring the green shirt reports as they pass through."

One of the younger guys chimed in, "You really pissed off a bunch of them with that stunt. They had borrowed those helicopters from up north and coerced pilots from a National Guard unit around here to fly them. You should have heard the storm you raised down here. It was crazy!"

The guys laughed and another one of them asked, "So what unit were you in?"

I looked back at him. "North Carolina, 3rd militia. Now, its 3rd battalion, 1st North Carolina Army."

The guys looked a little puzzled. "No, I mean before the war. Were you Army? Some guys guessed Marine."

I felt a bit ashamed in the presence of real heroes and knew the next few minutes may make the difference in the war. "I was a phone engineer before the war. I never served," I said honestly.

"How did you guys get so far without military guys in the ranks? You must have learned all this from somewhere."

I looked at the men and tried to explain. "Seriously guys, we had a few men that served, like Gunny, but for the most part we did all this with farm hands, grocery clerks, bankers, and the like. We learned from a few vets and then came up with methods that suited people that were not seasoned veterans." The looks on their faces was that of amazement. They couldn't believe we had done so much with so little.

"But, did you actually do all the things from those stories?" the man asked. I could tell they wanted confirmation of our skills. Their whole military career was based on training and more training. It was hard for military to believe civilians had skills that did not come from military or law enforcement programs.

"Yes, as far as what I have seen from Data's web site. He didn't embellish," I told them plainly.

The major said, "Guys, I think we have a challenge. Let's settle it on the range." I looked around as everyone went to a locker and pulled out their choice of gear. This was the thrill of a lifetime for me. I only hoped I could match their skills enough to prove what I had done.

I followed the major through another series of doors that led off the main floor. We walked down a set of steps that led to the floor below in partial darkness. The sounds of boots followed us as the major flicked a series of light switches by the landing. The indoor range lit up and exhaust fans could be heard pushing the air from above. The range itself was only 100 feet or so in length. It was maybe 40 feet across with some bays off to the right that were separate. This whole place was underground and surrounded by thick concrete walls.

The major addressed us, "Men, let's show the good Colonel here what it means to be a good shot." I laid my rifle on a nearby table along with my pack. The Major pulled a buzzer off the same table. The buzzer signals you to start shooting while it records the sound of every shot and the time elapsed. Everybody grabbed ear plugs and stuck them in their ears.

"Hell, yes," came a reply from one of the men. "I'll go first." He was wearing a Sig 226 in a Safariland thigh rig.

Three man sized targets stood at various distances on mobile target stands from 5 yards to 9 yards away. Each center was pasted over with a replacement paper. Any shots outside the center paper didn't count as a hit was my guess.

The volunteer held his hand over the Sig and waited for the buzzer. When it beeped, he drew and shot Blam blam, blam blam, blam blam. He double tapped each target. Each target had two clean holes in the center section of the paper. The Major shouted, "4.28 seconds."

I tried not to smile as I walked to the line. The major looked at me and said loudly, "Go ahead and make ready."

I replied, "Ready!" without looking back at him. My hands were relaxed at my side, no weapon in sight. Outwardly, I had on a multicam field shirt with a button up shirt underneath. My pants were 5.11 with my M&P in a Blackhawk Serpaholster underneath. The buzzer gave a loud beep and I swept the multicam shirt back and drew the M&P with one motion. I too double tapped the three targets, but my shot cadence was different. It sounded like one continuous string instead of three distinct targets being engaged.

I finished as the Major shouted, "3.41 seconds."

Several of the men swore loudly at the time. They used language I won't repeat in this book. Let's just say they were surprised to see a civilian, someone without formal training, do such a thing.

The first volunteer went back to his friends amidst a few jeers, but others watched quietly. A second SF soldier stepped forward to the line and said, "Try this." He nodded to the major who nodded, ready. He drew an M9 from a plate carrier holster set up as a cross draw. He blasted two to the body and one to the head of each of the three targets, nine shots.

The major announced, "6.48 seconds."

I walked to the line and drew my spare magazine and reloaded my M&P. After re-holstering, I nodded to the major.

My draw was not as clean the second time. I shot the furthest head target first and continued to the closest targets with faster and faster follow-up shots.

The major announced, "6.22 seconds."

A few more jeers for the defeated SF soldier issued. I ejected the magazine and pulled the other partially loaded out of my pocket. "Guys this is great and all, but I don't have much ammo for the M&P. It's kinda hard to come by nowadays."

One of the soldiers looked around and opened a steel locker with cases of ammunition. He brought an open ammo can back to the table and thudded it down. "Here."

I reloaded my magazines and took off my multicam shirt, "It's my turn guys. Somebody move all three targets to the seven yard mark. Let's shoot an El-Pres variation."

Two of the men walked downrange while the others asked what in the world I was talking about.

I told them, "You start up-range downloaded with 6 rounds in the pistol. On the buzzer, you turn, draw, and shoot each target 1-1-2-1-1.That is, you shoot each target once before any targets gets two hits. You reload when empty, and shoot the targets the same way again 1-1-2-1-1.Each target will have four shots in the end."

We discussed it a couple of times where I emphasized the point of the drill was to train the shooter to concentrate on the transition between targets. Reloading with speed under duress and engaging multiple targets, were added benefits.

I stepped to the line, looked to the major and nodded ready. The buzzer beeped and I went to work. I blasted just about as fast I could with the M&P. This was still a fairly unfamiliar pistol to me and I lost track of the font sight sometime after the eighth or ninth shot.

The major yelled out, "7.16 seconds, with two hits outside the center."

I looked and saw he was right. A couple of my shots were just outside the center of two targets.

A parade of SF soldiers lined up to shoot the scenario. But in the end, only one or two men could get close to my time. Most of them were closer to nine seconds with some of them above ten seconds.

The major and I watched the SF guys as they tried the stage over and over trying to match my score. We spent a lot of ammunition in that session, and it lasted for hours as we changed to M-4s and sub-machineguns. I didn't do as well with the sub-guns because I had such little experience with them. I did show them a thing or two with the M-4, however.

By the end of the session, a couple of qualified snipers took my Thor sniper rifle next door to a series of long range tunnels. Once there, they introduced me to another Thor they had purchased a couple of years before. They also had several examples of Army sniper rifles with a variety of optics and night vision gear. The underground tunnel offered us a 300 yard range where we tested my Thor against their rifles. The SF soldiers used the same ammunition, from a ballistics point of view, as the Federal Gold Medal Match 175 grain I used. They graciously offered me several boxes of their ammo to supplement the limited supply in my pack. It was like a bullet Christmas.

The men made their way back upstairs after a while, and the Major welcomed me to sit in their operations center for a chat. It was really late by the time we sat among their computer systems and maps. Sergeant King and Sergeant Blake joined us.

"You men have quite the setup here, Major. Thank you for all the hospitality. By the way, what was this place?"

The Major pointed around us at the concrete walls, "This was a test bunker for new prototype artillery back in World War II. This bunker was abandoned right after the war and stayed vacant for decades. When Vietnam rolled around, Green Beret A-Teams started to use them as individual team ready rooms. The artillery ranges were no longer in use, but the unexploded ordnance served as training for explosive ordnance disposal. The special forces were new back then, and this was considered little more than the hind end of the base."

I asked, "How long have you guys been down here?"

Sergeant King responded, "Only some of the men you see here were even stationed at Bragg. Some weren't even in the country when the chaos started. A few were stationed here, or Camp Mackall, others were in transit between Iraq and Afghanistan when the power failed. They made their way back only to find their units dismantled and their fellow soldiers arrested. They had seen this in other countries and recognized what was going on fairly quickly. Some of the guys traveled for months to get back. Others, like that guy in the black t-shirt, were from other teams. He was a SEAL from team two down here for training. Two of the guys were Marine Recon out of Lejune. We are a real mixed bag around here."

I looked at them earnestly. "I always wondered how it was for soldiers. My home town was so isolated for so long. We didn't understand what was going on for ages. You don't know how many people we lost finding out how the prisons worked."

Sergeant Baker looked at me. "You were part of the operation to retake the capitol, weren't you, Colonel Huck? What was that like?"

I sat back and tried to tell him. "We attacked them out of the blue. The green shirts were caught off guard and we had downtown Raleigh secure by late afternoon. The green shirts put up a fight at the Wake County Sheriff's building and their political headquarters, but we had them dead to rights everywhere else. That is when the green shirt armored task force showed up from up north. The planes and tanks were just too much for us. We lost the majority of our commands and barely made it to free territory by the end of the day. That was back in the spring, but it feels like ages ago," I recalled.

The Major sat listening intently before he spoke. "Your operation in Raleigh made a lot of this place possible. Only SF groups used these bunkers. The green shirt's military liaisons had no idea these places even existed. We took the opportunity of the militia operation to steal gear and move weapons to our bunkers. The hope was that our people could make it back in due time and be a part of the resistance. Unfortunately, not very many did."

I asked the Major what I had been dying to ask him all night. "What about the 5th militia guys? Have you guys tried to work with them?"

The Major looked the slightest bit hesitant to answer. "Huck, we worked with them since they formed up. They haven't known it all the time, but we tried to pass them information and give them support from time to time. But every time one of our guys volunteers, it's the same old crap. Their operations were narrow-minded, their plans are short term, intelligence is not used effectively, and the mindset of the militia does not allow for training from the outside." He had been very honest and forthright with me. I think he wanted to see if I was the same way.

I made sure to assure him. "You took a big risk contacting me, Major. I hope I can make it worth your while. There are some strategic operations in the works and I really want you and your men to be a part of it. With the stuff you have here, we can make a real difference."

The Major looked at me. "So, where do you see us fitting into the militia? Do you want us to work with your 5th battalion and supply them with heavier weapons?"

I knew his question was a test of my command ability. He wanted to see how much vision I had and if it was worth the risk to his people.

"No Major, I don't. The 5th is not able to utilize your people's full potential. Nor would they accept a new command structure from people they don't know or trust. My general has given me a wide berth on how to get my missions accomplished and he allows me to staff the jobs as I see fit. Our sniper program is top notch, but our resources are limited. We can train men in the ways of militia operations, but if we are going to take this fight to the next level, we will have to bring bigger guns to the battle. I can't do that with untrained farmers. I need force multipliers like yourselves. With your help, we can train the men we need and run operations of our own. But, that is only the beginning. There are missions that need experienced operators that can work independently. I need real SF soldiers for precise missions. "

The sergeants looked to the Major and shook their heads in approval. The major said, "Well Huck, today might just be your lucky day."

"Yeah? It's been pretty lucky so far, Major," I admitted.

The Major was about to reveal something he had been keeping back and it showed in his face. "Colonel, this is only one of four such facilities. This is just the showroom, if you will. I beg your pardon, but I wanted to see just what kind of person you are. We had to see if the stories were true about you as well. Not many civilian understand that SF work is not all Hollywood blood and guts. We put a lot of effort into our men and we don't want to waste them chasing some squad car through bumfuzzle in the middle of the night. Our capabilities go well beyond regular forces and we have been waiting a long time to give the green shirts some real payback."

I was shocked to say the least. They further explained that they had weapons, ammo, grenades, some light armored vehicles, and missiles. They promised me a full inventory, but for planning purposes they gave me a copy of their gear and capabilities on a secure flash drive.

"Well gentlemen, if we have the bullets, it's just down to hitting the green shirts and Sandys where it hurts the worst," I told them.

We sat there at the operations table and shared intelligence information for hours. It turned out that the SF guys had a vast network of computer systems with some serious encryption capabilities. Their gear was on par with anything I had seen from the foundation to the green shirts. I gave them codes and methods of contact for reaching us in North Wilkesboro. Data would have a hard time keeping up with all the stuff the SF guys would send. Sergeant King gave me a series of methods for SF volunteers that I might find in hiding. If an SF operator needed support, he could use the information from King and make contact with the men at Bragg.

We passed information back and forth for quite some time about various subjects in the immediate area. The green shirts were really putting some effort back into Fort Bragg and Pope AFB. The SF guys showed me where Pope was reconstructing fuel tanks for aviation fuel. There had been increased green shirt air traffic in the last few weeks which was a bad sign for us all. There were serious rail-line security operations going all the way from Charlotte to Wilmington, presumably to support the Sandys.

Our mutual opinion was that the Sandys were a bigger threat than the green shirts at that point of the war. The SF Intel pointed to Wilmington as the largest concern in the state and correctly guessed we would have to take out the port city very soon. The Sandys must be stopped from landing more heavily equipped army groups before they had too strong a foothold. Otherwise, we might never be able to drive them out.

After reviewing the information on the current 5th battalion officers, I chose to recommend that Bull limit them to small raids on train tracks and trestles for the time being. They were wasting volunteers left and right to fight for non-strategic goals inside Fayetteville. The SF had been monitoring their progress closely and gave me more details than any 5th battalion report I had seen so far.

I filled in some gaps in their maps from what I had heard from other militias. We passed information back and forth for hours until our voices were hoarse and our eyes were bloodshot.

I finally looked at my watch. "Holy cow guys, I have to get back to my unit. They are expecting me back in an hour."

I scrambled around and collected my gear as I wished the men good luck. The Major walked me outside to our waiting bikes.

He shook my hand and said, "Huck, we will defeat these green shirts, and then we will drive out the Sandys, or die trying."

I added, "But not before we take a lot of them with us." The Major grinned broadly and gave me directions for my return trip. An SF member led me for several miles until he pointed me to the paved road near the edge of the base. My ride back to the horse farm seemed to take forever. Even in the sunshine of day, it was all

I could do to keep awake amid the rush of ideas on how to use an entire Special Forces unit to its full potential. To make things worse, I hadn't had any real sleep in two full days.

Chapter Nine
The Meeting

I checked in through our security checkpoint only thirty minutes before the unit was to leave me behind. As I passed, I heard the guard notify Gunny of my arrival via the radio. Gunny's response included several words that were not in the Marine Corps manual, but did not exceed four letters. I parked the bike behind the tent where I was met by my people.

Gunny marched out of the tent and addressed me, "We were just about to leave your ass behind. I hope whatever you did was worth it."

"Well, it was not what I expected, Gunny. How is the recruiting drive here?"

"You've been out recruiting all night, Huck?" he clearly wanted more detail than I was prepared to share in front of everyone.

"Gunny, I'm going to sack out for a few hours. Come by my truck in ten minutes and brief me on the number of recruits we rolled into the 5th last night." I did everything but wink at him, suggesting he drop the subject.

He picked up on my evasiveness quickly and helped by ushering all the people nearby to their duties. When he met me later, I filled him in on the meeting with the SF guys. Few things in this world impressed Gunny outwardly. But when I told him of the secret facilities, he commented on how he would have to be nicer to the Army guys. Of course, his next suggestion was for us to divert to the Camp Legune area for recruiting. He said if the Army guys could do it, there must be twice as many Marines ready to fight. I hoped he was right.

I did the rally that evening on pure adrenaline and some really strong coffee. A lot of the men from the previous night came back and several of them brought friends. Word was getting around that the militia was serious and we had our stuff together. We did, too. Things were really looking up for the whole movement by the time we finally packed our bags that night. After the rally was over and the new volunteers went home, we hustled around and packed our gear. Our convoy was gone by 22:00 that night. Later, we received reports of green shirts probing around the area only hours after we left. It must have been frustrating for them. They finally catch wind of militia activity, and by the time they showed up, the party was already over.

In the quiet of my truck, I sat back and tried to get some rest. The next leg of our journey was going to take several hours as we turned west from Bragg and headed for the Uwharrie National Forest. The small towns of Mt. Gilead and Norwood were next on our list of visits. These were small towns much like the first few stops we made in our trip and I hoped they would be quiet little rallies. To tell you the truth, the sniper from Yanceyville was lurking in the back of my mind. The thought of getting on stage was daunting to say the least, especially when it is the last thing in the world you should do with an enemy sniper gunning for you. Someone in the team had a bullet-proof vest which I wore for the speeches. Otherwise, the vest made me itch and sweat too much and I took it off after every event.

The rally at Mt. Gilead went on without any fuss. The two remaining rascals did their jobs well. They were fitting into the group as well as could be expected by then. We had been on the road for a week or so. I am sure Spanky and Darla would agree that they were not military minded and could only expect to fit into a highly motivated group like the people I had with me. Gunny said that Darla reminded him of a girl he knew back in the Philippines and kept a close watch over her. I'm not sure what he meant until one of Rocket's motorcycle scouts got a little fresh and more than a little rude with her one night. After Gunny made his objection noted to the gentlemen in question, nobody dared tell an off color joke around her for the rest of the mission. Guys actually asked Gunny's permission just to talk with her. Let's just say, the scout had to wash out his underwear when Gunny was through with his objection. I hated I did not get it on video; it could have been a great training tool for how to scare the hell out of people with just your voice and a pointed finger. The scout was lucky he was not picking Gunny's boot out of his….well you get the idea.

The next day we did the rally in Norwood. When the event was nearly done, a man strode up to me and shook my hand with earnest. At first, I looked at him oddly and didn't recognize him until he called me by my real name. This shocked a few of my people as they had only ever known me as Huck. The man's weathered face didn't ring a bell though. He had a scraggly beard and his clothes looked like something homeless people would reject.

The man's appearance threw me, but his voice was unmistakable. He had a thick country accent that only a real southerner can appreciate. Most others simply conclude the speaker ignorant at such inflection. Make no mistake and confuse a drawl for stupidity. My friend had two degrees or more and fist full of acknowledgements.

"How in the world did you get down here, Bo?" I asked. Bo was not his real name, that's just what I used to call him back in the day, as it was shortened from Bowman. He had been a cop back in Burlington or Graham before the war. Bowman shot with some of us in pistol matches on occasion, but was world-class with a bow. There was no fish he had never hooked, no deer stood a chance, no turkey, or any other game animal he couldn't bag. He was a first rate outdoorsman.

"I walked," he said with a toothy smile as he hugged me in recognition.

"No, I mean how did you get down here in Norwood?" I asked hoping to make myself clearer. The militia around me gave us a little space as we talked like a couple of old school chums.

"I walked all the way from home to get down here to dad's old cabin. Just got here a couple of weeks ago, Huck."

"You're kidding me?" I asked, not knowing what to think. "You walked 130 miles through green shirt territory to get to your dad's old hunting cabin?"

"Where is the old man?" I asked as I looked over his shoulder, expecting to see another friendly face.

"They got ol-dad last summer back home," he said with tears welling up in his eyes. Mine had tears hearing about that as well. We had been friends for years. "Yep, they had me'an dad on the list when this whole business started last year. Burlington was all bottled up from day one. Police all scattered to hell and gone. Some were arrested right off. Others were packed off to who-knows-where. They rounded up folks left and right. Between riots and arrests, folks couldn't keep track of their own kin. I spent near about a year in a work camp under an assumed name. Escaped this summer and been on the run ever since."

I was amazed to say the least. "You hungry, Bo?"

"I could eat," he said as he looked around at the men gathering into our team tent. Some of the scouts were getting off their bikes and walking through the doorway as we approached.

One of them looked at Bo and immediately dismissed him with a glance of disgust at his appearance. Then he noticed Bowman's rifle slung over his shoulder.

"You loaded there, Grizzly Adams?" the scout mocked.

Bo looked at him square in the eyes without the slightest hint of fear or hesitation. "What good is an unloaded rifle?" I waved to the scout to let it go. Bo had been through a lot and I was not about to lose a scout for having a smart mouth.

We sat around the table where we were served the evening meal. Our cooks were pretty good at making a feast out of the local resources. Bo ate hungrily I noticed. His appearance and odor were noticed by some in the tent. We pretty much had the whole end table to ourselves as we ate.

Bowman unslung his rifle and laid it across the table as we caught up on the past year. "The cabin must not have a mirror in it," I joked. "I didn't recognize you with all that hair on your face."

Bowman scratched his face, "Nope, it don't. Been meanin' to clean up. Been too cold lately, creek froze over," he admitted. Until then, I hadn't really considered where Bo was living. The old huntin' cabin was rustic to say the least. No running water, no electricity for miles, and I am sure there were few creature comforts.

I looked at him seriously. "Why don't you come out to North Wilkesboro and run our wilderness survival course? We have a whole basic training thing set up for guys coming into the militia. They need somebody with real outdoorsman experience. You could teach them all sorts of stuff, even write your own curriculum."

He looked at me. "I just got to the cabin, Huck. You don't know what it took to get there."

"I do, Bo. But up there in North Wilkesboro you will have a home, good food, it is free territory where the green shirts have no offices. You can start over," I offered.

Bo was considering it. "I don't know, Huck. I'll have to think about it." We kept eating for a few minutes as the hum of the tent continued in the background.

I noticed Gunny walk over and begin to sit on the bench beside Bo. "Nice 30-30 you've got there, son." As he said this, Gunny reached down to touch the rifle in admiration of the immaculate finish. Unlike Bo, the rifle was clean as a whistle. The flash of bright steel reflected as fast as lightning. Bo's bone-handled knife slammed into the table between Gunny's index finger and thumb. Gunny was not cut, but shocked to say the least. Bo had drawn his knife with the speed of a rattlesnake without warning. If his aim had been off, Gunny would be short a few fingers from the razor-edged blade.

Gunny froze as did the whole tent. Then Gunny's anger rose like the fury of a typhoon. "Just what in the hell?" He pulled back his hand and got to his feet, ready to throw down.

I jumped up to hold back Gunny as Bo kept eating. Gunny got red faced as he blurted oaths and all manner of uncivilized speech. It was all I could do to keep Gunny from having a stroke as he blurted curses.

Bo didn't look flustered in the least as he finally looked up at Gunny, "This ain't no 30-30, Pops. It's a .44 Magnum, a Browning model 92. Nobody touches my rifle." He went back to his plate just as calmly as if nothing had happened. I think that pissed Gunny as much as anything.

The entire tent watched with their eyes wide open staring at us. A couple of men actually had their spoons halfway to their mouths, waiting to see these two go at it. We finally got Gunny to settle down after a few minutes. If you ever got him riled up, it was something you wanted to see from a distance.

I sat back down with Bo after Gunny left. "Would you mind not doing that?"

"Huck, maybe I just ain't fit to live with nobody," he looked dejected, and I knew that his spirits were low because his tone suggested that he meant what he had said.

"I looked at him. "You just need a purpose again. Sometimes, things get us down and we need something to pick us up again. My wife just had our first baby and…"

Bo looked surprised for the first time. "You're married? You have a kid already?"

"Yeah, that's a kick in the head ain't it, Bo?" I asked, relieved of the stress.

"Is it that ugly girl you were dating last time I saw you?" Bo asked. Oh, tell me it ain't her."

I looked at him conspiratorially. "No. She's the hottest thing you ever saw. Blond hair, gorgeous, whew!"

"You don't say? She must have pretty low standards to have married you. I need to meet this gal. She might get to likin' a real man for a change," Bo suggested as he acted to comb his beard and hair. It was such a drastic change from only a couple minutes back when I thought Gunny was going to lay into him. Nothing seemed to get Bo's dander up.

I looked at him. "You better come to North Wilkesboro to find out for yourself."

It was right about then, a man walked through the tent door that none of us knew. He was a courier which visited on special occasions with special orders. They usually hand delivered these important messages for special missions we didn't want electronically broadcasted. You could never be too careful about sensitive information like that. I heard the man refuse to deliver the package to anyone but Colonel Huck personally.

He was directed to my table and apologized for the interruption. "Colonel, Sir. I have a message from the General for your eyes only. Sir, the General told me I had to deliver it by 19:00 hours today or he would skin me alive."

I looked at my watch. "You did well, bud. Looks like we will have to skin you next time," I told him, seeing the deadline was still 15 minutes away. The man looked relieved and sat down at the table. He had obviously been riding hard and fast to get me this packet. I opened the seal on the packet and read a hand-written note from Bull. It read:

Colonel Huck,

Report to the Stanley County airport by 20:00 hours for transport. Stand by on 22R. Have Gunny take over current mission and proceed to Lejune.

Code: Raven

General 1st North Carolina Army Group
Bull

I looked at the packet front and back; there was nothing else. Bull wanted me to go somewhere for something darn important. The Raven code was reserved for aliens landing on the planet or finding a nuclear bomb under your kitchen table. Above all else, my mission was secret to the point I couldn't tell anyone.

I looked at Bo who watched this take place with a curious eye. "Bo, you have 30 seconds to decide if you want to be in the militia." I walked to the waiting men as I jammed the paper into the wood-burning stove. "I need a ride, who wants to drive?" One of the men jumped up with his jacket and I told him to fire up my truck.

Spanky asked, "What's up, Colonel?"

"I can't say, Spanky."

"When will you get back?" he asked, confused.

"I don't know. Where is Gunny?"

Spanky simply pointed out of the tent as I grabbed my rifle from the rack. They knew I had to leave and didn't ask a lot of questions.

I found Gunny and explained that I had been called away. When he heard he was heading to Lejune to recruit, his mood brightened up a bit.

"I can't tell you anything other than *Raven* about this mission. You know the drill. Gunny, you are in command until I get back. Do as you see fit. Get us as many Marines as you can find. We may need them quick."

I went back into the tent with the last of my gear and Bo stood at the end of the table. "Well?" I asked.

Bo looked a little hesitant. "I might as well join up, I reckon."

I was glad to hear it. "Jump in the truck."

We made our way to the airport like a bat out of hell. Even though it was only 20 miles away, I had to be there in under an hour. Albemarle was not exactly free territory, either. There may be some green shirt office in town, or we might catch some Sandy patrol by accident. Most of the trip was run with fog lamps only. If you don't know how fun that is, try it doing 80 on back roads. Wow! Not good for people with anxiety disorders. We made our way around town and kept to the east until we reached the northern end of a small town called Badin. From there we continued north as we raced to the airport along highway 740. The airport lights were on and could be seen from a distance of a mile out. I wondered just why in the world we were using this place. Then it got worse. Only a half a mile from where we guessed was the end of the runway, we crossed the railroad tracks. This line was most likely well guarded by the Sandys or the green shirts.

We turned left onto Barnhardt road as headlights flashed in the distance. My driver swore loudly and said we may have company real soon. I looked up to see flashing lights in the distance and knew our time was short.

"Keep on Barnhardt until we get to a big curve ahead," I was looking at the GPS map as the driver gunned the engine. We raced even faster down the road, knowing that our time was running out.

"Bo, stay on my butt as soon as we stop. The runway is on the left side of the road. Driver, you get out of here as soon as we get out. Keep running north, then head east, and don't look back."

The driver looked back, "But sir, you will be all alone out there. What if the plane doesn't come?"

"Then I will walk!" I told him as I looked over to Bo. He just shook his head and looked out of the window behind us. When we made the bend, the driver slowed and let Bo and I jump out. Both of us made it to the ditch before the green shirt squad car rounded the corner. By then, my truck had continued down the road as fast as the thing would go. Twice more in the next ten minutes we heard sirens off in the distance, but there was no telling what had become of our truck and driver. Bo and I jogged along in the dark until we reached the outer fence surrounding the runway. After we scanned the area, we made our way to the flat paved surface of the runway.

I don't care how many times you load onto a plane, the runway always make you feel small. All that concrete and flat open ground makes me feel like a very small fish in a great big glass bowl. We didn't have to wait long in the cold by the edge of the field, though. Right on the dot at 22:00, a small twin engine plane crossed over our heads and turned sharply over the trees. This pilot had skills. He dipped the plane's left wing and made a tight turn as he approached the opposite end of the runway. Almost immediately he touched down, I heard security vehicles from the tower blare their sirens. The plane taxied without lights and turned 180 degrees as the side door opened right over the letters on the runway. Bo and I sprinted to the plane as it rolled down the dark concrete. We climbed aboard as the pilot gunned the engine and rolled onto the tarmac. From the tarmac, we gained enough speed to launch into the air with all the thrust the engines could manage.

We banked hard to get over the trees and hangers nearby; we were airborne. In a few minutes, Bo and I sat upright as the plane flew low over the trees bouncing along the air currents. We were hugging the ground so close, I imagined twigs hitting the propellers. The airfield's lights were soon out of sight as we passed into darkness. There was a man in the back helping us close the door and get our gear squared away.

"Colonel Huck, Sir? Welcome aboard," he greeted me. "We weren't expecting your friend here."

Bo looked around at the empty plane. "Should I have brought a parachute?"

The man didn't answer Bo, but looked at me. "He can't come on the next leg of your trip." This was not a suggestion, it was a statement.

I asked over the engine noise, "Where are we going?"

"I can't say, sir," he responded.

"Can you get Bo to the North Wilkesboro command?"

The man looked at me and thought for a second. "Yeah, I think so. It may not be a direct route, but I think we can get him there in a couple of days."

All this took place in the dark among the seats in the rear of the fuselage. The plane was totally dark as we banked left then right. Each time we banked, those of us in the back, grabbed seats and hung on for dear life.

Then a voice came over the intercom, "Hang on back there. We have a couple of helicopters in the area. They may have spotted us." The plane passed over a lake and dipped below the tree-line. We grabbed seat belts and sat, trying to keep our guts intact. The pilot was using every ounce of power the engines could muster. After another 30 minutes, we finally slowed at least somewhat. The pilot backed off the power a bit and was flying straight and level for another 45 minutes. The pilot's voice came back over the intercom, "We are landing in five minutes, get buckled up."

We landed calmly enough, but my knees were wobbly as I gladly stepped off the plane's step ladder. A security detail immediately drove up and ushered me to their waiting Suburban.

"Sir, we have orders for you. Your companion can't come with us," one of the men told me.

"Can you get some transport arranged for him to get to North Wilkesboro headquarters?" I asked.

The man looked around and finally said, "He will have to stay here at the field. I will see what I can do, but I can't promise anything soon. It might be better for you to cut him some traveling orders so he can hitchhike on a supply truck."

I wrote out some quick orders and instructions for 3rd battalion HQ so Bo could go ahead and get started as an instructor right away.

"Bo, you may have to get creative to get there, but these orders should get you started. They will get you housing at one of the schools." I laughed. "It will most likely be a farm where you can run and play."

"Thanks Huck, don't worry about me. I can get there." With that he got out of the truck and walked over to the men milling around the plane. I didn't worry about Bo, to him all this civil war stuff was just an extended hunting trip where the game shot back. He didn't get too excited about anything.

My security detail sped us off the small grassy runway after making sure the Thor and my pack were stowed on the seat beside me. It was getting close to midnight as we drove down deserted two-lane roads through unknown little towns with only a few lights.

"Where are we?" I asked the driver.

"We will be there in a minute, sir," the man responded evasively.

"That's not what I asked," I told him.

"Sir, I have special instructions and can't say any more," he responded again with no more information.

"Just who am I supposed to be seeing," I asked, knowing the answer.

The driver turned the Suburban down a residential street with his lights out. "Sir, we're here." He pulled into a driveway that was completely dark beside a house that was equally non-assuming. This place looked like a safe-house for a witness protection subject. A grandma most likely lived here. I doubted the neighbors even knew this place was occupied at the moment.

The security detail secured the perimeter of the house and opened the porch door for me. To tell you the truth, I was a little concerned about these guys. I didn't know them at all, and if they would have demanded me to disarm, I would have resisted. However, since they made no such request, I thought them at least on my side.

I walked through the back door with my gear in almost complete darkness. My security guys walked back to their truck and said, "Just knock on the door. They won't open up until we are gone."

The suburban left as I looked around in the dark. What in the world is going on around here? The place was silent as I knocked on the back door. The sounds of my knuckles on the wooden door were louder than anything in the area. It felt weird to say the least. The door opened immediately to a small kitchen where a security officer I recognized welcomed me. "Colonel Huck. I'll take your pack and rifle and put them on the table." I handed him the gear and he pointed to a hallway. "He's waiting for you down the hall on the left."

I walked down the hall with at least some trepidation. Who went to all this trouble to talk with me? I rounded the corner of the hall and entered a comfortable living room that was well lit. A group of chairs surrounded a coffee table. Doilies covered nice end-tables over wall to wall carpet. Sitting in the chairs were three men, only two of whom I knew. All three stood as I entered the room.

"Bull, Data, just what the hell is going on around here? What's with all the cloak and dagger business?" I asked.

Bull smiled blandly at me as he introduced the third man in the room. "Colonel Huck, this is my internal security chief, Moriarty."

I shook hands with him and looked back at Data with a lump in my throat. "Is Seven alright?"

"Oh, she's fine," Data stammered. "She's back home."

I looked back at Bull. "Okay, what is all this about if Seven is fine? You take me off mission and fly me to wherever we are. What is so important?"

All three men were dressed in plain clothes. Bull had a Harley Davidson t-shirt showing his large biceps and barrel chest. Nobody was in camo other than me. Whatever was coming was big. I don't think we had ever had such a secretive meeting in the past.

Moriarty started, "Colonel, we are having some serious breaches of security lately."

I interrupted him immediately. "Yeah, I noticed." I looked over to Bull. "You sent me a freakin spy on my recruiting mission."

Moriarty broke in, "We didn't know the man you coded Alfalfa was the mole. It could have been any one of them."

I looked back at this chief of security. "You could have compromised hundreds of volunteers. Everybody we visited before Yanceyville is at risk because nobody briefed me on a potential security threat. You're lucky I got a clean shot at the guy!"

Bull added in before I got too wound up, "Huck, they messed up big time. They won't do it again. We have a lot to cover and we don't have much time tonight."

I took a plush seat as the others sat around the coffee table in the chairs.

Bull started, "Gentlemen, our commands don't know we are here. Our wives don't know where we are. That is how important this conversation is. We are about to share information that nobody knows and it must stay in this room until the time is right to share it with everybody." Bull motioned for Moriarty to start.

Moriarty cleared his throat. "The militia, by nature, is not a standing army. We have volunteers coming and going all the time. We have open borders for the most part and towns that are learning to be free again. We are having one heck of a time keeping insurgents out of our small towns because we cannot maintain a perimeter around Charlotte *and* keep the free territory secure. The Sandys are just waiting for spring to open up on us with more military power than we can resist. It's a straight up numbers game. They will have us outgunned in a matter of months if the ports in Wilmington continue to stay open. In the mean time, they will be willing to sit back and consolidate their strength until a large scale operation in March.

The green shirts have pulled back to the major cities in North Carolina for a reason. North Carolina is going to be the northern border of the new Muslim nation recognized by the People's Planetary Revolution. Their council of countries has ratified a treaty with the green shirts to partition off the southern United States and make us into a fully recognized independent *Muslim* state. From North Carolina to Tennessee, from the Mississippi River all the way through to the Atlantic, has been officially declared, Salidin's Teman. I suppose they are invoking the name of the medieval conqueror there. Temon means city of the South. Florida will remain under the control of the league of Caribbean States.

Data looked around to me. Bull folded his hands in his lap, thinking. He had not known at least some of this before now. I was not too surprised.

"So, we guessed a bunch of this already. What's changed lately? I asked.

Moriarty continued, "We have access to some of the highest level information to date, thanks to your intelligence analyst Data here and the computers you captured from Yanceyville. From all the information we gathered, the Sandys plan a full invasion in late February or early March. The Sandys here now are just the ones that set up camp as it were. That is why they are content to stay in Charlotte for the time being. That is why they keep us occupied with small raids in obscure towns while keeping pressure on our defenses daily. They want our attention diverted from the real threat. The operation in late February or March will be the start of millions of foreigners immigrating to their new country. Those of us that remain will be converted to Islam or dealt with under Sharia law as infidels. And I don't have to tell you what that means."

I looked onward thinking how little firepower we really had against a real army. It was daunting to say the least.

Bull looked sullen as he spoke, "Data, How much cooperation is there between the green shirts and the Sandys to right now?"

Data sat up straight, "From what we monitor, not much. The Sandys have made requests from time to time, but there does not seem to be a very cooperative effort going on. In fact, half the messages from the Sandys have been complaints about support and access to smart grids. We discovered that their cyber intelligence efforts have been focused lately on all our smart grid information. They can track movements of our militia by when and where water or electricity is turned on and off. By following our own usages, they can determine where our troops are housed and how many there are. We of course, are shutting them down at every opportunity, but with so much of the country getting power back, it's hard to keep them out of the loop.

Secondly, the Sandys want more of a military effort from the green shirts to keep the militia off their backs. Some of their emails read more like demands, rather than requests for cooperation. There have been some disputes on where exactly the border will be drawn, but otherwise, they don't communicate through many channels that we have access. Either they are communicating outside our networks, or they aren't talking that much."

We all sat still for a minute with all that information. I was impressed how far Data had come in the last few months. Six months ago he would have tried to explain PC language to us in mind-numbing detail. Now he ran a department and gave great briefings with the information we needed.

Bull was quiet as he spoke, "Well at least we have that in our favor. I imagine the local green shirts will want to keep the major cities where they have complete control. Maybe we can get them fighting between themselves or something, but even then it will only get us to summer, at most."

The room fell silent as we contemplated the thought of millions of people coming in as an invading army. It was overwhelming to consider.

Data reached down beside his chair and pulled out a packet of papers. "Here you go, Huck. It's a bio of that sniper you call Tigger." While the other men talked, I flipped through the pages briefly. Data had at least some of the guy's information as well as a grainy photograph. I stuffed the packet in my jacket pocket for later.

Moriarty said to Bull, "If we only had more time to train these new recruits, we could send a task force to Wilmington and close the ports."

Bull looked frustrated. "It's all the 2nd can do to maintain their pressure on the Sandys now. Shutting down the ports for any real length of time would require some serious soldiering. The reports on my desk say that the 2nd has no chance of penetrating their defenses. We would need some serious firepower to change the status quo. If the Sandys send air cover into this fight, we will be in a world of hurt quick. We need a real army."

I stood up and paced behind the couch. "Bull, I may be able to help you with that."

Everyone's eyes locked on me.

"What do you mean, Huck?" Bull asked. "Do you have an extra army you haven't told me about?"

I looked back at him. "As a matter of fact, I just might."

The other men in the room looked at each other, waiting for the punch line.

I told them, "Three days ago, I spent an evening with some special forces in hiding around Bragg. They have trucks, missiles, personnel, guns, ammo, and the works. If Data were to check one of the accounts we use for secure communications, he will find a report on what materials they have available."

Moriarty and Bull's mouths dropped open. Data whipped out a laptop from nowhere and began typing at his usual light speed.

We talked for a few minutes while Data retrieved the email. He read through several reports and asked me, "Is Arrow somebody you know? His attachment requires some military grade decryption."

"Yes, that's the Major's report. Use the key "Archer1987" on the attached document."

Data typed away while the rest of us sat and waited without saying a word.

In a few seconds Data's eyes widened, "HOLY crap!"

Bull and Moriarty got up and looked over Data's shoulder. Each of them scanned the screen trying to read through the document.

Bull pointed to the screen, "They have some AT4s, Javelins, a few stingers, good heavens, the list keeps going!"

Moriarty pointed, "That can't be right. How can they have that many M-1 Carbines? They haven't been in service in years."

I told Moriarty the history of the M-1s that Major Arrow had shared with me. I also shared the concerns about the 5th battalion militia leadership from the perspective of the Special Forces in hiding. Then I followed up with my vision for how they could be used appropriately. I wanted to make sure he and Bull understood what an opportunity these men were to the resistance. We discussed plans for quite some time and hashed out several key objectives over the following few hours.

After much debate, our planned attack on Wilmington was scheduled for mid-February to early March. Bull would communicate our findings to all the other resistance groups in the region so they could start preparing. I was to be sent back out on the road for the next few days to see how many Marines I could get to come on board. As soon as we could, we would assign fresh recruits to the task of containing the Sandys in Charlotte. Our more seasoned troops would be sent up to North Wilkesboro to train with the SF guys from Bragg for a few weeks. I wrote out a bunch of orders and instructions to the people running our basic training schools. They must have thought I had lost my mind with some of the stuff I was writing. New instructors coming, give them full access. Weapons and ammo will be arriving by truck. Ex-military coming, we need to integrate our regulars and their people into small combat teams and start new training cycles.

Chapter Ten
Tigers and Bears, oh my!

By the time the sun rose, Data and I were on our way back up to North Wilkesboro. Bo had already hitched a ride and was nowhere to be found. Bull arranged for a plane to pick me up in 24 hours to help me get back on mission. That gave me a small window to go home and see the family. It was hard to imagine having a family at that moment. All I could think about was how to prepare for the upcoming mission to close down Wilmington.

Somewhere in the back of my mind, having a family seemed to make me more vulnerable. I felt guilty for having those feelings, but I couldn't help it. But, that was not the time to dwell on emotions and lose sleep over them. None of us slept much over those weeks.

As we drove up to North Wilkesboro, I wondered how Gunny was getting along. He was supposed to be driving to the outskirts of Lejune, which was no small task. From Bragg to Lejune was further than 100 miles of spotted green shirt control. That was, of course, passing through areas also covered by Sandy helicopters on patrol. The thought of losing members of my team while I was back home disturbed me to no end. The thought that they might be hurt while I was home was impossible to accept. I tried to tell myself that my work was really important to the cause and that everyone understood the risks they took, but none of that helped much.

By mid-day, Data and I reached the 3rd battalion headquarters. We parked and checked into the main building where we were flooded by questions from everybody passing. What should have been a beautiful reunion, turned into a detailed explanation as Seven found me in my office.

"Huck? What are you doing back here at headquarters? Seven began her interrogation. "Where has Data been for the last twelve hours? What is going on with your recruiting mission if you are not there?"

"It's nice to see you too, dear. Let's see, I can't tell you, somewhere I can't tell you, and I have no idea," I answered her questions as accurately as I knew how. She was neither impressed nor humored by my lack of detail. "So, what are you doing here? Where is Punkin?" I asked.

Seven had her hands on her hips. "You are not redirecting me, mister man. Now, give me a kiss before I hurt you."

I did so gladly. In the background, people came to the door of my office as word got out that I was back. It turns out a week or so was quite long enough for a great deal of paperwork to pile up. Department heads showed up asking all sorts of questions on everything ranging from menus to staffing changes. For the first time in a while, I felt it was better to be back on the road. Seven tried to help me for a few hours and made everyone a ten minute appointment for the remainder of the day. They were all given a time and strict orders to not be late.

Seven left for home as I sifted through the small mountain of work on my desk. My mantra became a simple series of one-liners, "You decide. Make it work. Pass him to another squad, then. Go ask that person, then. Yes, I'll have another cup of coffee."

Most of my work over the first few hours had been for the local basic training courses. But as evening drew near, my first operational appointment arrived. Rocket had come back to town with the fuel trucks to re-supply our recruiting mission.

I hollered out of my open office door, "Rocket, come in. Have a seat. We only have a few minutes, so let's get down to business."

Rocket came in and sat on one of the chairs. He looked up at me with question and confusion on his face like a kid that had been called to the principal's office. Although this time, he looked like he couldn't remember why.

"Yes sir." He sat and looked back across the desk.

Rocket, you have done a great job so far with your motorcycle scouts. The guys you've trained have come out and have done their jobs as well as anyone could expect. They know our procedures and they can sniff out green shirts like blood hounds. You've trained them well."

He was waiting for the hammer to fall from the looks in his face.

I continued, "But the war effort needs you elsewhere for a while; I need you to name your replacement."

Rocket took a big gulp. "What did I do?"

"Do?" I asked back at him."You didn't do anything bad Rocket. This is a promotion."

He looked relieved and then skeptical, "Don't they usually promote guys that can't do a job, just to get them out of the way?"

I knew what he meant, but I played it up. "You mean like these Eagle's wings here?" I flipped my collar at him.

Rocket instantly backtracked, "I didn't mean you Colonel Huck. I just meant, well sir, I never meant to make it sound like you aren't, well...."

"Easy Rocket, I knew what you meant. No, this is a real promotion that some might question whether or not you are up to the challenge. I'm betting you are."

Rocket breathed for the first time and relaxed a bit. He was eager to contribute, which was something to be admired on its own merit. Further, Rocket was a lot like his Dad. He had a natural air about him that people were attracted to. He was the miniature version of his father, General Bull.

"Rocket, I'm about to tell you some of the most secret plans in the war to date. This conversation must stay between us for now. Understand?"

Rocket gulped a bit and said, "Okay?"

I paced back and forth behind my desk for a second or two and tried to think of a way to explain things to him."Rocket, are you familiar with the Red Ball Express of World War II?"

He looked back at me in utter confusion. "Uh, no."

I sat back down and told him, "Europe was destroyed. The trains were all bombed out and there weren't enough planes to haul the tons upon tons of gear to support the army fighting the Germans. So, we organized a supply line comprised of trucks in large convoys to transport all the gas, bullets, and beans for the war effort. It stretched across all of Europe. They ran non-stop day and night to supply the front lines. They got creative on how they shipped the goods and how they kept the men going even after long hours on the road. I need you to gather a team of drivers and set up our own Red Ball Express."

Rocket sat back in his chair, thinking. I could almost see the wheels turning behind his eyes. "Sir, this won't be a regular supply train, will it?"

I looked back at him, "No, it's not. I need your team to open a route that gets all the recruits from the other commands up here in a week. Then you will open a route that gets all our recruits and their gear to a staging area, here." I pointed to a place on the map behind me.

"Sir? We are hitting Wilmington in force?"

I answered back, "That's right. Our success will depend on getting enough of our people there in one piece to make it happen. They will need to travel at night, covertly, and you will have to do it in such as way that the green shirts have no idea we are coming. You will need primary routes and backup paths. All of this has to be detailed out where you can manage hundreds and hundreds of passengers over great distances. Estimate fuel usage, timetables, etc."

Rocket's eyes were fixed in thought. "How much time do I have to get all this up and ready?"

"You can hand off the scout training class today when you name your successor. We are scheduled to have recruits coming in by New Year's Eve. The big operation needs to be ready by the end of January, with all your drivers trained and positioned along the route. All your park areas need to be operational by then as well. It will be a massive undertaking."

Rocket sat back in his chair, "Hmm. Well, I need to research this a bit."

"Give me your plans by 07:00 tomorrow and I will start the operations officers on getting your orders together. I want your personnel lists as well. Go by Intel and have them give you what you need for contacts with the other battalions. They may be able to help a bit with facilities, but this must remain quiet. Nobody can know our destination target. Only use drivers you know personally and trust. Some of the other commands don't even know as much as I have told you. Get it done, Rocket."

"I will do my best, sir," he assured me as I ushered him to the door.

I felt bad for giving Rocket this assignment with so little instruction. What I had just given him was overwhelming to say the least. But there was simply no time to do more. I had to trust my people to do the job they were assigned and keep moving.

I looked down at the schedule. "Data, come on in," I yelled through the crack in the office door.

Data and three of his people came into the office and sat around my desk. I plopped down in my chair as the door closed.

"Okay, Data, who do you have here?" I asked.

Data pointed to each person, "This is Tinker, Repo, and Princess." The last person in the group was a girl in her mid-twenties. She was wrapped up in enough layers she could have survived in Alaska. I don't like to call people names, but I would have identified these three as mega-geeks. Before the war I have to admit that I was judgmental. During the war, I had a great admiration for the people that could hack their way through the telecom grids with complete anonymity.

I looked to the girl. "Princess?"

She looked back in explanation. "You see, online I was the Elvin Princess of Mysteria. You know, in Worlds of Middle Earth." Undoubtedly, I was supposed to understand completely by this revelation. She continued, "I was the level 49 head mistress of the lady of light…."

I interrupted her due to time constraints. "Ah, so that was you?" All of them looked to me with instant interest. "So all of you are well versed in telecom hacking?" I asked. All three nodded their heads, "And you are ready for field work?"

They again nodded their heads. "I assume Data has filled you in on what we need. We must have secure communications from fixed installations in the east back here to headquarters. Tinker and Repo, you two are assigned to the staging areas outside our objective. Princess, I am assigning you to the midway point. I will cut orders for you to go out with the Intel groups in the next couple of days."

Data spoke, "Colonel, could we get them into a class or two on field survival and maybe some basic handgun? Nobody here has any real-world experience in either."

That reminded me of Bo. Where was he?

I nodded my head. "Yes, by all means. Do you have enough tools and trinkets for field kits? Do you have jumpers, wires, patch cables, multiple power sources for the PCs, tools for cabinets, etc.?"

Data handed me a list. "We need a few more items. We don't have them locally."

I looked at the list briefly. "Pass this on to Intel, not standard logistics. If you can't find them here, steal them somewhere enroute. Don't take anything near your objective. I can't tell you how sensitive your mission is to the cause. Above all else, stay off the green shirt radar. If you are compromised in any way, bug out. Start fresh from somewhere else and use every security protocol known to man. With any luck you will survive this mission."

All three of them went wide-eyed as they sat there trying to catch up to the speed of information thrown at them. I scratched orders for them and handed out the papers as they walked out of the door. There just was not more time to do a better job. Everyone would have to learn as they went.

I walked out to the office as Data and his people left. The office manager was on the phone with security and I overheard part of the conversation.

"Tell him that the Colonel is very busy right now and without the right password, he cannot enter the building. If he doesn't go, call the constable and have him arrested."

"Who wants to see me that bad?" I asked.

"Some homeless guy with a rifle, the way security describes him. One of our drivers dropped him off. Maybe a hitchhiker or something."

I smiled. "Tell him to identify himself."

A few seconds went by. "Sir, he says his name is Bo. I will call the constable."

"No, send him to my office right away," I ordered. I could see the looks of incredulousness as they complied. Boy, were they on for a surprise. I had Data's folks stand by as Bo made his way upstairs. Within a few minutes, Bo found me.

"Just what in the blue hell is goin' on round here?" Bo asked my administrative assistant. "That crazy driver nearly killed me with all his back road drivin'. Security don't know nothin'. Wuz it you that suggested for them to arrest me?" Bo asked the lady.

Before he got too wound up I walked over and handed him a piece of paper making him a Lieutenant. "Take this to security and they will get you squared away. These are your first students,

Tinker, Repo, and Princess. They need some field training and basic pistol shooting in the next two days. Can you handle it?"

Bo looked back at me. "Wha'? I just got here and I don't even know where the toilet is."

"Down the hall and on the left. After that, go see the operations Captain over the basic training courses. He's somewhere on this floor," I waved incoherently. "Give him these orders and he will get you the gear you need from the logistics people downstairs."

I turned back to my office with my next appointment waiting for me around my desk. Everyone in the waiting area looked down at their pieces of paper trying to figure out what to do next. It would have been funny if not as much was riding on the outcome of those meetings. At 20:00 my itinerary read: COME HOME. The rest of the paper was blank until morning when I was due to leave on a plane for Camp Lejune.

I caught a ride back to Wooten Valley on time for a change. It caught me completely off guard as I loaded onto the van where fellow resistance leaders talked about Christmas. I had completely forgotten it was close at all. It seemed more like a distant memory than the holidays. I hadn't seen a properly lit tree in a couple of years. There had just been no thought towards celebrating Christmas with all the things going on with 3rd battalion. I promised myself to remember to take time away from all the work and see if Seven and I could spend extra time with little Punkin.

The van pulled off the road and parked, allowing us riders to cross the creek over a little foot bridge almost a half mile from the nearest home. Our main road was closed off to vehicle traffic for security reasons. The gravel road felt like home as we walked along in the darkness. Stars guided our footsteps as we walked along and talked in the freezing night air. Some from Wooten Creek had elected to move to town during the winter. Several of us remained with limited electricity and our wood burning stoves just because it was more comforting. City life was not that appealing to some of us. Our numbers dwindled as we passed from house to house.

My personal security guard patted me on the shoulder. "Colonel Huck, I will be here before sunup so you can make your flight in the morning. A truck will meet us back at the bridge to get you to the airport."

"Thanks Mac," I replied. "Go get warmed up. See ya tomorrow."

The light was on in my little cabin as I stepped up onto the stoop.

"Hi honey, I'm home," I said loudly as I walked through the front door. I heard footsteps from above in the loft which was our bedroom. In a few seconds, Seven walked quietly down the stairs with her fuzzy slippers on. Her hair was done up in her usual pony tail but strands of blond swayed freely as she walked to me.

"He's sleeping," she motioned with her fingers over her lips.

We spent that night doing much of nothing. Between feeding the baby and sitting by a crackling fire, life was good. Fred called once to see if I was in, but he wisely did not call back when Seven hung up the phone on him. She was not impolite mind you, it's just that we were having family time and I'm sure Fred understood. Yeah, that night was calm and peaceful for a few short glorious hours. The next day was nothing like we expected.

I awoke some time before dawn in the foothills. Dawn may come a little earlier, but it depends on the side of the hill you live on that determines when you see sunshine. Seven and Punkin were asleep as I dressed. Seven woke as I started down the stairs and wished me a safe journey. Just as I kissed her goodbye, there came a knock on the door.

Mac stuck his nose through the door. "Colonel?"

"Come on in Mac," I told him. "I'll be down in a few minutes. Go ahead and make us some breakfast." I told him. Mac had done this before and it was customary for him to start breakfast on the occasions he escorted me from our little house.

In a little while, the smell of bacon and eggs wafted through the house and I fed Seven, who was still upstairs nursing Punkin.

Mac called up to me from below, "Huck, we need to go ahead and walk to the bridge. The car will be here in ten minutes. I'll get your pack."

I called back, "Okay. Hey, grab my old sniper rifle too. The armory thinks they have a new barrel for me."

Mac responded, "Okay." I heard the front door open and Mac's boots walk down the front steps.

As I knelt to kiss the baby goodbye, I heard a series of thumps and bumps with the unmistakable sound of clamoring metal hitting the wooden front stoop or steps. At first, it sounded like Mac had slipped and fell on icy steps. Then, the rifle report echoed through the valley. In an instant, I knew it was more than slippery steps.

Seven's eyes darted throughout the room franticly. "What was that? Was that a rifle?" She strained to look through the windows as I raced down the stairs.

I told her, "Stay away from the windows!"

With my pistol in hand, I made my way down the inside steps into the room below. It was quiet, nothing was out of order. The sounds of the early morning fire in the stove popping and hissing were the only sounds. From a distance, I looked through the side window to the left of the door. Mac lay just off the steps in a heap. I could see he was shot cleanly through the center of the chest from what could only be a sniper.

"The Tiger!" I said as the words as they bit through my clenched teeth. "That SOB found me! Us," I corrected myself in dismay.

Seven called down, "What is it, Huck?"

"Honey, wrap the baby up and bring him down here. Get your pistol and get tucked into the pantry. I think that Serbian sniper just shot Mac." While I said this I pulled on my heavy jacket and jammed stuff into my pockets. There was only a single magazine for the Thor and whatever ammo it contained. The rest was in my pack lying beside Mac out in the open. There was no way I could tell if the sniper was still on the prowl or not. Mac and I were about the same size. Perhaps the sniper thought he had gotten me and was gone by now. I had no way to know for sure. My heart raced as I thought hard what to do next.

Seven came down the steps with the baby in one arm and her M&P in her free hand. I hated the look of strain on her pretty face. She was terrified, but calm. I tucked the phone into the baby's blanket as Seven headed for the pantry. "Call the store. Let them know what is going on and that I am on channel one on the radio."

Seven knew to keep calm in these situations and was collected as anyone could be. As she dialed the phone, she looked over at me. "Huck, he knows where we live. You must get him before he escapes or kills someone else. Go!"

I raised the Thor and slapped the bolt down on a 175 grain Matchking. "I'll get him."

One of the reasons I chose the little house off to the side of the road was the thick patch of mountain laurel on this side of the hill. My back door was not useable for anything other than getting firewood or climbing the hill covertly. From the front of the house, or even the sides, the door was all but invisible. With my elbows and toes digging into the dirt, I crawled up the side of the hill under the thick green laurel.

As much as I dared, I peered through the thicket to see the opposite ridge across the river. A lot of the trees on that side were hardwoods. The leaves had fallen months ago, leaving the ground a light tan bathed in the morning sun. I heard sounds of shocked people as they peered out of their doors and saw Mac lying in the road. Quickly, loved ones grabbed the onlookers back into their homes for safety. The minutes wore on as I crawled through the thicket towards the top of the ridge. Shouts echoed from below.

After a short while the radio crackled. "Huck, are you alright?" The voice was that of the local convenience store proprietor. This was our unofficial 3rd battalion headquarters mind you. Almost everyone that ran the 3rd battalion lived right there on Wooten Creek. The convenience store is what we called it, because that is what it was before the war. Over the last 7 months or so, it had become a grill, a gathering place, our store, the center of our community. Nobody but militia lived there in the valley with the exception of a few family members related to those serving. The Tiger had swatted a hornet's nest and it was my bet that he didn't even know it yet.

"Yeah, Mac is hit and it looks bad. He is on my front porch and I can't get to him out in the open. I think the sniper they called the Tiger is the one that shot him and he did it from across the valley," I replied back quietly into the handset.

There was a pause. "What do you want us to do, Huck?"

"Call headquarters and get security here now. Tell them to setup counter-sniper posts two miles out, on every logging road and path leading away from here. Tell them this guy has talent and should not be underestimated. Collect whoever you have at the store and send them to all the bunkers on the Ozark, Bunker Hill, and Loblolly Trails. Tell them to haul their butts to those bunkers and sit tight. Keep an eye out for a motorcycle, car, or whatever. Over."

The voice came back, "We're on it. Do you want somebody at your house?"

I said, "Yeah, send someone from over the hill through the laurel and go through the back door. Just make sure Seven knows it's our people so she doesn't shoot them."

"You want us to send you some backup?" he asked.

I replied, "No, just get a perimeter set up to the west. I have a hunch he went that way."

"Okay, Huck. Good hunting."

I made my way to the top of the ridge and rounded the crest. Feeling safe, I ran the ridge on the side facing away from the valley heading north. From time to time there were sounds of traffic as cars and trucks passed along the roadway below me. Some were vehicles positioning themselves at washouts, logging roads, trail heads, and the paved roads. We knew these woods like nobody else. We had been training sniper groups almost non-stop along these trails for the last six months. That's how they became named trails in the first place. A squad of recruits would use some pre-designated trail each day of their training cycle. We set up known and unknown shooting distances, bunkers, booby traps, and all sorts of other things to teach the recruits the art of sniping. The Tiger had really picked the wrong place to ambush me.

He must be one cocky turkey to come calling me out at home like this, I thought. From the northern bend in the valley, I slowly looked over the top of the hill back towards my little community. All was quiet from what I could see. My watch said it had been close to 30 minutes since the shot that most likely killed Mac. I hated not knowing for sure if he was dead. The choice not to try and rescue Mac was a hard one that I was not sure about. I did know that if I had tried something foolish, I would be lying there beside him just as dead. As a sniper, you always back the other guy in the corner and dare him to do something stupid. When he does, you have him. Although this time, my advantage was that the sniper was the one fooled. I had bet that he saw Mac with my sniper rifle and shot before verifying it was me. That would be his undoing. I was getting payback today.

After a few minutes, I ducked back behind the hill and jogged along the outer trails. The whole time I wondered how he found us, if he had been able to communicate our position, or how much he really knew about us at all. If I were him, I wouldn't strike on a guy's home turf like that. I would pick a place in transit where he is most vulnerable.

In an hour I was several hills north and west of our valley, perched under a cedar tree beside a fallen oak tree. My radio crackled as men checked in periodically according to standard operating procedures. The roads were blocked and monitored. The trails were manned and guarded. I scanned the hills lying in front of me. Four little valleys issued from a single ridge to the south allowing a view of each.

Slowly, I covered the lens cap of the Thor's NightForce scope with a leaf covered bit of sniper veil. This kept the light from reflecting off the objective lens and betraying my position. The NightForce was an amazing scope. I could see minor details of the woods four hundred yards away.

I lay with my belly on the ground and cold seeping through my jacket. I was painfully aware of winter that day. Birds picked through leaves nearby making all sorts of racket in their morning feeding ritual. Deer drank in the river and ate clover a half mile away. But there was no sign of my prey. It was getting under my skin to stare at nothing.

The radio chatter was constant for more than another hour as teams got into position. Our security had been set, now it was a matter of waiting.

Around noon, I heard, "Team four to base."

"Go head, four."

"We found a motorcycle over here parked under some bushes off of Mertie Road. We pulled the spark plug and are setting up a sniper to watch over it. There are a few tracks that lead up the road towards our valley, but we lost them on the hill. Fella must be pretty tall. His boots are size 13 or more."

Whoever was manning the base radio said, "Roger that team four, good work. Be careful and watch out everyone. Our target is still on the loose."

I was elated at the news of the motorcycle. Finding it meant that it was likely that the Tiger was not brought in by an escort team. It also meant that there was a possibility that the Tiger had not communicated our location to his employers either. Unless he had a satellite phone, I doubted he could use any other form of communication because we monitored them. If he acted like a classical stand-alone sniper, he might wait till dark and make his move to get through our dragnet. He undoubtedly thought he could get a shot off at me, then make his way from hill to hill until he reached the motorcycle. From there, he could escape before anyone was the wiser. Our lockdown of the area must have surprised him to say the least.

While the day wore on, I found another fallen tree off to my right some 20 yards away. My hide and this fallen tree were connected by a ditch that allowed me to move unseen between positions. Under that tree, I planted a dark stick to poke out from underneath the main trunk .I placed my compass on top of the stick and held it in place with my camo hat. If my judgment was right, the sun would set off to the west and reflect off the compass. From the opposite ridge the compass equipped stick would look like a sniper that had forgotten to shade his objective lens. During the middle of the day, the fake rifle barrel was in shadow. By evening, it would be exposed and visible from the opposite ridge. I might just fake him out with my trickery and get a critical second or two for a clean shot. That is, *if* the Tiger was still out there. I hated guessing what someone else was thinking. There are just too many possibilities.

By the time evening rolled around, our teams were on their third rotation. Patrols monitored the roads and snipers were replaced with fresh eyes. North Wilkesboro sheriff deputies had several road-side checkpoints and monitored everyone's coming and going for miles. My stomach growled from the lack of calories and the exertion through the hills. My pack usually contained a couple of days worth of food, but Mac had taken my pack as he walked out of the door. Even though I was dressed for winter, the cold had infiltrated every spot that had gotten damp from lying on the ground. The only thing that kept me warm was the determination I had for getting this guy. He could not be allowed to get away this time. He had shot at me once before back at the old headquarter building some months ago. Fred shot at him with the MP5 at the airport less than three weeks ago. The Tiger grazed Fred in the dark and nearly killed him. This guy set up in Yanceyville and killed a couple of our scouts. Now, he shot my personal security guard thinking it was me on my own front step. He had to be stopped before his buddies showed up.

From a distance, I saw headlights appear on roadways far off in the distance. The sun was setting off to the west throwing dark long shadows into the valleys. Smoke rose and hung in the air like thin clouds from wood burning stoves. I watched through the NightForce scope as the shadows stretched across the opposing ridge. A dark unknown object moved high on the ridge at an incredible pace. I panned the rifle to the right to zoom in on the object. A black bear loped over the peak of a smaller ridge through the leaves with ease. Bears were not that uncommon here, but something had spooked him enough to send him running for cover. Most people never see bears because they are so private a creature. They typically don't wait around for people to get too close. I pointed the rifle in the direction from where the bear ran.

Far off on the largest ridge another dark shape moved. This object was not as dark as a bear. I could just barely make out the outline of a man trying to make his way from the top of a saddle down into the bottom. I had anticipated this and waited for a few minutes for the man to re-appear. The man kept to the dark shadows as I expected he would. My bet was that he had detected the sniper bunker on the Ozark trail and had decided to make for the little gap between it and the fork of the river. That would bring him out right in front of my leaf-covered slope. He would feel safe being able to see the whole empty side of the hill and I would get my shot at him.

Precious minutes worth of shooting light faded as I waited. Then, just about where I guessed, the Tiger emerged at the base of the hill. His Soviet SVD sniper rifle pointed as he scanned my ridge. He was looking things over as he should. I pressed the Thor into my shoulder as I took closer aim at the figure below and to my right. It was a really hard position at an extreme awkward angle to see around a giant oak between us. Maybe that is why my first round was not exactly on target. Kaboom! The Thor cycled the next round into the chamber as the sound of the 175 grain match round sped down the slope towards the Tiger. I watched through the scope and saw him hobble forward to thicker cover and darkening shadows on my side of the river. He looked wounded, but certainly not out of the fight.

The radio crackled as the teams tried to figure out where the shot came from. My earpiece fell out as I put my plan B into motion. I crawled hard and fast off towards the right along the ditch. Within a few seconds of passing it, I heard a crack and the Tiger's round slammed into the fallen tree trunk behind me. Pieces of my compass flew through the air and landed in the leaves. He had shot my fake sniper barrel stick just as I hoped he would. I cut my elbows and hands scratching my way further west to the ravine on my stomach which kept me out of sight. If my plan worked, he thought that he had dispatched another militia sniper. My hill sank towards the west into a wide basin where a tributary of the river flowed from streams above. If I were the Tiger, I would make my way up that tributary and keep under the mountain laurel so I could continue north until was clear of the area.

Once in the outlying shrubbery, I crouched and ran the remaining 200 yards to the small stream flowing down the ravine. In the shadows of the laurel, I waited. My heart was pounding at the sudden exertion. My arms and legs ached at the prospect of sitting still again. 30 seconds later, I sat with the Thor across my knee. The Tiger made his way up the slope just as I had predicted. It was almost dark. It was too dark to see through the NightForce scope because the laurel obscured almost every source of ambient light. By the time the Tiger made it to my position, I was considering to use my M&P on him. But, as I sat there trying to keep out of sight, I realized my M&P was not on my hip at all. It sat on the counter at home with half my gear that did not make it to my pockets. The Thor was my only choice even though the crosshairs were completely invisible.

The Tiger kept his SVD at the ready as he steadily marched up the hill. The babbling stream a few yards away masked his footfalls as he approached closer to my position. He walked in silence toward me I sat, crouched, waiting for him to get close enough so there would be no question of my shot. The Thor sat across my knees turned slightly counterclockwise. I could just make out the end of my barrel as I watched the Tiger climb the hill towards the very spot where I sat. My heart beat as if I were running a marathon and my ears strained at the silence of his steps. I was almost holding my breath just to make sure I did not tip him off early to my presence.

I would to say that I was chivalrous and offered him a chance to surrender, but I didn't. I double tapped him as he neared my position along the side of that little creek. The Tiger reeled backward slowly as his body stiffened briefly at the shots. He bounced backwards until he sprawled upside down on the hill there on the bank of the sloping mountain stream. His face showed the most bewildered expression of horror and recognition on his face. I can't say for certain if he really knew it was Huck, his target, that killed him or just that he knew he was dead. Either way, it didn't matter. The Tiger was no longer a threat.

I fumbled around and found my radio's earpiece at last and called, "Base, this is Huck. I got him, the Tiger is dead."

A myriad of cheers echoed in the background.

Base to Huck, where are ya? We will come pick you up."

I told them, "Tell the Ozark trail bunker guards to head east until they get to the fork in the river. I am 150 yards up the ravine. Bring an ATV." The radio voices responded with cheers over and over.

"Good going, Huck."

"Good shooting, Huck."

"Way to go. Whew!"

I, however, sat down and tried to collect myself for a few seconds. My adrenaline was wearing off after all the stress of the last half hour. The Tiger lay at my feet sprawled backwards upside down with his head facing downhill. For the first time in months, I remembered the night Pan was killed taking down Old Joe and the foundation. I guess the thing that got me most was how similar this guy was to me. We thought the same way and conducted ourselves the same way in the field. If he could make a fatal assumption, I could do the same and be lying here instead of him. It was unnerving to say the least.

After a while, the scouts found me and we hoisted the Tiger onto the back of the ATV. We took him back to our valley and collected all his gear for intelligence. The Tiger's custom SVD sniper rifle hung over the door of the store for a long time after that day. It was the focal point of stories for years. We did discover four wounds on him. Fred had hit him in the leg, barely, back at that little airport. That wound was still stitched and bandaged. My first shot had grazed him along his left side and arm. And of course, my last two rounds that had hit him square in the chest. He had multiple scars over him as well. This was not his first rodeo, but it was his last. We didn't find a satellite phone on him or in any of his gear. That was the best part of the whole mission in my opinion. We really didn't want to relocate our whole valley.

The Tiger's body was buried in the corner of a field in a wet swampy area that nobody used. He was lucky not to have been buried in the pig pen. Just as we finished burying the sniper, we noticed a single lantern coming up the gravel road. It was our preacher, Darin. We stood there in the light of an ATV with our hands resting on shovels as he made his way to us.

"Evening Darin," I greeted him.

By the lamplight Darin looked at our small group. "Boys, we will have services for Mac tomorrow in the church around 10am."

Well all acknowledged this by looks of remorse and silence. Some of us had only suspected Mac had been killed. Everybody knew him and liked him. His loss was difficult to say the least.

Darin looked down at the fresh dirt. "Is this the sniper?"

"Yep," one of the men answered solemnly.

Darin pulled out a Bible and passed off the lantern to the closest man beside him. He quoted several passages before one of the younger men in our group spoke up, "Preacher, this guy was a Muslim. I don't think he would like it too much having a Christian service spoke over him."

Darin looked up at him in the gentlest manner. "We are all God's children, even if we don't recognize it."

After a little while, Darin finished and we all made our way back to the convenience store. We knew everyone would be gathered there for news and to see us return. Seven was glad to see me as I arrived. Even though my clothes were covered in leaves and grime from being on my belly all day, she nearly toppled me over as she hugged me. While I was being fed, I learned that Bull had called several times during the day to get updates. It turned out that a lot of people were following the sniper duel with great interest. I'm sure Data would write something fancy about it all.

Several people told the story of how others risked their lives to reach Mac out in the open, but it was to no avail. He had been shot cleanly in the center of the chest and was dead within 20 minutes of being shot. The crowd was happy to be rid of the threat, but also somber at the loss of someone that had been with us so long.

My flight was rescheduled for the next morning, which gave me an extra night to spend with the family.

I recounted every aspect of how I tricked the Tiger into coming up the draw along the creek. I mentioned everything of the day except for the strange emotions I was having. I felt both glad to be alive, yet almost ashamed to have just killed a guy that may have been more experienced and was most likely a better sniper than I ever hoped to be. I hated losing Mac at my expense. Call it survivor's guilt, I guess.

Fred sat opposite of me on the bench in the glow of the few convenience store lights after most everyone had left. "Huck, you got him. What's eating you?"

Fred knew me too well. "Fred, that should have been me instead of Mac this morning. He just happened to be the one that walked out of the door first. It's just dumb luck that he got shot, and I'm sitting here."

"Yeah, but you got him in the end. That's all that matters," Fred tried to reassure me.

I looked him in the eyes. "He found out where I live, he staked out my house. Somebody else could do the same thing. Seven or the baby might get hurt next time. We were darn lucky to survive this guy. You got shot, and if my rifle hadn't taken the hit, I would have been dead months ago."

Fred looked back at me just as earnestly. "But you are sitting here now. The family is okay and you are okay. Don't you think on it. You always were a head case, Huck." I knew he meant to cheer me up. It felt good to have someone on my side that understood.

I smiled back at him. "It takes one to know one, Fred."

Chapter Eleven
Temporary Assigned Duty

Stepping off my front steps was done with at least a little trepidation the next day. Mac had died there only 24 hours before. Memories of him lying there weighed heavily on my mind. Seven claimed to be okay, but I could see the strain in her face as she wished me a good trip. Her eyes warily scanned the opposite ridge as I walked down our front steps. I made my way to the airport without any trouble and boarded with four or five replacements destined for my mission group. The plane took off right on schedule and headed out for an airfield outside of camp Lejune. An hour outside of our designated field, Sky Manor, we diverted to Albert Ellis field.

The pilot spoke over the intercom, "Okay everybody, I have a slight change of plans. We are diverting to Ellis field. Your operations officer radioed us a few minutes ago and said that the green shirts have shut down our primary landing zone. Ellis is under their control too, but we have a cover story all set up. We are going to have an accident."

Those of us in the passenger seats looked around at each other with more than a little concern.

The pilot continued, "Don't worry guys. We are going to land safely and claim an emergency. When we open the door, you climb out quickly onto the first emergency truck as we stop. The tower should not be able to see you. We have fake courier documents ready for this as well, so don't worry about us. We run shine down here from time to time and they let us pull this kind of stuff every once in a while."

Our concern turned to humor as we considered we were running boot leg liquor along with a handful of heavily armed militia. Those were weird times to say the least.

Sure enough, we approached the field and landed as we expected. And, just as promised, a couple of fire trucks met us at the end of the runway where we unloaded without trouble. Our militia security met us back at the emergency services building near the tower. The same van that dropped me off several days before picked us up at the back door of the building. There was a fair amount of mud on the sides of the doors and the tires were brown.

"Colonel Huck, sir, good to see ya again," the driver met me at the door.

I recognized the young man. "Good to see you too. Last I saw you the green shirts were hot on your tail. How did you get away?"

He took my pack and loaded it into the van. "Well, it was hairy there for a while. I ended up hiding behind a barn for a few hours until everything settled down. "He pointed at the tires. "I nearly got stuck in the field, though."

I liked the young man and his energy. "So, how was your trip here?" I asked. "Have you met up with the local militia yet?"

The driver loaded the last of the gear as he spoke. "I'm not sure, sir. It took us while to get here. The Captain had to change our base of operations. It looks like the green shirts have been working hard around here lately. Things are not as open as Bragg."

In just a few minutes we were heading out of the airport complex. After a mile or two, I noticed we were heading north and west.

I asked, "Where are we going? Isn't Lejune to the east?"

The driver responded, "Yeah, we had to move the rally due to green shirt patrols. They have closed the roads around Jacksonville. Lejune is completely locked down. They're even moving the locals."

We drove for a while longer and entered the town of Maysville sometime in the afternoon. Maysville was a typical coastal town outside of a major military installation. There were four or five rows of streets off the main road. Trailer parks lined both sides of the road as far as you could see through the pine trees. Kids played in yards as the weather was warmer here by the coast. Within a mile, we were pulling off onto a dirt road by a series of fields. We passed through our checkpoints and pulled up to several of our vehicles as they were parked in a tuft of evergreen trees. This area was too flat and sandy for my taste.

Spanky met me at the door of the van. "Good to see you Huck, uh, Colonel, sir," he added.

"Spanky, where are we set up?" I asked as I looked around at the men milling around.

Spanky scratched his head. "I don't know yet. We just got here a couple hours ago. There have been a lot of green shirt patrols. The scouts are still out, but what we saw of Jacksonville, I don't know if Gunny will have to move us again. You should see the posters they have all over town."

"Where is Gunny?" I asked.

Spanky looked unsure. "Well, he went out a while ago and I haven't seen him since breakfast. He was looking for somebody, I think."

I didn't like what I was hearing so far. Jacksonville and Lejune were really important to our overall plan. We needed to recruit a lot of Marines if we were going to make a real effort on Wilmington. That fact was close to my heart since we stood maybe 65 miles from Wilmington at that moment. If the green shirts were expanding to Lejune, we might have some strategic problems.

It wasn't until evening that Gunny showed up. Our position was secure enough for the time being, but I couldn't see holding major rallies here. It was just too close to occupied territory for my taste. If we were spotted, we would have only five minutes of warning at best. Without any Intel on the area, I didn't want to make any decisions on where to go just yet. Gunny may have the answers.

That evening Gunny pulled up in his truck with a security escort.

I looked to Gunny as he stepped out of the truck. "Gunny, good to see you."

He looked at me with a little surprise. "Huck, what are you doing back here? I thought you would be back home sitting on your butt for a few more days," he joked.

I said slyly, "Well, I've been Tiger hunting."

That got Gunny's interest. "Yeah? Do any good?"

"I bagged one near the house. Mac was killed though."

Gunny's eyes showed unusual shock as he asked, "Mac from the personal security detail?" I could tell the news bothered Gunny a great deal. He had personally trained Mac and the first squad of personal body guards for the officers of 3rd militia. If you didn't know Gunny, you would have thought he was just thinking. But I could tell the news hit him hard.

Gunny looked shaken. "Well, you got him. That's what's important."

I led Gunny away from the group and told him, "Gunny, we have a new mission. We need to finish up our recruiting tour within the next couple of days and get back to North Wilkesboro. Rocket is building up a transportation network that stretches across the state and we have to start training for a major operation."

Gunny listened, but was shaking his head. "Huck, from what I have seen around here, there are a lot of people that need our help. I just got back from town. The green shirts are shaking things up on a scale we haven't seen in a while."

I looked around to make sure nobody could hear us. "Gunny, Lejune is not our mission right now. The general himself gave us another priority."

"But Huck, did you see the trailer parks down the road? There ain't nothin' but kids half starving, running around in the streets. The green shirts have started up some sort of sweat shop making the mothers work all day."

"I realize what you are saying, Gunny, but we have to prioritize here," I told him. "Our orders are to work up to a major operation that has to take place in March! We cannot mass an attack on Jacksonville in the mean time."

Gunny continued, "Look here Huck, these are Marine families. These are Navy wives and the kids of Marines. I can't just turn my back on them." He pointed off towards town, "There are hundreds of kids without their parents, all day wandering the streets just like in some freakin third world country. I have seen this in India and Iraq, but this has no place in the U.S. We have to do something!"

I turned around several times trying to compose myself before speaking. This was uncharted territory for us. Gunny and I had always gotten along. Oh yeah, he was rough around the edges, but this was more. Gunny was not budging. I turned to face him, "What can we do about it? We can't transport a couple hundred families to North Wilkesboro. We barely have enough gas to get the job done now. And that is if we are lucky, Gunny!" I said, heated. "The operation coming down the pipe is strategic. It may change the whole outcome of the war."

Gunny looked at me. "I can't leave them to rot, Huck. Not this time." He was determined and frustrated that he was not getting the cooperation he expected to get.

I nodded my head in recognition. "We have a couple of days. Let's see what comes up. Maybe we can do something. But, for now, we have to leave in two days. You have until then to come up with a plan."

We walked back to the trucks in silence. The guys looked at us. "Are we setting up here or what?"

Gunny growled back that he had found a better place down the road a ways and we better make camp there. We traveled quietly in the dark to our next hide. The men set up camp as we met with some locals to get a feel for green shirt activity. The men in our trucks suspected something because they had never seen Gunny and I so at odds with each other. Morale can be wonderful or destructive depending on the mood of the men. We were already under enough stress. The men didn't need to see their officers arguing out in the open. In the militia, that can be as destructive as bullets.

The locals gave us a readout on the green shirt activity. The green shirts had shut down the air station at Cherry Point back in the beginning of the takeover. They feared the Marines. Lejune and Jacksonville were populated with displaced military families, like Gunny described. All the senior members of the corps were long since carted off to fictional mental hospitals or supposedly working overseas. We knew from the Army Special Forces that these were familiar cover stories used on the populous. People had no choice but to accept the crap they were being fed.

Most people didn't know anything about the labor projects, but they heard a bunch of rumors. The green shirts were using the local workers to re-start small factories. Women were conscripted into service as little more than slaves. They were tasked with making green shirt uniforms, patches, insignia, as well as those horrible grey worker uniforms. The stories of supervisor brutality and outright sexual harassment were also a common theme.

Over the next 24 hours we met several younger Marines that had managed to stay "off the radar" as you might say, but there were very few. Most of the guys had served a year to maybe three.

All the others were gone for the most part. The men that came to our rally were subdued and looked at us like they did not trust a word we said. We quickly appealed to their sense of patriotism and called them to defend their country as it was founded. It made a difference to a few, but these guys were really young. They had grown up in schools where global warming was never questioned. Collectivism was commonly taught as a good thing. Carl Marx and Hitler were just stories in a textbook the teacher never covered. It was amazing to watch as the people most affected by green shirts, did not attribute the problems of the day to their strict authoritarian rule.

Don't get me wrong; we recruited several dozen Marines around Lejune. Just, not as many as we expected or hoped to get. It was heartbreaking for Gunny. In the back of his mind, I'm sure he imagined an entire army marching behind him. He imagined them to be waiting for someone to come and get them all organized for some serious Marine-style green shirt butt whipping. But that was not be. Not yet, anyway.

On the last day of our scheduled trip, Gunny met me at my truck as I prepped my gear for the return home.

"Huck, let's have a word for a minute," Gunny invited me. It wasn't really an invite. It was more of a nice command. I didn't resent it though. Gunny and I had an understanding.

"What's up Gunny?" I asked him, curious. The sun was up and the last of the gear was being packed into one of the panel trucks. We walked out of earshot as the men hurried about their work. Everyone was anxious to get back home. Christmas was in the next few days.

"Huck, I just got a report that you might find some more SF men up around Moyock. It seems the green shirts have declared that whole area off-limits. It's my guess that somebody has re-occupied the old Blackwater facility up there. Whoever it is, the green shirts are scared to even go near the place."

I looked at him, still curious, and took the paper. "That's great Gunny. What else?" I knew there was more.

I had never seen Gunny so hesitant. "Huck, we've been through a lot this past year. We got the militia up and running. Gave the green shirts a black eye or two....."

I interrupted him, "You're leaving, aren't you?"

He looked back at me. "I got to."

I was devastated. Gunny had been everything to us. He knew so much, he taught us how to tie our shoes, for crying out loud. He kicked our butts when we didn't work hard enough. He was our salty dog, our veteran that understood what it took to turn civilians into fighters.

I looked at the anguish in his face. "You are not quitting the militia. You are being put on Temporary Assigned Duty (TAD)." I scratched out orders on my notebook as I spoke slowly, trying to keep the orders as open-ended as possible. "..assigned to support the greater Lejune area until further orders…"

It was more of a gesture than anything else. If Gunny chose to leave, nobody deserved it more. I couldn't really blame him. He wanted to watch out for the wives and children of the Marines he considered family. He just hated to leave us right before the launch of a major operation.

We talked for a few minutes, and I wished him well, letting him know what a great help he had been. A few minutes later he took the spare scout bike and shook a few people's hands. Then he left with a pack on his back and a rifle over the handlebars. Everybody hated loosing Gunny, but each of us also expected to see him again someday. We just didn't know when or under what conditions. I want to say that people stayed in the militia and never left. However, that was not the case. Some needed to get back to their families just to make sure they were cared for and fed. Others developed attitudes that were not good for team spirit and let their pride get in the way. Some arguments got out of hand and fights broke up entire units as cliques formed. Personnel changes were a constant as we tried to match personalities. Our team leaders were the very backbone of our movement. A good team leader is essential to a civilian army. We all hated to lose someone like Gunny.

Chapter Twelve
Naval Special Warfare

Gunny's report on Moyock left me hopeful, to say the least. The green shirts did not avoid areas unless it cost them more in materials and people than they were willing to sacrifice. In the old days, you could expect the green shirts to circle an area and smash all resistance. By the time the second winter rolled around, the green shirts were more interested in the defense of major cities and the interstates that linked them together.

I looked over to one of my team leaders as I wrote, "Get this to headquarters through the Intel department. Tell them we need a contact in this area. Send it to Major Arrow. They will know what I mean."

The man ran off to send the message. It would be hours before would hear back on anything. I called the team around and said we were staying a bit longer until we could get a response to our message. They were not thrilled at staying any longer, but the weather wasn't bad in that part of the state. If you have to be on the road, be someplace nice.

The hours passed slowly as we waited for word back from headquarters. Night fell as my team sat around by the trucks trying to keep from being bored to death. A couple of my scouts finally rounded the bend and made their way to us. Rocket pointed them towards my truck and their lights bounced our shadows among the pines.

"Colonel Huck, we got word from headquarters." One of the men handed me a sealed envelope.

I took it and ripped the paper. "What? This is all they said?"

The scout looked blankly at me. "Yes sir. They said since we were on a level 3 non-secured line, they had to be brief."

I looked at the paper. It read "34.2 miles, 043 degrees from point Yankee." I knew that those were the coordinates based off our internal maps. You didn't give out GPS coordinates over a non-secure line. The message continued, "Arrow made contact. Friends waiting at cords. ID Code, Anchor. Go alone. Look for blue van."

I looked the scout and the men that gathered. "Men, I have to go meet some friends. Make camp for the night about five miles north of here. I will meet up with you sometime before Christmas."

The men went about the boring task of moving the camp in the dark once again. I knew they were ready to be home, but there were some really critical people I needed to see. I pulled my stuff from the truck and loaded the Thor into the cradle of a scout motorcycle. My guys were well trained by now. They knew I needed certain pieces of gear for the meeting. They handed me a radio and tuned it to the scout channel so I could talk to them when I got back. My pack was loaded onto the back and someone handed me the airport map which had all the preset locations marked. Point Yankee was not exactly close. It might take me hours to make it there. I wished the team well and made sure they knew to be careful in setting up the new camp. They assured me they would, gesturing that I was number one in their books as I drove off. My guys were really funny.

I drove through the back roads of rural North Carolina as if the green shirts never were there at all. I don't think I saw a green shirt cruiser until I got within five miles of Elizabeth City. By the time I worked my way around town, I realized the green shirts had physically blocked the roads leading north to Moyock. That is expressly why I chose a motorcycle for these little forays into the wilderness. You can go just about anywhere, and I did. I'd like to say I bogged the bike down only once, but that would be a lie. The low lying swampy areas around that area were deceptively deep. It was all I could do to find paths dry enough to make my way to the designated area. Maybe that is just the reason the green shirts were willing to block off the roads in the area and ignore the rest of the open country.

It wasn't until 01:00 before I made my way to where I expected to find my contacts. Several times I stopped to look and listen, but all was quiet. I drove through the outskirts of a little township called South Mills guided by my GPS. The old Blackwater facility lay to the east still several miles away. Blackwater is where a lot of the ex-military, turned civilian contractors, trained for operations overseas. They had gotten a lot of bad press over the years which made them re-brand themselves a couple of times. But for all the negative political posturing on the subject of State Department contractors in the press, operations were expanding in an era where government bureaucracies hindered the military from acting decisively.

There were very few street lights in South Mills, which made sneaking easier. There was no traffic other than my silenced engine as I cruised the back streets looking for a blue van. I checked and double checked until I read the note again. It said something weird, "cords." I looked around at the street signs but to no avail. Then I realized it might be a house name on a mail box. After another fifteen minutes of searching I discovered what I was looking for. A quiet little house sat off in the dark surrounded on three sides by trees. Two small garages made a small courtyard behind the house and the mail box read Cords. As I drove around, a blue van was parked just behind the house. It was barely visible from the road. Bingo!

I edged my way around the house and turned off the bike's headlight while I was still 200 yards away. The place screamed empty, but the hairs on the back of my neck suggested differently. Even though the driveway looked clear, I could almost feel the military presence. The bike's tires crunched the small gravel in the relative quiet of the star-filled night. My breath produced small puffs of visible air as my bike rolled to a stop beside the van. With the engine shut off, I pulled off my helmet and listened. You can tell a lot about a place by the sounds. Sometimes it's what you don't hear that gets your interest. The normal sounds of bugs and critters hummed off in the distance. But this place was quiet.

I looked around to find a man standing beside the small garage on the opposite side of the driveway. He had an M-4 draped across what looked to be a T.A.G. chest rig similar to my voodoo tactical. His was desert tan and was equipped for carrying ballistic plates. These were rigs common to Special Forces and I recognized the design immediately. The same time I decided say something, the van's side door slid open and two men stepped out only feet from me. There was no time to resist. If these guys were not my contacts, I was in for a world of hurt. Adrenaline flushed throughout my body as I tried to put on my best poker face.

"What's your name?" a man's voice came from the inky blackness of the van's interior.

There was no time for coy disguises. "I'm Huck. Code, Anchor."

The unknown man paused only briefly. "You're late."

It was my turn to think about what to say next. "Well, my directions were a bit vague and the green shirts put up a perimeter just down the road."

The voice from inside said, "Jump in. We don't have much time."

The two men helped me into the van with hands like vice grips. It was more of a toss, really. As I landed onto the middle row seat, the van started and we threw gravel down the driveway. I looked behind me to see the rear seats empty. The driver and passenger were the sole occupants.

The passenger started, "My guys will get your bike under cover. The drone will pass over in less than 5 minutes."

"Drones? As in U.A.V.s you mean?" I asked. I looked through the window to look among the stars. There was nothing to see.

The passenger responded, "Yes, the green shirt military has one parked over this area most of the time. They would very much like to come and visit us, you might say. That is something we need to talk about, but not yet. First, Major Arrow tells me you have made an impression on him and his men."

"Is that right?" I asked, trying to conceal my approval.

The passenger looked back at me and moved to sit beside me on the middle seat behind the driver. He was eager to speak to me directly. His eyes were piercing, as if he was using x-ray vision to see through my body and read what was going on in the back of my mind. It was almost creepy the level of intensity of the guy. "They don't like it when civilians show them how to shoot."

I grinned. "Everybody likes to think they are top dog from time to time. A little dose of humility keeps us all in line."

The man nodded his head in agreement. I could almost see the thoughts whirring behind his eyes. He was guarding his statements carefully.

He said, "You can only begin to learn when you understand that you have everything *to* learn." He paused, then began again. "I want you to know that we have been watching the militia movement for quite some time."

That got my curiosity.

He continued, "You guys have done a great job so far and it has gotten our attention."

I smiled, but I was tired with all my travels and I just wanted to get down to brass tacks. "So, what are you guys all about? Contractors? Or, are all your men ex-military in hiding like you?"

The man sitting beside me didn't even blink at my statement. "What makes you think I am military?" he asked calmly.

I looked forward "Well, your driver wears his Sig on his hip like they train FBI and SF guys. The rest have level three Safariland thigh rigs. Their M-4s are slung so that they can transition and go right to their secondary without hesitation. The driver's left wrist has a barbed wire tattoo that I know to be common with divers. I can tell you guys have operated for a while together because you don't need to do more than glance to communicate. My guess is that you guys are from the Teams." I sat back and watched him wiggle for a change.

The driver looked around to me without saying a word as he drove. After a second or two he turned back to the road.

"That's very observant, Colonel Huck. My men and I have operated for quite some time through various branches of the armed services. Some come from the teams in Naval Special Warfare. But we don't like to announce ourselves as a general rule. Not many people can appreciate the nuances of our work. We had a lot of press over the last few years before the takeover and it has gotten us too much attention during this new regime."

I looked back at him. "I can appreciate what you and your men must have gone through. You guys must have been on pretty nasty lists very early on if my guess is right."

The van continued along the dark road without lights. I noticed the driver donning a set of night vision goggles as he drove with the lights out. We pulled into another farm area where there were a series of small barns. As we approached, one of the barn doors opened and then a second set of doors revealed a second smaller interior room large enough for a vehicle. The van pulled into the interior room in complete darkness. I must admit that my apprehension was not helped by this change of status. The van stopped inside and the driver jumped out to close the interior room doors.

My counterpart clicked the van's interior lights as the barn doors closed behind us. He was perhaps ten years older than me, but had an athletic build much like a triathlon competitor.

He spoke as if at ease now. "Sorry for all the secrecy, Huck. I will see if I can explain in the next few minutes and perhaps you will understand why we are so cautious."

I was curious, alright. I sat there trying to ask a relevant question. "What should I call you? We use code names in the militia."

"Call me Captain Nemo. I know how you guys like code names from movies," he said as he took a final look around.

I felt more comfortable as he relaxed, but more wary because he seemed to know a lot about how the militia did things. I asked, not really trying to be funny, "Nemo like the little fish or the Captain from 20,000 Leagues Under the Sea?"

The Captain took it in stride as he responded, "Let's go with the Nemo that James Mason played in the Disney film."

For the life of me I couldn't remember the actor's names of 20,000 Leagues under the sea other than Kirk Douglass. I hoped it was the guy that played the Captain.

Nemo pointed to the ceiling above the van. "This barn is insulated so that drones equipped with infra-red will not see our body heat or our van's engine heat. We added a layer of insulation over the roof of the interior room."

I nodded in recognition. "How many drones are in use? We haven't seen any."

"That's one of the areas I wanted to talk to you about. The militia is depending on electronic communications way too much nowadays. The green shirts have access to computing capabilities that will quite frankly amaze you. It is not safe to continue to using the internet in any shape way or form. They own it. It is their playground. I cannot emphasize this enough."

I wanted to let him know we were being careful, so I said, "My computer geeks are pretty good at breaking and hacking into networks. There are not many layers they cannot break through. Our encryption is pretty cutting edge, as well."

He looked at me patiently. "I understand what you mean, Colonel, but what I am talking about is a whole other world." He reached into his jacket pocket and pulled out a piece of paper which he handed to me. I took it and unfolded the paper to see a list of names. My real name was on top. Below my name was a pretty comprehensive list of militia officers. I recognized most of the 3rd battalion leadership on the page. My eyes bulged at the revelation.

"Okay, You've got my attention. How did you get all this information on us?"

Captain Nemo looked me dead in the eyes. "I copied that list from the green shirt intelligence bureau."

My heart took an extra beat and I breathed hard. "Oh my." I couldn't think what to say. Everything seemed hopeless. If they could gather this data on us, how could we survive? Were we just pawns allowed to think we were going to resist a little longer only to be disposed of when the time was right? I finally asked, "They have us pretty well covered don't they?"

Captain Nemo elaborated, "The green shirts were just the construct of the PPR movement as the takeover became eminent. The PPR had their claws into all branches of the US government well before the attack on Washington. How else could there be 100 Muslim brotherhood advisors to the White House? We even funded the brotherhood for the last three years out in the open. That was the price for the oil embargo and it fit the radical environmental agenda of the PPR. It was a marriage made in Mecca."

I chimed in, "Yeah, some of our militia intelligence confirmed the PPR's involvement in the oil embargo. Do you know who set off the nuclear device in Washington?"

The Captain sat back in the seat. "Not really. We think it was someone in the administration or with homeland security that got the device into the country. Those were the only people able to get all the nuclear material warning sensors ignored. We are pretty sure it was a

Russian suitcase nuke that had been sold years ago to someone in the Middle East. We don't know much more than that. We doubt the Russian's had any direct involvement, though. Everything beyond that is just conjecture."

I listened intently, trying to keep up.

The Captain continued. "That's all window dressing though in the greater scheme of things. What most people still don't realize is how far along the U.S. Government has been in data-mining its citizens. The media gave lip service reporting on conspiracy theories under project names like Echelon or Five Eyes. These projects were ostensibly used for tracking terrorists and following their funding, right? Well, there is a lot more to it than that. Hacking, gaining access to private servers, web surfing, email, wire tapping, they were all just components of the real objective. They were merely a means to an end. A lot of people heard about the data mining in the news, but they didn't realize how far it could be taken. The software packages constructed over the last ten years could take in ALL your electronic information and form it into profiles. Your debit card purchases, who you called, what sites you went to on the internet, your friends on social media, your party affiliation, your entertainment choices, your debt, all of it was collected to form a digital profile of every person. With the software package, Snapshot, they can determine who is a risk to the state based on your digital profile. You are the sum of your parts as it were."

I thought for a second. "You mean like the movie Minority Report? They supposedly had pre-cogs that could see the future. Are you saying this is the same thing?"

The Captain nodded. "Yes, but they don't need to see the future. They know everything you did for the last few years. They know more about you than you might even realize about yourself."

I asked, "How far did they take it? I know they could monitor communications, but how integrated did they get it before everything crashed?"

Captain Nemo interrupted, "Crashed? You make it sound like the project is dead and buried. It's not! It is more powerful than ever today. The printout I gave you was produced only a few weeks ago. The power outage removed the last of what they called dark areas or networks outside their influence. Every computer network that came back online has the light of Snapshot shining over it. They don't have to read your encrypted emails or listen to every GMRS radio conversation overheard from NSA antennas. Snapshot captures it all automatically, takes it in and plugs it into your profile. Couple that with your purchase of camo clothing using a debit card three years ago, watch Red Dawn five times from your Netflix account, and boom, they know all they need to about you. You have been flagged as a potential lthreat to the state. The more you use electronic means, the more they know about you. Every electronic interaction increases the accuracy and efficiency of your personal Snapshot profile. The more you do online, the more they collect about you until they can gobble you up."

I thought for a second and asked, "How much did they do in facial recognition? Can they couple our profile with our facial images?"

Captain Nemo smiled because he knew that I was catching up to all the possibilities, "Yes. That started in the Community Service Centers about a year ago. They needed a way to update their profiles so they started a program to film everyone while they were at mandatory community meetings."

I laughed at the flurry of memories coming back to me, "I was there and saw the equipment they were using. They came to our community last year during the really bad ice storm. They actually took me aside to fix the system when they overloaded the data collection server. I had no idea what they were really doing though. I knew they were filming, so I had a kid pull the fire alarm and we all went home."

The Captain chuckled. "That is most likely why they didn't know your identity sooner."

I admitted, "Yeah I was pretty lucky a few times. What do you mean sooner, though?"

The Captain pulled out another piece of paper that had been folded several times and looked to be older. He read it to me, "The resistance militia sniper must be from one of the following geographical areas, X, Y, or Z. The autopsy from our security specialist revealed a 5.56 caliber weapon was used at extreme range. The twist ratio of the barrel is consistent with a Krieger AR-15 barrel and the bullet used was of 68 grain match grade Hornady. The attached list is all the people that have purchased this bullet, this rifle barrel, and related components in the last 4 years."

Nemo continued, "The intelligence report says that you should round up the attached list of people as suspects. Your name was second from the top."

I looked at the list with amazement. It had my old name before my stepfather adopted me. The computer had spit me out of its systems over a year and half ago. The only thing that saved me was incomplete data. The local green shirts couldn't find me because they had my name wrong from a clerical error a decade ago. It was incredible that I had survived the initial sweep for dissidents. It explained how the green shirts seemed to know who to arrest and from what town. They knew where to find the gun owners and hunters. They knew everything about us from our Snapshot profiles. They had left very little to chance.

The Captain and I sat there in the dark van with only that single dome light illuminating us on the van's seat. I was overwhelmed to say the least. It seemed there was just too much to handle. How could we fight with such a complete collection of information?

"A bit overwhelming, isn't it Huck?" the Captain observed. "We operate in this area because the pencil necked paper-pushers expect it from our profile. We do not want to teach them different until we have to. But the time has come to close down the ports of Wilmington and we must act soon."

I looked at him, knowing that I had not communicated the militia intention to attack Wilmington.

He raised his hand in defense. "If we know it, the green shirts and their Muslim friends you call the Sandys, know it too. They caught wind of you using that facility up there in North Wilkesboro and they bombed it. They did that out of revenge for their allies you guys took out quite unexpectedly. The green shirts don't like surprises in their new utopia. But here is something you may not know. The green shirts and Sandys are not as cozy with one another as you might expect. The green shirt leadership is a hard core secular new-age collectivist form of government. It's kind of like a modern version of the old Soviet Union from the 70s but with a rather odd twist of commercial endeavors. Someone once called it State sponsored Capitolism. Whatever they call it today, it is not about to let the militia muck up the works for them. There are two reasons the green shirts have let you guys operate without resistance. One, they have the bulk of their military trying to contain Texas. They have very limited, yet powerful, resources. The rest of the major units are spread throughout the north keeping all their core states in line. Second, they might just want to let the Sandys take care of you when the bulk of their forces arrive in a few months. We have been tracking their shipping from foreign ports and see that there will be a lot of immigrants coming into the country very soon."

"Yeah, we've expected they will be coming in force, sometime in March according to captured intelligence. It makes a lot of sense why the green shirts have pulled back to the major cities and left the rural areas open for the most part. We are still a fly on the wall that can be swatted later," I said disgustedly.

Nemo said, "Don't underestimate the conflict between the green shirts and the Sandys. The Muslims are not secular in the least. In fact, there is a bit of tension between the two when it comes to the role that religion plays in society. The green shirts debated long and hard on whether or not to give North Carolina to the Sandys. It was thought that the Sandys might be too close for comfort and may try to unseat the PPR at some point in a few years."

I looked surprised. "They plan on North Carolina as a border state, don't they?" He nodded in agreement. I continued, "What makes them fear the Sandys so much? Didn't they just help the PPR to bring down the U.S.?"

The Captain responded, "Don't underestimate the destruction of our military and how it influenced their thinking. The green shirts feared that our military would intervene during their takeover. That is why they dismantled our fighting capacity so quickly. They destroyed all but the absolute minimum amount of equipment to subdue our population. Now that these foreign nations are planning to bring in entire armies, it scares the hell out of the green shirts."

I asked, "Is that why the green shirts are staying close to the major cities? They want to create a solid border and solidify their power as much as possible before the bulk of the Sandys get in country?"

The Captain replied, "That's what I think."

I sat and tried to comprehend everything we had covered. My brain was sure to be emitting steam as I tried to comprehend it all. Finally, I asked the Captain, "How are you so plugged in? You may have been a SEAL at some point, but my guess is that you worked counter terror at JSOC or the Pentagon before the war."

The Captain's face took on an expression of pain like a man who had to admit something. "Colonel Huck, your guesses have been pretty good so far. Let's just say that I share in the blame for all this just like Captain Nemo in the movie. Snapshot was a project that I helped bring about. Counter terror groups needed to track individuals using the web to communicate within our own borders. The Pentagon decided to build adaptive profile networks and we were assured it was for tracking terrorists only. Then it was expanded for criminals, serial killers and the like. We were promised that it would be used in extreme case only. It progressed from there until the takeover. By then it was too late to reverse. "Share this info with your General." Nemo reached behind the seat and withdrew three small sealed cases. "Spread these out and make sure they reach your general at all costs. Don't worry; there is nothing in there that will compromise me or my men. Maybe someday we can work out a way to disable Snapshot. I don't know."

"Thanks Captain," I told him. "Will you come out to North Wilkesboro with your men next week? Major Arrow and some of his men are coming to train our volunteers for the upcoming operation in Wilmington."

The Captain rubbed his chin. "Yes. I will do something up here to keep the green shirts busy for a while and we will show up three days after Christmas. But make sure you do not communicate electronically about us. The green shirts must not be allowed any more information on us than they already have. Use only secure telephone systems and stay off the internet until you can have a plan of deception in place."

We talked for a few more minutes until one of his men showed up on my motorcycle. I thanked Nemo and his men and then got directions on the drone's rotation schedule. I sure didn't want to eat a hellfire missile on my way back to my team. The trip back to camp was uneventful for the most part. The air was getting very cool as I drove mile after mile with the three cases of information strapped to my back. The information Nemo had given me flowed though my brain until I was exhausted. The conversations replayed over and over as I tried to get a handle on what to do next. There was so much to do and so little time to get it all squared away. How could we do it all? How could we expect to defeat such an entrenched enemy? Could we even stop the Sandys at Wilmington? Did we have enough troops? Could we get them trained fast enough? How could we defeat both the green shirts and the Sandys? It was maddening to think of it all.

It was nearly dawn before I returned to the people in the tent awaiting my return. My sleeping bag awaited me and I was not going to disappoint it. My head hit the pillow and I was out. Or, so I thought, anyway.

Winter

"Revelation"

Chapter Thirteen
The Machine

"Colonel Huck, it's a message from Rocket. He says he needs to talk with you as soon as you can get to a secure phone. He sent the message via courier on the last personnel transfer. It is marked priority urgent."

I looked to the person handing me the note with my eyes half open. "Thanks." What was it now? How much sleep could someone go without? I didn't want to find out the hard way, so I dozed back off in my sleeping back for another 15 minutes. Noise in the tent told me that dawn had broken and the men were busy with the day's chores. Smells of breakfast prompted me to reluctantly unzip my bag and get dressed. The note simply read what the man told me earlier. Nothing particular, just "call me when you get a chance."

I was tired from the night before, but thrilled to have made contact with more special forces. If the Seals were to come on board, we might have a real chance to do some serious damage. The Sandys would not know what hit them. That was my hope, anyway.

After breakfast and the normal orders for patrols, I had the scouts find me a local telephone cabinet. These are the cabinets you see on the side of the road and never notice. Some are colored beige with dark brown legs with a power meter attached to one side. Some are open below, while some have additional battery compartments in the free space. These are telephone cabinets that house the DLCs(digital loop carrier) devices such as the SLC-96 and the SLC-5 (subscriber loop carrier). Everyone's home twisted pair phone line goes through a box like this, unless you are close to the local switch. In essence, these devices allow the phone companies to operate hundreds of phone lines off of a couple of trunks or T-1s without having to run everyone's phone line all the way to the central office. It's even more complicated, trust me.

Well anyway, my driver took me to one of these cabinets and I got out of the truck with my secure telephone kit. This kit contained a little specialized wrench that allowed me to open the side door. Once inside, I looked to the electronics within. The cabinet was luckily powered up an operating. That was good. This cabinet was an 80D type and had several SLC-5 channel banks inside. Based on the little green lights, the blue group of one of the units was in operation and humming along nicely. I rummaged through my little bag and pulled out a test clip that plugs into the line interface unit or LIU. This allowed me to tap into the actual telephone card faceplate and have access like I was plugged into somebody's house. If I were traced, they would go to this person's address and I would have time to get away clean. All the warnings from the night before flashed through my mind. Yes it was a risk. But it was necessary.

Next, I clipped the test lead to the laptop I carried and started a "Data" session. Yes, that quirky goofball named the encryption protocol after himself and put an icon on the laptop with his picture. I decided to use it once more since Rocket was not one to rush messages around. In the back of my mind, I wondered how this would look on my digital profile.

After several seconds I was given access to our secure phone system back in North Wilkesboro. Another minute or so later, they established a link with Rocket who was evidently waiting for me.

"Rocket? This is Huck. Can you hear me?"

Rocket's voice sounded far off. "Sir, is that you?"

"Yeah Rocket. What's up?" I asked as I sat in front of this big cabinet on an old crate.

"Colonel, I have something you have to see."

I paused, "What? You called me off a mission to tell me you need me to see something? Rocket, I have a lot going on over here....."

"Sir, let me be clearer. You aren't going to believe what I found over here. We are setting up a transportation station in one of the old green shirt truck parks. They left a bunch of their old gear stacked up in the back of the lot that was junked. The place was filled with old semi trailers and used tires. We found it when we were scrounging..."

"For goodness sakes Rocket, what did you find?" I begged him, slightly irritated from lack of sleep.

"Sir, I think it's a Reaper."

My heart double tapped in my chest. My mouth went dry. "Really? Is it intact?"

Rocket replied, "Sir, it has the Department of Recycling on the side and all. I think it's all there."

I couldn't believe it. I hated the next question on my lips. "Was it used?"

"Yes sir, I think it was," Rocket said solemnly.

"Where are you, Rocket? I will come by on my way back to base," I told him rapidly.

"I am just outside of Oxford," and then he gave me the GPS coordinates.

I will see you in a few hours, Rocket, good work. Keep it safe. Huck out." I hung up the phone with my hands shaking. My driver helped me pack as I rushed back to the truck.

"Let's get back to the gang. We have to get to Oxford as fast as we can get everyone packed."

My driver rushed around, throwing things into the truck as he asked, "Sir, what's going on? Is Rocket in trouble?"

As we pulled off the side of the road and made our way back to the rest of the team I explained, "Rocket may have found a Reaper."

The driver was doing 90 miles an hour and looked from side to side. "A what?"

"Slow down, son. You are going to kill us both if you don't take it easy," I told him.

He slowed to normal breakneck speed and asked, "I don't get it. What's a Reaper?"

I looked over at him. "You never heard of a reaper?" He shook his head no. "Where were you recruited" I asked.

He looked over to me, "I joined up in Murphy, North Carolina, 4th militia, over the summer."

I stared at his young face. "That explains it, you weren't around back then. You're area didn't have any federal prisons did they?"

He responded, "No, sir?" He was confused.

I stared at the road as we drove. "Back when the green shirts first took over, they emptied the prisons. They gave the prisoners an opportunity to gun up and do their bidding as payment for their freedom. The green shirts went from town to town disarming the people and arrested anyone that was not cooperative to the new regime. Then they sent in the ex-prisoners to rape, pillage and plunder a town until there was nothing left. All the stolen stuff was collected and sent to giant warehouses for redistribution. Cooperative people in the major cities were essentially bribed with goodies from the state. Nobody knew the goods were stolen or how many people had died by the hands of the gangs. None of that was common knowledge outside the militia."

The young driver gulped, "Wow, it's hard to believe how they could get away with it."

I reminded him, "The green shirts controlled all forms of media. For a long time there was no power, no radio, no paper, and no television. There was no way for the story to get out. Of course, the gangs became the next target and poof, they were gone almost overnight."

The driver asked, "So, where does the Reaper come into it?"

This time I paused, remembering what it took to get the information. Rooster and the special intelligence squad I had put together during the first summer of the war came to mind. How they infiltrated the prison system and how the operation went sour. Finally I said, "We sent in a team to scout the prisons back in the first summer of the war. The militia was new; we were barely wet behind the ears. Information was next to impossible to get. So, we sent organized teams to see if we could find the people in our towns that had been arrested. The intention was to find them and rescue them somehow. There was very little gasoline for trucks or vans back then. The team infiltrated the prisons but could not find any of our people. What they discovered was worse than they had imagined."

The driver asked quietly as I paused, "What was worse?"

I continued, "The team found out that everyone that was arrested in the early days was eliminated or executed. We uncovered how the department of recycling was behind it all too. They ran the programs from Raleigh. They were the true fanatics that considered the human race to be killing the planet. It was the Department of Recycling that justified the killing of tens of thousands of people in order to save the planet."

The driver sounded scared. "The Reaper?"

"Yeah," I replied. "The Department of Recycling was evidently really smart in a couple of areas. They knew that no person could witness the killing of hundreds of people day after day. It would warp even the most devout fanatics. They couldn't allow witnesses to run around free, either. So, they devised a machine that would do the job without witnesses. It was an automated killing machine. We referred to it as a Reaper in the militia. We didn't know what the machine looked like or how it worked exactly because we never captured one. Everybody guessed the green shirts destroyed them all when they shut down the prisons last year. We never recovered any bodies either. Rocket may have one of the last of these devises intact. This may be the crucial linchpin of a war-crimes case if we ever defeat the green shirts."

The driver swore under his breath and increased the speed. In no time we made it back to our camp site where we checked in. In a little while we packed and set our scouts ahead. Our recruiting drive had been less than we hoped for in Lejune, but better than we expected in Moyock. We should have a better idea of our capabilities in a couple of weeks with all the recruits beginning their training. Our hopes were high one day and frantic in fear the next. But, that was the nature of our movement.

We left for Oxford mid-morning and did not get there until late that same day. It was dark as our convoy approached the GPS coordinates Rocket had given us. We radioed the advance team to let them know we were coming through their perimeter. It was a good thing, too. This was a great place for an ambush. The outer buildings of the complex were deserted with only a small access driveway leading to the yard behind. Overgrown trees surrounded the property. You could park a dozen or more semis back there and never know it from the outside.

The back of the yard was littered with trailers parked one beside the other. Wrecked cars and SUVs were piled in heaps. These had once been green shirt vehicles. Their paint was worn in places and bullet holes riddled the bodies. I considered them militia marksmanship trophies. Parts had been stripped from the cars, only hulks remained.

My truck stopped in the yard as the rest of the convoy was directed to park.

Rocket came to my door as I stepped out. "Colonel, Huck. Good to see you."

"I like this place Rocket. Good spot. Good defenses, too."

"Yeah, we just got here yesterday morning. We are the advance team. We find a spot, check it out, then decide what the place needs. I call back to HQ and they send in a team to man the place in a few days."

"Great going, Rocket," I praised him. "You are doing a great job. Tell your people the same, okay?"

"Yes sir," he said proudly.

"Now, where is the Reaper?"

Rocket pulled out his flashlight as all the convoy was parked and the lights were off. "It's over here; second trailer from the left behind the stack of cruisers."

We walked around the heaps of car rubble and crawled over small hills of litter to get to the trailer.

I waved my flashlight beam to the side which looked like any other 53-foot truck trailer. In the common emerald green lettering it read "Department of Recycling." The outer rear axle tires were missing and the remaining rims were banged up pretty badly. The area behind the landing gear was a drop down box. These normally hold air conditioners or freezers for refrigerated units. This one did not have access panels, but rather appeared to be one piece welded to the bottom of the cargo area.

I shined my flashlight around to Rocket, "What makes you think this is a Reaper?"

"Sir, the other side of this box has two 7-inch large-capacity drain connections. I never saw these on a truck before so I opened the hatch and saw a black residue. It might be dried blood."

I walked around the cargo doors and looked where he pointed. Sure enough, the drains were suspicious. But what did they do?

I asked Rocket, "What is this door on the driver's side of the cargo bay? Have you opened the rear doors yet?"

Rocket looked towards the rear doors. "No. we just cleared the crap from behind the door just as you guys pulled up. You can go inside the side door, though. It's open. Looks like an engine compartment."

I climbed through the side door from a stack of pallets that made a crude ladder. The interior room was only about nine feet in length overall. Instantly there was a mixture of smells. Diesel fuel along with some very strong chemical smell blasted your senses as you walked in. Very distantly there was an odor of old staleness. The engine was a high torque electrical generator that connected to a series of large electrical motors nearby mounted to the floor. The motors were then connected to chain drives that reached into the adjacent compartment through the wall partitioning the cargo area.

Rocket followed me in. "Colonel, the rear doors are locked. I sent one of my guys to get a bolt cutter so we can take a look inside."

I kept panning the flashlight around looking for answers. "Rocket, what do you make of these motors?"

He beamed his flashlight on the largest one mounted in a bracket off the floor and nearly on the roof. "I don't know for sure. I think they are used on large conveyor belts. You know, like you get in rock quarries."

I pointed my beam down to the floor where a second motor was mounted in the center of the room. "They must be spinning something in there that has extremely high torque." I pointed the flashlight to the chain drives both top and bottom leading off to the rest of the cargo area behind the wall. Other motors seemed to be power pneumatic driven pumps that operated steel rods also passed through the wall. There were power panels, control switches, and all manner of gizmos.

One of Rocket's men passed by our open door and announced he had the bolt cutters. His boots crunched the gravel as he walked to the back of the truck. In a few seconds I heard the metallic clank of the lock being cut. Rocket and I made our way to the back of the truck as the doors swung open. I noticed Rocket trailing behind me hesitantly. Neither of us was anxious to find dead bodies or anything back there, but we had to look. All I could think of were pictures of dead Jews stacked in railroad cars from WWII. I remembered how the allies freed camps and made horrific discoveries of the death camps. The thought of what I would find behind those doors was intimidating to say the least.

I walked around the corner and we all shined our lights at the same time. The view was unremarkable as the men gathered to see what all the fuss was about. Several of us took a deep breath. The confusion started immediately.

Rocket's man looked inside. "I don't get it. What is that?"

We shined our lights at an object inches away from the doors. We still could not understand it completely. A large steel or aluminum drum was mounted in the rear cargo area. Its diameter was the same as the truck's width. Presumably it turned on its axis and spun around. However, there was no door showing. You could not see around it, nor could you see above or below the outer wall of the drum.

I looked to the men, "I guess we will have to fire it up to see how it works. Do you think you can get it going?"

Rocket looked around to his guys. "Get the truck over here with the tools. We will check out the engine first and see what the fuel looks like. Check the filters and then the breakers."

"How soon can you do a test?" I asked Rocket, a little let down. I wanted to confirm this was really a Reaper and see how this thing operated.

"Give me a few hours, sir. This thing looks custom and I will have to work on it a while before I know if it will run or not. That building over there has our gear in it. Your guys can sack out in there for the night."

"Thanks. We have been up for a while. Let me know when you have something. Oh, and be careful. If we are right, that is a true killing machine."

I ushered my folks into the building and we got squared away for the night. I had every confidence that Rocket could fix just about anything. His first toy must have been a box end wrench. My head hit the pillow and I was asleep. The adrenaline rush had really aggravated my fatigue from the last few days. Gunny leaving, the road trips, flights, midnight meetings, it was getting to me.

I slept soundly for hours lying in my sleeping bag. My dreams were dark that night. Images of the machine in use raced through my mind. I awoke with a start. Coming from the parking lot was the most agonizing screeching noise I had ever heard. It sounded like metal fingernails on metal chalk boards. You wanted to curl up in a ball and try to avoid it. It was deafening. Luckily the sound only lasted 15 seconds. I quickly got out of the bag as one of Rocket's men came hurtling through the door.

"Sir, we got it running," he informed me.

"No kidding. I'll be there in a minute," I told him. The sun was up, but it was early. Everybody in the room rushed to follow me to the yard outside. Only guards on watch stayed at their post.

My radio chirped as teams called in, "Did you guys hear that?"

"What the hell was that sound?"

"Are you guys in trouble over there?"

I replied to the teams, "Stand your post guys. We are testing the machine. Report any green shirts within five miles of this place. We might wake up the neighborhood."

As I said that dogs barked in the background. Their sensitive ears did not appreciate our experiment. I walked over to the side door where Rocket stuck his head out.

"Colonel, we got it going. When it made that sound I shut it down right away."

"Do you know how it works yet?" I asked a red-eyed Rocket.

Well, I understand the controls, but I haven't seen how the back end works yet. We walked to the back and looked. The rotating barrel seemed to have opened to the doorway a little bit. There was not enough room to see inside.

I said, "Rocket, have one of your guys fire it up and we will watch what it does from the back. In a minute we were ready. Rocket gave him some instructions and the motor started. The metallic screeching started and the large drum spun around to reveal a doorway leading to the interior of the drum. The drum stopped in the center of the truck and did nothing. The metallic sound of pure metal on metal screeching was unbearable. I waved for the man to shut it down.

"Is it broken?" I asked, trying to stop the ringing in my ears.

Rocket looked perplexed. "The controls indicate that the unit is working correctly. It must be waiting for a command of some sort. Something must trigger the cycle, but I can't tell you what that is."

Rocket jumped up in the back of the truck and felt his way carefully through the doorway.

"Geez, be careful Rocket!" I warned him. If we were right, this thing was designed to kill you quickly and efficiently.

Rocket looked back, "It's off. I'll be okay." He looked around for a minute at the floor of the drum. This is weird.The bottom isn't one piece, it's like a series of flat panels like you get on turnstiles at baseball games. Hey wait a minute, I see a pressure switch." Rocket called back to one of his men, "Get me a roll of duct tape and the camera from my pack. I have a theory."

I was clueless. What the hell did this thing all do? Rocket worked alone for a few minutes and came out wiping his hands.

I asked him, "You find any blood or anything?"

"No sir, but I think I may have something here in a minute, if I'm right." He looked around to the side of the truck, "Okay, fire it up and let it cycle twice before you shut it down."

The guys waved okay and started the machine. The screeching sound started and the drum immediately spun around closing the doorway. In a few seconds the drum door reappeared and stopped only briefly. Again it spun around and finally opened again as the engine was shut down.

We watched the drum stop as the screeching noise subsided. Everyone held their ears for several seconds.

After the engine shut down, Rocket jumped into the drum and came out a few seconds later, "Let's take a look at this," as he pulled the camera from the duct tape."I think we have something."

We started the camera's video and watched intently. The recording showed Rocket start the recording and attach the camera to the upper portion of the drum. As the machine started, the camera bounced a little as the drum rotated. From its vantage point, the camera recorded the most amazing series of events. When the drum rotated 180 degrees, the door opened to another compartment between the engine room and the rear drum. This compartment contained a pair of ominous looking rotating cylinders with spikes. The only way to describe them was to call them giant graters like you use on cheese or fruits for slicing. They were horrific so see even on camera. An instant after the rear drum stopped, the floor turnstile poles shot up through the floor and raked everything inside the drum to within inches of the rotating graters. Once the cycle was complete, the rods retracted and the drum rotated to face the back doors once again.

We watched the video several times. The engineering was incredible in its terror. Anyone inside the drum was forced into the graters with the power of steel rods. Nobody could resist. There was no escape, no place to hang on, anyone inside would be instantly thrown into the graters. The pressure of your body weight activated the cycle.

Grown men that had seen combat, shed a tear at the devise's gruesome nature. Words could not describe the feeling you got just standing near the thing. You felt dirty to be near it. The desire to blow the thing sky high was overwhelming. We sat in silence for a few moments.

"It's beyond anything I ever thought. How could you send people into that?" one of the men asked.

"You wouldn't need many of these things to wipe out a thousand people, would you?" one man commented. "How many of our friends were killed this way? How many of the people in the prisons went out this way?"

We sat down and tried to take stock of what we had learned.

One of Rocket's men summarized, "The drum spins and lets you in. The drum closes and opens you up to the rotating wheels. Then the floor throws you into the grinder and you are mashed into paste. The drains are hooked up to pipe out the blood, guts, and bone fragments. You could kill maybe five people at a time. As fast as you could get people to walk in."

Spanky had been standing at the back of the group. He lurched away with his knees wobbly and threw up. We all felt the same way.

The man continued, "There is no blood in the drum, so people feel safe to enter each time. You are dead and in the pipe, before the drum swings around for the next victims. That's why we never found mass graves at the prisons! They were no bodies left. The dozers were cutting trenches for the sludge."

The revelation of all this was astounding. Someone piped up, "You smell that? It some sort of chemical released during the cycle. Do you think that is what covered the smell?"

Several people agreed with the assessment. We were all in shock.

Someone from my group spoke up. He had been in the 3rd for over a year and had been with me on several missions. "I always wondered how they could get people to send others into a killing machine like this. Who could do it? This machine explains it by its design, don't you see? They pull it up to a doorway somewhere. You get some flunky to start the engine up front and run the piping to a drain or ditch. You tell him anything, it's a sewer system, a bio-compost thingy, or whatever. Who knows the difference? Who could tell what it really does? Then, you get the guards inside to march people inside what looks to be a little round room. Nothing to fear, maybe it opens to the outside for all you know. Then wham, whoever is inside is dead and the room is empty for the next person to walk in. Nobody knows anything, nobody shot anybody. Everybody walks away with plausible deniability."

Wow, he was right. This machine took away all the guilt. You never saw anything happen to anybody. You didn't kill anybody. You never see anyone killed by the machine. The only people that knew the details were the special police from the Department of Recycling.

Someone else asked, "What is the screeching sound? Is it broken?"

I said gravely, "That was to cover the screams."

After a while, I ordered Rocket to secure the trailer and get it ready for transport to the general's headquarters. This discovery was going to be shared with everyone. We documented with video and pictures of the site where the Reaper was recovered. Everybody in both our units witnessed the machine so there would be as many eye witnesses as possible. They did the same thing in WWII. Armies and civilian populations were paraded through the death camps to witness what the Germans had done. Thousands of people were there to see the bodies. Yet, before the war was even over, people denied the scope and tragedy of the holocaust. Some people could never believe their fellow man was so brutal.

All of us were glad to leave that place and head towards home. Our recruiting drive was finally over. We made a few stops on our way back, but they were small rallies that were treated more like rest stops. Thankfully, the trip back to North Wilkesboro was uneventful. A few times we turned to avoid green shirt patrols, but mostly the trip was filled with tedious miles of boredom. None of us complained about boredom though. I took the opportunity to write up a bunch of directives for the various militia departments. I fell asleep with my pencil in hand imagining the folks back at the convenience store talking about everything we had discovered on this mission.

This trip, as well as the past year, had been hard on everyone. We were in need of a break, so I made note to send as many as I could home for Christmas. At the time I didn't feel the need to ask permission for such things. Later, Bull reminded me that he was in charge of big decisions like that.

Chapter Fourteen
Christmas

Our caravan drove through the streets of North Wilkesboro a couple of days before Christmas. The streets were relatively crowded considering the low quantities of fuel that were available. The town had the distinct smell of burning wood as people had converted to stoves in most of the houses. The streets were lined with people trying to get through the market for the last time before the holiday. Decorations were hung on street lamps and there was a festive mood among the folks walking along the sidewalk markets. This was an area that had never really known what it meant to have the green shirts in charge of every aspect of life. Folks here had been free for the most part.

People in the major cities were not preparing for Christmas. The whole idea of celebrating the birth of Jesus had been long since banned. The green shirts would have no rival. Worshiping a power greater than the state was not allowed in any way, shape or form. Of course, they used the excuse of tolerance and freedom from religion or some such nonsense. I wondered how many people in the big cities really bought into all that garbage. But they obeyed.

Our convoy passed slowly through town, trying to keep attention away from our weapons and camouflaged vehicles. Even militia who swore an oath to keep people safe, were still viewed with concern if weapons were openly displayed. The conditioning of the last 20 years through the media had taken a toll on our psyche. People had been trained to fear guns of all kinds. The collapse of our economy and the blackout had confirmed all the irrational fears of guns. Funny how the very things they feared were just the things keeping them safe from tyranny.

We drove up to the militia headquarters and parked our vehicles. I felt at home even though the likelihood of rest was still hours away. The men stretched out miles of road as we collected our gear. I think we all felt lucky to have come back from such a trip with so few losses. We had traveled the state and fought Sandy Special Forces. The Tiger had bled us, but he had not been able to pin us down. Our recruitment had been successful. Perhaps we would have hundreds of recruits come to train in the next week or so. We lost Gunny, but gained some of our own special forces that promised to help us in our fight to free the state.

I walked towards the building with my pack and rifle as Spanky approached me.

"Colonel Huck, sir?" Spanky stopped me from behind.

I turned to him, "Yeah?"

"Well sir, I just wanted to say thanks," Spanky stuck his hand out to shake my hand.

I shook his hand. "Not a problem Spanky."

Spanky looked at me, concerned. "I hope we meet again, Colonel. Darla and I are supposed to head back to the general's headquarters in the morning and I wasn't sure I would see you before we leave. Anyway, thanks again for being open minded. I will never forget this recruiting drive."

I smiled and replied, "You did a good job, Spanky. You and Darla really made this a professional looking deal. You made it back; there is nothing more to be said. Thank you, Spanky."

With that, Spanky and Darla left in their truck. I saw several of my team that initially snickered at Spanky, shake his hand before they left. We had come a long way together.

The van dropped us off on the edge of Wooten Valley as per our normal procedure. It was good and dark before we walked the gravel road in the dark towards our homes. My thoughts raced at first, but then I calmed down and focused on Seven and our little Punkin waiting for me. What did Seven mean by a surprise visitor? I wasn't worried about bad guys or anything because our security was pretty tight after the sniper had infiltrated our valley. The last few hundred yards of my walk had me pass by a row of little houses that looked like something out of a Normal Rockwell painting. Warm little cottages with streams of light smoke issued from chimneys. Yellow light shined around faces as families peered through windows to see if loved ones would be home soon. It was good and cold too. My breath told me that it would be freezing soon. Fred's house was lit but it didn't look like he was home. I wondered how he was feeling and if he would be ready to rejoin the fight by the time of our planned operation. My pace quickened as I reach my front door.

I walked up my front steps hardly able to keep my eyes off the stoop where Mac had been shot. It was hard to keep the memories out of my mind as I climbed the few steps and worked the door. Voices and laughter could be heard through the walls as I opened the thick wooden door. Seven sat on our couch beside Bo. She was laughing hysterically as Fred and his wife sat across the small room in chairs.

"Hey honey, I'm home!" I called out to everyone.

Bo looked over at me in complete deadpan. "Hey sweetie."

Seven jumped up and threw her arms around me. "Good to have you home, Dear."

I put the Thor in the rifle rack by the door and hung my pack on the little iron hook. Fred shook my hand and patted me on the back. "Did you have a good trip, Huck?"

"Anytime you get home in one piece, it's a good trip Fred. What are you guys doing here?"

Seven waved at everybody. "We thought we would throw you a welcome home, Christmas, and anniversary party." Everyone in the house cheered and raised their glasses. Punkin cried a little at the unexpected noise. Everyone covered their mouths as he squalled like a banshee. Nobody minded it though; this was an occasion to remember and the mood was playful. I wished I had taken the opportunity to wash up back at headquarters. I wasn't nasty, but I felt grimy from all the road miles I had put in.

I walked over to the couch where Seven had sat back down. I smacked Bo's knee as I plopped down. "What lies have you been telling everybody?"

Seven laughed, all red faced and said loudly, "Bo here was just telling us about that fat girl you were dating in high school."

"Oh, that's a lie! She was not all that fat!" I claimed.

Fred almost choked on his drink. "She was so homely the dog wouldn't play with her." The room exploded in laughter. We joked on and on for hours, telling stories and just having fun. We ate, we sipped a little mountain medicine (translate as moonshine) and we had a great dinner party.

As the night wore on, Seven and Fred's wife went upstairs to put Punkin to bed. Fred was showing Bo his reddening scar with his shirt pulled up. Bo was raising a sleeve and comparing pains.

The fire crackled in the iron stove along with the oil lamps burning in the small room. Cinders bounced off the fire's door as we sat and compared scars.

While the ladies were upstairs, Bo looked over at me and said quietly, "You've got a good one there, Huck. You was right, she is way too hot for you." Fred laughed hard, trying to keep quiet.

"You're about right, Bo," I agreed.

Bo took a drink, which didn't help his intense country drawl. "Oh, thanks for sending me those computer geeks. I really appreciate you letting me get settled. I didn't know what the hell to do."

I broke in, "You know what Princess told me? She said, He made me eat squirrel!" I quoted in her squeaky voice.

Fred nearly peed himself. Bo chuckled loudly and I laughed so hard I thought I would bust a gut. Shushes came from upstairs and Punkin squalled a little at the disturbance. Fred was drooling at the mouth in his stupor and my eyes were tearing from the memory of Princess and her indignant attitude.

After we got settled a little, Bo looked around. "You've got a nice little setup here, Huck. I heard about that sniper from the folks at the store. They say you're getting about famous around here."

Fred said, "They've heard of Huck all the way in Texas. The head of the Texas Rangers gave him that rifle," Fred pointed to the Thor beside Bo's Browning on the rack. Bo got quiet in his memories for a second and sobered up somewhat. "Yeah, Huck always was the lucky one."

Bo asked Fred, "So whatchya been doing lately?"

Fred looked solemn for the first time that night. "Well, I've been working with the local town council representing the militia. I had to have something to do while I have been out of action."

Bo and I looked each other not believing what we were hearing. To be honest we had never considered Fred to be a politician. But when you thought about it, he was as straight forward as you get. Folks might actually find that refreshing.

I sat back on the cushion of the couch and thought out loud. "Look at us now, fellas. I'm married with a baby, Bo has been eating bugs for a year, and Fred is going to be Mayor someday."

Bo spoke, low and flat. "Then there are the fanatics down the road trying to kill us every other day."

We were all tired and ready to call it a night as we sat there in the quiet with our thoughts.

I looked over to Bo. "Have you got a place to stay tonight?"

Bo struggled past some internal thoughts and responded, "Yeah, they got me a cot in the back of the store. Its lumpy, just the way I like it." He got up and stretched. Fred's wife came tiptoeing downstairs. The baby was asleep and it was time to call it a night.

"Seven says to tell you all goodnight," Fred's wife said as she helped a lethargic Fred to his feet. Bo grabbed his rifle and jacket and waved quietly to us as he headed to the front door.

We said our goodbyes and I turned down the lamps as our guests closed the door behind them. That was a night to remember. We had such a good time just relaxing and sitting around without a care in the world. It was as if the green shirts didn't even exist. Those memories are the ones that really matter. How many shots I made, or how accurate they were, were not as important as my friends and how we spent a great evening together. Those were the times you remembered when everything else seemed to fall apart.

I went into 3rd battalion headquarters the next morning so I could get some work done before Christmas. There were a lot of preparations that had to be coordinated for all the volunteers coming in the next week or so. But it was right about then that I realized the value of our people spending Christmas with their loved ones. We all needed a recharge of our bodies and spirit. Seven brought Punkin in and we worked in my office as a family most of the day. I passed out all my notes for the department heads to consider during the break. The first bullet point in each memo started with directives to develop procedures so they could operate their respective departments without any electrical forms of communication. There would be a lot of discussions over that one in the next few days.

I sent out a standard report to the generals' staff on the recruiting drive. It lacked detail on purpose. Nobody realized how critical our communications security had become. So, I sent a written packet with all the details to Bull and copied his chief of intelligence. In the packet, I relayed the warnings and the need for an immediate review of all communications methods. I found it hard to stress the importance of the warning and urged the discussions surrounding the issue to be off-the-grid completely. I only hoped my warnings were sufficient and everyone that read them would treat the issues as if their lives depended on it, because they did.

In mid-afternoon, I issued orders to couriers telling all of 3rd battalion to rotate their staffs to 50%. Half of everybody would take the next three days off and the other half would take the second three days off. I had been working on my own so long, I never considered asking the general's permission. That was a mistake, as I was to find out later. Everyone in the command was thrilled at taking a few days off. Our stress level was always on alert with brief periods of sheer pandemonium at the best of times. Intelligence reports said that enemy activity was at the lowest point as it had been all year, so I felt the opportunity to give us all a little down time was an acceptable risk.

Rocket was still on mission, as well as several intelligence teams sent to recon the major cities. These were high risk missions that never leave the back of your mind as a commander. Any time you send people out there is a chance they will not return. You do everything you can to keep them as safe as possible, but in the end it isn't up to you. We were in a shooting war. If you were captured, or got caught by green shirt special police, you were in for a world of hurt. I had the security guys rotate their people on and off to make sure we had complete coverage during the holidays. There was no way I was going to allow the command to get too relaxed.

Seven and I packed up as the last of the headquarters staff finished for the night.

Seven told me, "Huck Dear, we have dinner plans with my folks tonight. Then you have to be in tomorrow for the officers review board."

I joked back, "Don't you need me to go fight some Sandy out in Hawaii or something?"

She played it off. "You just want to see me in a bikini."

I hadn't thought of it before. We had never been to the beach. We were married during the war and the idea of a sunny vacation away from everything was just foreign. But the idea of Seven in a bikini made my thoughts stray. She was getting her figure back and nursing didn't hurt either. Whew!

We had dinner with her folks that night. Her folks were great. They lived in Wooten Valley along with the rest of us. Seven was working at headquarters while they watched Punkin during the work days. Seven's dad ran one of the beef farms in the valley. It sure was nice to have a beef farmer in the family; you eat well.

Or, medium rare if that is your taste. Ha!

We tried to supply our own food needs from the valley while the recruits were fed by supplies coming in from our trades with neighboring counties. The logistics people were always hard at work keeping us fed and ready to fight. It was no small task in a time when field were plowed by hand and tractors were few and far between. Gas was coming in slowly and never on a regular schedule.

The Officer's Review Board (ORB) was not something that I looked forward to as I made my way into town. All the way into headquarters I wondered what crimes had been committed by the men that should be protecting others while under my command. The ORB was held every so often to review people that had been accused of criminal behavior. The officers of the 3rd battalion would review each case and make a determination on the appropriate punishment based off the case. It was like a court-martial, but a little more informal in its format because we were after all, militia, not lawyers. Most of the claims were small in nature. Somebody stole chickens or broke someone's property. The local person could make their claim and air their grievances. The officer's board would punish the volunteer and make them pay back whatever the damages plus interest. We tried to be creative about it too. If a young man were doing wrong, we made him work for the person he took from. Mostly it was harmless stuff. Once or twice a farmer's daughter was brought to the review board with a little bit of belly showing. That issue was occasional, but not too often. Preachers were better in those cases.

There were a few cases where the crimes were more serious. A person in the militia had to always keep the mindset of a police officer. We always tried to weed out individuals that were too eager to dish out force. We tolerated none of it. If someone exhibited signs of hatred, they were gone. If we found out that someone committed a real crime like a rape or something, they were handed over to the authorities in town. I would like to say that there was none of that, but we were made up of regular citizenry. Out of any given population, there will be some real criminals. Frontier justice was sometimes harsh in those early days of the war. A confirmed rapist or child molester did not have to languish in jail very long before their sentence was carried out. It was brutal at times, but very affective at curbing crime.

I issued directives and met with department heads most of the day after the review board. Bull was coming to meet the SF guys after Christmas and we were planning on a conference to be hosted by 3rd battalion. Rocket reported that he could start transporting volunteers from about 20% of the designated pickup points. Everything was right on schedule.

The days before and after Christmas were a blur. Seven and I spent the down time with Punkin. We celebrated our first anniversary together and our first Christmas in Wooten Valley. The convenience store was a buzz every night with families gathering and people coming and going. We marveled at how far we had come in the last few months. When we came to the valley, we had nothing. Now we had a thriving community with electricity and quite a few comforts of life compared to occupied territory. We prayed for a good spring as well, but no matter how you tried to get away from it, the pending operation to shut down Wilmington was on all of our minds. We tried to play it off, but we all knew what a hard and lengthy battle in Wilmington lay in wait for us. It showed on people's faces as they tried to have fun without outwardly showing fear. But we all felt the same way. We knew how vital that mission would be for us in the future. If we failed, there may not be a tomorrow for any of us. Those thoughts were sobering. But we managed to make the best of the brief holiday.

By the time Bull arrived, most of 3rd battalion was up and running again. The first convoys of volunteers arrived to find their camps a bit chilly compared to their homes in lower lying country. The foothills can be a challenge in the winter and living in a tent or barn can get old real fast. Our housing people had that covered though. They had a plan to rotate volunteers from place to place every week. That way nobody would have to spend three months in a tent waiting for the operation. Empty houses, barns, tents, dog houses, and whatever else we could find made our encampments. Bunkers along the hillsides provided shelter during bad weather for roving patrols. They also served the purpose of keeping an extra watch on the surrounding countryside. I didn't want any more snipers-for-hire to show up unexpected.

Almost the entire command was at headquarters with news of the general coming the following day. We were proud of our schools and wanted everything to be in order if the general wanted an impromptu inspection. There was a buzz about the place and everybody seemed to be in good spirits. There were meetings going on all over the building as department heads and team leaders tried to work out ways to get everyone fed and bedded down for the night. The first groups of 4th militia were trickling in by units about platoon size. Everyone was trying to get a handle on using written forms of communication between headquarters and the surrounding farms we used for camps and training facilities. It was organized pandemonium there for a while.

I walked down to what we called the motor-pool. It was really an eight-bay garage for busses that we used to work on our vehicles. To say the place was busy, was a gross understatement. We were constantly fixing and upgrading all sorts of vehicles so they would perform any number of tasks suited for militia operations.

"Hey Goodwrench, get this placed cleaned up before the general arrives." I joked to the man in charge of the garage.

With his back still to me he called out, "If that freakin general wants a clean garage, I will give him a broom." He turned around to face me. "Your man Rocket has made a heck of a list for me to fill. Just where will I find all the trucks he wants?"

I milled around the tables as mechanics worked under hoods with all the bays full. Goodwrench had a great team of people working for him. It was great to have someone so well versed in all things vehicular. I hated what I was about to tell him.

"Goodwrench, Rocket has priority over all other orders right now. Let the operations officers help you with the people you might need. We are pulling in a lot of folks from all over in the next weeks, but we gotta have these vehicles on the road in the next couple of days. You can get more mechanics when they come in. Oh yeah, you have to move operations out of this garage."

Goodwrench pointed a large shiny box-end wrench at me from across the table filled with parts. "That ain't funny, Huck."

"I wish I was joking," I told him. "But I'm not. There will be 20 or so guys coming in the next hour and we are packing you up and moving your operation to a new warehouse about eight miles away."

Goodwrench was upset already, and now he was mad. "Just how in the hell am I supposed to get all these trucks ready in time with you moving our butts to some new warehouse? It will take a week to get up and running good."

I responded in the way of a commander in charge, "Well you don't have a week. Get your hands off the wrenches and direct your department. Make up teams of your people and give them specific tasks. Delegate to your subordinates and let them work out solutions to get their job's done."

Goodwrench looked around at his men who were staring at the two of us. "Get back to work you guys. I didn't call for a break." His men suddenly got real interested in whatever task they were doing before.

I could see him working out ideas in his head. Or perhaps he was contemplating hitting me with the wrench. Either way, I interrupted his thoughts. "Oh yeah, and I need a bunch of new recruits for couriers as well. We are going to start courier runs all over the place and I'm thinking we will use street bikes and muscle cars."

Goodwrench scrunched up his face again. "Just where am I supposed to get a bunch of crotch rockets and drivers? Rocket already picked through the cream of the crop and stole everybody he could lay his hands on. There ain't nobody left but the local hotrod association and they ain't nothing but a bunch of punk kids with tattoos from head to toe."

"Sounds good to me," I responded coolly.

"So how do I get them into the militia Mr. Colonel, sir? Where do I find the hot-rodders, if you don't mind, sir" he said sarcastically.

I thought for a second and told him, "Host a car show and drag race in town. Offer 20 gallons of premium gas to whoever can do the fastest road course or something. Put out flyers. Use my office staff to help. Whatever you do, do it by day after tomorrow; we need those couriers." I walked back to the headquarters building as more trucks rolled through the parking lot. Goodwrench was a great mechanic, but now was the time to find out if he was a good leader. I'm sure his people heard that the Colonel had finally lost his marbles. Maybe he was right. It was a pretty tall order by anyone's standards.

I walked inside the headquarters which had the buzz from before, if not more. My next meeting should have started five minutes prior and I was likely the only one late. I walked downstairs to where the intelligence department had set up shop in the basement.

Seven met me at the door. "Huck, you're late. Everybody is in the conference room." She shuffled me towards the door as I tried to explain my tardiness.

The conference room was lit with several computer screens projected on several walls. Maps hung in various places with information marked on clear overlays. I noticed routes in red, yellow, and green markers covering several roads linking us to the other parts of the state. It must have been Rocket's planned routes underway.

"Thanks for you guys showing up on time. A Colonel's work is never done."

Seven stood by the white board and started the meeting. "Colonel, we have prepared a series of briefings on the various projects underway. You will see over here the greater Charlotte area with our estimated strengths and disposition of the Sandys. On this wall, you will see Rocket's effort underway. We have teams collecting Intel on all the major cities held by the green shirts, Raleigh, Durham, Greensboro, and Winston Salem. We have some information on Wilmington coming in soon, as well as the suggested staging areas. We also just finished reviewing that case of information you sent from your recruiting trip. I asked our IT specialists to sit in on this meeting as well."

It sounded weird for her to refer to me as Colonel, but 'honey' did not seem appropriate either.

I stood by the podium and looked at the room full of sullen faces. They looked as if they were in shock.

I looked to them and asked, "First impressions?"

The room was silent except from the hum of computers and lights. Everyone was silent until one young gal along the back side of the table said, "How certain are we of this new information from your source?"

I responded, "My source is most likely more hunted than even the people in this room. If he were working for the green shirts, in any capacity, I would not be standing here to tell you about it."

Seven tilted her head at me with a little look of concern.

Data asked, "Does this mean we will have to shut down all electronic communications?"

I could see the concern in his face. Everyone in the room was thinking the same thing. How much could we do and how would we do it.

"We are going to continue to use the internet and we are going to maintain the pace you have been doing over the last four months. In fact, we are going to increase the usage another 10-15 percent over the next two weeks and then again two weeks after that."

The room was bewildered. Everyone looked at me like I was a crazy fool.

They asked once after the other:

"Won't they know exactly where we are?"

"Aren't the drones already flying overhead?"

"How long before they bomb this place to the ground?"

I smiled at them. "I hope they do; we are leaving this facility within the week."

While their mouths hung open I took a marker and wrote on the board as I talked. "Our IT department is about to start the largest disinformation campaign in the war to date. Every electronic form of communication will be fake. We will continue to do business as regular as it is monitored by the green shirts. However, the content of those messages will be completely manufactured by people in this room. You will fake radio communications, emails, web sessions, hack attempts, everything you did before. We will create fake units, fake targets, and the goal will be to do it in such a way that the green shirts will not know any different. You will live in the fake world you create."

Another intelligence operative asked, "How will the militia communicate? We are spread throughout the state."

"All the departments have been ordered to begin using a new courier service we are putting together," I told them. They sat, scratching their heads in deep thought. It was a lot for anybody to take in. "Now that you know the extent of the green shirt capability, we can use it against them. There is always an angle that can be played. When someone gets too dependent on one source of information, you have them. Let's turn their efforts into our advantage; make them suffer for their reliance on electrical intelligence gathering."

After another hour of conversation with Seven's Intel group, I retreated back to my office. Seven would have them all squared away and working in teams by supper. My operations officers jabbered in my ears for another few hours as they attempted to handle all the men coming in from units in Bull's command. Now that I think of it, it was like the first day of summer camp. Except these campers came with rifles.

Bull's caravan blocked the streets outside of the headquarters building for five minutes. After a bit of shouting, the roadway was cleared and our people ushered Bull up to my office. Bull shook hands with all the staff as he made his way to my door.

"Who are you, Patton?" I asked Bull as he finally made his way through my door. Several of his majors and staff followed him through the door. Everyone sat where they could, but it was a small office and some had to stand. We traded greeting for a few minutes before Bull started.

"Huck, just what the hell were you doing calling a break at Christmas like that? You should have cleared it with me first. We can't have 3rd battalion out of it for a week like that."

I looked around at the stern faces staring back at me. "We were down by only 50% for three days at a time. There has been no enemy activity in our area other than that sniper."

One of Bull's officers asked, "What percentage of your people did not come back from that little break?"

I looked at him hard, "Our attrition rates are way under yours. Just where do you come off asking me like that?" I was red-faced and mad. I was not about to be lectured on my command decisions like that from some staffer in another command.

About the time I considered shooting the guy, Bull interjected, "Just check with me next time, Huck. We have had some Sandys making some fuss around our power plants trying to shut down our electrical grid. We have been fending off attacks on water plants and farms for the last month. We may have needed some of your people, that's all."

I was not over the attitude yet and told the major, "My people are spread razor thin as it is. We are recruiting local kids out of high school to run courier for us. If you think we can train hundreds of men in a month and a half, *AND* go around chasing the Sandys, you have another thing coming."

Bull went into his commander mode on me for a minute or two and we settled it. I was wrong. I let it go, he let it go, and we continued our meeting.

After we got back on track, the next topic was the Reaper that Rocket had recovered.

"Huck, we got that Reaper you guys found." One of Bull's people stated. "We have never seen anything like it. It must be the last Reaper in the state. We have been showing people and parading it around to as many folks as we can."

"Rocket was the one that recovered it. His team found it in Oxford among a lot of junked green shirt cars and so forth. The green shirts must have missed it when they destroyed the rest of them," I told the crowd before asking, "Have you guys filmed it and put it on the web?"

Bull said, "Yes, and the green shirts have already put out a claim that the militia built the thing and put it on the internet for propaganda. You know, their typical BS. But, with so much crap on the internet, there is a high level of skepticism."

Bull continued as we sat and thought about it. "What we need to focus on is our communication lines. That little box of information your contact sent was incredible."

Another of Bull's officers interjected, "Just how trustworthy is your source? All that seems pretty science fiction if you ask me."

I looked at him seriously. "Tell me you are not my intelligence liaison." Several of the men in the room snickered. He looked offended, good! "Gentlemen, everything done via any electronic means is being used against us. We need to turn the dial back to 1880 and not use any electricity whatsoever. If we use a computer, it better be filled with deception from start to end. The connection better be off-site and the more remote, the better. My team is working on a whole series of deception tactics that we will pass out to you in a couple of days."

The first officer in Bull's staff chimed in, "So what are we supposed to do, use carrier pigeons to direct our units in the field?"

I looked at him, "We are creating teams of couriers right now. I suggest you go find your own hot rod club and get them signed up as soon as possible."

The officer shot back at me, "That will take dozens of men out of the ranks. We have to direct the actions of too many units to wait for curriers. New orders will be delayed way to long!"

I had enough of that guy so I told him, "Then you had better train your team leaders to think on their feet and stop asking permission to go fight the green shirts. What were you, regular Army before the war?"

He answered proudly. "I was a Captain in the National Guard and we moved only when we had direct orders."

As Bull shifted in his seat, I responded, "What, were you an asphalt paving crew or did you manage porta-potty distribution?" Some of the men in the room choked back some outbursts at that one. Evidently his counterparts thought just about as much of the guy.

Bull called the meeting until the next day and strolled around from department to department the rest of the afternoon. I didn't see the NG officer again during Bull's visit. Bull visited all three farms where we housed men and did our training. One of my men escorted Bull's party in a non-descript van as we were implementing precautions in case the area was being monitored by UAVs. Switching vehicles may slow down the tracking process, but I doubted it would be enough to completely get off their radar. I only hoped we could make the necessary logistical changes covertly and not tip our hand that we knew about green shirt observation. Time was not on our side and a lot had to be done before we were ready to assault Wilmington.

The next day Bull was back in the headquarters building since he had walked through the camps the day before.

Bull said, "Huck, you and your men have done a great job with what you have. The camps are just what we hoped for. You make the 19th century seem comfortable even in winter."

"Thanks, Bull. Boy, did you get the right codename or what? "I asked as he laughed.

Seven came into my office as she knocked. "Guys, we just got one of our operatives back from the Durham team and I wanted to let you know."

Bull looked around. "Hello Seven, how is the baby?"

Seven produced a bundle of pictures like they were from a fast-draw holster. Bull took the pictures and oohed and awed as we walked downstairs to the Intel department.

Chapter Fifteen
Durham, Green Shirt Utopia

As we reached the bottom floor, Bull asked, "What kind of team is reporting?"

Seven looked to Bull to explain. "These teams have been trained to infiltrate green shirt territory and collect as much data as possible. They are usually out three days to a week before our extraction teams pick them up. Their job is to blend in, make contacts, and report what they see as soon as they get back. This is the first mission inside the downtown area of Durham."

The intelligence specialist was a fairly wiry young man in his mid-twenties, sitting at a small table in a sparse room we used for briefings and assignments. He could fit into any college campus with his youthful good looks or he could pass for just another worker at any local factory. I guessed that is why he was offered a job in intelligence. Several of our Intel team hovered around him with some fresh water and food. He ate and drank like a man that had been living in Ethiopia for the last month. His clothes were tattered and soiled to the point I imagined burning them instead of having them washed.

The young man stood as the general and I entered the room.

Bull told him, "Sit and eat son, we can wait a few more minutes for your report." The young man sat quickly and returned to his food.

"Sorry, sir. My ride didn't have anything to eat and I just had to get back here right away."

"So, how long have been in the militia?" Bull asked him trying to put him at ease.

The young man responded, "I joined the fourth back last winter, but was hurt down in Charlotte. I was up here with my folks when I joined the 3rd's intelligence group last summer."

Bull and I knew that this was common for volunteers. When someone was hurt, they often went to stay with family until they recovered. Sometimes the volunteer would rejoin his unit, but just as often, they would join a team nearer their home.

"Alright, what was your mission? I asked as he finished the remainder of his bowl.

"Sir, we were assigned to scout Durham. That is, Johnny and I were to scout Duke campus and the hospital complex. Johnny's codename was Blue Tic because he was a real hound. But they got him sir. The green shirt special police got him. There was nothing I could do. They got him!" The young man was rambling and his body shook from the recollection of the stress. I doubted he had slept in days. You could tell he had been on the run. He was covered in a variety of mud and filth. This was normal for sniper teams, but not covert operatives unless they had to evade capture. Evidently his mission had not gone well.

Seven put an arm around the young man and held him for a minute which seemed to calm him down considerably. A woman's touch can do that to a man, you know?

After a few minutes, Bull asked, "What is your name, son?" We all gave him some room and tried not to pry too much.

"Yes, sir," he said with a hiccup. "They call me, Beener because I used to do a lot of climbing. You know, like Carabineer? We just spelled it differently. "

Bull asked to prompt him, "What happened?"

Beener sat back in his chair and ran his fingers through his hair. "Blue Tic and I were assigned as one of the teams to go in and scout Durham."

Bull sat back and looked at the young man who was still distraught, but trying to keep his composure. We were all anxious to hear his report.

Seven prompted him. "Tell us what you saw; start from the beginning."

Beener recalled, "We drove through the outskirts and everything was kind of normal for nowadays. Wood burning fires in homes produced a fair amount of smoke in the neighborhoods. It was cold out, the smoke lay over the road, it was real peaceful. We passed through those areas and headed closer to town when we hit the slums. Houses were in pieces and people stood by burn barrels in the street. The place looked like downtown Beirut or something. We nearly had to shoot our way out, but our driver was able to get us closer on some back streets where it was quiet.

Our escort team dropped us off about a mile or so north of I-85 with our bicycles. We had our fake state-issue ID cards, cameras, everything we trained with. It was somewhere on Cole Mill road around some boarded up churches. The streets were quiet, not a sole in sight. This was weird for northern Durham. There are houses all over the place, but they are all empty. Most of them looked like they had been ransacked and gutted of everything useful. It was freakin spooky to walk through the place. Everything I saw north of the I-85 was empty. The green shirts made a dead zone around town. Nobody is supposed to be there. Green shirts patrol the old neighborhoods looking for trespassers. Word is that they shoot anyone they catch." Beener gulped some water down between breathes. He was talking non-stop.

Beener continued, "We thought we could sneak in through the west side of town near Duke Forest and make our way towards campus and the hospital which was our main objective. But they have constructed a series of walls all along the inside of the roadway. The wall follows 15/501 until it meets I-85, all the way around as far as Cameron Boulevard. The thing stretched all along I-85 to somewhere off to the east. Maybe it goes as far as where 70 splits off, I don't know. We didn't get that far. But I bet they have a complete circle around town. The green shirts control all open interstate and the major roads." By then one of our Intel people sat a map in front of him so he could point out landmarks and so forth.

Beener organized his thoughts and kept talking. "Every entrance into town is blocked. They have a very stringent border and they keep it manned all the time. You don't just walk down the road; they have gates, checkpoints and everything. It's like going into a foreign country. In fact, it's just like that. Blue Tic tried to flash his ID at one of the checkpoints and they told him to get lost. They said he was not a citizen and should beat it before the next patrol came by and arrested him. At first we didn't know what that meant. We found that out later."

Bull looked around to Seven. "Have you heard about dual citizenship or anything from the green shirts so far? She shook her head no as we listened to Beener.

Beener recounted, "When night came on the second day, Blue Tic and I made our way to a nice little dark spot along 15/501 where we climbed the fence. It wasn't easy either. There was razor wire double thick and it was a high wall too. Green shirt patrols monitor the roads around there all the time. They are not playing when it comes to their perimeter security. The perimeter roads are patrolled all the time. Most of the time it is squad cars, but sometimes there were armored trucks that SWAT guys use.

Once we were over, we walked towards Duke campus. There is a curfew so nobody is out after 9pm. We were the only folks running around. We made good time and managed to make our way to our objective. All you see are green shirt patrols riding by in squad cars every few minutes. The place is a police state. Anyway, we made our way through campus and the place looked normal enough. Duke was repaired when the green shirts took over management just like we expected. Blue Tic and I hid in the trees until dawn. When 0:700 rolled around, the place opened up and workers started pouring from apartment buildings. They were not casually strolling around either. They were hustling to their work assignments. It was like a stampede of people."

I asked, "How could you tell they were workers?"

Beener looked over to me. "They were wearing those horrible grey uniforms. Everybody wore those things. Blue Tic and I found ourselves on the street watching all this and getting very self-conscious as people stared at us because we were not in the expected clothing. We stayed on the move and kept out of sight as best we could, though. More than once a green shirt officer showed up on a bicycle and people pointed to where we had just been. We kept to the wooded parking lots for the most part after that. We had to blend in so we made our way to the laundry facility behind the hospital. If we were lucky, we could steal some hospital scrubs and blend a bit better. That's when Blue Tic saw someone he knew from before the war. She was a nurse named Monica. We walked over to her and she recognized him immediately. But instead of nice and friendly hellos, she freaked out at the sight of us."

She asked, "What are you doing here Johnny? You shouldn't be here!" She looked terrified and kept turning her head as if she were about to be caught doing something really bad. She was near panic and was trembling. "You take your friend and get out of here, Johnny. They don't like it when people sneak into town like this. You are not a citizen."

Johnny, sorry, Blue Tic asked, "What is all this citizen business? We don't understand."

Monica repeated her warning and said, "They have cameras everywhere, you are going to be arrested any minute and I don't want to be caught talking to you." The fear in her voice was enough for me, but Johnny pushed it.

"Monica, My friend and I just need a place to bunk for a night or two. C'mon Monica, they might know we are here already and we have been talking to you. Hide us."

She looked around in all directions and told us to meet her after her shift was over that evening. We walked around as much as we could, but there always seemed to be a cop or two on the streets. By 10am am there were casually dressed people walking around. They were shopping and strolling around at ease. By then there were no workers other than in the shops that opened around 9 am.

Oh yeah, there were no regular cars on the streets either, just those little electric carts and lots of bicycles. Even service vehicles for maintenance were carts pulled around by an electric golf cart kind of thing.

All the workers walked from place to place. The casually dressed people rode bicycles, but most had those golf cart things. We did see a street car trolley, but that was only a couple of times at shift change for the workers.

We couldn't go into any of the buildings because they all had these RFID chip readers mounted beside the doors. You have to be beeped in everywhere. The workers are not allowed to walk around in just any building either. Your ID seems to have specific permissions built into your ID code. Otherwise, an unauthorized worker needs special permission by security to enter. It was weird to say the least. I have never seen that level of access control."

Bull commented, "It sounds like they have a couple of things going on. They have a worker class and who knows how many other levels of citizenship. So did the green shirt police use regular gasoline powered squad cars?"

Beener scraped the last of his bowl and answered, "Yes, as far as I know. I saw some real nice BMWs and Mercedes parked nearer to the faculty parking areas. Somebody must be using them. They were clean and in a secure lot that we couldn't get near.

There were just too many cameras and security people milling around. Every step you take there is a camera on a light pole or a roof top. We hung out and tried to steer clear of everybody, but it was hard. They have classes march through the woods all over the place. They plant trees, study plants, bugs, and stuff."

Seven asked Beener, "Did you get back to Monica that night?"

Beener looked solemn for a minute. "Yeah, we met her back at the parking lot where we saw her earlier that morning. She was late. We were about to leave when she came walking down the sidewalk. She motioned for us to follow her and did not stop to talk. So, we lagged behind and tried to not look too conspicuous. It was hard, but we made it to her apartment after several minutes. She waited by the door with her ID in hand. She didn't say a word and motioned for us to stand to the side. She waved the ID over the black box and a light shone in her face. In a few seconds, the electric door clicked and she was able to go inside. We walked through quickly and she hustled us up to her apartment by the back stairs. At her door, she waved her ID and the door clicked immediately. Blue Tic shut the door behind us."

She turned to us out of breath, looking at her watch. "We made it! We made it! Whew!"

Blue Tic asked, "What do you mean? Is there a time you have to be home or something?"

She looked at him, "Yes, you big idiot. I work first shift, duh! I have to clock in here at the apartment by 7pm."

Blue Tic looked at me, not knowing what to say. I looked at Monica. "Do you have a roommate or is all this your place?"

Monica's response was not what I expected. "I have a roommate, but I haven't seen her in a couple of weeks. She got too many reprimands and had to report to the education facility."

I asked her, "How long will she be there?"

Monica walked around the small apartment taking off her shoes to relax. "She will be back in another week or so, depending on her level of cooperation." Her tone was casual as if her roommate were on a cruise. Education center was a smooth way of saying she was being reprimanded until she submitted.

Beener motioned with his arms as he remembered. "Monica's apartment was small, man. There was a couch and some chairs, but no kitchen. "The place was pretty empty. The only entertainment was the TV. Oh yeah, the TV was on all the time, no need for a remote, it was nonstop. Monica said it ran until about 10pm every night with various shows, news, and so on. It was all green shirt programming with no other channels. I watched a piece on the militia and the civil war. We are regarded as murdering bands of thugs and keeping freedom from spreading throughout the state. Pretty much everything has been outlawed. No weapons, you must wear certain clothes based on your work or status, no political parties are allowed, no meeting of people in groups of four people or more, it's crazy. All the news stories were reminders of the laws, or just propaganda stories about us bad guys. The rest was environmental stuff. No commercials, it was all-state all-the-time broadcasts.

I heard Blue Tic ask about electricity as I rejoined their conversation. She said the apartment power shut down when she left for her shift every morning and came back on when she got home. Her building was not allowed to have pets, but she said some places had them. She didn't have a thermostat either. The building was kept at 65 degrees or so all the time. It was hard for us to understand the level of control over the people's day to day life."

Bull asked Beener, "So if she didn't have a kitchen how did they eat?"

Beener quickly replied, "I almost forgot. Monica said that her building had an assigned time to eat in the foyer downstairs most nights. Everybody in the building was assigned a time and a place to eat. When I asked her about the food, she told me that every meal was part of a planned out nutrition formula set up by the health services. She also commented on how it was helping everyone stay trim and how high blood pressure and diabetes were things of the past. They were not allowed to have food in the apartment because of rats. At least, that was the excuse. I don't think they wanted anyone to have food at home. The green shirts wanted people to be completely dependent on them."

We all sat around trying to get a handle on what we were hearing. We had never heard of a society so tightly controlled. The green shirts had managed to control everything eaten by the populous. They even managed to restrict the food supply and do it in such a way where the people accepted the control. It was incredible.

Seven asked Beener, "Do they get paid? We've seen state credits before, how are they used?"

Beener nearly yelled out, "That was the best part! The green shirts have created the exact opposite of working and getting paid for your job. As a worker, you are given housing and food, all the staples of life. Then, they pay you a small amount of credits for the little things like toothbrushes and daily stuff. Instead of paying you in money, they reward you with extra credits for good work and good behavior. If you do well on the job and don't get reprimands, you're allowed to go out to dinner twice a month. Its 100% taxation with you getting to keep a little for trivial pleasures denied to you on a regular basis. The people have accepted it hook line and sinker because they think they are getting all these things for free!"

Bull looked at me. "How could people just roll over and accept being wards of the state like that? The society is completely structured. I will bet the schools have already decided which kids will do which jobs in the future by the time they are in the fifth grade. How is it that people can be led around by the nose like that? It's been a year and a half since the takeover and they are worse than the old Soviet Union.

I added, "Imagine the old Soviet bloc with modern technology. The RFID box scanned Monica's facial features when she checked into her apartment. That is why she had the guys stand to the side."

Seven looked over at Bull. "I bet they have a complete database of all the citizens and workers. When a camera picks up someone from outside, the cops are called."

Beener listened to us intently. "I think you guys figured out what I was about to tell you. So that night, Monica went to dinner and did not come back. Curfew came and went and she was still not back.

Blue Tic and I were writing up notes in the apartment when the lights went out. A buzzer sounded in the hallway and the TV went blank. Then an announcement flashes over the TV and it's a picture of us standing by the parking area. We were wanted for questioning and everyone in the area was instructed to report our whereabouts.

Blue Tic and I looked out the window and there were green shirt special police everywhere. We went to the door and it was locked electronically. As the cops went in through the door leading to the lobby, we hauled out the window and onto the fire escape. Blue Tic and I made our way to the adjacent building as the cops swarmed up the stairs towards her apartment. Then we ran back towards the west, knowing we were going to be chased all the way back to the wall. Within minutes cars were streaking through the streets looking for us. The way we came in was blocked, so we changed direction and headed east.

Everywhere you turned there was camera after camera. We tried to avoid them all, but it was impossible. We tried to use our shirts as masks, but since there was a curfew, it didn't matter what you looked like. If you were out after curfew, you were arrested. That's most likely why they waited to nab us when they did. They thought they could lock us down in the apartment."

Seven asked the question we all wanted to ask. "How did they get Blue Tic?"

Beener rubbed his hands on his dirty clothes. "We ran to the east trying to keep out of sight as much as possible. There are old neighborhoods inside the fence that looked like they were being torn down. Some old houses were still standing, while others were piles of rubble. Labor crews must still be working on them because there are tools still in the area. We ran through empty streets where rows of houses once stood. It was freaky at night without anybody around. The place was dead, block after block of empty houses. We cut south and ran as far we could. There were more of the new apartments and their cameras. By morning the cops were getting close to us. They must have spotted us at one point because they cordoned off the area and started using dogs. Blue Tic and I had to split up just to draw the scent away. Five minutes later I heard gun shots as the dogs barked a block or two away. After that, the place went quiet again. Blue Tic never made it to the rendezvous for pickup. I spent the next three days working my way back to the slums outside the fence. Let me just say it was a hard three days. The slums outside the dead zones are dog-eat-dog and it was a miracle I got out at all. I met the pickup this morning and had him bring me here directly."

We had taken up enough of the Intel department's time for one day so Bull and I went back upstairs and let Beener finish the rest of his debrief. We talked for quite some time concerning the thought of living in such a structured society. We could never do it. The only way we could see other people actually living that way was through the prism over the last year and a half of chaos. The general populous was scared out of their wits after the financial meltdown and power failure. They needed help for the basics of life and all they saw was bloodshed from the gangs. The green shirts made it look as though the militia was responsible for the rise of the gangs and the war itself. Then an all-caring, environment-friendly government wants to feed you and house you for free. Heck, they even give you a little spending money on the side. What's not to love? All you have to do is live according to their rules and accept whatever edict they hand down. They are the ones feeding you. If you resist, you are shipped off to be reeducated or perhaps expelled to the slums. Your freedom and liberty are things of the past. It was nothing short of amazing.

Reports from other recon units came in from other major cities. Almost all the stories were the same; the green shirts had completely restructured society. Personal freedom and liberty were replaced with promises of security and food if you worked for the state. The slums surrounding the cities were intentionally kept just barely above the starvation level.Thisserved the green shirts twofold. The murderous conditions of the slums made the green shirt's utopia seem that much more inviting even if it was very limiting. People seek comfort more than you might think. Secondly, the existence of the slums meant that you always had an undesirable place you could use as a threat to your trustees inside. Work and cooperate with our rules or we will cast you out there with the murderers.You have the choice of starvation or being hunted like an animal by crazed thugs just on the other side of the fence.

The one surprising aspect of all this information was the green shirt industries that were popping up. It seems the green shirts were very interested in developing a global trade system with goods from our state. One example was the production of tobacco and cigarettes. Yes, even though tobacco had been deemed a health risk and therefore banned completely, it was once again a cash crop. The green shirts had put several of the old manufacturers back in business in the old Leggitt & Myers buildings in Durham. There were more facilities in Winston Salem. All of their production was shipping overseas.

Beyond cigarettes, there was the pharmaceutical business. Until our recons units reported, we had no idea the manpower the green shirts were throwing at the pharmaceuticals. The Research Triangle Park had been home to some of the largest labs in the region. Their products were also being shipped worldwide. It must have been part of the People's Planetary Revolution for economic development. Each region produces whatever it can for the collective and trade is established. As with all communist forms of government, the economic strategy of trade without profit, simply cannot sustain itself for everyone. People have demonstrated over and over that they need to work for their own benefit. Without the drive for improving your situation in life, you simply don't produce in quantities necessary to support everyone else. Then you have too many mouths to feed, and just like Stalin, you have to reduce the population. I guess they figured they would reverse things a little and reduced the population while the power outage had everyone freaked out.

I wondered if society would ever look and feel like it did back before the financial collapse. Everything was so foreign. Trade was so difficult without a formal uniform currency. If it wasn't a tangible item, you didn't have a trade. Money was strange for us even in free territory. Some cities tried to establish a local money source, but there were always squabbles about the actual value of each note. You simply had to do your best to trade fairly and not get taken. It was the wild-west with funny money half the time.

The next day Bull and I were invited to the road rally and street race our motor-pool guys set up. Even though the weather was cold, there was an entire parking lot full of cars and motorcycles. The parking lot was spotted with little bits of dead grass between the seams of concrete. The building had been a home improvement store before the war. Needless to say, the place had been closed for quite some time. Our guys had a quarter-mile track laid out on one side and a road course circling around the remnants of several old fast food restaurants on the other. The place was packed with young men standing around various hot rods with their hoods raised. The American love of cars was certainly not dead. Bull was dressed in a Harley T-shirt as we pulled up in several gun trucks to one side of the parking lot. We were not trying to go incognito, but we didn't want to parade around in camo either.

The Grand Marshal was our man in charge of the motor pool. He stood on a makeshift podium with a portable microphone addressing a group of mustang owners. "In fifteen minutes, the judges will come by to each of your cars. Please have your trunks and doors open for the inspection."

I let him finish and motioned for him to bend down so I could speak to him more directly. "How goes it?" I asked.

With the microphone off he whispered back, "Colonel Huck, its all I can do to keep up with all the events. There must be 500 people here and I have my mechanics trying to run races and judge hot-rods. If you want some recruiting, you will have to do it."

I frowned back at him, "Thanks!"

He just smiled blandly and continued to announce events to the crowds of people. At least the turnout was good. A lot of people wanted a chance to get out of their house and do something that resembled normal. There were not many opportunities for that kind of stuff back then. I took the opportunity to walk around the rows and rows of cars and listen to the conversations. Bull was doing the same thing along with the small entourage of security and operations officers we had with us.

As I walked past, I heard, "What are those green trucks over there?"

One of his friends looked to our gun trucks and replied, "Those must be militia."

The first guy asked as if he didn't understand completely, "What? Do we have a camo truck category?" His buddy snickered at the remark.

I walked by and said in a casual tone to nobody in particular, "I think I heard somebody say that this whole event was militia sponsored."

One of the guys looked over at me in surprise. "You really think so?" He evidently had never considered the idea that we were mainstream everyday people like themselves.

I said back, "Yeah, I here they want to recruit a bunch of hot rod drivers to run courier routes throughout the entire state."

The first guy said, "I ain't going to run as no courier. Those green shirts shoot at you if you get too close to one of their towns!"

His buddy laughed a little as I replied, "I hear they are only looking for guys with steel nerves and brass set of balls anyway. They might not take you."

I didn't mean to take it quite that far, but it just came out that way. My security escort had to step in before there was a full out brawl. I caught Bull's eye as he watched from 50 yards away. He didn't have to say anything. He knew Huck had struck again. After a little while, I decided that more than a little candor was just what this event needed. After the last of the events finished, I took the microphone and the platform.

The microphone squealed as I began to speak. "Calling all motorheads, gearheads, and drivers with heavy right feet. The militia needs drivers and fast cars to run courier routes. It ain't safe, it ain't no walk in the park. We're fighting the green shirts with everything we've got. We want men that can run routes and carry messages back and forth between units. We will provide the gas and whatever mechanics to give you the best edge possible. You will be helping your town, your state, and your country. We will train you, feed you, and give you a warm bed almost every night. But I only want the fastest, most daring men here. If you can't run 100 miles an hour in the pitch dark, I don't want you! If you think you can handle it, come over to the green trucks on the other side of the lot."

The crowd stood silent for a few seconds considering what I had said.

One of the guys shouted, "Who's asking?"

I looked over at him. "The North Carolina militia, 3rd battalion of the first NC army. Some call me Huck."

The crowd recognized the name as they looked from one person to the next, but they stood still, not knowing what to say.

Just then, a muscular young man raised his hand proclaiming, "I'll do it. Where do I sign up?"

I pointed to the trucks behind me. As he began to walk by, I recognized him to some degree. I turned to watch the young man walk by as the crowd murmured between themselves. That guy was familiar. When I turned back, there was Major Arrow's face among the throng of racers. That was one of his guys that had just volunteered! My SF guys were here and helping me to work the crowd.

I walked over to Arrow as a few stragglers wandered their way towards our trucks. "Thanks, good to see you guys."

Major Arrow shook my hand and said quietly, "We thought you might need a little help. Volunteers need to see that their peers are willing to participate. High-school type peer pressure can be a powerful tool." He motioned for me to look.

I watched as several of the race participants stood by our gun trucks with one of my operations officers. The hot-rodder's wanted to know more about the various modifications we made to the trucks. It was all started by one of Arrow's SF guys raising his hand first.

I asked Arrow quietly, "You guys bring a lot of toys with you? Did my operations people get you all squared away?"

Arrow made sure nobody was within ear shot. "Yes, I brought a few guys to help with the crowd here, but most are with the trucks. We brought enough rifles and ammo to equip all the volunteers. More will be coming in a few days. Our special toys are already on their way to the staging areas and other caches we have."

I told him, "Good, let me know if you need anything and I will make sure my people provide it. Rocket should be here in a few minutes and I want you and your men to come by Wooten Valley tonight for a special supper."

Arrow looked at his watch. "We need to go ahead and get moving. The drones will be overhead in another 45 minutes."

I asked, "Drones?"

Arrow spoke softly, "Yep, we just got word that this area will be swept tonight and they will continue cycling birds between here and Charlotte."

I reassured his quizzical gaze, "I think we have enough deception programs to keep them off balance for a while."

Just then Rocket arrived in his usual style. Rocket's bike blasted through the adjacent parking lot and jumped the berm separating the roadway from the fast food place. Rocket landed, sped around the side of the lot, then skidded to a stop next to the gun trucks.

I heard several of the motorcycle racers comment, "Hey, that's the Rocket. What? Is he militia now?"

Another guy said, "Let's go see."

A throng of the motorcycle guys headed over to see Rocket. I had nearly forgotten that Rocket was his nickname from his motocross days before the war. Evidently, he had made a name for himself on the semi-pro circuit. Based on the number of guys surrounding his bike, I was guessing we would have a few more recruits.

I called out, "Hey Rocket. See who can make it to the old foundation warehouse on Pearson Street the fastest. Offer a job to anyone that can make it in the next eight minutes without killing some old grandma in the street." I raised my watch looking at the minute hand and yelled, "GO!"

There was the slightest hesitation before a dozen or more eager young men scrambled to their bikes. You never saw such a display of raw horsepower and testosterone as they screeched out of the parking lot. I walked over to rocket and told him that we needed to recruit inside the buildings and get everyone under cover until the drones passed.

Several of the car racers stood nearby so I made the same type of offer to them. I yelled, "Anyone that can make it to that same warehouse using the old logging trails by the airport, in the next 15 minutes, will have a job too! Anyone that can't make it in 15 minutes can go home and pump up your tires with your mamma."

Mustangs, Camaros, Challengers, and even a few trucks peeled out of the parking lot. Those remaining looked onward at the sight and tried to stay out of the way as cars and trucks sped by.

I directed Major Arrow's people to their boarding houses so they could get settled.

Arrow headed towards his car and told me, "See you later, Huck."

I told him, "My security people will help you guys get settled and get your gear all squared away." Arrow and several of his men left shortly after. I was sure glad to see the guys supporting us their first day.

I radioed our recruiters to make sure they were ready to meet our newest volunteers. The recruiters would give these guys a briefing on what we expected and our codes of conduct. We had developed a speech that laid out what was acceptable behavior and what was not tolerated. The rules were pretty simple and straight forward. We don't kill indiscriminately. We shoot only to save ourselves or our people. We don't tolerate any supremacy group or gang kind of mentality whatsoever. The power of the militia would never be used for personal gain or to influence people to take away any amount of their freedom. We would not allow ourselves to become the bully.

Later that night I heard reports that we had done very well in our recruiting effort. We had a good first turnout which was expected to bring in even more local guys once their friends told them of the cool things they were doing. I wondered how they would feel about our dark green camo jobs on their cars and bikes. I was glad not to be there for that conversation.

Late in the evening Arrow and what I guessed to be most of his men came walking down our road in Wooten Valley. According to our intelligence, the drones had left the area and shifted south towards Charlotte. For now, we had some time to relax. Tonight was our last night before real training began. About 20 of Arrow's men walked through the convenience store with half our valley there to greet them. It was cold outside, but inside was lit and decorated for a party. We still had multi-colored light strings that hung from the walls from Christmas. Most of the electricity in the valley was being re-directed to that store for that event. The mood was instantly casual as Special Forces soldiers were warmly greeted as heroes by the people of the valley. In short, we had a ball.

Major Arrow came to my side during the party that night, "Colonel Huck, thanks for such a big welcome party. Tell everyone it really means a lot after being in hiding for more than a year."

I assured him, "I'll tell them. These people know how it is to be on the run. We have been half a step from the green shirts for so long we think we cast a green shadow."

Fred and Bo came strolling over to us. They had been busily filling the soldier's cups with some of the mountain special brew from up-the-holler.

Fred looked into Arrow's cup with concern. "You better drink that in the next ten minutes or so."

Arrow asked with his eyes watering from the first sip, "Okay. Why?"

Bo chimed in with red cheeks. "Cause if ya don't, it'll eat through the cup in 11 minutes! Whew!"

The guys stumbled off to complete their mission of giving everyone an unforgettable hangover.

Arrow asked me as we watched the scene repeat with some of his men, "They are a lively couple of guys. Are they here for training?"

I responded, "Not quite. The one on the left joined the militia the same day as I did. We come from the same home town, Fred, is his name. Bo on the right is another friend who just joined up a short time ago. He runs our wilderness survival training."

Arrow took another sip, "They see much combat?"

I knew he was dubious because of his first impression of their meeting. His first opinion may have been a little skewed, so I wanted to reassure him.

"Fred has been on a bunch of missions and planned secure routes from foot patrols to major convoys. He was captured last year and shot just a few weeks ago. Bo there walked 100 miles through green shirt held territory with that 44 magnum rifle on the rack over there."

Arrow's look said it all. "Okay, Huck. I was just curious."

I could understand his concern. At first glance, Fred's antics when we were on down-time, may have seemed strange. His depiction of a wounded duck flailing his arms while standing on a table was nothing short of hilarious to the rest of us. All said and done, the party was a success and Fred had accomplished his goal of extreme hangover. We packed it up for the night and shuttled the SF guys back to their barracks.

Chapter 16
Basic Training

The militia had early on recognized that military-style training was the key to a civilian fighting force. However, since we were civilians, we took into account the support of families as well as the lack of actual military equipment. We didn't exactly have a bunch of ammo either. Bullets were precious. Every round mattered. Shooting for training was careful and precise without waste or carelessness. When we shot, we hit our targets or else we faced running out of ammo. And in a gun fight, you don't want to be the jerk that runs out of ammo first.

Our new SF trainers were introduced to the militia trainers first thing in the morning after the party. There were some sleepy-eyed men when we started. But everyone was really amped to get started. We all knew it was game time and a lot was at stake.

We had the militia basic trainers go through their individual classes and give a summary of how things were taught in their respective fields. The SF guys listened intently and asked questions as the lecturers did their thing. It took most of the day for the SF guys to be bused from farm to farm seeing the extent of our facilities. From time to time during the day, truck loads of recruits came pouring into the farms. They watched as our camouflaged men walked from station to station. It was an amazing undertaking to see hundreds of faces gathered for the single purpose of freeing their state and their land.

Later that night I had a scheduled meeting with Major Arrow.

Arrow and a few of his men came to my office as a throng of logistics people left.

"Colonel Huck, you ready for us?"

I told him, "Yes, please, anything to get me out of supply briefings." Arrow and his men sat around the chairs in my small office and closed the door behind them.

"Major Arrow, what do you think of our little training program here?" I asked as I sat behind my desk.

Arrow plopped out his notebook where he had scribbled several pages of notes. "Colonel, I'm impressed. We figured we would have to spend the better part of a week getting the gear stowed and the camps set up for training. But we see you have built everything from toilets to field kitchens already. Your people have really been busy."

I looked at him squarely. "Okay, but where can we improve?"

I could see Arrow was glad to hear I was open to suggestions. Arrow browsed his notes. "Since we are equipping the men with M1 carbines for the most part, we need to have classes on breaking them down and cleaning them. Of course, you have the ranges set up already. We just need to use them while there is no drone activity."

He flipped a page and continued, "We need to start organizing the men into teams so we need to discuss how many men you want assigned to an operational unit. How does 20 sound?"

I folded my hands in thought and spoke after a minute, "If we have one of your men lead a small platoon size group in the actual operation, we can make teams of 20-22. That is larger than we are accustomed to in the militia, but city fighting is something that requires a lot more men."

Arrow agreed and we discussed how any more men than that would be hard to control in a combat situation with ex-military and militia.

Major Arrow said, "We need to expand the grenade course. We need some bunkers for door breeching as well as some other scenario based drills."

I told him that we had never done a lot of practice with grenades since we had never had many in stock. He told me how they brought along a lot of the practice grenades with the replaceable shotgun primers for bang-simulators. He and his men already had them ready for use.

Arrow continued with his notes. "We need to have a plan for how many men will use the M4 or the AR15 rifle so that we train groups of men together based on their rifle. We will cross train with the M-1 carbines, but I want men to train together based on how they will be equipped for the most part."

I told him, "I agree, but we will make an exception for the sniper teams. All my guys have been trained on various weapons and they will be detached from the platoon sized units."

Arrow questioned me, "We saw your sniper program and it's a good one. But don't you think it would be better to have a sniper team embedded within larger groups?"

I told him flatly, "No! My men are hunters; they will end up being used like designated marksmen. That is not what I want at all."

Arrow's eyes narrowed, "The Army has been using designated marksmen for years and the programs have been very good for the men."

I interjected, knowing his argument. "The only reason the Army had good results was because they were actually teaching shooting skills at those clinics. But designated marksmen are not snipers by a long shot. I don't want to hog-tie my snipers because the Army didn't train for real marksmanship like the Marines did."

My mouth always got me in trouble. Arrow didn't like my comments, but he kept his cool. You couldn't expect everyone to see eye to eye and we sure didn't on that subject. It was not really a big deal in the end. I just wanted to keep my snipers out of large groups that would hinder their ability to maneuver as needed. My guys knew how to hunt on their own.

As the meeting wore on we discussed a variety of topics. The weapons that were very specialized would be handled by the SF guys in our Wilmington mission. The SF guys had brought in training dummies for the AT4 rockets as well as Stinger missile launcher simulators. We would not cross-train everyone on all these weapon platforms, but we would make sure a platoon sized unit would have two or three people that could work each one. We also expanded our training on M249 and the M240 machineguns. The SF guys had several weapons to augment our relatively small inventory of machine guns. They also gave us enough ammo to train a little as well as stock away more for the upcoming mission. Our plan was to issue these weapons to our new ex-military recruits that were already familiar with care and feeding of such hardware. Our civilian recruits could learn from them so in case one man fell, another could take his place.

Arrow and I discussed the training cycle until we were blue in the face. By the end of the discussion I think we had decided on just about everything from shoe laces to rifle optics. At the end of the day, the SF guys reported that they were ready to begin the training of our new recruits immediately. I thanked them profusely and made sure our operations people had the local guys escort all the SF to their respective farms. It was a busy time, but we all seemed to manage.

Our training courses started the next day right on schedule. Most of our volunteers showed up as we expected in the first wave of transportation set up by Rocket's team. There were only a few no-shows, but that was normal for the militia. We were right in the middle of solving the normal first day problem when we had some unexpected company.

Nemo and several of his men showed up at our headquarters building in a couple of unmarked trucks. This was a complete surprise to my intelligence group and everyone in operations. In fact, Nemo and his assistant were not allowed inside until someone contacted my office asking just who the heck was knocking at the front door and if I knew him. I looked at the clock, and sure enough, it was during a cycle where we did not expect any drone activity.

Nemo stood patiently in the parking lot, slightly annoyed, then greeted me with a hand shake. "Colonel Huck, good to see you again."

I ushered him to my office and we sat quickly. "Sorry for the delay, but we were not expecting you today."

Nemo was not too concerned. "We had to up our timetable at the last minute. Back in our home town the green shirts changed their tactics and we had to put the finishing touches on some of our.....surprises."

I grinned at this. "I'll bet there will be some green shirt security guys checking their shorts for stains."

Nemo commented rather matter of factly, "If they don't have EOD assets, they will be tied up for quite some time. Let's just say that the ground will shake off and on till Thursday of next week."

I told him that we had an operational planning session lined up with Bull and his staff in about ten days. This is where we would plan for the operation in Wilmington and start building the action on paper. That would give our Intel teams enough time to recon specific targets and report on the current layout of the city and corresponding docks. I cannot state how important it is to have updated information when you are trying to shut down an entire city. This was not just another open city, mind you. You couldn't ride down the road on a bike, like in other places. The Sandys had the perimeter of the town all tied up and guarded 24/7.

Nemo sat with his companion, who had yet to speak, across the desk from me. Out of the blue he slides a package of papers and flash drives across the desk while holding his finger over his lips. Nemo evidently considered my office bugged or monitored in some way. The cover of the file read "Talk about something else, and read contents." I flipped open the first folder and began talking about our wounded militia program and the local hospital support. Nemo picked up on my new subject and discussed the topic at length while I read. The information in the package documented that two PCs in our headquarters were being monitored by the green shirts and at least some of the information had already been shared with the Sandys.

I was shocked to say the least. You tried to do everything possible and they were still able infiltrate your security. The rest of the package contained a detailed schedule of disinformation emails and phone calls to broadcast over the next two months. The flash drives contained massive data files containing pre-recorded messages and thousands of emails. Nemo was supplying us with a complete cover story for the entire command. Bull had been given a set of these as well with similar instructions. It was nothing short of amazing.

Nemo and I continued our conversation about the hospitals, but the whole time we passed notes back and forth on how to get Data involved so he could review the package and implement these resources. I am sure that if anyone was listening to our conversation, they were bored to tears by now. We talked about everything from sterile bandage weaving to potential use of ambulances. All of it was pure crap we were just making up to cover our written conversations.

During this discussion Nemo's note read, "Organize a power outage and bug out during the blackout. Now."

I walked to the office door and saw Seven in the hallway. She seemed to be coming to find me anyway.

I looked at her as she walked down the hallway. "Hey dear. How are you?"

She paused and stopped, "Oh, hey dear. You want to go get some lunch? Fred had the kitchen make cornbread again."

While she was speaking, I wrote her a note and continued my conversation about lunch. "That sounds good. I just need to finish up with the wounded militia hospital therapy support group."

Seven looked at me like I had just told her that Frisbees were shooting out of my nose. You could see the question rising in her gaze as she looked at the two men sitting in my office.

She looked down at my simple note which read, "Have the power cut to the building right now." She looked back at me with more than a little concern and drew her M&P from beneath her jacket out of sight from the men in my office. At the same time she continued, "You want me to call Fred in for lunch?"

I shook my head no and motioned for her to put the gun back in its holster which she did slowly. I told her, "I will meet you in the cafeteria in five minutes or so."

She waved and trotted down the hall to the operations office area to find someone that could get the power shut off. I could see that she already had a pad of paper and knew to keep the actual request non-verbal. Nemo and I sat there for another agonizing five minutes discussing whatever garbage we could manage. Seven came back to my open office door and listened to us yammer on and on. Several operations officers stood behind her, peering inside and knowing not to say anything out loud. We waited and waited until someone marched up the steps and announced, "Colonel, someone just ran into a telephone pole down the street and our generator is about to give out."

I said, "Okay, let's see if we can scrounge some more fuel to run another couple of hours."

At that point the man at the stairs waved to someone outside the window. Within 20 seconds the lights flickered and everything went dark in an instant.

Nemo held his hands up for everyone to be quite until another 30 seconds passed. "Good going Colonel, it should be safe now."

Several people exhaled as if they had been holding their breath.

I announced to a mass of curious faces, "We are bugging out the headquarters building ahead of schedule! Everybody go grab your bugout manual and follow the procedures. I want the deception team up here within 60 seconds and we will have the power back on in 15 minutes. Team leaders remind everyone that there is a radio blackout for the next hour. Be thorough, be calm, and let's get it done right the first time."

Seven stayed while the others took off down the hallways to their respective departments.

I looked over at Seven, "Where is Data? I have to get him up to speed on some new material."

Seven responded, "He is downstairs in the "Battle Bridge."

Now it was Nemo and his man that had curious looks on their faces. "Battle Bridge?" Nemo asked.

Seven led us down the hall as I explained, "You gotta understand Data somewhat. He really gets into the Star Trek themes. He set up a computer room that he calls the battle bridge from the Enterprise, you know, the Next Generation…."

Both men looked at me with mild blank stares.

I continued, "His code name is Data, she is Seven as in Seven of Nine?" I thought it was clear enough for just about anyone.

Seven piped up, "Finally some people that are NOT Star Wars freaks!"

I raised my hand to start to correct her. She interrupted me, "I know, I know, Star Trek, not Star Wars!"

Nemo's assistant asked Seven as we walked down the stairs, "What do you do around here?" His tone was charming and admiring.

She responded knowingly, "Most of the time I try to keep the good Colonel from getting into too much trouble since he is my husband and my baby daddy." She snapped her fingers as she spoke the last few words. It was hilarious to watch her attitude fluctuate like that after the baby was born. If it weren't for the occasional hormone tweak, she would never speak like that. Then she continued, "The rest of the time I focus on intelligence gathering. I send out recon teams and make sure the reports are sent to all the commands."

She led the way down the stairs as Nemo looked to his man. His man gave me an "oops-sorry" glance that men give to other men in this situation.

I took the opportunity, "Seven runs the Intel department. Don't let her fool you. She can be a real fire breathing dragon sometimes."

Seven looked back at me because my mouth had once again proven to be unreliable. She led the group in as I whispered into Nemo's ear, "Well, at least I didn't let her shoot you in the office upstairs." Both Nemo and his man raised their eyebrows at this statement. I continued quietly, "When I gave her the note, she drew her M&P and was thinking you two were a threat."

Neither of the men said anything as she led us into Data's computer room. Both men were impressed because they had no idea of her suspicion since she had wisely shielded the move behind me. I think it made a positive impression. If that didn't, Data's room did. Even though the lights were out, emergency flood lights near the stairs lit the room well enough. The place was painted and decorated with loads of his things from his apartment in town. The full size cutouts of Worf, Picard, and the Borg Queen stood along one wall. The room could pass for some Star Trek motion picture set, the way it was done up. I had no idea there was so much crap down here.

Data looked up from his screens that were still glowing. "Seven? Colonel? How long will the power be out? I only have so much UPS time here." He paused, looking at the two strangers with us.

Seven spoke first. "Data, this is Nemo and his assistant. We are moving up the bugout date to right now so you need to shut down everything."

I flopped the package of material Nemo brought along onto his already messy work station. "We need to implement Nemo's deception emails into our plan and get you up and running in the new location as soon as possible."

Data didn't say anything but reached down and flicked the UPS switch as the last of his screens shut down.

Before anyone could say anything else, Nemo's assistant produced a sheet of paper from a folder and handed it Data as he spoke. "Your system has been compromised in two places. Terminal 342 and 7013 were being watched by the green shirts right up until the power outage a few minutes ago."

Data sat down looking at the paper. Several of his people came in from adjacent work spaces as they watched. I felt sorry for Data, he had done so well. He had come so far and this must feel like a real let down. Nemo's man came out with another paper from his folder and passed it across the table, "Here is a copy of an email you sent from this office a few days ago. The green shirts sent this to the Sandys in the Wilmington headquarters yesterday."

I expected Data to respond, but he did not right away. All his people stood frozen from what I guessed to be intense hacker shame. There was a strained silence.

Data looked at the second paper with great interest as he spoke to one of his staff, "Quick, get me the black binder, #2!" The young man dashed off at the request without a word. Everyone stood silent there in that dark room with only the sounds of foraging emitting from an adjacent dark room. The young man rushed the large 5-inch binder to Data's outstretched hands as the few anxious computer geeks watched intently. Data rummaged through the binder with a flashlight in his mouth. "Read me that tracking number again."

Data's assistant held the paper Nemo's man gave us to the light beside the binder.

Data read aloud, "2..G..A...0..0..2!" The last two numbers he read at nearly a scream. The rest of the geeks cheered as if their team had won the Superbowl or NCAA championship at least. They clapped, they hugged, they threw each other high-fives that didn't connect all the way. It was pandemonium on one side of the table. The rest of us on the other side of the table, watched in utter silence at the display. I had never seen them so passionate without typing.

Nemo looked concerned while his assistant looked almost outraged as he glared through gritted teeth, "You have been hacked and you're headquarters is being monitored! What is this all about?"

Data took time out of his cheering to rip the page out of the book and hand it to Nemo's assistant. The assistant read silently for a few seconds, but was evidently not very impressed. He looked around to those of us watching the display of outright jubilation.

Nemo asked Data, "What does this message mean to you?"

Data stopped the geek celebration and started to explain in computer terms that were so far beyond anything that I had ever heard before, there is no way to remember or let alone record for this book. Nemo and his man seemed to understand completely, but Seven and I stood in the background and listened to five minutes of PC talk that would make your eyes bleed. We ended up sitting on an empty desk as they went through a whole presentation in rapid PC language. Nemo and his man were shocked to say the least as the revelation of Data's effort became clear to them.

Nemo said, "Okay, I see, but we only have another five minutes before the power comes back on. We need to start your deception program before power is restored."

Data responded, out of breath at the rapid pace of talking, "We have been on the deception program all week. This is all part of black book #2. All the real intelligence goes to our new HQ building. All this is stuff we made up weeks ago." Data pointed to the screens he had turned off only a few minutes ago, terminals 342 and 7013. "All we run through them is disinformation solely for the green shirts."

Nemo and his man cheered now for the first time as they realized just how far Data had taken them.

Seven and I sat with our arms crossed, feeling completely left out.

Seven sat watching the new whoops and congratulations, then asked, "Can we shoot them now?"

Nemo turned around playfully with his hands up in surrender. "Its okay. We are okay."

Seven wasn't real patient in her postpartum state and she was slightly aggravated. Her look was one of a menacing angel if there is such a thing.

Nemo's man walked around the room with the other geeks while Nemo came over to us to explain with Data trailing behind.

Nemo started, "We thought we had found an unknown monitoring program run by green shirt headquarters which was being shared with the Sandys. It is one of the major reasons we came early."

I looked back blankly. "Okay; that much is obvious." I pointed to the dark room with no lights other than the emergency floods on in the corner.

Nemo continued, "Well it is hard to explain, but Data has just done something that nobody has even considered, and it seems to work perfectly."

Data added some PC jargon that was supposed to clear up everything. It didn't in the least.

"Okay, shoot him. We can get another geek." I told Seven in a casual tone. Data had heard this many times before during his time with the militia. It was our little code for him to 'dumb things down, please.'

Nemo tried again, using his hands for visual reference, "Imagine the world of the internet like a large reservoir full of water. Each session, email, or phone call, is a drop of water. It gets passed around from here to there, going from place to place all within the big lake. The green shirts have been watching the passing of these droplets and making themselves copies of everything. They track where stuff goes, who sends it, who reads it, the content of the message is tagged for Intel, etc. It is all in the effort to build these probability profiles of people. We know they focus on the resistance with special concern."

"Okay, you told us that part before." Seven said slowly as if she was being talked to like a third grader.

Nemo continued, "Well, the green shirts have been copying this information and sending it to their virtual storage facilities out west for analysis. What Data has done successfully for the first time, is something none of us ever considered. He has worked out a technical way to arrange the information into self-identifying packets. It's like putting the droplets of water into pre-arranged order whenever it is copied. His algorithms make the stolen information the tag itself. Their parity checks will never flag an error, because to them, it is simply the message with nothing added or left out.

I asked, "So, you can tag the copied emails? How does that help us?"

Data replied, "With these tags I have turned the tables on them. Every time they copy our emails, I collect information on them. I am mirroring their tracking of us! As they copy our emails, I see where it goes and who sees it. I can watch it flow through their system. I can see where their terminals are. I can even use their own system to report on themselves. The 2-G-Aplha series was one of thousands of phony reports we generated to test the theory. We had to use test messages so we could confirm our algorithms were working correctly. We just didn't have a way to independently confirm it until the good Captain here, showed us the captured email." Data finished out of breath.

Nemo added, "Data has made the whole green shirt data-tracking effort into something we can use against them. If things check out, we will have the upper hand for the first time in the war! This could be the key to dismantling their whole campaign! We will finally be on equal footing!"

Seven looked appeased. "Well I guess congratulations are in order. Good work, Data. Oh yeah, thanks for letting us in on your little experiment. I am sure the Intel department-head would love to know about such things maybe before we blackout the whole building." She finished the last sentence with her hands on her hips.

Data responded back like a kid caught with a hand in the cookie jar. "Sorry, Seven."

Seven continued, "Captain Nemo, we have made arrangements for you and your men. Let me know when you are finished with Data and we will get you squared away for the night." With that she spun around with her pony tail whipping behind her as she marched up the steps.

I left Nemo and Data to work things out over the next few hours. They still had a lot of work to do, but all was well with our security. We went ahead and continued the bugout of the headquarters building that day. There was no point to stay there the remaining three days before the scheduled transition. If all went well, the green shirts would have no idea we had moved our actual headquarters. All they would see were fake emails and fake phone calls to empty warehouses nobody in the militia actually used. The only people there were assigned to keep vehicles moving around in the parking lot and to run the disinformation campaign from Data's PCs. Over the next few days, we started a whole series of campaigns to throw off any green shirts monitoring our communications. I could barely follow all the safeguards set up.

I took time to meet and greet some of the recruits as our instructors went through their paces. Memories of Gunny giving us log PT back in our home town were relished....somewhat. The winter months were cold in the foothills. Snow hit us a couple of times, which made training that much more fun to endure. Not everything was all fun and games either. Cold weather clothing was a supply challenge for a while until some stuff came in from an Army Navy store in Tennessee. Supply issues took up a lot of my time, but I won't bore you with that.

With ex-military recruits, there was more effort dedicated to teaching them small unit tactics and how to operate according to militia practices rather than how to be a soldier. It took some time for Army guys to conform, but with the help of the Robin Sage trainers, they came through in fine fashion. I took the opportunity of the start of the last training class to watch the last squad work through their indoctrination day. Most other groups had been going for a week or more by the time this group arrived.

"Colonel Huck, nice of you to drop by, sir," one of the trainers greeted me as I walked in the door of a non-descript warehouse. Several of the roughly 20 recruits inside looked over to me. This did not sit well with their assigned instructor.

One of the barrel-chested instructors that looked like he could eat tin cans, barked at the gawking recruits, "You can get his freakin autograph later! Right now your task, your purpose for breathing, is to draw the rest or your gear before the Damn war is over and we are all speaking Arabic!" His voice echoed throughout the building.

I have to admit, my first instinct was to grab a bag just to avoid his wrath. Gunny had been the same with us a year and half before. I missed him on days like this. Maybe it was just as well, he didn't care for "Army kids" as he called them.

The group hustled about their tasks as I took the opportunity to walk over to the last set of tables. M1 carbines sat in wooden crates waiting to be used again after sitting idle since Vietnam. For all I knew they could be date stamped from WWII. As I looked down at the rows of cosmoline-caked rifles, I imagined the Marines on Iwo Jima or the Normandy 101st Airborne troopers carrying these very same rifles. If Major Arrow was right, the last people to handle these may have been ARVN soldiers in Vietnam. But nobody had touched them since. It was incredible to see crates of them ready for us to use in this war to free our own land. I wondered what the WWII vets would think if they could see these rifles in our hands today fighting off the Sandys. The tables beside me held neatly piled stacks of 30-round magazines still wrapped in tan wax paper after decades of storage. Each man was issued six magazines for his training cycle. Beside the magazines lay the last few chest rigs the militia had custom made by a local sewing shop. These chest rigs were simple in their design but could hold a bunch of magazines over field shirts or jackets.

One of the trainers saw me admiring the rifles, "Colonel, these rifles saw more fighting than any 10 of us. They will get us through this war too." He grabbed a rifle out of the case and passed it to the fist recruit who looked at his greasy hands with distaste. The trainer announced loudly as the recruits filed by, "This is the M1 Carbine. It was developed in the 1940s to give support crews more firepower than just a standard 1911 pistol. It shoots a 110 grain ball round at 1970 feet per second. The effective range is 200 meters. Take your chest rig and put it in your bag. Bring your rifle and one stack of magazines over to these tables and we will show you how to clean that greasy crap off."

One of the larger recruits looked down at the rifle he was given and asked, "What good are these old rifles? This one has grease all over it."

The trainer looked at him with a stern expression. "These rifles freed France and all of Western Europe when your Grandpa was in grade school. Marines carried these carbines when they climbed Mount Suribachi and kicked the Japanese out of the Pacific. Then these rifles went to Korea and fought off 1,000,000 Chinese Communists. But before they could be retired, they went to Vietnam and fought in the jungles again. You just pray you last as long as these fine implements of war!"

The entire group listened to the trainer and his speech. I think each one of the guys sat looking at the rifles in their hands with a new respect. As the group left for their training farm, I watched them load onto a truck with their bulging equipment bags. One by one they filed out of the door to the waiting truck.

"How are we doing on equipment?" I asked the remaining logistics officer that was supervising the remaining stores. The warehouse was relatively quiet and almost empty.

The officer was a younger man with a clipboard. "Sir, it looks like that is the last group. We have plenty of rifles. Most of them are good; we only had a crate or two that was exposed to water at some point. Those rifles were rusted pretty badly, but the Army guys brought extra just in case. It's a good thing they brought extra magazines, too, because we had cases that were bad. Most of the time it was just the wax wrapping that would not come off. Others were rusted or had bad springs. Even with all that, we have equipped everyone to the standard." He continued to scribble on his clipboard.

I reached down and pulled a vintage rifle from the crate. The wood was dark green from the prolonged exposure to cosmoline and the finish on the metal parts was a clammy dark grey. I looked at the back of the receiver and read the serial number. The stock had dings from a sling that had bounced across someone back in some foreign land fighting other people's grandfathers. I could only imagine the fighting this rifle had seen.

The officer was watching me as I examined the rifle. "Sir, do you want one? We have several cases left."

My mind was blurry as I caught up to his question, "Yeah, have someone clean up a dozen of these rifles and a case of magazines. Then have them delivered to the new headquarters building for the armory," I instructed him.

The officer quickly responded, "I will make sure you have them in the next day or two."

"Thanks," I told him. "I'll take this one with me."

The officer asked, "Do you want me to have someone clean it?"

I looked at the grease. "No, if we are going to get acquainted, I have to put in the effort first."

The young man looked at me with only mild interest in what I was saying. He just didn't understand what a rifle means to a shooter. If it is a foreign object in your hands, you will struggle to hit your targets. You have to know every quirk of that piece. You have to know how it works, how much oil it likes, how it shoots in the heat or in the cold. You have to find the ammo it likes. Well, we didn't have much choice in ammo because we were using military surplus tin cans or what they used to call spam cans. I took a break from my normal tasks and cleaned that rifle with all the respect I could offer it. By the time I was done, the wood stock was wet, but a much brighter shade of Walnut. The metal parts were actually the deep rich blue they had once been years ago. When I racked the bolt, the metal chimed back at me as it ran the bolt home against the barrel face. The quality of steel back then was impressive.

After an hour or so, I wished the logistics guys well and headed over to my next round of inspections. The day was overcast and cold with the wind blowing. My driver and security escort took me to several of the farms where recruits were quartered and trained. We drove up to a line of three squads of men using a 100 yard sight-in berm. Everyone had a carbine over their shoulder except for the men on the line. They were lying prone with sandbags to use as rests for target practice. Thick steel plates about six inches in diameter dangled beneath rebar U-stands on chains.

I jumped out of the truck and walked to the firing line instructor. "You have room for one more?"

He looked at me and quickly gave me a salute out of sheer Army habit. We didn't use salutes much in the militia and it felt kind of awkward.

"Colonel, yes, we can manage that. Position #1, move out and let the Colonel have your lane."

The men watched in silence as I lay down behind the bag. I pulled out a freshly cleaned and loaded magazine and held it up for the instructor signifying that I was ready to accept his instructions on the line.

The instructor looked up and down the line. "All positions, you are clear to load and continue sight in."

Several lanes fired quickly after the announcement. I made sure my sights were set center-windage with standard elevation. My first shot kicked up dirt low and right as the brass spun in mid-air. The brass landed back and to the right of the rifle showing the extractor was working properly. The recoil was snappy due to the relatively light weight of the rifle even with a full length stock. The instructor dropped his binoculars and said, "Shoot two more rounds and see if the rifle will group."

I shot twice more as dirt kicked up in the same place. The instructor reached down and turned the windage of my rifle a few clicks and said, "Fire another group."

I shot three more rounds to see dirt kick up right under the target. "She shoots a bit low."

The instructor asked, "Can I see your rifle, sir?"

I dropped the magazine and racked the slide to empty the chamber. He lifted the rifle and produced a flat file from his pocket, "Some of these older rifles were made with sights that had to be filed down to adjust the elevation zero." He scraped at the front sight quickly only taking off a slight amount of metal from the top. He then whipped out a lighter and blackened the exposed metal sight so that it would not gleam even in the low ambient light of that cloudy day. It took a couple of those filings to get the sights to match the dead center of the steel plate at 100 yards. But when the sight-in was done, I could hit the small steel targets with ease. In fact, I took the last six rounds of my magazine were used to ring the last six targets one after the other in rapid fire. Tang, tang, tang, tang, tang, tang, the plates rang out in sequence as the rest of the line stopped to watch and listen.

I thanked the instructor and promised to return when they were to do break-contact drills and team movement exercises. From what I saw of the recruits, we were in good shape. They were solid shooters with experience either from the military or from militia operations. Most of the teams seemed to gel pretty well, but there were always squabbles. Most of the problems were easily fixed by changing to another team. Rarely did we have to change squad leaders; most of them were picked because they were good with people. But as I always say, there were exceptions.

The third farm I visited that night was just one of those occasions. Fred had been working with logistics to coordinate food for all these groups as they came in for training. It was no small task to feed 100s of men every day. This was one of those smaller farms where there were a couple of barns for the men to bed down as well as a ranch house used for cooking and latrines. I made my rounds as darkness approached. Training had stopped for the day and everyone was preparing for a cold night in a breezy, but relatively warm, barn for a few hours of sleep. We were all tired from a long day and this was our last stop. I walked through the house and greeted the men. They were abnormally quiet as the evening meal was being eaten.

"What's up guys? You look like your mamma got slapped?"

This normally pepped up even tired men. These guys looked around kind of worried. "Sir, Fred is in the barn. It's that guy again. He is causing all sorts of trouble."

"Who? Fred? I asked in disbelief.

"No, No! not Fred, he's great. It's that guy that came in on the bus about three days ago," one of the younger recruits said. Then he stopped speaking as if he were afraid. This was a bad sign.

I asked, "Where is Bo?"

The young man looked up at me, "He's still out with the squad up on the hill. They aren't due back till day after tomorrow."

I walked out of the door sniffing trouble and said, "Ok."

I knew walking to the barn we were in for a real row that night. My driver and security guy unloaded from the truck as I waved them to follow me. From 20 yards away, I could hear a drunken voice that was unfamiliar. I walked into the doorway among a couple dozen recruits standing around the bunks that had been built out of 2x4s. One man was making all the noise as he stood in the center of a bunch of worried men.

The loud mouth was a tall guy in his early 30s, muscular, with tattoos showing over exposed arms. Fred lay on the ground with his mouth bleeding as this guy swung an M1 carbine towards another recruit.

"You little turd! You won sum of dis too?" he slurred at a scared recruit from 4th militia nearby.

The smaller and younger man stammered, "I don't want any trouble."

I bent down to check on Fred who sat up holding his mouth, "Huck. This guy has been drunk every night he's been here. Scares the crap out of everybody he can."

The man was intimidating and he was used to it; you could just tell the guy was trash.

"It's okay Fred, I am going to give him his discharge papers." I stood up and announced in my best drill instructor voice, "Colonel on deck!"

The whole place turned to look at me as I strode into the open space between men. The drunk recruit looked over at me for a second and thought what to do. He ambled over to me and got in my face. "I don't care what they call you. What you gonna do?"

I looked up at him. "Ground that rifle! You are not fit for this Army or any free man's military!"

The guy responded before I could finish, "I'll shove this rifle up your...."

He never got a chance to finish. I wrenched the rifle from his grasp with a wrist-tap that Gunny taught us so long ago. In one fluid motion, I grabbed the rifle by the barrel, spun on the spot, and swung the carbine until the trigger guard slammed into the guy's left leg. You could hear his fibula and tibia break on contact. The wooden stock split in two from the severe impact. The stock spun round and round as it slid along the floor. As he bent down in agony, I brought the front stock up to the guys chin knocking out a good portion of his teeth. I could smell the alcohol on his breath as he tried to scream through what was likely a broken jaw.

The man fell over in a heap, unconscious. I wondered if he would even remember the events of that night he was so drunk.

I looked down at the man curled up on the hard ground and said, "Discharged from service."

The barn stood silent as I breathed hard from the adrenaline rush. Fred got to me the same time as my security guys. They were not happy, but slightly impressed that I done so much damage to the bruiser.

I told them, "Take this man to the hospital and then to the brig. We can't trust somebody like this with our lives. He is to be in total confinement until our operation is over."

To the rest of the barn I announced, "I want good people who know what we are fighting for. If you are worse than the enemy, I don't want you."

One of the squad leaders approached me and spoke out, "Sir, these are all good men. He was the only one that was a problem. Thanks Colonel."

As I walked out of the barn, Fred walked along with me. "Huck, Seven is going to hear about this, you know?"

I continued towards the truck, completely worn out with my legs feeling like lead bricks. "Oh yeah?"

Fred raised his hand as if testifying. "Yep, I saw him your honor. He destroyed militia property when he broke that carbine's stock on that fella's leg."

I laughed a bit and said, "They will just have to court martial me I guess." We both chuckled our way to the truck, just glad the day was finally over. Fred claimed after that night that he had the drunk just where he wanted him before I walked in and stole all the thunder. I swore to let my security guys catch up next time.

Training continued for the next week at a rapid pace. Everyone knew we were planning a major mission in early to mid-March which was only a matter of weeks away. Winter was hard enough with limited power in the post-collapse era. It was harder on the recruits that were housed in tents between the relative warmth found in barns. The weather was cold again that year. Several nights hovered around 20 degrees, leaving a thick frost every morning. The cold affected everything from outdoor toilets to dead batteries in vehicles that were not used often enough to keep charged. Those of us in the 3rd tried to keep these difficulties as far away from recruits as much as possible. Their training cycle was short enough. We wanted them to get as much as possible in the way of tactics and procedures we used in the militia before the operation to shut down the ports in Wilmington.

While the recruits rested on a well-deserved night off, the SF trainers and the 3rd militia officers met in Wooten Valley for a special get together. The convenience store was reserved for us to gather for dinner and discuss how things were going so far.

I walked through the door of the convenience store, leaving behind a cold gravel road. The inside was packed with people, warm, and inviting. Dozens of conversations were all going on at once. The lights were shining brightly, the wood burning stoves were pumping out massive amounts of heat, and the mood was festive. Groups of men sat around the tables talking with one another. Seven had our little Punkin in her arms, entertaining a group of admirers. Fred and his wife stood by as SF guys examined the Tiger's sniper rifle which had been removed from its perch above the door. A picture of Mac hung on the wall along with pictures of other men that had died as part of the militia. The memory of the Tiger was painful to say the least, and it was frankly distracting to have that rifle hanging over the door, in my opinion. But, for some reason, some of the militia absolutely insisted we keep it on display.

I milled around the room talking with the different groups until I met Bo, who stood in the corner by the end of the lunch counter. His Browning lever action was propped by a stool, out of the way, but ready.

"Huck, whatchya know?" Bo asked me. He was clearly not comfortable in this room and was using the corner as an excuse to stay out of the way.

"Bo, you okay?" I asked.

"Yeah, but it's too daggon hot. They tryin to roast us in here?"

He had evidently been doing survival overnight trips for too long to complain about good stove heat on a cold day.

"Bo, how much time do you spend in camp?" I asked.

He looked around, "Well I spent three nights at the farm last week. The rest of the time I take the recruits out in the hills."

"Damn Bo, you can spend some more time at the farm. Take them out and come back in at night."

"They caint learn nothin if I ain't out there to teach-em." Bo was right, but I didn't want my friend to be so isolated.

I looked down at the freshly oiled Browning. "Bo, did you get a carbine yet?"

He looked down at the rifle. "I don't need one. The armorers found me some ammo."

I looked at him, a little concerned. "We are going up against machine guns. Aren't you worried about bad guys with 30 round magazines outgunning you?"

Bo didn't change in his countenance. "I had this same conversation with one of these soldier fellas last week. I was on the range with my rifle and he told me I needed to get me an M1. He told me how he could shoot five shots quicker than I could work the lever on two rounds. He rang the little plates ding, dang, pling, and so forth, to show me. I raised my rifle and blasted one of them 240 grain cast bullets into that little plate and took it off its hinges with one shot. He stood there with his mouth open as the plate swung side to side on the one chain left holding it up. He didn't say nothin after that."

I commented to Bo, "I'm glad you're on our side."

We ate dinner before the meeting started for real. I started off by telling everyone that I was happy with the teams so far. The recruits were coming along nicely in my opinion, but I didn't want this to be a happy ra-ra session. I wanted us to correct what was not going right and I wanted to fix it now before we got too far along.

I left the floor open to anyone with an observation.

One of the older trainers stood up. "Sir, I think if there are any teams that need to change out people, it needs to happen now. After we make the changes, the teams need to be finalized for the operation. This way the teams train and operate together as a unit."

I responded, "Good point. Do we have any last minute changes?"

It became evident that I had just been set up. Another trainer approached my table with a large display plaque for hanging on a wall. Mounted on the plaque was that same M1 carbine with the broken stock and bent trigger guard I used on the drunken recruit. The whole room looked on in anticipation as the SF trainer held it out for everyone to see.

The trainer announced, "The trainers and 3rd militia command wish to present this rifle to Colonel Huck." The crowd cheered. He continued, "The brass plate reads, "For Innovation in Creative Discharge Policies.""

The place was in an uproar with cheers. Seven sat beside me with a quiet expression as the baby cried from the noise. Fred's wife took Punkin and said it was his bed time anyway. She promised to get him home and in bed until we got home. Now that I think on it, she may have been the key to a lot of the successes the militia had after Punkin was born. Fred's wife took him while Seven and I were busy running militia operations instead of changing diapers. Without Seven, I know our intelligence operations would have been way less effective and we would have been hurt way worse than we were. I appreciated Fred and his wife from a friend perspective and that is why they were Punkin's Godparents.

I accepted the award and hung it on the wall of the convenience store among the other decorations lining the walls. It took some time, but we finally quieted down and continued the meeting. Our training plans were hashed out that night for the next month. Team leaders were selected and specialized training started in demolitions, CQB, communications, and weapons systems brought in by the SF guys. Firearms training expanded to break-contact drills and team by team covering movements. They trained during the day until the teams got the concept; then integrated those skills for use at night. We had warehouses set up for room to room clearing techniques with removable walls. When the recruits mastered a floor plan, the set would be adjusted to give completely new scenarios. From all the feedback of the recruits, the trainers were nothing short of awesome. They gave recruits good solid information based on real world experience that could not come from a book. The SF guys brought in some weapons commonly used by the Sandys so that we could do some cross training. Nobody got much sleep in January.

Chapter 17
Breaker One-Nine

Rocket came into my less-than-lavish office in the new headquarters building. "Colonel Huck, I'm back."

I looked up to see Rocket standing in the door. "Rocket, you look tired. Everything okay?"

Rocket sat at the desk across from me and ran his fingers through his short hair. "Huck, I am here to report that Red Route One is open and ready for use. You told me that our little super highway needed to be up and running by the end of January; it's February 1st."

I asked, "You have all the staging facilities set up?"

Rocket leaned back in his chair. "Yeah, the fourth is sending food stocks this week. The kitchens are ready, we have enough toilets, and we have the gas pre-positioned."

"How do the routes look?" I asked. "Are we going to have any problems with green shirts?"

Rocket leaned forward and said, "The green shirts are the wild card. They might send a squad car or two when we don't expect it, but I think we are trained to handle just about anything they throw at us."

I liked his cavalier attitude because I know he could back up his bravado. "How are the new drivers?"

Rocket smiled. "They didn't like it when they saw their cars all decked out in that black stealth-mode paint. They were surprised when we spayed down the test car and it went back to the original bright red color. They have all been trained on certain segments of the highway and they know how to get out of trouble. Oh, yeah, and tell Seven I appreciate her giving us the intelligence report we have to fill out after every trip. My guys don't write too well."

I promised to pass along the message and asked, "How are we on vehicles for transporting the army? Where are we lacking?"

Rocket looked concerned for the first time, as if he really didn't want to cover that subject. "Huck, I am scrounging everything I can get my hands on, but I am not there yet. A lot of these trucks and busses have been sitting so long that the batteries are toast. I can't go to Advance Auto and get any, so we are making do for the time being with jump starters."

I asked, hardly wanting to know the answer, "How short are we on vehicles?"

Rocket took out a piece of notebook paper he had written on by hand. There were lists of figures based on the information I had given him. The paper read like a laundry list of trucks, vans, busses, cargo trucks, motorcycles, and sports cars.

Rocket reported as I read. "We barely have enough to transport the army in a 24 hour period. And from what I have seen, we can't move everybody in such a short period of time. The green shirts aren't on every corner, but they will surely notice that many trucks rolling down the road all at once. We need to move the men to staging areas over a three night period at least. Otherwise, we risk some green shirt sympathizer selling us out."

I asked, "How many more vehicles do we need to account for breakdowns and so forth?"

Rocket looked around. "We need another 20 big trucks at least. We are okay on motorcycles for close in courier missions. But we need a couple dozen more ATVs, some vans, and another 10 pickup trucks just to have enough operational units for the mission. The SF guys and I have worked out a way to get the HUMVEEs to the staging areas. That will be done in another week or so."

I rubbed my chin and thought. "We could steal some right before the mission, I guess. But it could tip off the Sandys to a buildup in our staging areas."

Rocket and I sat silent for several minutes, thinking. Finally, I said, "A solution will present itself. Have faith, Rocket. How cooperative have the local sheriffs been?"

"Most are willing to help us. There are a couple that may or may not turn a blind eye to our couriers blasting through their towns, but they are usually tied up with more important things than handing out speeding tickets." Rocket said as he looked out of the window, "Dad will be here in a couple of days."

"The general, you mean?" I mocked his lack of respect for a superior officer.

Rocket sat up in his chair. "Yes, sir. That's what I meant, sir." He saluted with a true Benny Hill kind of satire that he only shared around me when we were alone. He was young, but he understood when and where to be relaxed. It was the sign of a good officer. I could see him being in charge someday.

Then he asked what he had been thinking since he walked into the office. "Colonel Huck, do you think I have done a good enough job with the transport effort and the couriers?"

I looked back at Rocket, who was surprisingly serious. "Rocket, you have done a great job. I gave you a near impossible task and you have done it as well as anyone could hope to do. Why do you ask?"

He looked reluctant to answer, but did so quietly. "I don't want anyone to think I got the job because my dad is the general."

I reassured him, "The men in your command have not complained the first time. Trust me, if they were not happy, I would hear it every day. You are just like your dad though, the men respect you and never question who you are. You just do your job and everything will work out."

Rocket looked pacified at my comments. "I just want this all to work out. If the Sandys catch wind of one of my staging areas, they could blast everybody in one attack. I have a lot of people depending on me to do a good job."

I shook his hand. "Congratulations, you just learned lesson one of being a good leader. Care for the people in your command. Guide them, support them, and never let them down. But in the end, you cannot decide if they live or die. You have to lead the way no matter what happens and live with it forever."

Rocket thanked me and left my office with promises of doing everything possible to bring all of his people home someday. Rocket had only lost one man, working in his team on that mission to destroy the bridge outside Charlotte. I don't know if before that point he had ever lost anyone under his command. I wondered how it would affect him.

February 3rd saw us roll out of North Wilkesboro as the 3rd battalion's officers left for the big mission briefing held in Taylorsville. Major Arrow, along with Nemo and few of his men, left right before we did that day. The rest of the 3rdbattalion leadership stayed behind to continue the regular training cycle underway. Fred and Seven joined me in a small convoy that left only hours before the beginning of the conference. We were being very careful to keep our profile unanimous, given the known use of drones in the area. Nemo and our Intel staff were monitoring the drone activity, so our convoy was scheduled to travel while they were between surveillance orbits. In the back of my mind, I wondered if we would ever realize it if we were wrong. I mean, the last thing you might see would be a trail of smoke leading to your vehicle. The next thing you would see would be the pearly gates leading to Heaven. I kept those thoughts to myself and sat back in the seat of the Suburban.

Taylorsville was a relatively small town that managed to recover nicely after the financial collapse and power outage. They would play host to our meeting. It also helped that the green shirts had shown little interest in a town so far west and deep in militia held territory. The local sheriff was quite cooperative because Bull had wisely supported him early in his effort to bring back civility to an otherwise lawless environment. A lot of our food came from Taylorsville. Money was a very regional back then and the economics of the day were much more centered on tangible goods. Taylorsville was turning into a central hub of trade and resources since they were one of the first larger cities in free territory to get a handle on the lawlessness that plagued so many other places. Once order was restored, the infrastructure was repaired and electrical power supported roughly 80% of the town by that winter.

We made our way into town and pulled into the designated coordinates we had received just that morning. The 4th battalion and the general's staff had procured a small office building and warehouse on the edge of a very active marketplace that was bustling with cars and trucks. Our security personnel followed the directions of some local deputies to an outlying pair of buildings on the edge of the complex. The large doors opened as we approached, and closed quickly after we drove through. My security detail made sure the area was secure and ushered my Suburban to park among a dozen or more various SUVs. The warehouse was wide open inside with small windows providing light for the concrete floor below. Guards stood at all four corner posts and looked through windows with scoped rifles. From the outside, this place looked like any other warehouse during those times. Inside it was all militia business.

Our group was escorted to the attached office building through a series of hallways which had minimal lighting. We followed the directions of the security people and walked up a couple of flights of stairs to an open hallway. The windows of the building were covered in two layers of coverings. The outermost covering was light colored and had vertical lines painted on them. The coverings on the inside were the customary black curtains used to shield from unfriendly eyes. I supposed the lighter coverings would look like any other empty walls if you saw them from the outside. Simple black curtains would be a dead giveaway that someone wanted to be left alone.

The conference room was a buzz of men and women in small groups. Nobody was in much of a uniform because this was supposed to be completely incognito.

I heard Bull say in his usual saw-mill whisper, "We choose to use this place in the daytime because of all the activity in the area. It was the only way to mask all these SUVs coming in today." He held a coffee cup in one hand and the man he was speaking to with his other massive hand. The guy was a good inch shorter than usual because Bull had him by the shoulder in a friendly gesture.

The officer understood. "I know what you mean, general. None of us want an armed drone to fly over and send a hellfire through the window. We have had a hard enough time keeping our command one step ahead of those things."

I waved to Bull as he looked in my direction. He nodded as he greeted several more groups on his way to shake hands with me.

When we finally shook hands, his grip was like iron. "Huck, How are things going up in North Wilkesboro?"

I responded, "Keep the supplies coming, I have guys living in tents. If we run short on food, we will have to eat Fred." Fred stood nearby talking to some people by the conference table. With his spare hand he made a rude gesture with his middle finger behind his back towards us. I was glad he was well enough to rejoin me at those meetings.

Bull took the time of the levity to whisper in my ear, "You have to get me that new *discharge* policy you created up there." He squeezed my shoulder until I thought he would break my arm. He loved every second of it.

I stood there trying to keep an air of professionalism. "You heard about that did you?"

Bull chuckled under his breath. "I'm sure the guy deserved it. They tell me you hung the carbine on the wall too. Is that true?"

"Yeah, they gave me a plaque and everything," I told him. Bull snorted.

A man approached Bull and I about that time, saying, "Gentlemen, everyone is here. We are ready to begin." The guy seemed like a waiter the way he spoke. It was as if he was showing us to our table at a fancy dinner. We sat around the large conference table with real coffee in our cups. You would have thought we were all millionaires to drink actual coffee with real sugar. Most of that stuff was long gone. I overheard a couple of men discuss that there had been some shipments making their way into the deep-south lately. That was a surprise until Intelligence began the meeting with an update on the country based on reports from other states. It turned out that the people that held Florida were willing to do business with the southern states even though the People's Republic of America forbade it. Shipments of coal and natural gas came from free southern territory while food goods came in from Central American countries. Evidently the PPR movement's control was not 100% complete. How long this would last was uncertain, but for now, we had coffee and a few pleasantries like sugar.

Reports from Texas were encouraging. The Rangers reported that they had made several blows to the green shirt Army groups on their northern border with Oklahoma. The southern borders were still plagued by Mexican Federalis, but the Texans were not losing any ground. Production of fuel was up and Texas anticipated an increase in the amount of gasoline we could expect to see in our area. More and more trucks were making it out of the refineries and delivering to non-green shirt held territories.

That was the good news. The bad news was that the northern part of the country was under more and more control by the green shirts. Outlying freedom groups in upstate New York, greater Ohio, and Northeast Virginia were almost silent by that second winter. Very few reports came from those areas, and the ones that did, were not good. The green shirts turned on a lot of power to the smaller rural towns along with access to what was thought to be free internet. Unwittingly, the users were being monitored through the Snapshot system and were thoroughly thumped for it. Arrests were the last thing you heard on standard government radio or TV programming. This kept the greater population in green shirt territory ignorant to the arrests of their neighbors. People simply vanished overnight without a trace. Resistance to the green shirts vanished almost instantly as they unwittingly identified themselves and their resistance movements by trying to communicate or search for information. We all wondered what it was like to live in towns up north where the state dictated your behavior and monitored your every move. It was unnerving to watch even from a distance.

The intelligence teams gave us an update on North Carolina as well. Things were mainly the same as they had been over the last few months. Charlotte and Wilmington were the key Sandy strongholds. What few Sandy aircraft were in country were being used to keep the militia off the major roadways and train tracks. The green shirts controlled pockets of the key larger cities along the Highway 40 and 85 roadways linking Charlotte to Wilmington. For the most part, the green shirts were not very interested in securing the rural zones outside of their little micro-utopias. All the green shirt cities were marked on a wall-sized map hanging on the conference room wall.

We knew the Sandys were waiting for their full invasion force to arrive in March. Nemo told us that his people in the region were watching for signs of the pending convoys of ships needed to transport tens of thousands of new residents. That was a sobering thought to say the least.

The 2nd battalion had the Sandys bottled up in Wilmington for the time being. But the 2nd's Colonel was not happy at all with his directives. Bull ordered him to slack off containment operations for the next few weeks and slowly pull back his people. The idea was to give the impression that the militia was not as interested in the place. However, the 2nd's Colonel wanted us to take a different approach. He wanted to drive the Sandys as far back as he could before our main assault. His point was that he wanted to push hard for a day or two and hit them with the assault force as a knockout blow.

Bull wanted a surprise attack instead of a prolonged assault, though, and refused his request. Bull's 4th militia had learned the hard way how difficult it is to contain such a large enemy force spread across such a vast geographical area like a city. Charlotte had been contested as far back as our failed Raleigh mission and it was still draining our resources. Raleigh proved two things to us; you can win *and* lose in a single day. Wilmington could not afford to be lost or the ports to stay open. If we could not close the ports, we would eventually lose the state and our resistance might as well leave the area completely or risk being eliminated entirely.

Fred walked to the Intel desk, deep in thought as he reviewed the maps hanging on the wall. The rest of us discussed the situation on what was meant by strategic goals and tactical goals for the Wilmington operation. I watched as Fred rubbed his chin in deep contemplation.

More Intelligence people talked about various subjects. Nemo gave us an update on the capabilities that he and Data had worked out over the last few days. They were optimistic about a few things that made us in command take notice. They had learned that the number of drones available to the green shirts was rather limited. The green shirts had been directed to use drones in other countries, at the direction of the PPR, to support their willing accomplice heads of state. A local dictator can't trust a pilot or even his own air force, so he has an ally kill his rival by remote control. This was becoming very popular from what we gathered. The net affect was a lack of drone support that the green shirts could afford domestically. This was also another topic of contention for local green shirt authorities because they could see us building our strength and they knew sooner or later we would contest them for real.

Nemo gave us highly-classified details on how the green shirts were only begrudgingly helping the Sandys. He read us transcripts of emails going between green shirt commanders concerning building projects to be completed by the middle of March. There were some heated words between the Sandys and green shirt local governor over which airports would be allowed to reopen in the spring, as well. But the big fight was over Fort Bragg and Pope AirForce base. The Sandys claim it was within their territory and the green shirts claimed that they never agreed to hand over the place."

The 2nd's colonel spoke up. "It sure would be nice to know their expected borders so we can fight for the key positions. Do we have any email traffic showing the actual borders the green shirts and Sandys intend to use when the invasion force comes in?"

Our Intel department admitted that it was a top priority to find out, but that it was a complete mystery at this point.

Fred suddenly became aware of our conversation and spun around. "That's it! What was that?" His confusing question was rather loud and it stopped all other talking instantly.

Seven looked over at me kind of worried because this was typical Fred behavior that some people found unprofessional. But luckily everyone listened to him to clarify.

Nemo responded, "We don't have any border information, the bases are in question, and they are arguing over what airports will reopen in the spring."

Bull asked Fred, "What is it, Fred?"

Fred moved the table that was in his way so he could get right up to the regional map of the Southern States on the wall. He grabbed a nearby marker and drew a large green line from the Virginia border above Henderson all the way through the state to the west side of Ashville. The line followed the major interstates exactly. Fred continued the line from Asheville over to Knoxville, through Nashville, Memphis and finally Little Rock."

The 2nd's Colonel watched him with contempt, "Okay that's a pretty picture, but how do you know that is where they intend to draw the line?"

Fred stood there for a moment thinking, "We have approached everything through the prism of the militia fighting for our own state. We see things from the point of view of people that lived here our whole lives. We have border we know and respect all the borders drawn up on maps that we learned in grade school. The green shirts don't see it that way at all anymore. The old state lines don't mean anything to them at all. In fact, they have already agreed to the resettlement of the South because they detest all of us Bible thumping rednecks and so forth. That's why they so willingly let the Sandys have this area. But we also know that they are not comfortable with the Sandys so close to home, even if they serve a purpose now."

One of the 2nd's intelligence guys said, "That is about as clear as mud. Can we continue please?"

Seven got up and walked over to the wall where Fred stood, silent. He could not grasp how the others could not see it so clearly. I thought Seven was there to escort him out of the room for minute until she grabbed a marker and said slowly, "What Fred was trying to say is that the green shirts are telling us exactly where the border is drawn.

The 2nd's Colonel was dismissive. "Okay, let's not spend too much time on this because we have to plan for the mission in Wilmington today and this is all academic anyway."

Bull said, "Let's hear what Seven and Fred are talking about for a minute before we go on. It was Fred that anticipated the armored column last year that saved our bacon in Charlotte. Continue," he ordered.

Seven spoke, "Fred has drawn a border line based on the interstate highway system and the construction projects underway. Almost all the towns and roadways along this line are currently held by the green shirts. Everything south of the line must be for the Sandys. The green shirts are building strongholds in these cities to make it clear to the Sandys where they intend the border remain after the invasion. They have chosen roadways because they make a great wide open partition that can be monitored day and night. We have seen them devote a lot of effort to making sure the roadways between cities are kept open for their traffic. "

Seven circled Raleigh, Durham, Greensboro, and Winston Salem according to reports of construction activity. At Hickory, she changed the colors to blue and drew the line from Hickory to Knoxville. In Knoxville, she continued back with the green line all through the remaining states signifying green shirt control. She and Fred were right. It was clear that the new borders were going to be drawn by the roadways, not some lines on a map before the takeover.

Seven looked at us all. "The green shirts have only one section of this line not under their direct control." She pointed to the 4th's territory linking Hickory to Knoxville, "They will not let this patch go empty and let the Sandys draw the line themselves."

Fred found his voice. "That's right. This clearly shows us two things. One, they know they must have a definite border before the Sandys get here. If they don't, they are scared of where the Sandys will draw the line and claim too much land that they will never get back. No matter what they say, they fear the Sandys. Second, they are bound to establish a link from I85/95 to the coast somewhere south of Norfolk.

An intelligence officer asked, "Why not just draw the line right under Norfolk and be done with it?"

One of his counterparts was watching this unfold and said, "Because we have to know exactly where to position our troopers to block any advance from reinforcements."

Others quickly opened up. One man observed, "The Sandys want Bragg and Pope for obvious reasons. They want a base on the northern border where they can house aircraft and troops after the pacification of the state. The green shirts don't want them to have it for the same reason. They want to keep it for the same reason. It is the perfect spot to launch operations going north or south. Whoever controls the ports and Bragg will control the state."

Bull asked the Intel team, "What do we have on construction projects going on in New Bern or Jacksonville areas?"

Teams of people shuffled through papers, trying to find references. As they found reports, Fred and Seven drew dots on the board showing both green shirt activity and Sandy held locations.

Nemo watched as the pattern emerged and commented aloud, "The Sandys would never agree to the green shirts having Lejune open so close to their chief port city of Wilmington. They must be thinking the border will be drawn much further north, perhaps around the Virginia line. There is just no way they would ever accept for the green shirts to have every major base in the state. That reminds me,....." His voice trailed off as he flipped through a couple of folders. The room was a buzz of activity with only a few of us sitting and watching the show of brain power at work.

Finally, one of intelligence people announced, "We have reports of green shirt rebuilding activity going on at Lejune and Cherry Point. But strangely, there is no green shirt activity in Jacksonville itself. They have an office in New Bern and they have been constructing walls and barriers like everywhere else, but not in Jacksonville.

Nemo looked over to Bull. "I think we may have just discovered something that will help us a great deal. I have an old intercept between the Sandys and one of the government officials in charge of commerce in Raleigh. The Sandys wanted the docks around New Bern to be used for commercial shipping only. At the time, they referred to it as the eastern border which we didn't understand and thought it was a misunderstanding in translation. After what we just realized here, I think the Sandys agreed to New Bern as the most southern and eastern border city to be held by the green shirts. That is why they wanted it to be commercial shipping only. They want Norfolk to be the closest green shirt naval base, not New Bern."

One of the 2nds Intel officers blurted out, "So, okay. You want us to hit New Bern now?"

Nemo looked across the table at the man with more patience than I would have offered. "New Bern is not the issue. The fact that the green shirts are working on Lejune *is very* important. I will bet that they are doing this without the Sandy's knowledge or the PPR's approval. Remember, all this construction is taking up a lot of green shirt resources and manpower. The fuel that would otherwise be used to solidify their hold on the region is being used to build border cities and haul workers across the state. If they use gasoline on it, it's important. Right now the green shirts need to finish the border before tens of thousands of Sandys pour in through the ports next month. We are seeing the manifestation of their natural fear. Perhaps we can use it to our advantage. "

The room fell silent, as everyone looked at the board once again. The pattern was clear; from Raleigh Fred drew a line along highway 70, through Goldsboro (Seymore Johnson AFB), Kinston, and all the way down to New Bern. Everything north was green shirt territory while everything south was supposed to be under

Sandy control. All the reports of construction corresponded to the pattern in exact detail.

Bull sat with his fingers crossed as he pondered the new understanding of all the construction. The green shirts were putting everything into the southern border cities and that is why they left the rural areas alone. They did not have the time to deal with us because they needed to concentrate all their efforts into making their southern border as secure as possible. Finally, Bull spoke. "When and where can we expect an attack from the green shirts to open the section between Ashville through to Knoxville?"

Everyone sat silently, wondering the same thing. 20 minutes ago, we didn't consider the green shirts as a remote threat to militia held territory. Now it seemed almost eminent.

People made comments about the strength and disposition of green shirt elements in Winston Salem. They were mainly police, without much in the way of heavy equipment. Greensboro was about the same; a few armored cars or swat vans, but nothing major. There was nothing identified in the green shirt police force inventory that really worried us too much.

One of the Intelligence officer commented, "If it weren't for the Sandys, we would have a good chance of wiping out the green shirts completely."

One of Bull's operations officers had been taking notes and asked the group aloud, "Why haven't we seen the green shirts start to position troops down here? I mean, right now they have a bunch of patrol cars and some armored vehicles, but no tanks or planes or anything. If they are so worried about this area, why don't they move some troops to the border before the Sandys land in force?"

Nemo responded, "You have to see this from their perspective. The green shirt leadership sees North Carolina as a border state that has been relatively quiet for the last four months. The militia has not challenged any of their strongholds or building projects in any meaningful way. They are willing to abandon the smaller towns to concentrate their resources towards their larger cities that they can occupy at the last minute."

Nemo was in his element and his arguments were convincing.

Nemo continued, "With the militia keeping the Sandys occupied in Wilmington and Charlotte, the green shirts can amass forces somewhere north until it is prudent. Politics has a part in this as well. The green shirts and Sandys are supposed to be friends and future neighbors in this wonderful utopian society imposed by the PPR movement. If the Sandys see a buildup of forces before they arrive, it will be seen as gesture of distrust. The Sandys will be outraged and the whole American green shirt contingent will reflect badly on the PPR in general."

Nemo had the whole room's attention with his analysis. I am sure I was not the first one to wonder how high up this guy was in the government, based on the sophistication of his remarks. I don't think anyone would be surprised to find out he had briefed the Pentagon or presidents at some point in the past.

Nemo continued, "The green shirts have been relying on their drones and their internet surveillance to watch us fight the Sandys. They rely on this information completely and trust it like it was gospel. They base all their decisions on what these spy programs tell them. The green shirts won't risk their troops until the last minute because they are spread out trying to consolidate the north and contain Texas. Remember the whole train load of equipment you destroyed last year? They can't afford another repeat because they don't have the military manpower or expertise to lose like that again."

Several men in the room thought long and hard about what Nemo had just said.

The snotty intelligence office from the 2nd spoke almost under his breath, but loud enough for everyone to hear, "When we hit Wilmington, it will give the green shirts the perfect excuse to deploy troops. They have to quell the uprising and provide security for their new neighbors."

We sat there stewing at the attitude of that guy. But one thing was worse, he was right. A lot of us sat stunned at the correct assessment. The green shirts would surely use our Wilmington operation to bring in a permanent border guard.

Bull took it all in as he listened to everyone's opinion, then asked, "Fred, where do you see them coming from to hit us?"

Fred looked at the map. "There are three main roads leading from the north. Highway 81 at Wytheville down to 77, then over here along the east coast where we have I-85 and 95 that run all through the south. If they are going to send in an army, it will be from the west or north. They will need to bring forces from Nashville or Knoxville, if they come in from the west. If they come from the north, it will be down highway 81. Either way, Wytheville will be their key position because they will need to drive in supplies from the north. That is, unless they bring in stuff from the west, but I don't see that happening. They want Texas contained and they can't go around stripping resources from that effort. If I were the green shirts, I would secure Wytheville so that I could secure the major highways of 81 and 77. If we are right, the buildup will start there."

Bull took the opportunity of silence to announce his decision. "Huck, send me 100 men from the first groups to finish their training. Make it a mixture of talents. I want some ex-military, demolitions people, and so forth. I will contact the resistance movements in West Virginia and Western Virginia so they can lend a hand as well."

Bull looked around the room for someone particular, "Colonel Beaumont, this is your job. Bring your command from Gastonia and pick up Huck's people in North Wilkesboro. I will cut you orders tonight and send you the plan as soon as we can write it. I want you to recon Wytheville in force and see what resistance they offer. This is not strategic, *YET*. Shoot, move, and communicate for now."

Beaumont looked wide-eyed. "When will your people be ready, Colonel Huck?"

I thought for a second. "We have some guys that will be finished in two weeks."

Bull said to us both, "I want them on the road in 10 days equipped to stay for a month, if need be. Make it happen."

We agreed, even though we were not sure how to do everything. Several logistics officers shared our views as well. How in the world could we get it done in time? Conversation finally broke out as the operations officers questioned Bull on some details for the orders they were to issue to our commands.

Bull called for a short recess so we could all talk among ourselves. This informality let people express their opinions a little more freely and it made a big difference in the long run. Bull stood by the table with Fred and Seven, looking at the maps. Every corner of the room was filled with chatter as commanders issued work out letters for their commands.

I walked over to the mass of people standing by, listening to Bull.

I heard him say, "Seven, I need you to get me pictures of the construction effort going on at Bragg and Lejune. I want people on the ground taking photos of those locations as soon as you can get them there. Oh yeah, and start up a courier route to Wytheville so we can get some of your snipers up there right away as well."

Nemo stood by my side as we listened. "Colonel Huck, it's amazing for me to see civilians, from all walks of life, organizing a resistance effort like this. Do you know how many generals I have briefed that could not make a decision about what pot of coffee to serve at a dinner party without assistance? You are very lucky to have the good people around you."

I commented rather darkly, "All the people with limited vision are already dead. It's a matter of attrition, really."

Nemo looked over at me with a strange expression and didn't say anything as Bull made his way to us.

Bull looked over to us and motioned for Nemo and me to follow him. At the same time, he announced, "Break for lunch, we have food downstairs. Nemo, Huck, follow me."

The adjacent room was empty for the most part and smelled of musty air. Security wasn't even allowed in the room. It was just Bull, myself, and Captain Nemo.

Bull turned on the spot and looked at Nemo. "Looks like we may have to consider Plan B after all." I didn't know what he meant, but Bull's words were anxious. It was as if he was really reluctant or hesitant to even consider this Plan B. Nemo stood rigid, thinking about Bull's comment.

I looked Bull square in the face and asked, "Ok, what is plan B?" What could cause Bull to look so apprehensive? I had never seen this level of concern in him before. Just what had he and Nemo been discussing?

Bull was lost in thought and didn't answer right away. Instead, he began on what seemed a tangent. "What if we change our thinking on the whole Wilmington operation?"

I looked to Bull and commented, "In what way? No matter what the green shirts do, we have to close the ports."

"That is absolutely essential," Nemo agreed and nodded as he stood with his arms folded. The man was hard to read.

Bull paced around, thinking out loud. "From the beginning we have anticipated sending 2,000 men or more to close down the ports and see if we can wrestle the Sandys for the city. What if we make the Wilmington effort more about the ports and not try to free the city? Do you two think it is possible for a Special Forces group to shut down the docks so the Sandys can't land their people?"

Nemo considered Bull's request as we stood there trying to grasp the possibilities. "I don't know, Bull. I see what you are getting at, but the port has to be closed or else we will lose the war. If those ports stay open, the south will eventually fall. The entire war depends on the ports of Wilmington."

I knew Bull realized this. Why was he even considering not attacking the city in force? What would make Bull so willing to risk the Wilmington operation just to head off another green shirt armored force we couldn't see, yet? Granted, it was a real threat, but not one as daunting as we faced in Wilmington.

Nemo observed, "The 3rdbattalion can support a sizeable special operation contingent with their sniper teams and logistics. We can pull units from Major Arrow's command and augment my teams. I think that will suffice. We will not have to go to plan B unless we fail."

Captain Nemo looked around. "My men have done missions like this before and we learned a few things over the years. If we do this, it has to be our way. No local militia units getting in the way. Huck's 3rd and Arrow's men will be enough to support us. But Bull, know this, we don't have a lot of time here. Security is going to be a big factor with all these people knowing we are planning a major operation in Wilmington. I will bet the green shirts and Sandys have at least some inkling we are coming already."

Bull said forcefully, "I am counting on it."

That took Nemo and me by surprise. Bull decided to let us in on his plan. "I am going to leak information out about the green shirt construction at Lejune and Bragg. We might even make some junk up and Photoshop some real racist stuff in the pictures. By the time we are done, the Sandys will be outraged at the green shirts in this state."

Bull continued, "That little snot from the second is right, as much as I hate it. The green shirts will send in a major force some time in the near future and we will be caught in the middle of two opposing forces. All the green shirts need is an excuse like a militia attack on Wilmington to justify sending in troops to secure the southern border of their territory. If you two can shut down the ports, I will take the units that were supposed to assault Wilmington, and I will ambush the green shirts at Wytheville."

I looked to Bull and Nemo like they were crazy. "Now, wait a minute. We have been training for a major assault in Wilmington. The men are all set to go and we have begun training on sand tables. What if we cannot close the ports with just special operations? What if they find a way around our little sabotage and get the ports going in a couple of weeks? What is you fall back plan if we fail?" I was heated by the time I finished. Nemo and Bull stood silently, waiting for me to complete my thought.

Nemo took my frustration in stride and said, "We have a couple of contingencies of which you are not aware, Colonel. First, we have an ingenious Captain of a nuclear attack submarine that was able to save his boat after the collapse. He has been able to stay clear of the worldwide PPR movement but is well aware of the Sandy threat. He is going to try to cripple the Sandy's fleet somewhere in deep water after they leave port. Secondly, some of the special warfare teams in Norfolk have a plan to use some of the remaining SEAL MKV support boats in a coastal defense posture. They have the ability to float MK48 ADCAP torpedoes off the fantail and remotely pilot them to hit surface ships as they near the channels leading to the docks."

I was amazed at the revelations, but not convinced that even these measures could guarantee any level of success. Surely the Sandys would have escort vessels for so many inbound troops. How could they be so certain these defenses would be enough to close the ports? I was comforted somewhat, but by no means satisfied. My expression must have given my apprehension away.

Bull leaned on a table's edge and spoke. "That is where Plan B comes in. If the special-forces mission is a success, we can shift those SEAL boats south to close off Charleston and/or perhaps Savannah. That leaves *us* to fend off the green shirt troops at Wytheville. If Wilmington is still open after your attack, we have only one remaining option to stop the invasion."

Bull looked at Nemo, who began slowly, as if giving a lecture in a university. "I have in my control a nuclear device similar to the one used on Washington DC. It's a small unit, but would be enough to destroy the city if everything else fails. That is Plan B. Of course, that is a last resort, worst-case scenario."

I was shocked to my core. Nemo had access to resources I had never dreamed of, if he was in control of a nuclear weapon. But how could we even consider using it? Everyone living inside Wilmington would be dead. We would take out the Sandys and all the Americans used for forced labor. There would be thousands of American casualties.

I looked at Bull. "We can't possibly use a nuke on our own country. Tow the thing out to sea and we will hit their fleet before they come in."

Bull hung his head while Nemo answered me. "I wish we could, Colonel. Believe me; if there was any way we could get this bomb off the coast, we would do it. But NSA tracking would have us pegged before we got three miles off the coast. The only way we can hide it now is because there are hospitals with x-ray machines working again. Otherwise, we would not have been able to keep it under wraps this long. If it gets out in the open, the space-born radiological defense nets will pick up the bomb's signature. We can camouflage it for a while, but it would have to be used in the city itself to inflict enough damage to make the ports unusable."

All three of us sat there, contemplating the depth of this discussion. How in the world did I get here? A couple of years ago I was at a steady job, getting through life, things were pretty good. Today I was standing in an abandoned building with two other men who had a nuclear bomb at our disposal. And worse, we were considering using it. I had a wife in the next room and a baby at home who counted on me for everything. "How did I get here?" was all I could think.

I said the last thing that popped into my mind. "Well, I guess failure is not an option. Our mission to close the ports will have to succeed. Anything else is too horrible to consider. Nemo, the 3rd will support the mission to close the ports or we will all die trying. I swear it."

Nemo nodded his head, accepting my commitment. I was shaking like a leaf. I think everyone else in the room brushed down the hairs standing on end.

I asked Bull, "When will we tell the men about the change of plans?"

Bull paused, "Cross train all units on the Wilmington operation and the Wytheville plan. When they get on the bus, we will announce which operation they are headed for. Otherwise, the three of us are the only ones that know the real plan. Not even Seven can know about plan B, though. That must stay with the three of us."

Nemo looked a little concerned. "Do you think your people will accept a change in orders so easily?"

I had to admit, that was good question. I didn't relish the idea of changing missions on the men, or worse, keeping a secret from Seven. She would not be fooled for long in my estimation. I told him, "They will have to."

We stood there until Nemo suggested, "I will start making plans right away for shutting down the ports. I will send Data all the information he needs to spread the disinformation leaks when the 3rd's Intel team gets those airport pictures. My teams and I will move into one of the staging areas outside of Wilmington and start our recon. I will let you know what I hear from my contacts in Tripoli and Cairo when they report. They should be able to tell us when the main body of transport ships leaves. Otherwise, Huck, we will meet you at the staging area in a couple of weeks."

Bull looked at Nemo. "You would make a great Colonel in the resistance, Nemo." His tone was very suggestive.

Nemo looked Bull in the face. "Let's see if we make it through this operation first; then we will see."

Nemo shook hands with Bull, who understood that Nemo was willing to fight the green shirts, but he was not ready to join the militia. A part of Nemo was still linked to the formal national defense structure. It was in his very nature. That mentality was not something you just abandoned when the bad guys came knocking. Bull and I estimated that Nemo was a unique mix of spy, warrior, and politician that could not be nailed down to one character trait. We liked him and trusted him, but he was driven by motives we could not see on the surface.

We rejoined the conference and went through the motions of planning a large scale assault on Wilmington as everyone expected. Bull also insisted that all troops learn the Wytheville mission just in case they would be needed as a backup. At the time, everyone accepted the concept and never questioned the directive.

We spent the rest of that day deciding a bunch of things. We laid out plans for deception assaults on various places. Intelligence groups were assigned so much work, I was sure they would never sleep again. Logistics people were briefed in such a way that they would be able to re-direct Wilmington-destined supplies towards Wytheville without anyone sending up a red flag. It was sneaky, but we thought we pulled it off in such a way that was not conspicuous.

On the way home, Fred, Seven and I wrote notes and orders for all the department heads in our command. It was a hard grueling day before we finally walked the last leg of our journey down Wooten Valley's gravel road.

As we trudged home, Fred announced, "I'm going up to Wytheville with the scouts." It was a statement rather than a request."

We walked down the road with every step crunching the early night's frost. Our breath made little clouds of visible vapor as we walked along thinking about Fred's statement. The stars were out; goodness it was cold.

I asked Fred with Seven under my arm, "Are you well enough to go out on the road like that?"

Fred quietly said while looking forward, "I'm okay, Huck, but Bull has everything riding on what I told him. I have to go up there and make sure I didn't make a mistake."

Seven said, between her gloved hands covering her mouth, "You wife is not going to like it. She doesn't want you going out any more."

Fred acted like he didn't hear her and tried to lighten the mood. He said, "I always wanted to be a trucker." He mimicked a trucker driving a big rig and held his hand like he was talking on a CB. "Breaker One-Nine, we have ourselves a convoy!"

With that, we continued to walk down the road nearing home. It was up to me to give him the approval, but it was hard for me send him into what could be a meat grinder. He was my best friend asking to do something really dangerous. If he was hurt, it would be my fault for sending him. As we neared home, I told Fred, "Work with Rocket's group to create the couriers leading up to Wytheville. Over engineer the routes and make sure we can *truck* people up there at a moment's notice. You have my approval, but keep your freaking head down. You wife will kill me if the green shirts shoot you again." Fred thanked me, which didn't help.

Seven and I picked up Punkin from Fred's house and left relatively quickly. We didn't want to hear Fred's wife when she found out he was leaving for a month or more.

As we went home, Seven admitted, "I know how she feels. You and Bull are cooking up something with that little meeting with Nemo. Don't deny it either. If he is going to you, Bull is really going to pull a fast one on the green shirts."

I looked to her in mock surprise and swore I would behave and play nice with the other boys. But she knew my lack of information meant that there was nothing I could tell her about our little meeting. Seven took that stuff well, given the circumstances. I think my silence freaked her out more than anything else, though. As we walked through our door, she said, "I know you can't tell me anything, but don't get yourself in over your head. You like Nemo, but I think he has his own agenda. He has a lot of secrets."

I agreed, "He does indeed."

Chapter 18
Be Prepared

The day after the meeting with Bull and the other battalions, I met with the training leaders to give them all the new directives. I detailed the Wytheville operation with as much detail as I could imagine and mapped out the details as I knew them. Some trainers really took notice of the shift in attention to the Wytheville operation, while others took it in stride. I must admit that the ex-military took it better than the civilian militia. Soldiers were more accustomed to changes in orders at the last minute.

I drilled into the instructors how they needed to emphasize flexibility in which operation they would be assigned. "Pass it along to your teams. They need to be prepared for anything," I told them. It was all the heads up I could give them. My thoughts were more concentrated on the troops themselves. If they took the change of plans poorly, there would be a drop in morale that could hurt them and their mission.

The trainers assured me they would do their best to get the men ready before the operation. February was approaching quickly and everyone knew they would be in a major fight within a month.

My notebook had scribbles of notes where I started to make lists of men that I wanted on the Wilmington operation. These were men that I knew well from the 3rd militia as well as specific SF soldiers from Arrow's men. This list was always in the back of my mind. I ate on it, I slept on it; it dominated every conversation.

My days were complete mayhem as I tried to get everything set up for both major operations. My operations officers were split into two groups with orders that must have made them think I was a loon. Half of you will run the Wytheville operations and the rest will work the Wilmington mission. They had more than suspicions when their staffs were split 70/30 with the emphasis on Wytheville.

One day, several of the senior operations officers came to my office. "Colonel, can we have a word?"

They closed the door on my shabby little office in the new headquarters building. I offered them a seat among piles of paperwork held down by the bipod and stock of my Thor sniper rifle. Someone joked it was a 7.62 paperweight. The operations chief spoke first. "Colonel, we want to talk to you about the staffing arrangements."

I looked to the men as they sat there across from me. "Okay, what's the problem?"

They looked more apprehensive than usual and my suspicions were confirmed when the chief of staff said, "Well sir, frankly, we are concerned that too many of the operations staff is focused solely on the Wytheville operation. More than half of Rocket's couriers have been re-tasked to support the Wytheville operation."

I continued for him, "You are concerned that you don't have enough people to properly plan for sending 2,000 troops all the way to Wilmington and conduct a city wide assault. Is that it?"

They all agreed whole heartedly and were relieved to see that I understood. I looked the men in faces and made sure they knew I was serious. "Gentlemen, I agree completely. That is why I am shifting you (I pointed to the chief) to this facility as your permanent post. You will not be going on either mission. You will be promoted to my second in command as light Colonel and will assume those duties forthwith. Bull has already approved you, congratulations."

The men looked at each other in utter shock.

Before they could speak, I continued, "Captain, you are assigned to the forward operating base we are setting up near Fort Chiswell. You will make sure the couriers are set up in a tactical formation that follows the task force wherever they go in the region. We will continue written messages for every aspect of the missions. No form of electronics whatsoever."

The men finally understood and each one of them went from confusion to realization in moments. They knew I was operating under instructions that I could not pass along. My sudden assignments meant that we were not hitting Wilmington in force and I could not say anything about it directly. It was then that one of the younger Captains asked me, "Sir, which mission will *you* be assigned?"

I thought for a second and paused, trying to decide on the right tact.

The chief of staff cut the young Captain off and began to tell him that it was not for him to know at that point.

I responded anyway because he deserved to know. "I will be in Wilmington come hell or high water. But gentlemen, our troopers don't have a need to know that right now. They need to complete their training cycle with as little interference as possible. They need to be as ready as we can make them. In nine days our first recruits will be heading out on their first assignment. Fred will be leaving tomorrow or the day after with the advance team. Orders will be coming very soon if they are not already on the way."

The men appreciate the amount of information I had given them and knew full well I couldn't say more or risk all of our lives. I suppose military people have this type of thing happen more often than us civilian soldiers. It was harder for us to change gears, but we were getting better at it. The operations officers left just as Data came in for his scheduled meeting with me. Data waited until they were down the hall then knocked on my door.

"Colonel Huck, you wanted to see me?"

"Yes, Data. Come in and have a seat." He did so as I looked him over closely. He was disheveled and looked a bit worse for wear.

"Data, how are you sleeping? You feel alright?" I asked him. My question was out of concern for his health because he was more pale than usual.

He rubbed his scraggly beard. "Oh, well, I have been putting in some long hours since that day Nemo came by. I was able to incorporate his entire disinformation packet into my plan because it had a bunch of things that will drive the green shirt security people nuts. We are working on fake photos that will piss off the Sandys something fierce. We made it look like green shirt are painting slogans that say stuff like: Allah eats hamburgers. They are also working on a bunch of gay stuff too, about *the profit*. It's not politically correct, but it will get the job done. Nemo might be a pain, but his stuff's pretty squared away for a bureaucrat."

I poured Data a drink and sat beside him by the desk. "When was the last time you slept in a real bed for eight hours?"

Data paused, "Well...I...let's see. I have the cot over at the ....hmm. What day is it?" he finally asked.

I put my hand on his shoulder and said, "Go sack out and get some real food, then come back tomorrow. Let someone else handle things for a while. You've trained your group well; let them do the job while you get some rest."

Data bowed his head and rose to his feet. He must have been too tired to even argue when he said, "Okay, Huck. Oh, here are the preliminary reports from some people somewhere. Seven wanted me to pass them straight to you as soon as the couriers came in. I'll see ya, Huck."

I thanked Data and sat behind my desk again as I rifled through the papers. In essence, the courier groups were pretty new and there would have to be some tweaking over the next couple of weeks to work out all the kinks. Seven's first choice spies had departed that morning and would be reporting back in three days if all went well. Rocket had been made aware of the mission, dubbed Concord, and all units were already at least one leg down the routes Rocket had set up. That was good. The rest of my paperwork consisted of my usual head honcho crap. People asking permission to switch teams around, logistics wanting estimations on supply issues, and the usual requests for clarification on orders.

Nothing was really urgent so I packed up the Thor sniper rifle and walked down the hall to where the security station was manned 24 hours a day.

"Hey guys, let's get over to Wooten Valley. I want some range time on the sniper course." My detail rounded up a few people for escort and we headed out in a plain Suburban after we checked the known drone schedule. Luckily for me, there was no activity for the next few hours and most of our ranges would be open for training.

In 25 minutes, the Suburban rounded the last corner on the side of the road leading through the hills to the east of our little valley. This was our trail-head that wound its way down the ridges and across the lower hills leading to the sniper training post we set up. This trail kept recruits from walking down our little main street among what few families lived along the river. We just didn't want the place to look like a police state at all hours of the day.

Two of my security detail climbed out of the truck with their M4s at the ready. Once they were satisfied, they signaled for me to exit the vehicle. I slung the Thor over my pack straps and zipped my jacket. The cold spurt had not let up and the wind blew through the hills as if the intention was to freeze you to the bone. The sky was overcast, but fairly bright because the clouds were thin in the higher elevations. We walked the narrow paths heading over the hills and finally to our sniper staging area almost a mile from the road. The woods were as bare as the trails. Fallen leaves covered the ground among left over strips of snow that had not thawed since the last storm.

My security element and I turned the last corner of the trail where we startled a small group of men huddled together with their hands in their pockets. They paced in place, keeping the blood flowing to their feet in the cold. The group was dressed in an assortment of BDUs, ACUs, and various camo patterns from Realtree to dark green DPM jackets. Looks of concern at our unexpected presence spread through the men as their conversations stopped immediately. Their rifles were slung or lay on the ground around them.

This little flat place was a spot at the base of all three trail heads where recruits waited to be assigned a mission based on the training of the day. Once the mission assignment was divulged, a recruit would be assigned to one of the trials where he has to complete a set of tasks based on the topic of the day. Examples of these missions included: Lone Wolf – This was a lone sniper drill against any number of targets at various ranges. Sniper/Spotter – As you can guess, a Sniper and spotter worked as a team to hit targets. Of course there were variations that taught recruits how to patrol with three or more in a team, there were sniper break-contact drills, stalking drills, traveling at night, and of course they had to go see Bo at some point to get a feel for wilderness survival. The final task would be a full mission profile where recruits hiked out of the valley and hit a designated target without being caught by the instructors.

A dozen eyes looked in my direction, but not a word was said.

I walked among the men, looking up the trail head for an instructor. "Where is your instructor?" I asked the men in general.

One of the recruits said, "He just went up the trail with the first group."

"Who is you instructor of the day, recruit?" I was in drill instructor mode that even Gunny would have been proud to witness. Before they could respond I said, "You guys are standing around like this is a Boy Scout jamboree. Would you like me to build a fire for you so you can roast some marshmallows? You have no security set and none of you have as much as a sharp stick in your hand as we came around that corner. You train like you operate. Practice makes permanent!"

It was about that time when the instructor came jogging back down one of the trails out of breath.

"Colonel, Huck, they didn't tell me you were coming today." Several of the men in the group had not realized I was the Colonel and their eyes widened at the nugget of information.

"GT, this group of recruits needs a refresher on posting security at all times. This might save their lives someday. The more they do it in training, the more they will do it when they are on mission."

The instructor's name was GT because of his absolute love for the Mustang he drove before the war. I swear the guy had a picture of that car in his wallet at all times. He had requested to be a courier when that program started up, but he was a good sniper instructor and I could not spare him.

"Sir, I will kick their butts until they get it right." GT assured me.

"You do that, GT. And after they get it, make this group your aggressor team to hound the other sniper teams during their drills. Work them day and night until they teach all the other teams the lesson as well. Maybe they will learn from other people's mistakes."

"I'll do it, sir."

I focused on the trails ahead. "What is your skill of the day?"

GT responded briskly, "Loblolly is open. We are doing Sniper/Spotter unknown distance drills. We are using man-targets along the river, base of the hill, right side. You want to go next, sir?"

"All I need is a spotter," I told him.

None of the recruits dared to move since I had come around the corner and most stood solid like their feet had frozen in place.

GT looked over the men in the squad and picked one of the younger guys. "Colonel, Opie here has an uncanny knack for judging distance."

I looked to the young man and understood how he got the nickname. Opie had big ears and freckles which made him look somewhat like the young Ron Howard. I said to him "Code names suck sometimes, don't they?"

He grabbed his rifle off the ground. "Yes sir, Colonel Huck, sir," The rest of the men stifled snickers at his expense as I led him up the trail. Opie had a Remington 700 PSS rifle chambered in .308. The rifle was painted with some bands of peeling green and tan stripes of spray paint. A burlap bag was frayed and tied in various places so it would blend in with the winter woods better. This rifle had been used quite a bit from the looks of it. His scope was a Millett of one variation or another. Overall, the rifle was a good one in my estimation.

We walked the trail, leaving behind the other recruits with my security detail following 20 yards behind.

I said quietly to Opie while scanning the opposite hill, "How is the militia treating you?"

Opie was two steps behind me in his cover position just as we taught. He too was keeping his head on the swivel as we put it. It meant that we kept watch in all directions as much as humanly possible. We joked about how we looked like a bunch of bobble head dolls when we patrolled. Opie kept up his scanning as we walked. "It's has its ups and downs, but good so far, Colonel."

I asked, "Getting enough to eat?

We walked a few more steps in quiet when Opie answered, "it's fine. Not like before the power went out, but I'm not hungry." His tone was quiet, not in fear, but it was just like we trained. We stayed quiet while on mission.

"Good," I told him. "How are the men in your squad? They all seem a little …older. They treat you okay?"

We walked around a few bends and Opie answered, "Yeah. It's a pretty tight group, really. We are all from the same area, Chimney Rock, west of Charlotte. My Dad and I joined up about this time last year. He always said this war would come sooner or later."

I noticed that Opie's footsteps were careful. He had the nature of a hunter, which is something you either have or you don't. You can train some hunter techniques into people, but you know the difference when you see someone with real hunting skill. Opie had some experience from what I could see.

"Did you serve in the 4th's sniper teams around Charlotte?" I asked.

Opie responded with more ease in his voice. "No, sir. They had us in a regular line unit, the 5th. But when our platoon was hit by a company sized element back in the early summer, our squad fended them off."

I stopped in the trail and knelt down. Opie followed suit as I looked to him. I was interested to hear the rest of his story because I had heard about the mission as an example of incredible militia determination.

"Was that the King's Mountain operation? Where you a part of the 5th company, second platoon then?" I asked him.

Opie looked to me and answered, "Yes, sir. You know about that mission?"

"Everybody in the militia knows about that mission. What your company did there was nothing short of amazing," I told him.

Opie kept scanning while we sat on that cold trail on the edge of the hill. The wind whistled and blew from every direction because the mountains have no shame. He finally admitted, "It sure didn't feel all that special. We were just trying to survive. The Sandys had us dead to rights that day. I don't know how any of us got off that mountain."

I noticed that my security element settled nearer than normal so they could overhear. The story of 2nd platoon's effort was legendary. This squad of recruits had most of the original survivors of that fateful mission. They had been reassigned as part of a sniper company due to their skill with rifles. These men were bound for the Wytheville operation, but they didn't know it yet. The hairs on the back of my neck were standing up as I asked Opie, "Can you share some of it?"

Opie kept watch and started to tell his story without looking in my direction. "2nd platoon was assigned the southern flank of the railroad tracks that ran through town. We dropped off and contained the area and shut down the roads. The major part of the mission was further north and the company commander took some units south along the tracks to hit some switching station. We were told to hang tight and be the 3rd platoon's backup in case the Sandys showed up unexpectedly. All the major highways were shut down and the area was quiet. The green shirts didn't have much there in town. 3rd platoon had all the green shirts wiped out by 09:00. It was looking like a real smooth operation."

Opie's voice had a lump in it, if you know what I mean. It was like he was watching the events replay in front of his eyes as he spoke. "Dad and I joined after Mom died. She was diabetic, and....well, you can guess what happened with the medicine gone and all. Dad was our squad leader because he had served in the Army back when he was young. He set us up in a small warehouse off the Andrew Jackson highway where it meets highway 85. The place must have been a truck park before the war. Greens shirts used it at some point because it had a lot of their banners on the walls. Maybe their highway patrol used it since it was a strategic intersection before militia got strong in that area."

Opie caught his breath as I looked back to my security escort. They tried to look cool, but they were eating up every bit of the story as much as I was.

The kid didn't seem to mind though, his thoughts were on autopilot. He continued, "It wasn't too cold that day. I remember that the clouds parted and the sun poked out. We had been on the move half the night getting into position so we were all pretty tired. We didn't have a lot of gas back then. Our trucks and busses were parked on the west side of the interstate so they could be closer to 3rd platoon. We were just there as a blocking force so we didn't have any heavy weapons or demolitions people with us."

"It was right around noon when the first gunfire was heard off to the east. The Sandys were coming down the Andrew Jackson highway in force. Our platoon leader sent scouts from 1st squad to go see what was going on. At that point, we didn't know how many Sandys we were dealing with. For all we knew, it might have been a squad car or two, full of green shirts. We were wrong about that. Our radios weren't working, or they had some jamming going on that day, I don't know which. The platoon leader couldn't reach any of the scouts or any of the other platoons we were supporting. He kept yelling into the handset trying to get anybody he could. But all he heard was static. He turned to every frequency he had ever used in the past, but it was all the same. Dad told him to just stuff the code book and command the men.

By then we were hearing heavy machinegun fire from the eastern approach of the Andrew Jackson highway. We all stood by the roadway on the edge of the pavement when this one guy was seen walking down the guardrail towards us. It took him what seemed like an hour for him to walk the $1/3^{rd}$ of a mile from the bend in the road. At first, we didn't know who it was. It was just a dark silhouette coming closer and closer. Meanwhile the gunfire raged just a mile out of sight. You could hear the occasional booms and thuds of RPGs. I had never heard anything like it before. It was so loud and intimidating. Like a wave that got closer and closer until it engulfed you.

I was the courier for the group because I ran track in high school right before we joined up. The platoon leader sent me to find out who that guy was coming down the road in the open like that. A lot of the guys were already finding road signs to crouch behind for cover. But there was nothing solid near the road.

I ran out there and caught up with…the guy…and I couldn't even tell it was Harry. His right arm hung from his shoulder like a puppet or something. His whole right side was burned to the point where I couldn't tell where his clothes stopped and his charred skin started. His web gear was in pieces and disappeared into his side. Burnt blood was caked all over him, but somehow he managed to walk all the way back to us. I didn't know it was him until he spoke. All he said was, "run."

Opie paused at the memory and I was tearing up at the sheer magnitude of his story. He told it so vividly that I could feel the description of his friend's wounds as if I were there. It made me think of Fred and how he must tell the story of how he carried me after that tank shell almost killed us in Raleigh.

Opie saw my eyes out of focus and offered, "Sorry, sir. I heard you went through stuff like that, too."

"Don't apologize to me, son. The Lord has seen fit for me to live long enough to hear the stories of true heroes and I am honored to have you share them with me," I told him.

Opie decided to continue instead of recognize the compliment. "We tried to bandage Harry, but he died there on the side of the road. There was nothing we could do. The Sandys must have decimated 1st squad and they came looking for the rest of us. Two of those Russian armored car/tanks with eight wheels rolled down the road, one on each side. By the time the platoon leader could see them, we were eating machinegun bullets. Bullets skipped off the road and bounced off the signs like it was gravel being thrown by truck tires. Then the freaking mortars started to rain down on us and all you could see behind them was infantry. There must have been a hundred and fifty of them coming straight for us.

The platoon leader ordered everyone to cross I-85 and join up with 3rd platoon. Dad grabbed him by the collar and jerked him around to get in his face. "That is 300 yards of open terrain. They will tear us to pieces before we make it half way!" They argued for a few seconds as the other squad showed up from the north end of our blockade. A handful of the men ended up following the platoon leader across the road while Dad took the rest of us south into the woods. None of the guys headed for the road even reached the median between the lanes."

"Dad took command of our squad and the other partial squad as we raced south through the woods for cover. More of the Sandys were running down this power line cutout as we tried to cross. We fired while others ran through the clearing. A couple of men went down, but we didn't have time to stop for them. The Sandys were only a few hundred yards away and there were just so many of them.

Dad called a halt a little while later when we reached a clearing that turned out to be a graveyard. The sign said Pisgah Graveyard and there were like a half dozen rows of stones in neat little rows. The men were out of breath trying to gulp down some water. Others reloaded their rifles. Dad told us we had to keep ahead of them or they would flank us and kill us all. To the southeast lay a road with a golf course on the opposite side. Dad put us into a picket line with instructions to bound back 100 yards in two lines.

It was like a squad-sized break contact drill. Every time the Sandys got close, we killed ten or so and dropped back. We ran 100 yards past the line behind us and dropped again. We reloaded while the other line fired.

It took an hour for us to get to the road. By then, the Sandys weren't sure exactly where we were and must have thought we turned back to the west. We filed across the road without so much as a shot fired. But by the time our last man crossed, the Sandys had caught sight of us. We used the irrigation ditches to spread out and make our way to the tallest point on the map. You could see the hill peeking through the trees of the golf course. We knew we had a chance if we could get to the hill for cover. Dad split the group up so we could cover the open fairways. We punished the Sandys every time they got out into the open. Some of our guys could really shoot. Before long though, they realized how few of us there were and started to follow us through the ditches. We ended up running the last hundred yards just to keep far enough ahead of them. They were so close at one point we saw their armored car fire on their own guys."

"By the time we got to the base of the hill, we were exhausted. The sun was starting to set and most of us were running really low on ammo. We were nearly out of water; even the junk water in the ditch was looking pretty good. None of us had eaten all day; we were running on pure adrenaline.

Luckily for us, there was a thicket running up the side of the hill and we used it for cover as we climbed. Almost everybody was bleeding at least a little. Dad had been hit with bullet fragments and flying tree bits a few times. I pulled a chunk of bark out of my leg at some point that day. Others had been shot in the arm or leg, but they were still going.

We got up the hillside and spread out to catch the Sandys making their way through the golf course. We bled them good. All I had was a Remington hunting rifle with iron sights, though. Nobody had any serious firepower on our side. The Sandys pulled back around dark and sat by the road out of range. We watched them eat as the light faded. They threw some mortars at us for a while after dark, but we were spread out pretty good by then. Their aim wasn't so good anyway.

We thought they might lose interest or that they might decide to leave for town at dark. We hoped 3rd platoon would come and get us, but they couldn't and we knew it. They hit us again around midnight. The Sandys came in from the north trying to flank us. Dad had us move up the hill while they dropped mortars to the south. The whole mountain wasn't 1,000 yards across. The Sandys just kept trying to work their way to the crest so they could get us in a cross fire. You shot one and two more came from behind a tree. They were so close you could smell what they had eaten for supper."

"Dad caught a round on the north side of the hill while he was moving between rocks. I had just run out of ammo and was trying to get another magazine for my captured AK when it happened. I ran over to him and held him through the rest of the attack. They were not going to overrun that position. I took his rifle…after."

Opie motioned that the rifle he held was his father's. I had never heard an account of that mission first hand. Opie said that he could not remember too many details after that. He fought the rest of the night and most of the next day, keeping supplied from dropped Kalashnikovs. Late the second day, the Sandy's pulled back. What was left of 2nd platoon was rescued and escorted back to a militia safe area. By the end of the mission, only seven of the 2nd platoon walked away from it. The Sandys losses were estimated between 80 and100 troops based on the casualties they left littering the hill. Our intelligence groups claimed that the Sandys expended their whole ammo compliment in the vain effort to kill the remaining fighters on the hill. They fired every round they had with them to the ire of their officers. It may have been one of the longest running gun battles in the war to date.

"Opie, you may look like a young Ron Howard, but you are a man of steel in my book," I told him. My words felt empty, but they were all I had.

Opie smiled blandly as we continued along the trail to our targets. He was quiet, but efficient, as we marked our targets. GT was right. Opie was good at distance estimation. I practiced several shots with the Thor and recorded the hits in my data book. My concentration was less than it should have been, though. My mind raced at the story Opie had shared. It was nothing short of amazing the way their squad held on against 7 to 1 odds. So many times a small militia group would get split off and just annihilated. It was a shame, but it was the side effect of having civilian soldiers.

We ended up our shooting session and walked back down the trail to the waiting group. I looked to them with great respect as we passed through their waiting security. I shook hands with all the men and promised I would do everything in my power to make sure they were kept together as a team. Whatever equipment they wanted, I told them to come see me personally. As I walked back up the trail, I noticed that my personal security detail shook each of the men's hands as well.

I returned home that night and hugged Seven and the baby. My prayers that night included a special request to protect my men as well as their families. So many of our people had been through so much over the last couple of years. I knew *I* could not protect them from harm, but I prayed to the One that has the power to watch over us all.

Chapter 19
Last Deep Breath

Fred had been gone for three days before his couriers brought back the first messages from Wytheville. Our analysis was a little behind the times. The green shirts had already commandeered several locations along highway 81. They were working hard to convert three truck rest-stops, and a small factory outlet mall into a major staging area outside of town. The truck stops were freshly repaired and surrounded by new fencing. Portable generators were used to light the empty lots at night for security. The lights were correctly pointed from the center of the lot and faced outward. Patrols ran up and down the interstate at all hours of the day. The town of Wytheville itself was well underway to becoming a large scale dormitory for a sizeable force. Fred estimated that there were more than 150 security police with another 200 forced laborers. He was convinced the green shirts were preparing for a major force to use Wytheville as a staging area. Fred had sketched several maps of where the police forces were deployed.

I laid that report on my desk and wondered how come we had not heard from the militia movements that were already working in that area. They knew the highway 81 corridor was strategically important and they had been monitoring green shirt activity along highway 81 for more than a year. We didn't have regular contact with these groups, but we counted on occasional communications on major events to see these events coming. I directed my Intelligence team to make contact with groups like the Sons of Liberty militia based in the hills outside Pulaski. There were other groups based in Blacksburg and Radford, but we had evidently not heard from them in a while. We received after action reports from them from time to time, but we had heard nothing about this level of construction in the last month or so. The closest green shirt held city was Charlottesville, which was 180 mile from Wytheville. Seven promised to get us some answers in the next day or two.

Data and Captain Nemo were well into their Piss-off-the-Sandys campaign (P.O.S.). Emails were going out on non-secure web sources from fake militia PCs. Some daring intelligence officers actually made their way into green shirt offices and planted the manufactured emails into green shirt computer systems. They emailed the P.O.S emails to everyone in the user's address book just to kick things off. Data reported that green shirts were already sharing the emails between each other and soon would make the emails viral by themselves. He estimated that the Sandys would have captured enough of the P.O.S. program in the next 36 hours that we should see some results soon after. Data also mentioned that his tracking package was delivering so much information that he was having a hard time storing all the information he was collecting.

Days passed at the same light speed until the first units from the 4th arrived. Captain Beaumont met me at one of the staging areas where we had men and materials ready to go. Bull and I agreed to increase the expeditionary force to 500 troops as the initial assault. We may have sent more, but logistics could not support the movement of that many men all at once. We were limited on vehicles and fuel, not to mention ways to feed all those men during a time when food packaging was rustic.

Beaumont looked at me as he loaded into his SUV, ready to leave. "Thanks, Colonel Huck. The men look ready and I am more than happy with their readiness. I thought it would take hours to load up all these men and their equipment. From what I have seen, I think we can have everyone at the Fort Chiswell staging area by dawn."

I shook his hand through the window of the truck. "Thanks. All these men are some of the best we have fielded in the war. They are all dedicated soldiers who will never give up. Lead the way and they will bleed the green shirts like never before. Now, get out of here before the drones change their rotation. All these trucks have to be out of here in the next two hours."

Beaumont chose not to respond and simply saluted. I returned his salute as his SUV led the way down the road. I stood there and saluted every truck that passed until they were all safely down the road. In the distance, I could make out the tail lights shining down three different roads as they headed north on three different routes. I stood on the open field and prayed for every one of those men.

The sun fell behind the western hills as several of the men took field implements to obscure the tire tracks of the departed trucks.

Even if someone photographed this field, it would look like a farmer was planting winter wheat or something. By the time the scheduled drones were back overhead, the remaining units were under cover and the last of the supply vehicles were miles up the road.

I sent Bull an update via courier that night to let him know the latest information. He was not going to be pleased to hear that the green shirts were so far along in Wytheville. We had all hoped we could assault these places well before this level of construction could be completed. None of us in command got much sleep that night.

The next day empty trucks returned to the various warehouses where we parked them out of sight of the drones. Immediately the logistics crew readied the trucks for another run. However, if all went well, the operation to secure Wytheville would not start for another week. The advance team was to pre-position troops to recon the area and lead the main assault when the time came. Our intention was to coordinate the attack on Wilmington as close to the Wytheville operation. The resulting confusion would serve both operations. Our remaining recruits were itching to go, but we wanted to risk as few men as possible at that point. I think Bull also wanted to keep some men in reserve in case the Sandys tried to pull something unexpected.

With more recruits ready in a week, and more following the week after that, we were confident in the plan of action. Data reported that Captain Nemo was set up in one of the forward staging areas outside of Wilmington with some of his men. Major Arrow accompanied the Wytheville team to assess demolitions projects and advise how his SF soldiers could support the mission. Arrow was scheduled to return to North Wilkesboro in the next few days to make sure we had everything we needed for Wilmington. I remember the conversation with Arrow when I gave him the directives.

I told him, "Major, you are assigned to the Wytheville operation. I need some commanders with real world experience." While he was taking in what I said, I handed him a list of six names.

Arrow looked at the scrap of paper and asked, "Okay, what are these guys all about?"

"I responded, "Those are your men that I need on the Wilmington mission."

Arrow flipped the page over looking for more names. "That's it, Huck? Are you sure you don't need more of my men?"

I waved him off. "Major, you are going to need all your men in Wytheville. Our recruits need every ounce of experience your guys can muster in this upcoming fight. My men have trained with your guys and they respect them. If I take more than that, it will hurt your mission."

Arrow did not look satisfied. "Colonel, Wilmington is a big city. Nemo might need some backup and once you stir up the hornet's nest, they will come down on you like a freakin anvil."

I told him, "It's okay, I have a secret weapon."

Arrow stood there, wondering what I was talking about.

"I'm taking a special sniper squad and I have Rocket's couriers to get us there and back. The Sandys won't know what hit'm." My remarks were carefree.

Arrow heard me, but suggested, "Let me tell Rocket to keep a couple of the HMMWVs to give you some firepower."

I waved him down again, "It's okay, Major. I told Rocket to keep the Tactical Toyota down there at the staging area. All the other vehicles will meet you in Fort Chiswell in a couple days."

Major Arrow was frustrated with me, but accepted the fact that I was going to keep the unit *very* small. The Tactical Toyota, as I called it, was just that. It was a six-cylinder turbo diesel pickup with armor plating surrounding the fenders and doors. Ballistic glass replaced the stock windows and windshield. A swiveling gun mount housed a Dillon Aero so that a gunner could stand in the rear seat area of the extended cab to fire 360 degrees. The Dillon Aero was a six-barreled Gatling gun that fired so fast it looked like a continuous string of lead being poured from the barrels. I had only seen pictures of the truck, but it looked so cool I had to use it for the Wilmington mission. I only hoped we could do our mission without needing support by something as conspicuous as a minigun. My chief worry was how the tracers themselves would make the truck a target in the seconds after it fired. We knew the

Sandys had significant artillery assets covering the entire city. The opportunity of shooting up a major weapons system like a militia gun truck would be a juicy opportunity that the Sandys would not resist. I counted on their enthusiasm in my plans.

Arrow wished me luck and went about the preparations for his mission. I am sure that to him I was just another annoying militia officer that did not fully understand the importance of what he suggested. But in reality, I agreed with him in principle. We should be hitting the Sandys with 500 men just to have a chance to demolish the ports. Captain Nemo said he had a plan using just his men to get the job done. For the life of me, I couldn't see how he intended to shut down the whole city. Even from what I knew of Wilmington, there were perhaps dozens of docks and ports for all sorts of cargo. How could he ever have enough explosives or the time to damage all the docks? Quite frankly, one of the reasons I chose so few men was simple. The more I thought about it, the more likely it sounded like a one-way trip. There just didn't seem to be a way to survive the mission. Nemo's plan needed to lean heavy on miracles in my opinion.

Training resumed as the next few days passed. The men were more quiet than normal. The intensity turned up as the recruits felt the urgency to get as much information as possible. It was almost as if the men strained to hear shots off in the distance. This of course was impossible, but whenever you walked outside in the dark, people always looked north and stood still.

Couriers from Wytheville brought back copies of maps that were hand drawn by snipers in the observation posts. Fred wrote some letters detailing how the task force set up outposts on the overlooking hills and ran operations from Fort Chiswell. The SF guys made plans for bridge demolition at key positions to shut down the highways. They also made up a preliminary defense strategy for holding off an armored force indefinitely. All indications suggested the green shirts preparing for a major convoy to come through the area quite soon. Luckily for our groups, they had not been spotted by any of the green shirt patrols lurking through the valleys. How long that would last, was another concern.

Seven's spies returned from Blacksburg and Pulaski. The news was not good. In the 24 hour time period our spies were given to scout the towns, almost no militia could be found. The reason was evident when the first groups reported to my office in the new headquarters building.

Seven ushered in a young man and a petite young woman in laborer outfits.

Seven walked through my door. "Huck, one of my teams just got back from Blacksburg. You need to hear this." She introduced them as Jack and Jill, with her eyes daring me to comment on their code names. I tried not to smirk as they walked in.

"Okay, report." I told them.

Jack spoke first. "Around 18:00 the day before yesterday, the courier dropped us off just south of Blacksburg. It took us hours just to get over highway 81. The green shirts have stepped up patrols using aircraft and now they have started to monitor the creek underpasses. We saw crews searching under bridges for signs of demolition, I guess."

I asked, "What made you think they were looking for explosives?"

Jill responded, "Sir, they shined a light on the metal joints of the bridges and looked between the girders to see if anything was there. We saw them do this on one big bridge and some smaller ones that just crossed creeks."

"Okay, proceed," I ordered.

Jack continued again, "The first thing we noticed were the lights on in the houses. We weren't expecting to see the houses all lit up. We were under the impression that the Sandys had shut down the power plant a couple of months ago in that raid we heard about."

Jill piped in, "We made our way into town to find a couple of militia addresses we memorized from our previous contacts. But every place we found was destroyed. They all looked burned to the ground and, from the signs, it looked recent. A couple of the surrounding neighborhoods looked like there had been some fighting as well. Green shirt police are everywhere up there. We tried to stay clear, but every corner had some sort of security. We didn't see any heavy equipment, but there were plenty of squad cars and busses. Our count was 42 special police in various squad cars with only one or two armored vans that they use. Whatever fighting took place was over and done there in town."

Jack must have felt a little insecure because he interrupted Jill, "But sir, what we found out the next day is the kicker. The green shirts were going from house to house making sure the power was on. They wanted the people to use their lights and stuff. We would pass by as groups of green shirts went door to door. When the door opened, the families were instructed to line up on the porch and everyone was scanned using those had-held pads. From the looks of it, they were doing retina scans of all the people. ID cards were swiped, and the busses followed along in the street to pick up anyone who resisted."

I asked, "Were you able to talk with any locals?"

Jill said, "Yes, but everybody is pretty scared up there. They hadn't seen green shirts in force like that in almost a year. The militia had kept them at bay so long; the people had forgotten how harsh the green shirts were. Everybody was really freaked out to talk with outsiders, but I did talk with a woman who was claiming to be on an arrest list. She said she was informed that, due to her age, she would be relocated to a care facility if she could not work in her assigned state job. She also told me that the green shirts mandated internet connectivity in every home and that it looked and felt like the old internet before the crash. All her friends were shopping online with the promise of state credits to pay for everything."

Seven asked Jill, "Were you able to see the internet home pages or anything?"

Jill said, "No. We saw some broadcasts from a distance though. It seems that some of the programming overrides anything else going on in the house or business. From time to time the normal feed stops and a news program or state message flashed up. All the approved-to-be-open businesses have screens for their patrons to watch. We noticed that the monitors all have cameras in them. I wouldn't be surprised if they were doing facial recognition from those cameras to see who goes where and who you are friends with."

"Thanks for the report. Go ahead and give your full debriefing in the Intelligence office," I ordered. Jack and Jill had nothing else earth shattering to report, so they complied and walked over to the Intel department.

Seven stayed behind looking at me. "So the green shirts have changed their tactics a bit. They turn on the power to all the homes and mandate internet access. The people unwittingly shop and do searches on their home computers like they did before. The internet looks and feels the same as it did before the crash. What's the harm?"

I completed her thought. "You have no idea that everyone in your address book just got sent to the snapshot system. Every search you did back then, and now, is monitored and recorded for your personal digital profile. All the emails that they could not see before are now accessible because the power is back on. How hard would it be to round up every potential dissident in an entire city? Snapshot would have enough data in a matter of hours to identify the most likely threats to *public safety*."

Seven added, "They give you enough rope to hang yourself, and you end up tying the knot."

I thought out loud. "I bet they shut the power off once they are done. Or perhaps they will shut down everything but the community service centers. Remember that in our town? Then they will grab every worker they can to go work in their factories. The age thing seems to be cropping up over and over, doesn't it?"

Seven stood by with her arms folded. "Now that you mention it, yeah. Every time we get reports, there are very few people over fifty left walking around. Everybody we run into is young, for the most part."

I sat back in my chair and commented, "It's part of the *whole lives* program they spelled out years ago. The very young and the very old should not take up disproportionate resources against the value of their labor. In other words, you are valuable as long as you produce."

Seven and I paused, looking at each other, thinking. Seven broke the silence. "When are you heading to the staging area?"

Her approach was tactful and measured. She wanted me to know that she was aware of my decision to go to Wilmington. She knew she couldn't talk me out of it and was not going to try. Her eyes were filled with tears. We hugged after she rounded the desk.

"Maybe four days, no more than a week though," I told her.

She covered her face and sobbed for a minute. This was not normal for her and I attributed it to baby hormones for the most part. I was also well aware that she was scared to death of the Wilmington operation. She knew how strategic operations went most of the time. Men died on those jobs and there was no way around it. She knew how hard it would be to shut down Wilmington.

We went home that night and did not speak of the war or the 3rd militia that night. We just needed some time away from things as much as possible.

The next day was just about like the days before. The weather was still cold and skies were filled with clouds. First thing in the morning I had my security truck escort me to a house near Wooten Valley. We drove up to the front porch as faces looked through aging windows needing a fresh coat of paint. As I stepped onto the porch I could hear boots rushing on hardwood floors inside.

I knocked on the door. "It the Colonel. Can I come in?"

A single pair of footsteps came to the door and turned the knob. As the door swung open, a line of men stood at attention. It was early in the morning and their appearance showed it. Most of the men were in sweats and various cold weather underwear. Wet clothes dried by a fire that popped and crackled in the wood stove in the corner. The house was full of gear. M1 carbines were lined by the door with magazines at the ready. Most of these men must have just come back from night exercises from the look of things.

I marched into the room and looked among the men until I saw the face I was looking for. "Opie, at 10:00 hours, I want your squad to report to logistics warehouse number two. I am assigning you guys some extra duties. Say goodbye to the nice dry farm house, you won't be coming back any time soon. Bring all your gear."

Opie looked at me. "Yes, sir. *My* squad, sir?"

I eyed the men I knew from the sniper range. "That's what it sounded like to me. See you there at some point later today."

I turned on the spot and marched out of the front door. As my boots clunked down the steps, I heard voices from the house hooting at Opie's promotion. I smiled to the security detail as we loaded back into my truck and headed for another day of work.

By 10:00, I had the official ceremony to assign my second in command. Major Crackerjack Bushing was assigned the official duties and responsibilities of second in command of 3rd Battalion 1st Army Group. We had a ceremony there in the new headquarters building with all the major staff. This was done for several reasons. One, the men needed a firm command structure before we took on both major operations. I wanted everyone to be clear on their roles and responsibilities. Most officers by then realized we were not hitting Wilmington in strength. I think a good portion of the men did as well. But not many asked me about it, because they knew we were doing things quietly for a reason. You don't live through green shirt occupation and go flapping your gums about stuff. You tend to take things as they come and you gut through whatever comes your way. I must say, it was impressive to see such fortitude out of people that had grown up in comfort their whole lives. By comfort, I mean running water, televisions, electricity, and cars.

By noon I made my way to the logistics warehouse to find my "Mayberry" squad. Logistics warehouse number two was used to support the loading of all the trucks and men that had already gone to Wytheville. What remained was almost nothing. About six tables stood in an empty floor right in the middle between all the loading bays for trucks. In the corner lay several of those big green plastic deployment containers that it takes two to four men to lift.

I walked through the doors as my security detail followed behind. "Gentlemen, how are you today?"

Opie and the men said, "Good, sir." Each of them stood at attention.

I walked up to them and shook all their hands. As I did this, I spoke out loud to the whole group. "Men, I have a confession. You are not assigned warehouse duty. Rather, I have a job opportunity for you. I cannot tell you what it is until we talk things over. First, I am not ordering you for this mission. It is a volunteer mission because it will be extremely dangerous. Anybody that has a family to support, or for any other reason, can back out now with no hard feelings. I am serious about that, gentlemen. Nobody here will think differently about you because you opt out. But if you choose to come with the rest of us, we may change the power structure of the entire war."

The men took my words to heart and looked from man to man in each other's faces. They knew I was not kidding about the danger. All seven stood still and nodded that they were in.

I looked at them and could feel the surge of adrenaline they were all experiencing.

I continued, "Okay then, your in. From now on I am Huck. Behind me are T-Rex and Shady, my personal security detail. Shady was Army before the war and did a lot of personal protection contracting in Iraq. He is also our chief combat medic. We call him shady because he always wears those freakin sunglasses. Beside him is T-Rex. T-Rex was also ex-military and served as a contractor in Iraq and Afghanistan. He has personally inspected more whore-houses than anyone in Southeast Asia."

The men laughed. I even got a chuckle out of T-Rex, which was rare. I called out Opie front and center then had him introduce each of the men one by one. As he did so, I gave them their new code names for the mission. Oh yes, I gave them all new names like we did for every special mission. My Mayberry squad had Opie, Andy, Barney, Floyd, Gomer, Howard, and Otis.

Half the men though I was kidding until I barked my first orders, "Ok men first things first. Each man take a table and stow you gear bags on it. Spread out so we have five or six feet between each table, you are going to need the room."

The men scrambled around as if their butts were on fire. The legs of the metal tables screeched across the concrete floor as the men went about their tasks. T-Rex found another two tables stacked in a corner and brought them over with one hand. Did I mention that T-Rex was a big guy? Yeah, he was someone that played some college football for a while. He didn't get in many fights because the look of him sobered most other men.

Shady picked up where I left off according to our plan. "Everybody that has an M1 carbine, bring it to this table. That includes your magazines and chest harness' too. Bring whatever carbine ammo you have as well. If you have a personal pistol, magazines, and ammo, stack them on the table over here."

The team looked more than a little surprised at the request.

Andy spoke up, "Huck, do you want our sniper rifles too?"

Shady looked to him. "Not now. Leave them at your tables." I nodded in agreement.

T-Rex helped men carry armloads of gear over to the table where they unceremoniously piled it. It was a collection that would have made any gun-nut drool at the mouth. All the men completed the task and looked around as if they had just been emasculated.

T-Rex and Shady walked briskly to the far wall and beckoned the team to lend a hand. They all did so and carried the containers back over to the mostly-empty tables. Locks on the latches were cut off and the contents revealed. Inside was a warrior's toy box. Each container revealed one treasure after another. Flattop M4 rifles with ACOG TA-31 illuminated-reticle scopes lined the interior of one case. Each rifle had a sound suppressor. They were not silencers per se, but they took out flash and made the gun less ear abusive when it fired. Another case held three M249 squad automatic machineguns along with specialized OTIS cleaning kits and spare barrel packs. Another case contained stacks of Tactical Assault Gear (T.A.G.) plate carriers with dozens of various magazine and grenade pouches. A dozen M9 Berettas with boxes of magazines came with Safariland drop-leg holsters. Each man was instructed to grab his own gear and start the process of fitting the gear to the person. Shady brought in a large cardboard box of camo clothing that had just been procured from our logistics department. Each man was issued two sets of new olive drab BDU pants and shirts. I would have preferred multicam, but it was a miracle that we were able to supply these men with anything at all in the way of camo clothing. All camo had long since been scarfed up.

I announced to the men, "T-Rex will carry one of the M249s. We will all cross train on the M249 over the next few days as we do squad exercises. We will need two Mayberry volunteers for the other gunner positions. Go beg T-Rex, but in the end, he will have the last say on who gets it."

The men were busily fitting their first-class assault gear when two SUVS pulled into the parking lot. This got Shady's attention as he walked to the doors to peer through the small windows. He slung his rifle and worked the manual stop on the garage doors. He pulled the chain until the large door lifted off the floor allowing the trucks to roll into the massive warehouse. Their lights flashed across the men as we stood and watched the trucks park. As the bay door closed, the doors of both vehicles opened as the men from Arrow's team climbed out.

I took the opportunity to introduce everyone. "Men these are some of Arrow's boy's from Bragg. Each one of them is an experienced operator and soldier. They are here to help us train and they will also accompany us on the mission." The men shook hands and greeted one another quickly.

I addressed Arrow's men, "You haven't been given a squad of cherry, cake-eating civilians here either. These guys fought one of the longest running battles of the war to date. These are the surviving squad members of 2nd platoon, 5th company from the King's Mountain operation. They shot more Sandys than most other people have seen. And they did it with hunting rifles." The SF soldiers took the news in stride. They would be more impressed when the training started.

I continued, "We are hereby sequestered from all other units until we deploy. We will train together, eat together, and share toilets. Our mission is critically important to the war, and if we succeed, we will stop the Sandys from landing a major force on our east coast. We are shutting down the port city of Wilmington."

There was silence until the militia man I code-named Andy looked around, counting, then asked, "Just the 16 of us?" He pointed to us standing around the tables.

I took the opportunity and said, "Oh no. We have several of Rocket's drivers and couriers, as well as Captain Nemo's SEALs. We might have 40 total."

Otis looked a bit worried. "Shut down *all* the ports in Wilmington? Forty of us?" He couldn't believe what he was hearing. "Don't the Sandys have thousands of their top soldiers in Wilmington?"

I looked him dead in the eyes. "They do. Reports tell us they may have as many as 5,000 troops down there. They have artillery, several light tanks, APCs, and every bit of Russian armament you can imagine." Everybody took in what I said and thought about it hard.

Finally, one of the SF soldiers asked, "How do you want us to split up for training, Colonel?"

I looked over to him and said, "We are going to do things backwards, so please bear with me a moment. When it comes time for the operation, The SF guys will be first squad, the Mayberry gang will be 2nd, and my team will be 3rd squad. I want to do this because I want you to operate with people you know and trust. We are not going to rebuild teams in three or four days. But I do want the Special Forces guys to share what they know on a one on one setting. Over the next three days, we are going to pair off man for man so that the militia guys get a feel for how you do things in SF. Consider the next few days as a final exam for the militia and a refresher for the SF guys."

Opie looked at the numbers and I could see the math was not working out for him. "Huck, there are seven of us and six of them."

I looked at him. "That's because I'm going to be your spotter. For training you will be a part of 3rd squad so you can get a feel for how I do things."

Opie's eyes widened. "You are going to be *my*...spotter?" I nodded back in the affirmative as he looked around at his team. Several men chuckled at his reaction.

"Alright; finish up here in the next hour and we will start vehicle drills between drone cycles," I ordered.

I collected an M9 and M4 like everyone else so we would all have the ability to share ammo and magazines on our mission. My intention was to carry the Thor with the M4 as a backup slung across my back. With my gear packed, I wrote a note thanking Arrow for the great job he had done supplying us with the best gear available. I only hoped we could make it work well enough to give the Sandys a royal up-yours when the time came.

That afternoon, the teams practiced loading and unloading SUVs, pickups (gun trucks), and various cars. Part of that training included how to carry your rifle while in the vehicle as well as everyone's zones of fire during ambush situations. Training halted briefly during supper and regularly scheduled drone fly-byes. Drills resumed after night fell so the same lessons could be repeated in the dark. It is like starting all over again when you add the difficulties with doing tasks in the dark. Once satisfied with our progress, the team stopped for the night. We rolled out our bedding and slept in the warehouse.

The next morning started with physical training from the Army manual. For us militia, it was a smoke session. The SF guys worked out according to their regular routine after the rest of us tried to throw up our breakfast. I swear some of those guys could eat a plate of bacon and eggs while running ten miles. I don't know how they did it.

The second day of training took place on an empty farm where we practiced with the M4s. Each team member marked his M4 as his own and zeroed the rifle at 100 yards. From there we drilled in team reaction tactics. The militia men had just gone through the basic course and surprised the SF guys with their proficiency. In fact, they did so well our SF team leader suggested we cut our rifle work short and start door breeching techniques. We also drilled on room clearing techniques and how to stack in hallways. It was a cram course in urban warfare. The day was long and hard as we crashed back into the warehouse where supper waited for us. One of Rocket's couriers handed me a message bag as we sat around the tables for dinner. Between slurps and grunts from hungry men, I read. We were thankful to be inside after a long day of training outside. Winter was not friendly due to the dark gray rains that had been keeping us miserable all day. The courier left with promises to return for my response in an hour.

A note from Data caught my attention so I read it aloud to the men sitting at the tables.

"Hey fellas, listen to this. It's a note from Data."

The note read:

"The Psy-Ops mission is working like a champ. The Sandys are going nuts over the messages we implanted on the green shirt internet. They are flipping out over the anti-Muslim photos like you wouldn't believe. They are so pissed there have been some un-coded messages out in the open as they rant and rave over what they think is green shirt treachery. The PPR is already scolding the governor in an official capacity. The Sandys have requested the green shirts stop all work at the Raleigh airport and pull back all drones anywhere near Sandy held territory."

The team cheered at the news. I must admit, it was no small victory. We had just convinced the Sandys how the green shirts were severely insulting them before they could even land their forces.

Unfortunately, there was no update on the Wytheville operation due to green shirt activity in the area. This was common more often than not. Our couriers were trained to make runs as it was prudent or tactically necessary. Our idea was to keep as low of a profile as possible before our attack.

The outside of the message packet had Seven's writing. "*I miss you already*." We had said our goodbyes the night before and I will not chronicle those conversations. Those are private.

The third day of training touched on demolition equipment. The SF guys wanted us to know how to work each of the detonators so we could operate them in a pinch. Halfway through the third day, I took the opportunity to stop our cross training and put the men back in their normal groups. We finished with an easy day and stopped our training for the upcoming mission. I wanted men that were well rested, fed, and hydrated before this mission. Even if things went well, the physical hardship would take its toll on us all.

Late in the evening, a motorcycle courier sped up to the outside doors of the warehouse and hastily parked. The rider rushed through the doorway as we prepared to bed down for the night.

"Where is the Colonel?" the courier asked out of breath. You could hear him across the warehouse. Everyone was on alert in an instant. Men sat up in their sleeping bags to see what was going on.

"I'm over here," I told the young rider with a wave.

He ran to me with a bag in his hands, "Sir, this just came from headquarters."

I opened the bag and read the single page of hand written notes. The contents were simple.

They read:

Operation Rockslide began one hour ago. (That was the official name of the Wytheville mission)

Have units reporting to your warehouse in ten minutes, recommend your team proceed to staging area.

Good luck.

3rd Battalion acting C.O.

I looked up from the note, "Gentlemen we have to find a new place to sleep. Pack up your gear; we are moving out in ten minutes. Move the trucks to the side south side of the parking lot so they won't get stuck in the yard. This warehouse will be crawling with hundreds of men and dozens of trucks in the next fifteen minutes."

My men scurried to grab all their gear. Men crammed sleeping bags with spare gear into deployment bags. Within the ten minute limit, my entire team fired up our SUVs, and cargo truck as the first militia units reported to the warehouse. I waved to the operations officers as they pulled into the parking lot among a string of panel trucks and semis waiting to load men. The officers looked to me and saluted, knowing we would not see each other until our operations were over.

In the back of my mind, I wondered if any of us would make it back to North Wilkesboro. We were really sticking our necks out on these missions. If operation Rockslide failed, the green shirts would have an open lane to roll in troops throughout free territory. Our only hope was that our offensive would catch the green shirts and Sandys completely off guard. My little family was all that really mattered, though. As long as I could come back to Seven and our little Punkin, nothing else mattered.

We pulled off the main road and killed the lights as we headed east towards the first relay point and our fate.

Chapter 20
On your mark, get ready....

We drove for a couple of hours before one of the trucks flashed his lights. The other SUVs did not see the flash and continued down the dark road as we stopped on the shoulder. Radios were too risky to use and this was a side effect by not having direct communication. I jumped out of the lead SUV and walked back to the stopped truck, "What's up?" I asked amid the engine noise.

"Sir, we have to shift people around. The guys are freezing back there."

I looked to the men climb off the back of the truck nearly frozen. I said, "Guys, go get in my truck. Send the others back here so you warm up for a while. All we have to do is get to the first rally point. We will steal one of Rocket's vehicles when we get there."

Opie volunteered, "Huck, I will ride back there with you too." The doors closed as the rest of us climbed into the back of the truck among the gear bags. By the time the truck got to speed, we were huddled as low as possible to get under the gear bags and away from the wind. Good God that was a cold night for riding in the back of the truck.

Opie sat beside me as we froze riding along the road. "Huck, is everything okay?"

I said loudly over the wind, "Yes as far as I know. Operation Rockslide started a day early. Don't know what caused it."

Opie's face reflected the interior lights of the truck as they shined through the back window. "Sir? What do you think of our chances?" The other men tried to look as if they weren't listening.

I told Opie vaguely, "By the time we are done, the Sandys will not be able to land their invasion force in Wilmington. Nemo has a plan that we won't get to see until we get to the staging area."

The man I coded, Otis, spoke up. "How long before we get there?"

I looked back to him and yelled against the wind, "Another hour or two. Why?"

Otis said, "I gotta pee." He wasn't kidding either.

Let's just say that we had him stand in the bed of that truck and face backward over the tailgate. I could only imagine someone seeing that sight as they looked out of their window, a whole load of militia barreling down the road with a man taking a leak off the back of the truck.

Sometime in the very early morning, we reached our first objective. The posts directed us to a secluded parking lot behind a couple of derelict buildings. As we parked among the other SUVs, armed security guards replaced the gate across the driveway. The gate itself was heavily camouflaged to make it look like the driveway was completely inaccessible.

The SF men greeted us and we explained our switched seating. "We had some guys freezing and needed to rotate the men."

The man we called Floyd chimed in, "Otis got to pee off the back of the truck as we rode in." He meant it to be a funny thing that would get people's attention.

One of the SF guys looked completely un-impressed. "I took a crap out of a HUMVEE window right in the middle of downtown Baghdad. We couldn't stop then either."

Floyd looked horrified at the mental image. "Really?"

"Yep."

We got our gear and made our way to the building as directed by a militia security guard holding an M1 carbine. The inside of the building was a lot different than the outside. There were tables and chairs for close to 200 men. The place was not what you would call clean, but it was not by anyone's definition, dirty. Lamps had been freshly lit which made the interior of the massive floor-space usable.

I asked the security guard, "Is this your post?"

He responded, "Yeah, we busted our butts to get this place all set up and some head honcho takes all our trucks. How are we supposed to get 500 people through here a night with no freakin trucks?"

Floyd was just about to give away my identity so I clapped him on the shoulder to shut him up. I quickly said to the guard, "Those officers up there in North Wilkesboro really take the prize, don't they?"

The guard thought he was in safe company as he said, "Don't get me started. All this cloak and dagger stuff; it's for the birds. Any green shirt shows up, I will wear him out with my carbine."

The men sat back listening to this bravado as if they were entertained. Most of the SF guys were spread across two tables with their feet in opposite chairs trying to get some rest.

I looked to the guard and asked, "Who's in charge around here?"

The guy puffed up his chest a bit and said loudly, "Some hot shot kid they call, Rocket. He should be here any time now." The guard wanted to look tuff for the Army guys, I think, and demanded, "You boys don't get too comfortable there. We have 500 men coming through here tonight and this place will be packed. You guys move out to the back of the room." With that he kicked the chair of the nearest SF soldier as he sat with his eyes closed and arms folded.

Just as the SF soldier sprang to his feet, I rushed over to keep the guard from becoming a greasy spot on the floor. By the time I took two steps the metal entrance door opened loudly and in strode Rocket with a pair of other men behind him.

Rocket looked at me, "Colonel, good to see you."

I looked back to the guard as recognition flushed his face red. The SF soldier flicked him in the skull which made a dull thwack before he sat back down.

Rocket and I shook hands as I said, "We were just listening to the heroics of your security here, Rocket."

"Sir, can I have a word with you in private?"

We walked out of earshot. "What is it Rocket?"

"Sir, how are things going in Wytheville?" he asked.

"Don't know. We just got the word that the operation started. I haven't seen a message since then." I told him.

Rocket looked concerned. "What do you want me to do?"

I thought for a second. "Do you have any extra vehicles and drivers?"

Rocket said, "Yeah, I left enough to take you and your men throughout the network until you get to the staging area. Nemo has his men there and the equipment that didn't get sent to Wytheville. The rest of my drivers left for Fort Chiswell a few hours ago."

"Good," I told him. "All we need is enough men to escort us along the safest routes so we can get as close to the staging area before morning."

"What then?" Rocket asked.

That was his real question all along. What were my plans for *him*?

Rocket listened as I said, "I see from your people, they don't know the whole story here, which is good. We need to keep it that way for now. I need you and three others to make the last leg of our trip with us. Send the rest of your couriers back along the routes to stand by so they can run messages and ferry us back when this is all done."

Rocket understood and we got the men going again. Within 15 minutes we had our vehicles refueled and offers were made for the truck bed riders to tag along with the couriers in nice warm cars. I had the misfortune of riding in a Mustang whose driver thought that incredibly loud smasher-style heavy metal was good for keeping awake during his speeding sessions. By the time we reached the second station, my eardrums were numb.

None of us reached the second rally point together. Half the vehicles took a separate route which was longer by 20 minutes. The building was similar to the one we had stopped at before. The exterior looked like a place where missiles had been tested. But the inside had massive amounts of seating for only the 16 of us. I hated all the work that was wasted to prepare these places for hundreds of men only to have us sitting all by ourselves in the quiet.

Rocket and the next set of drivers looked over a map as the rest of us tried to sleep. After a little while, I got up and walked to the table where they sat.

Rocket asked a courier, "Is the northern route open, then?"

The guy pointed, "Well, I don't know. Jackrabbit saw a green shirt squad car up there about midnight."

Rocket thought for a second then said, "It's getting too close to daytime to try the southern route. They usually have their convoy move through in about an hour. That won't work."

"Problems, Rocket?" I asked sleepily.

"Well sir, there was some green shirt activity through the quiet routes last night. It might be clear, but it is hard to say for sure."

I asked point blank, "Is it safe to move?"

One of the smart mouthed couriers answered, "Nothing is safe with green shirts around."

I asked him, annoyed, "Would you like to take point on the next run then, Sparky?" We were all a little tired and the stress of trying to guess the safest route had us all on edge. Knowing the Wytheville operation was underway and hearing no word from them, wasn't helping either. While we stood there I decided not to push the situation any further with all of us so tired. I ordered, "Send out motorcycle scouts on all routes when the sun comes up. Rotate the watch and we will choose the best route when things are clear. For now, everybody get some rest."

Rocket had the men stand down for several hours so they could sleep. The sentries were rotated and we slept as best we could. By midday the scouts were back on the road searching for anything that would be a threat to our trucks. Rocket had us switch out of our militia Ford F350 with utility body, for one of his vehicles. He gave us a panel truck which would blend in with the local civilian traffic common to the area. His couriers had fake green shirt travel papers just in case they were stopped.

Between scouting runs, I noticed that a couple of the motorcycle scouts were using what I called super bikes that were not camouflaged. The riders claimed that they fit in a bit better without their bikes looking all tactical. It was weird for me to see so much civilian traffic on the roads nowadays. I say civilian because a lot of the vehicles were not armed. The green shirts had passed laws that prohibited just anybody traveling at will like we did before. If you left town, there had to be an official purpose that somehow served the state in some fashion. Checkpoints at main intersections determined if each vehicle had the right people with the proper authorization to travel to specific destinations. Most on and off ramps leading to the major interstate highways were closed to traffic all together. When a vehicle approached a check point it was time stamped with a card the driver had to keep on hand. When that vehicle got off the highway the card was scanned into the system and you were logged off the road. Nothing was left to chance. Thankfully, that level of restriction was applied to the major cities and the interstate highways between them. The rural roads were free for the most part. All we had to worry about were the occasional green shirt patrols or convoys that passed through at irregular schedules.

By the time night fell, the scouts reported all routes clear. With our gear all tucked away in a panel truck, I thanked Rocket. "You have done a great job here, Rocket. I know that it is a real let down now that the Wilmington operation is not coming in force, but I am confident the places you prepared would have been perfect." I shook his hand with as much appreciation as I could relay to him.

Rocket looked at me while nobody was within ear shot. "Colonel Huck, I will bring the F350 to the staging area myself in a day or two. We will be ready to bring you guys back."

I clapped him on the shoulder and said, "You do that. But as soon as you drop us off, have your men clear out of here. Use the Intelligence safe-houses near the waypoint stations and check them every 12 hours. Whatever you do, don't linger around Wilmington. Drop us off and leave."

Rocket knew me well enough to understand the direct order I had given him. He was a good man and I didn't want him to stick his neck out for us if our mission failed. Our plan B did not allow for people to be anywhere near that city, or else.

Our vehicles took several different routes that night. Some swept off to the north. Others followed a more direct path. Somehow, I got in the back of the panel truck to ride along with the equipment. I wasn't the only one, several of the SF guys mixed in with me and a few of the Mayberry gang. It was just too conspicuous to see a whole SUV full of men riding somewhere together.

It had only been an hour into our ride when we hit some traffic. We drove along loaded down with the various weapons, grenades, gear all of which would get you a one-way ticket to green shirt hell if they caught us. We could see lights from other cars shine under the rear door of the truck. It was spooky knowing that anyone outside the wall of that truck was actively incentivized to point out militia in green shirt territory. In fact, if the regular citizen did not report seeing us, they would suffer the same fate as us. Public hangings were becoming things of legend in the areas surrounding the green shirt utopian cities.

Traffic stopped dead. Those of us in the back were on edge because the driver beeped his horn twice, then paused, and beeped the horn once more. That was our signal to remain quiet. We were coming up on a green shirt check point. Rocket's team was supposed to have given us a clear route. How could this be? If they opened the back of this truck, we would have to fight our way out. The men and I in the back donned our tactical vests in near silence and readied our weapons. There could be anything out there. The green shirts might have armored cars, concrete K-rails blocking the road, anything. Maybe they knew we were coming. Maybe Rocket's security had been compromised. None of this was good. We sweated in the dark, waiting for the slightest sign of trouble. Every sound of the following traffic made us look left or right in anticipation.

Minutes crept by at such a slow pace, I was sure we had been there hours. My watch said we had been in traffic 15 minutes. It must have stopped due to my freakin irregular heartbeat is all I could figure. The six of us in the back of the truck kneeled in two rows facing the rear door. Cardboard boxes had been placed on pallets just behind the doors so that we would have a chance to use them as cover if we were discovered by an inspection. None of us wanted there to be a gun battle though. We would be the fish in the barrel as it were. Our only hope was to charge headlong into whoever opened that rear door and shoot everyone in sight. Minutes ticked by.

Over the hum of the trucks diesel engine, a voice could be heard from the road on the driver's side. "Let's see your manifest and travel orders."

Our driver sat in the cab and talked through the truck's window, "Yeah, I got it here."

Seconds passed by as those of us in the back listened for the faintest hint of trouble. Search lights shown through tiny cracks in the truck's side. This could be a large intersection if they had roadside lights working off of portable generators.

The green shirt officer's voice was that of a younger man, possibly mid-twenties. He said, "Your travel orders expired yesterday! You have to get these renewed when you don't use them." His tone was one of annoyance rather than suspicion.

My driver stammered for a second. "The truck broke down and I had to get someone to replace the radiator hose. My supervisor told me I had to make this delivery or he would kick my butt."

The green shirt officer said harshly, "Pull over to the side and let these people go by."

My driver put the truck in gear and we moved slowly over to the shoulder. The fear in the back of the truck was mounting. Nobody dared breathe because it might have made too much noise. The truck pulled over and stopped again. You could hear two sets of boots walk to the driver's door.

An older voice asked, "Okay, what is the problem here?"

The younger officer said, "Their travel orders are expired."

There was a pause. The older voice directed his question to my driver, "What are you doing on the road tonight without the proper travel permits?"

The cab door was opened and my driver was being hauled out of his seat as he pleaded, "The truck broke. I had to get it fixed." It sounded like they were pushing him around. The older voice barked at the passenger of our truck who was Opie, "You sit tight, boy!"

Opie sat silently. Our driver continued, "Our supervisor told us we had to deliver this truck to the warehouse or else."

The older officer's voice was demanding, but not overly so. It was as if this was all some sort of regular routine with him. A set of boots walked to the back of the truck, which got our attention. If they opened the back, a gun fight would be the result.

About that time, we could hear Opie call out to our driver, "Oh, give him the jars why don't ya?"

Everybody paused. The man at the back of the truck stopped to listen.

The older man's voice asked, "What jars?"

Opie continued as if talking to the driver, who was silent. "You know, the stuff we get from old pappy. You aren't supposed to have it anyway."

Our driver played it up. "Shut up kid. Those are the last two jars in the whole county. It's mine. You can't get it no more."

The older voice demanded now, "Where are these jars?"

The man that was at the back of the truck walked towards the cab. His footsteps crunched rocks as he walked on the shoulder of the road beside our parked truck. The sounds nearly echoed against the metal side walls. It made the hair on the back of our necks stand straight up as he passed by only inches from us.

The younger voice said, "Look at that! When you shake it, the bubbles are tiny. It must be 80-proof or better."

The older voice forcefully said, "You can't have contraband liquor on this road! Give me that!"

I heard the sounds of a nylon backpack sliding across the truck's vinyl seat. What I did not hear was the sound of breaking glass from mason jars.

Finally the older voice ordered our driver to get back in his cab and get out of his sight. There were warnings and rebukes, but nothing further.

Within 30 seconds of handing over the illegal liquor, we passed through the checkpoint and continued east. As the lights dimmed in the background, those of us in the back sat against the truck's walls to breathe deeply for the first time in ages.

One of the guys exclaimed, "I thought we were going to have to fight our way out of there." Sweat poured from his forehead as he leaned back. The rest of the trip was uneventful as we drove down dark road after dark road.

By late in the night, or rather not so early in the morning, our truck came to a halt. Darkness was giving way to light off to the east as the sun was daring to peek over the horizon.

The driver and Opie opened the rear door along a nondescript section of woods that was still fairly thick even for winter.

The driver told us, "The staging area building is straight through the woods about 200 yards. Rocket told to me to drop you here and let you walk the rest of the way. He didn't want the truck to be seen coming and going out of the parking lot."

The rest of the men started to unload the bags of gear as I looked at the driver. "That was a close one back there at the checkpoint."

His response was not what I expected. "Colonel, the local green shirt highway patrol likes to set up those roadblocks as a way to make some extra money. They were just looking for something to steal."

Opie walked around the side of the truck and heard our conversation. "Yeah, we worked out the whole mason jar thing about 20 minutes after leaving the warehouse last night."

I looked to the two of them. "You sure had the rest of us pissing our pants. Thanks for that!"

A sentry from the staging area hurried us along as he grabbed a bag to get us moving. He said we needed to get inside just in case there was a passerby walking down the street. I noticed as we walked through the woods, the air was much warmer this close to the coast. You could tell it was winter, but you didn't feel like you would freeze to death 20 seconds after getting out of the truck.

The staging area was another large structure that looked like it had been bombed out and left for scrap metal from the outside. The woods behind the building contained a secluded parking area not visible from any road I could see. The lot was empty for the most part. Weeds grew waist high between the sections of asphalt. It looked desolate and completely deserted.

As we neared the building, the sentry led us under a section of tin roof that appeared to have collapsed. As we walked under, I could see there were several vehicles parked underneath and out of sight. The tactical Toyota and two of Arrow's HUMVEEs were parked under camo netting. We rounded a few corners and were ushered into the red brick building itself. Like the other facilities, this one was nothing like what you would expect before you walked through the door. The interior was dark even though the sun was up outside. The windows were shrouded from the inside with what seemed like shadow boxes. From the outside of the window, it looked like the room was full of trash and debris. Nobody would ever guess this place was intact. There were rows and rows of various cots and beds in a very neat grid patterns on the floor. We could have housed hundreds of men easily in this place. I made a mental note to thank Rocket and his team once again for all the effort even though it was completely wasted.

I walked further into the room among men with gear strewn about the bunks. I didn't know any of them, which felt strange after working with the Army guys and my militia team so closely.

They must feel the same way about us. Their eyes watched us as we lugged our gear into the massive room. In the opposite corner I saw lights and a gaggle of the Army SF personnel sitting around tables eating breakfast.

Once again my truck was the last to arrive and we looked like a group of heavily armed vagabonds.

"Colonel, Captain Nemo is in the operations office there. He said to come on in when you got here."

I looked down at the Army soldier who was digging into an MRE packet. "What's for breakfast?"

He slurped the brownish gunk down and said "Beef enchilada, breakfast of champions."

Suddenly I was not as hungry as I thought I was. I dropped my gear on the last row of bunks and walked into what used to be the office of the warehouse before the lights went out, before the war. I could hear a portable generator humming along almost inaudible in a room on the opposite side of the corridor. They must have the exhaust vented because I could not smell any fumes.

I walked into an interior room that was packed with PCs, various radios, and cabling that led to a parabolic dish antenna outside. The room had six men inside already as Opie and I walked through the door.

Nemo looked up from his map as men on either side of him pointed to references with pencils. The table was littered with notes and highlighted sections of data. The walls held various pictures of specific structures and what looked like blueprints of flat-bottomed boats of some kind.

Nemo smiled. "Colonel Huck, good to see you made it here in one piece." The other two men simply nodded at our presence without saying anything. Nemo continued to give the men at his side instructions for a couple of minutes as Opie and I stood there and took it all in. There were mounds of information and pictures from Wilmington. Somebody had flicked about a million digital pictures in my estimation. Some of the images were thermally enhanced and from a vantage point at least 5,000 feet above ground. Most likely they came from UAVs. There was even an old tourist map lying on a side table with the North Carolina seal and state bird on the front. Opie pointed out the map to me and opened it up see what was history. The Sandys had been in Wilmington so long, I was betting that nothing was the same any more.

Nemo finished and the two men he had been talking to left the room with their orders. Nemo stood and stretched, then said, "Huck, sorry for the wait. We have an operation going on. The team is on their way back. We had to use a couple of the couriers to help get the men back here. They should be back within the hour, though."

I looked at Nemo. "What operation?"

Nemo pointed to the wall full of pictures. "This bridge, the Cape Fear Memorial, over the Cape Fear River. It links downtown to the outside world." Nemo swept his hand over the roadway. "Highways 17, 421, 76, all merge at this intersection and cross over that bridge. I have a team scouting the outposts at the intersection and the bridge itself."

I studied the pictures closely and saw a lot of changes since the last time I had driven through Wilmington. We used to drive through on our way to some of the beaches on the coast like Carolina, Kure, or Fort Fisher. Now the roadways were completely blocked. There was no driving anywhere near downtown Wilmington. The Sandys had the roads blocked with serious amounts of firepower behind concrete and steel abatements. Foreign made tanks lined the critical highway overpasses in re-enforced tank pits. These pits allowed the turret to cover the surrounding area without exposing the rest of the tank. More pictures on the wall showed anti-aircraft guns mounted to the roofs of tall buildings. Other pictures showed buildings being used as barracks, new Mosque construction, artillery pieces in protected fighting positions, and various outposts along the major highways. It was overwhelming and my face must have shown it.

Nemo stated, "It's amazing to see how far they have come in such a short time."

Opie was speechless and I was only able to get out, "Yeah." Where was Fred when I needed someone to blab something completely inappropriate? Then it occurred to me to ask, "What have you heard about the Wytheville operation? We know it started, but none of the couriers have come back with any updates."

Nemo turned to a PC screen that was blacked out. He typed a few keys and the screen lit with a map and overlay that someone had been working on. Nemo pointed to some lines. "Here is a map we copied from the green shirt database about three hours ago. According to this, your militia force has taken a section of highway 81, from the town of Wytheville, all the way to the intersection of highway 77. The green shirts have lost all communication with the town as well as their advanced scout unit that was sent two days ago."

I looked at Nemo. "How in the world did you get this? I thought all land line communications were strictly forbidden." My tone was accusatory and slightly heated.

Nemo raised his hand as if to calm me. "I chose to burn one of my assets to do this. It was a satellite burst transceiver request that was done from a sat-uplink on a one-time channel. They can't trace it."

I hoped he was right because even with my engineering background, how he had done what he said he had done, was a complete mystery to me.

Opie looked down at the screen. "Can you see what the green shirt plans are from this map?"

Nemo looked as concerned as I felt. "I can see what they saw about three hours ago, but not really more than that. We haven't gotten any word from the operation, either. But that is not necessarily bad. We can't have couriers running around in and out of this building or else we will draw more attention than we can handle."

I didn't like not knowing about such an operation with so many of my people involved. To me it meant more than just who was winning or losing. My friends were fighting up there and I was not beside them for the battle.

I stated to Nemo, "Last we heard, the Sandys were freaking out over the disinformation stuff you guys put out."

Nemo looked relieved at the change of topic and reached for a stack of papers. "Here, look at these. These are copies of official PPR memos between the Secretary of the Republic (Jones) to the global PPR parliament just yesterday. The Sandys are livid, and the green shirts have already executed a dozen or so of their own people trying to pacify the rising tensions. The green shirt drones have been pulled back with threats that they will be shot down if they get anywhere near Sandy-held territory. The Sandys have also issued expulsion orders for all green shirt officers in their territories. In general, the tensions are so high; anything could start a shooting war between the Sandys and the green shirts. It is that delicate."

I looked at Nemo. "I have a few ideas on how we can help start that fire, too." Nemo was now the curious one.

Nemo folded his arms and asked, "Okay, how do you propose we do that?"

I pointed to the map on the wall. "The couriers and scouts have dodged a couple of Sandy helicopters around the former Raleigh Durham airport."

One of Nemo's aids added, "Yes, they are running a regular patrol to check on the status of the airport since the disinformation campaign. They don't trust the green shirts to use the place for commercial traffic only."

I pointed to the road on the southern end of the western-most runway. "We take about six satchel charges on a couple of motorcycles and stage them off in the woods before the next patrol. As the Sandy's helicopter does its flyby, our guys get onto the runway and drop the charges a few hundred yards apart. We set the timers of the charges a few seconds in sequence and let them rip."

Another one of Nemo's men observed, "Those charges wouldn't do enough damage to the runway to shut it down for very long."

I agreed, "You're right. But we just want to make it look like an attempt by the Sandys to shut down the runways. We can even add in a few fake emails talking about how the local green shirts planned the whole thing to frame the Sandys. It will be mass confusion and nobody will come out of it completely trusting the other side."

Nemo looked around at one of his men and ordered that a half dozen of these charges be prepared immediately. I told him that I would find a couple of courier volunteers and send them that night if at all possible.

We spent the rest of the morning getting our gear squared away and ready for an operation if the need arose. A few of Nemo's men returned from their recon mission around lunch time.

One of Nemo's scouts reported to Nemo as we stood there watching. "Sir, I left team two and three by the river. They had such a good observation point; it was a waste to move them this morning." He walked to the map where the bridge crossed the Cape Fear. "Here is the battleship memorial, the bridge to the south, and the barge docks. At 06:00 this morning there were five barge-strings docked and loaded. Team two said they would try to get on board as laborers. We already have two of the barge strings disabled." With that he pulled from his pocket a collection of fuses and various electronic components that looked to be stolen from a ship's control panel.

I picked up a part and examined it "Okay. You don't want the barges to move. Why?"

Nemo paused and then began, "We don't want the barges to move until *we* move them and *we* are ready." Nemo moved a couple of maps around and pointed with his pencil, "This is the Cape Fear River; it dumps out into the Atlantic down here by Bald Head Island. All shipping has to come up this channel, past Southport, and up to Wilmington a few miles upstream. From everything we have gathered, the Sandys intend to use the docks at the M.O.T. just north of Southport."

I looked at Nemo, "What is a M.O.T.?"

Nemo pointed to the grayed-out blot on the map. "This is the Military Ocean Terminal at Sunny Point. The railroad lines come in from the west and this whole area is a marshaling yard. You can literally park hundreds of trucks and tanks at this place. It is designed with revetments to minimize the effectiveness of air power or artillery." Nemo pointed the three strands of white that extended into the blue part of the map. "These are the three docks that serve the M.O.T."

I asked, "Can we destroy them or render them useless somehow?"

Nemo patiently answered, "No, these docks are 1,000 feet in length each. It would take truck loads of demolition to make those docks unusable. Even if we could destroy them, the Sandys would just divert their fleet to the dozens of docks up here towards downtown Wilmington." The map was dotted with docks all along the river. Some were fuel line docks, others were for loading grains, and a few were dedicated to the barges.

I looked at the map symbol that read (USS North Carolina BB-55 memorial), "I wish we could haul the old girl out of mothballs and send her down the channel. That would send the Sandys hauling."

One of Nemo's men took me a little too seriously. "Colonel, the battleship is moored in 20 feet of mud and she was decommissioned decades ago. It would take a year and a billion dollars to make her float again. There is no way to use it."

This time I showed patience. "I know that. I was merely admiring the size of the ship and thought how nice it would be to have a 750 foot long, 36,000 ton portable reef." Then it dawned on me. Nemo's plan was just about as genius.

I pointed to the river, "You have disabled the barges because you intend to pilot them down the river and plug up the channel. Don't you?"

Nemo looked taken aback. "Yes, I do." His demeanor was more of shock than anything else. He looked as if I just cheated off his high school midterms. I don't think he expected me to figure it out on my own so quickly. The guy had a slight air of prestige about him and I think he resented someone coming to the same conclusion by only seeing a few maps and a stray report.

Nemo continued, "We will take the next two nights laying charges under the hulls of each barge compartment in all five barge-strings. On the third night, we take over the barges and sail them down the channel to here." He pointed to a narrow spot between a small island and the southern end of the M.O.T. Opposite of the island lay the state park of Fort Fisher. "Once we get to this point, we nose over the lead container and blow the first charge. The current will push the back end around and we blow the rest of the compartments in sequence. We line up each barge end to end and stack them on top of each other. The current is able to flow around each unit and allow flow over the top. But the channel will no longer be deep water serviceable. No ship of any size will be able to go upstream without hitting the sunken barges. We will close off the channel to all the docks instead of trying to destroy them."

I was amazed at the simplistic and downright inspired bit of thinking that had gone into the plan. Then it dawned on me. "How are you going to plant the charges?"

Nemo looked back at me, "Divers will carry limpet mines and place them in key positions. Why?"

I looked at his man who spoken earlier. "I remember the battleship memorial and seeing alligators all over the place down there."

Nemo thought for a second. "It is still mid-winter. They should be dormant for another couple of months at least. We should be okay." There were several looks from his men, but nobody objected.

We talked about how the barge pilots planned to escape. The plan was for them to scramble onto life rafts and paddle towards Fort Fisher after blowing their barge. One of the coastal patrol boats from Norfolk was supposed to pick up the men via motorized zodiacs.

It wasn't until late that I asked Nemo, "Have you heard from your people in Cairo or Tanzania about the convoy?"

Nemo looked ruffled for a split second. "According to my contacts, a major convoy was spotted passing through the straits of Gibraltar 48 hours ago." You could hear a pin drop in the room it got so quiet.

I broke the silence. "Weren't we supposed to know a bit sooner? Did your contacts fall asleep or something?" It was dumb luck that I was here this soon anyway and that was because they needed our warehouse for the Wytheville operation. I paused, thinking about more relevant matters. "How long will it take them to get here?"

Nemo looked at a printout that had a timetable. "We estimate they could be here in another five days, seven at most. Most likely it will be five days from tonight because the tides will be right." He didn't address my remarks about his contacts.

The room fell silent again with only the hum of the PCs for background noise. I sat in the nearest chair and pulled the largest map to me. "Okay, Nemo, where do you want me and my guys?"

Nemo pointed to the bridge named the Cape Fear Memorial. This was the large bridge that highways 17,421 and 76 all shared. "This bridge is causing us a lot of trouble. The barges are docked on the western side of the river with the bridge only a few hundred yards away. If they catch onto what we are doing, they will shell the hell out of us before we can get out of sight. They have lookout towers and checkpoints all over that bridge."

I added rather bleakly, "You need us to give them another target instead."

Nemo said, "Yes, that's just about right. If you can insight enough fear and panic further north, we will have time to get away with the barges to the south."

"I get the tactical Toyota then?" I asked.

Nemo nodded. "That should keep you one step ahead of them, but I can't guarantee that even that will help you. All the areas on the west side of the river have been reduced to rubble. The second militia has been using the area as a dead zone and the Sandys have shelled every structure within two miles of the bridge. There are few shrubs and the buildings are little more than three or four bricks high. The surrounding grounds are littered with ditches and canals which will bog down any truck."

I looked at Nemo. "This is sounding better and better all the time. What else?"

Nemo spoke slowly, "Huck, We need some of your men to augment our airport team. Have three of your men report to Lieutenant Alpha; he is in charge of that mission."

I looked at Nemo. "You are kidding, right? We only have eight in my team now. How much mayhem can I manage with five guys and myself? We might as well go to plan B now and get it over with." I was heated. I was not about to waste my men for just a few minutes worth of artillery practice. We had to get a lot sneakier than that.

Nemo looked upset at the same time. I could tell he was not used to people questioning his command authority. He thought like a soldier, and from his perspective, I was just undisciplined militia with no clue about command chain.

Luckily we both recognized the situation and continued calmly. "Okay then, what do you have in mind, Colonel?" I didn't like his tone and for the first time wondered if this would work with mixed teams. Maybe we just needed to do our thing and let them do theirs. After several minutes, I pulled a couple of maps and looked things over, determined to make the plan work.

"Nemo, let me get back to you on that. I need to do some of my own recon and see what the terrain looks like. I want to go see for myself and then come back with a mission that has more escape routes."

This seemed to work for him. "Okay Huck, let's talk when you've had time to walk the battlefield. But, Huck, we need to hurry. I don't know if our sub commander has the ability to attack that convoy. He might hit them hard or not at all. Either way, we have only three more nights to have everything in place. H-hour is 20:00 March 2nd. We have to have the barges in the river by 22:00 or we are in for it because the tides will change on us if we are any later."

I added, "Plan B?"

Nemo looked sullen. "The device is local and it is secure. It will be on a Humvee the night of the mission and will follow us to a pre-designated area. If we have to use it, I can start the timer using a remote crypto device we have for such things. The pre-arranged detonation time will be 04:00 March 3rd. Everyone has to be out of Wilmington by then and at least 10 miles away to be relatively safe."

I asked while looking at the map, "And if there is no time for a time delay?"

Nemo answered in a hushed tone. "There is an immediate detonation option with a five minute countdown in cases like that." He pulled a thick tablet-like device from a drawer. The exterior was rubber coated with a very thick screen. This was one of those military-grade tablets that could be submerged in mud, frozen in ice, or some other calamity. Either way, the thing worked in any condition and in any environment. It was spooky knowing this little thing could detonate a nuclear device. You didn't feel confident to even touch it for fear of some freak accident.

We broke from our discussions and I wandered back into the cavernous space of the staging warehouse. I found half my men lying on bunks. They had just come in from sentry duty while the other half had gone out. It was late, but we were on that adrenaline rush that does not let you fully rest or sleep.

Opie looked at me as I plopped down on an adjacent bunk. "Colonel, we are ready. Our gear is ready for an operation whenever you give the word."

I was on my back staring at the dim ceiling. "Okay, sounds good." I wasn't really listening though. My mind was racing at the idea of the mission and what part the militia could play in the event. Finally, I asked Opie, "When do the next round of couriers go out to pick up Nemo's teams?"

Opie answered, "I heard one of them say an hour before dawn."

"Alright Opie, we are going out with the couriers then. We'll be gone all day." I told him. I was barely aware of anything at that point. Images of that bridge swam through my thoughts. The Toyota with the Gatling gun, sniper rifle ranges, the USS North Carolina sitting there as just one big lump of steel, incapable after such valiant service through WWII, all passed through my visions.

Opie said slowly, "Yes sir."

I don't know if I slept that night at all.

By the time the guards changed, I was up and arranging my gear. The Thor lay on the empty bunk beside me as I arranged the contents of my pack. The recon mission was going to be light. I made sure my pack contained a few essentials just in case things got ugly. Spare magazines for the Thor went into my pockets, a sniper veil and some MREs went into the pack. My belt held my personal M&P in a Serpa holster. The left side of my belt held a flashlight, knife, and spare magazines for the M&P. My spotting scope went into the pack along with some water. It was just the bare essential for today.

Opie was up and watching me pack. He picked up on the fact that I was not taking my M4 and plate carrier rig. His pack was loaded like mine by the time I was finished strapping the contents tightly. We let the others sleep while we walked outside to an older Camaro painted in a deep slate grey. The courier was not expecting us as Opie opened his passenger door.

The driver looked to us and said, "I'm going to pick up the patrol from yesterday; I got no room for you two."

Opie didn't bat an eye as he said, "It's okay, we're not coming back."

The driver paused, confused as Opie folded the seat forward and sat in the back. His sniper rifle lay on his lap cross ways. I sat in the passenger seat and elaborated. "You just pick us up after the shift change tonight is what he meant."

The driver nodded and looked like he understood. We left the secure parking lot after our sentry signaled the road was clear of vehicle and foot traffic. We sped along for miles through back roads and small streets trying to remain as inconspicuous as possible. It was hard though, most vehicles were derelicts the closer we got to our objective.

The once beautiful coastal neighborhoods were now dilapidated shacks with ghosts for occupants. This was the same as we saw near the outskirts of the other major cities controlled by the green shirts. Inside the city was nice and clean with running water and electricity. Outside the city was a rotting barrier of wasteland with destroyed buildings. Only the strongest thugs lived anywhere near here. The Sandys must have used these people the same way the green shirts used them as occasional labor forces. The PPR and the green shirts were the architects of this new America, but instead of taking credit for their work, they blamed the woes on capitalism. Their TV and radio programs continued to spill out propaganda about how this calamity was brought on by the wealthy and big business.

The sun was up as we made our last few turns down a secluded street. In the distance, some woods or high grass that had not been mowed in a couple of years engulfed a secluded cul-de-sac. We approached slowly as a few men lingered at the corner of the street watching us drive by. I looked at them and immediately reached for my rifle. They were up to no good and I was sure there would be a flurry of bullets at any moment.

Our driver turned off the radio and continued down the street. After a few moments he looked over at me as he pulled over. "Okay, this is where I pick up the team."

I could not believe what I was hearing. "We better get the hell out of here before we have to shoot our way out!"

The driver opened his door and popped the trunk open, "It's okay, you guys are just some extra muscle to back up the sale. That's all." His tone was cool and confident.

I opened my door and got out with the Thor at the ready, "The sale? What are you talking about?"

The driver pulled out a half dozen mason jars filled with white lightning and started to walk towards the bad guys. I was near speechless.

While they were still 30 yards away I said under my breath, "Just how much of this stuff do we sell anyway?"

The driver responded, "Well, this stuff is like liquid gold around these parts. Money don't mean much, but good corn squeezings can go a long way with the locals."

Opie and I walked on either side of the driver until we reached the thugs. After a short barter session, the driver handed over the jars and an exchange was made. We walked back to the car as the thugs jogged out of sight with their treasures. On the way, I asked, "What did you get for those?"

The driver handed me a crumpled sheet of paper that was covered in filth. On it were scribbled notes and time tables. A crude map was penciled on the back with more crude writing. There were a couple of names and street addresses in different sections.

"What is it?" I asked as I handed it back to the driver.

The driver pocketed the paper. "It's a list of the local green shirt offices outside of Wilmington. They were kicked out a few days ago and have set up some temporary places outside the dead zone here. These are their daily patrol schedules."

I looked to his other hand as he pocketed something else. "And those?"

We reached the car and the driver held out a hand filled with junk silver coins. "Well, we have to make a living somehow. If you don't tell the Colonel, I won't." He laughed at his joke. Opie's mouth opened for a split second and then turned to a sly grin. The driver sat back in his car, waiting for Nemo's team to arrive.

I waved at him through the door. "He won't hear it from me."

Opie followed behind me as we walked down the small trail leading south. We got off the path and continued along several small canals which were covered by tall grass. My guess was that the tide was out and we would have several hours before the water rose again. The day was warmer than we had been used to up in North Wilkesboro. The sun was out, with only a few high clouds. There was the wind, though, constantly whipping and blowing. It was as if we were walking a maze of weeds that had no end. I pulled out my compass and made sure of our intended direction. This was very difficult because there were no visible landmarks to check out progress. We continued like this for a couple of hours before we saw the first signs of human activity.

We reached one of the main tributaries of the Cape Fear River that connected the two main branches. The border of Sandy held territory lay to the south another half mile. The border was the main roadway of highways 17, 76, 421, and so on, which led straight into downtown Wilmington. I looked around, wondering just how we were supposed to cross a body of water like this. It was not fast moving, but would be dangerous to swim with all this gear that weighed us down.

Opie looked around thinking the same as me when he said, "A rowboat." He pointed to a small wooden dock where three small boats were tied up. The house nearby was shrouded in tall grass. I don't know if anybody lived there or not, but we stole that smallest boat and paddled our way to the canal.

As we paddled, I told Opie, "Strip down to your t-shirt and hold up a stick like you are fishing. Take your hat off too."

Opie looked around quickly and stowed his gear as low as possible. He understood that if anyone was to see us, they would naturally assume we were trying to catch some lunch on a nice sunny day. The bottom of our boat was lined with all manner of military hardware, though. We would never get away with a close inspection. Luckily for us, nobody else was on the water in the back canals at that hour. We paddled our way east, following the canals as they led back to the main parts of the river. Through breaks in the grass we could see and hear the road traffic from the main roadways. There was very little civilian traffic. Mostly it seemed there were convoys of trucks heading east towards Wilmington.

We continued to paddle our way through a small man-made lake and into a ditch filled with water. If we were right, we could travel through the grass to our overwatch position on foot. We stashed the boat and covered it in cut grass. Once our gear was back on, Opie and I painted up any exposed skin and took a final compass bearing. From there we traveled slowly, without a word between us. We walked several steps, then stopped to listen. We walked further and stopped at the edge of our ditch. The sound of traffic was spooky when we knew we were completely on our own. If we were spotted, they would wipe us out with just a handful of Boy Scouts. Our only chance was to stay hidden.

I turned to face Opie, who followed me five yards behind. I gave him a hand signal to come to me. He did so as I cut grass and stuffed it into the rings of my boonie hat. Opie did the same with his as we both watched out for anyone else in the area. Once we had our rifles and heads covered as much as possible, we crawled the final 150 yards to a small knoll where only a few scrubby trees provided cover.

The highway 200 yards to the east was not what I would call busy, but the traffic was consistent. Every two or three minutes a car or truck would pass in front of our field of view. It was mid-day by the time we got to our little vantage point. The sun was out and the air was tolerable for winter. I thought back on the crawl to get there and was thankful it was winter. Otherwise the summer would have made the trips full of bugs and snakes as well as a stray alligator. The thought of that possibility gave me a cold shiver.

To my right (southeast) I could just make out the giant loops of the on/off ramps where the Sandys had cut all the low lying shrubbery. I could see several tank emplacements that had been photographed earlier. All the major highways intersected here on the west side of the Cape Fear River before going across to downtown Wilmington. The Cape Fear Memorial Bridge was a gray steel-framed structure that lifted all four lanes into the air to allow ships with tall masts to pass underneath. The roadway arched upward as the bridge spanned the river leaving me a clear view through the Thor's scope. Nemo's men were right about the number of checkpoints and security shacks on this bridge. There was no way to take out enough sentries with so few men at our disposal. Opie scanned off to the left towards the northeast. His elbow nudged mine as we lay side by side under the shrubs. I looked left to see the thin outline of a helicopter hover some two miles away. That must be the airport. I took the bearing of the helicopter and made a mental note. I oriented the map according to magnetic north and drew a line with the bearing and confirmed the airport's location. We watched the helo casually fly west as it rose into the air. I know we both wondered what it was doing and if our friends were in its sights.

After a while, the wind carried a few sounds of the rotor blades whipping through the air. Luckily the helicopter seemed to be heading further west and south. My guess was that it was a regular patrol for the railroad lines which lay to the south.

I looked due east, trying to see the landmark to beat all landmarks in the area, the USS North Carolina battleship. It was instantly apparent that billboards obscured the ship from my view. I didn't remember them being there when I passed by on my way to the beach years ago. That was the best part of the drive. You drove across a small bridge and looked left to see the whole front of the ship from the road. The large 16" guns stared at you with the large superstructure and antennae mast behind them. Here I was only a few hundred yards away and I couldn't tell the ship was even there. Then it dawned on me, the Sandys would not want anyone to see such an inspirational symbol of American firepower. I bet they mounted the billboards to the deck just to mask the ship. They sure couldn't destroy the ship or move it. The billboards must be directly mounted to the deck in order to camouflage it from casual observation. I bet the poor guy that was tasked with obscuring a battleship with billboards was wishing he was in another business.

I looked through the Thor's scope and noticed the hint of a squarely cut mast just peering from behind the center of three large billboards. Arabic writing was boldly displayed with colorful images of some dude with a long white beard and his hand pointed upward as if he were instructing pupils in school. I wondered what the writing said. I had no clue what it was about or the significance of this guy.

Opie and I watched that roadway until it was fairly dark. With the sun setting to our backs, we did not dare leave our hide until we were no longer back-lit. Back-lit is when there is a light source behind your position which draws attention to your darker silhouette. In the waning light, I tapped Opie and demonstrated putting away my map case and notebook. He did the same and recognized it was time to get back to our pickup point. Things were really quiet the last half hour before sundown. No trucks had come by in 20 minutes. Lights were coming on the bridge as well as the buildings in downtown. The wind stopped blowing for the most part and the evening was coming quickly. You could hear some seagulls squawk in the distance.

Then a loud speaker way off in downtown sounded the Muslim call to prayer. You could hear the chant from across the river as well as from the intersection to the south. We stopped dead because the sudden noise spooked us. We crouched and sat for a second before I said quietly to Opie, "Let's go while the getting is good."

We trotted down the canal, sloshing through the edge of the water, trying to make our way through the edge of the marsh as quickly as possible. By the time the singing stopped, we were a climbing into the boat. Without losing a beat, we paddled out into the canals and made our way west as best we could. In the distance several loud booms could be heard. In peacetime that could be a stray thunderstorm on the coast. Or, it could be Sandy artillery off to the south; it was hard to say.

In the daytime, navigating the narrow passages was cumbersome. Doing the reverse course in the dark was a nightmare. Several times we grounded the small boat because we could not see that we had shifted angles. The high weeds and grasses masked any and all landmarks. We paddled and paddled until I wisely strapped my compass to my sleeve and made us head west as I monitored the direction between strokes.

Finally, we came back to the main tributary where the way was clearer. Somehow we had managed to come out within 400 yards of our original position where we had stolen the boat. We chose to tie the boat under some small overhanging vegetation on the west side of the tributary. From there we took a compass bearing that would get us back to the neighborhood where our ride was supposed to pick us up. My watch must have been running at twice the normal speed, though. Every time I looked down we had lost another half an hour. We were nearly running the last half mile before we neared the pickup point. A few hundred yards away we stopped to take a breath and listen. There were a few candle lit houses here and there, but all was quiet. I could see a car's fog lights in the distance as someone parked in the cul-de-sac. We had made it.

"STOP WHERE YOU ARE!" a voice demanded softly.

I froze. Opie gave a short inhale at the sudden voice from nowhere.

"WHO ARE YOU?" the voice asked.

"Game Warden," I announced softly. I couldn't do more than that because my heart was trying to tear its way through my cammies.

"Colonel Huck, are you alright?" the voice asked, a little less demanding.

"Other than the heart attack you just gave me, I'm fine," I sputtered.

Two of Nemo's men stood near the path and ushered us to the waiting pickup truck. One of the men said, "We are your escort back to the staging area." Both men were wearing helmet mounted ANPVS 14 night vision. One man had a suppressed MP5 while the other carried a standard M4 with an Eotech 550 series weapons sight. Both men climbed into the truck with us as the driver started for the staging area.

The drive back was excruciating from the cold. Opie and I had gotten more than a little wet during our observation and boat ride back to the pickup area. The chill of the air and the wetness from muddy canal water made things ten times worse. Opie and I huddled behind the cab while Nemo's men sat on the bed by the fenders. By the grace of God we finally pulled into the dark parking lot through a small entrance I didn't even know existed until we pulled through.

We thanked our escort and went inside. I noticed there were two other cars and a couple of motorcycles parked in the lot which was rare for the staging area. We were trying to stay low profile. Opie and I peeled off our gear as some of our men came over to our bunks.

Floyd and Andy jogged over to us. "Colonel, good to see you made it back in one piece. We were worried."

Opie asked, "What for?"

Andy was slightly out of breath, "We heard there was some artillery fire tonight and thought you may have stirred up some trouble."

Opie said, "We heard it, but couldn't see where it was coming from."

I looked at the guys. "What's with all the couriers?" I pointed towards the wall and the parking lot out back.

Andy said, "They just got here. One of them just came from Wytheville."

That got my interest. As fast as I could, I changed out of my muddy fatigues and wiped as many layers of filth off as I could. I quickly dressed in some spare clothes and hurried over to the throng of men sitting in chairs just outside the operations office. Nemo and several of his men were standing around while the rest of the Mayberry team surrounded a young man sitting at the corner table. I recognized the young courier as one of those that we picked up in North Wilkesboro just a couple of months prior.

The men were hounding him with so many questions he couldn't possibly answer all of them.

I used my authoritative voice and told everyone to catch their breath. We were all interested to hear what was going on in Wytheville. The young man looked like he was about to be water-boarded if he didn't come up with some details pretty fast. The guys stood back briefly and let the young man speak.

"What do you guys want to know?" he asked.

I told him, "Tell us what you saw from the time you got there, until you left."

He gulped a little at the request and started. "Okay...I was on courier runs as the troops deployed. Most of my messages were between company commanders in Fort Chiswell and the 3rd battalion headquarters. They ran me back and forth about five times the first day alone." He looked at the faces of the men eager for his tales and continued with more detail. "On my first run I saw that our advance team had secured highway 81. The road was not clear, but it was ours all the way from the 77 intersection to the exit leading to downtown Wytheville. There were some burned-up trucks with the tires still smoking right there in the middle of the road. Some bodies were in the ditch. When I slowed down, I could hear gunfire from town."

"The rest of my runs that day were all to Fort Chiswell. I didn't see any of the fighting. They had us debrief after every run as well so we could report any green shirt activity. Most of us didn't have much to report, though."

I asked, "Did you see Fred at Chiswell?"

The courier looked over to me as he sat. "I saw him on the second day. He was updating the maps at the command center, but it was brief and I didn't talk to him."

The man we called Floyd asked, "Have you seen anyone from 4th battalion, 5th company?"

The courier responded, "No, most of the guys from 4th were still coming in when I was re-tasked to come here. Rocket said he needed a couple of extra guys for this mission, so I volunteered since I lived in Wilmington for a while. I know the place pretty well."

That peaked my interest. A driver that knew the area was a real find. Before the rest of the men resumed his interrogation, I ushered him to Nemo's command office. I wanted the courier to give Nemo a heads-up on any particular roads that may be useful for the operation.

But Nemo's reaction was not what I anticipated.

"Huck, get that man out of here," Nemo commanded in a not so friendly kind of way.

We turned on our heels and I told the courier to hang out just outside the doorway.

I went back in through the door by the time it closed. "Just what the hell is up, Nemo?" I asked indignantly.

Nemo responded a little on the hot side, "Huck, we know you. Your men are trusted resources, but that is a courier you barely know. There is information sensitive to our very lives in here and I don't trust that level of information to just anybody. Besides, couriers are dangled out there on the edge all the time. We could lose him to the green shirts just as easily as the Sandys."

In the back of my mind I knew he was right. But being right doesn't make my pride get in the way. My natural reaction was to defend one of my men from someone I didn't know much better. "Nemo, I know him about three weeks less than you. This guy lived in Wilmington before the war and may know a lot about the area." Dang, my mouth got me in a lot of trouble.

Nemo was bothered by my statement to say the least. "Huck, he cannot come in here and that's final. I will send someone to debrief him as soon as they are free." He paused and looked at me as he gripped a small stack of papers while leaning on the operations table. He looked tired. His graying hair was ruffled like he had not had a shower in a month. In fact, I was not sure when he had left the room at all. "I just got a flash from the sub captain I told you about. He has not located the fleet where he expected it to be." The news was hard for him to even say out loud. We both knew that plan B was an absolute last option, but the scenario for having to use it was becoming more likely if things didn't start going a little more right for us.

As I turned to leave Nemo asked, "Do you have a plan yet?"

I looked back to him over my shoulder, "Yeah, but I don't know how many of us are going to walk away from this one."

Nemo understood that our chances were slim at best when he said, "We will do the best we can with what we have. The rest is up to the fortunes of war." He and I paused, then he said, "See if you can get your men to rest tonight. They are going to need it. Operations meeting at 0:900."

I nodded and walked out of the door. The courier walked along behind me as we met the rest of the men by our section of bunks. They were all surprised to see me return so quickly.

"What's the story Huck?" one of the men asked.

I didn't feel like getting into too much detail; there was plenty of time for that tomorrow.

"Guys, bed down for the night and don't hound the courier with questions. Get all the rest you can because when we go operational, you won't sleep for a while. There is an operations meeting tomorrow at 09:00; we will meet at 08:30 as a team because I have some information to pass along to you. Now go to bed."

There were a few ugly looks but overall the men kept their questions to themselves. We bunked down for the night with only the promise of occasional guard duty and our thoughts to keep us awake. Both were plenty. I looked at my watch and calculated approximately 70 hours until the start of the operation.

The next day we woke early feeling at least a little refreshed. Not by any means well rested, but at least better. The men had begun a workout routine with Nemo's men each morning. My guys lay about the room after the first 30 minutes sucking in air. Nemo's men from the teams averaged almost two hours with a variety of exercises.

By 08:30 my Mayberry Marauders gathered around the bunks for our meeting. The men sat quietly looking at Opie and me, knowing that we were getting close to our operation kickoff. The tension was painted across their faces without need for translation. This team had been through hard times, they knew this mission was more important than all of us combined. If the Sandys landed their full force, nothing would be left of the state we called home.

Opie started, "The operational plan is going to be laid out this morning after we break at 09:00. Our team is going to split into two groups. Three of you will be assigned to the airport team with a group of SEALS. The rest of us are assigned to harass the Sandys the best we can after we attack the Cape Fear River Bridge."

The men looked concerned at the news. The whole point of me choosing this team was because they had been through so much together. Splitting up their squad was not what they expected or wanted.

Andy looked at me. "Colonel, do you really think it's a good idea to split up our team?"

I paused and said, "No, it was not my first choice either. But Nemo needs three of us and we are team players. It's as simple as that."

Otis asked, "What kind of support does he want?"

Opie responded, "Most likely you will be driving the humvees."

I added, "They need militia to show them how to shoot straight." My levity was not lost on the guys. As they considered the new information, I resumed. "Whatever mission or job you have, you do it to the best of your ability. If all they do is tell you to scrub a garbage can, you freakin make it sparkle. These men are all about doing the job as a team. They don't ask outsiders to operate with them very often. I want them to remember how professionally we conduct ourselves. Whatever you do, don't try to impress them. They have no time for bravado, it gets men killed and this is a numbers game. There ain't so many of us and this is going to be a hard mission. Study what they say and do exactly what they tell you to do. Remember this gentlemen, our mission is strategic. We succeed or we die trying."

The men nodded in agreement.

Opie looked at the men. "Andy, Floyd, and Barney, you are going with the airport team. When Nemo asks for our three, you raise your hands."

I could see the burden of command already showing in Opie's eyes. He would never admit it, but I could see it as he spoke their names. He knew the men might not make it back and it was his decision to send them on the mission. He was a leader of men at that very moment.

I concluded our little pow-wow with, "Go get changed into the operational uniforms, I want all our men dressed the same for the briefing. We are going to look like we are men that Nemo and his men can depend on. Wear your OD pants with your side arms and your black t-shirts. Briefing in ten minutes at the dinner tables."

The men broke to their gear in silence. All our men were standing tall and proud as the rest of Nemo's men, our Army brethren, came into the warehouse for the briefing. All the teams were in, only the couriers stood guard outside. I noticed it immediately because I was aware of the security risk they posed in Nemo's thinking.

Nemo started the briefing. "Gentlemen, we have a lot to cover in the next couple of hours; get comfortable.

Our operation will begin in different segments based off of the time it takes each team to get in place. For the purposes of this mission, the H-hour is 20:00 on March 1st, which is only 51 hours from now. That is when we need all the distraction teams to initiate their attacks on their designated targets. "

I was visibly surprised at the change of date. Nemo had taken a full day off our original plan. He must have new information on the Sandy's invasion fleet and it was my bet that the news was not good.

Nemo introduced a few team leaders from his group and outlined their missions in detail. Lieutenant Able was assigned the airport mission. His team's main objective was to cause as much damage to the airport facilities as possible. Aircraft and fuel stores were his main objectives. They would take two of the tactical humvees and one of our gun trucks to approach from the north. All of the Army SF soldiers we chosen for the mission. Previous recon missions to the area left avenues for approach through compromised sections of the perimeter fence. All a truck would have to do is just hit the bumper on a marked section of fence and it would fall over. After the mission, the trucks would try to escape back to the north and make their way to the secondary staging area.

Lieutenant Baker was assigned to lead the dive teams. He looked like he had just gotten back from another night of preparing the barges for theft and demolition. His team would insert into their inflatable boats from further north in the Cape Fear. At the drop point, they would send dive pairs to assault the five sets of barges with suppressed weapons. Once clear, they would repair the barges and wait for us to start the various distractions. If all went well, the barges would be floated down the Cape Fear until the designated channel south of the Oceanic Terminal and clog up the river. They would extract to the east and cross the sandy marshes south of Fort Fisher where the coastal patrol boat would pick them up.

Nemo emphasized the extreme time sensitivity and reminded everyone that the mission must be accomplished by 0:400 on the March 2nd.

Nemo assigned himself along with T-Rex and Shady to plan B. My guys shared some looks as he referenced the subject.

Nemo picked up on the looks immediately. "Colonel Huck, have you made your men aware of plan B?"

I looked at my guys and shook my head no. I said, "That should be your prerogative."

Nemo elaborated, "Plan B is if everything else fails. We have a small nuclear device just south of here that will destroy the city if we cannot close the ports. If we cannot get the barges in place, you need to be at least 10 miles out of Wilmington by 04:00. Let me put it another way; we cannot use radios on this mission. The Sandys have directional radio detecting gear and they have used it against the militia in the past. You will not get a warning. You must be clear of Wilmington by 04:00."

My guys went white eyed at the reference to the bomb. They had no clue we had resources like that at hand. Just the thought of being within striking distance of a nuclear bomb is hard to grasp for some. I wondered how they would react. Nobody said a word, but they all kept their mouth shut. I looked at the map when Nemo was talking and realized where the bomb was located. The only way to mask a nuclear signature was to shield it in some way or hide it close to another source of radiation. The Brunswick nuclear power plant was on the western side of the Cape Fear River south of the MOT. I bet he hid the thing inside the power plant somehow.

"Huck, you want to spell your mission details now?" Nemo asked as he handed me the marker for the dry erase board.

I took it and looked to my men specifically. "Opie and I are inserting 24 hours in advance of H-hour. We are going to attack the troops securing the crossroads in front of the bridge where all the major highways intersect. Our objective will be to take out their artillery spotters. While they have their heads down, the rest of my team will drive the tactical Toyota and get as close as possible to the bridge. They will expend all the ammo from the minigun on the bridge and its guard posts to clear the way for the dive teams. They will run west after the attack and lead any pursuers away from our objective. The Toyota will meet up with couriers staged about 15 miles west of the Sandy checkpoint here." I marked the spot on the map. It was a small country lane out in the middle of nowhere and should be easily identifiable at night. "The couriers will be given sealed orders as we disembark. Opie and I will meet you guys at the other staging area as soon as possible. But know this; when we leave here, we are not coming back. If you have left over gear, give it to the couriers. Take all the ammo you can carry. This is going to be a run and gun event, make no mistake."

There was a whole lot more detail in the briefing than what I described here. Nemo left nothing to chance. His men knew every aspect of the plan and how each man was supposed to do each job. After the meeting I met with Nemo briefly.

"How did we lose 24 hours?" I asked.

Nemo sat down at the table inside the office. "The sub commander reported that he found the fleet. It was a lot further west than he anticipated."

"What about escorts?" I asked.

Nemo said, "He says there are several ships from his sonar database. It's a mixed bag of former Nato ships they are using as convoy screening. The Sandys didn't have much in the way of trans-Atlantic naval assets before the takeover. Our good captain expects to make an attack in the next 12 hours or so."

The thought of our former allies running screen for an invasion fleet heading for the U.S. was unnerving to say the least.

Nemo turned to me and commented, "Huck, I didn't catch your exfil plan for you and Opie. What do you have in mind?" He was fishing for information because his command nature was very different from mine. He needed a plan, he wanted timetables and schedules. That was the proper way to conduct warfare in his eyes. He may be more right than I liked to admit, too. His people were survivors and they were disciplined warriors that made the most damage and got away.

I told him, "Opie and I are going to fill in the blanks. We will be the thorn in the Sandys side that will not go away. We will shoot and move wherever the best opportunity presents itself, then disappear into the weeds. They will think they are chasing a dozen of us by the time we are through."

Nemo wished me good luck and handed me a pack of papers. "Here is a map kit for your Toyota team. One of my men from

Able's team can spend the next few hours instructing your team on the use of the minigun. Do you think they can handle it?"

I told him, "Are you kidding? They are like a bunch of kids with a new toy at Christmas. They probably have played with the thing already. It is okay Captain, I saw my guys working with T-Rex. He used one when he was in service."

Nemo concluded, "Let me know if you need anything, Colonel."

The teams broke into groups for rehearsals and readying gear. My Mayberry team was doing a great job as they worked to prepare vehicles with the other teams. The mood was calm but deliberate. Everybody knew the time was quickly approaching. The rest of that day was a blur. We memorized timetables and codes as we loaded every magazine we had for the M4s. Green tipped SS109 ammo was loaded via stripper clips from freshly opened cans. The SF guys held magazines sideways and used them to mash the round down to the feeding lips of other mags. It was quick and if done properly could be done without damaging the magazine that was being loaded. Grenades were strapped into pockets on our vests and gear was adjusted to fit after all the ammo was loaded.

Opie and I sat cleaning our sniper rifles while half the Mayberry team loaded everyone else's M9 magazines from a couple of cans of 9mm 124gr. Nato ball ammo. The pile of magazines was impressive as they sat stacked four rows high. Ammo was scattered all over the table as men grabbed a handful and loaded the rounds one at a time. Once a magazine was full, it was tapped on the back to align the rounds. This would help to prevent jams, but not eliminate them entirely.

We watched as the Seals laid out suppressed MP5s and performed last minute checks on dry suits. Their gear loadout was awesome. They had to work out half the day just to lift the massive amounts of mines, demolition gear and night vision equipment.

Everyone was loading their water reservoirs when I noticed a couple of guys add a powder from packets.

"What is that, Opie?" I asked as he poured.

He looked over his shoulder and said, "The men from the teams handed these out. They say it is packed full of vitamins and stuff. It is supposed to keep you awake and give you the energy for long missions."

I looked at it a little skeptically and sniffed. "What is it, like, pure caffeine?"

Opie shook his head no. "No, the guy said it is not supposed to make you jittery like an energy drink. It's supposed to just keep you going without the crash like you get from and energy drink." He pointed to my pack. "I put three of them in your pack. You only need one for a 100oz. bladder."

Opie and I worked on our gear next. He would take his sniper rifle with an M4. I wanted to carry the Thor, but I debated on taking my M4 as well. It may be too much weight to carry overall. It was the age-old debate. Do I carry both weapons or do I carry loads of ammo for just one? In the end I chose to take the M4 as my primary weapon and haul the Thor in my pack broken down. Since I only had about five magazines for the Thor, my options were limited. I had plenty of ammo, but I would have to reload magazines if I wanted to shoot more than 100 rounds. I took an extra 150 or 200 loose rounds in a zippered pouch. All the Thor ammo was standard 175gr. match ammo.

We both carried our M9s with five extra magazines. As always I took along my laser range finder, a large strand of 550 cord, a couple of smoke grenades, four fragmentation grenades, two MREs, my flashlight with spare batteries, and a few carabineers. Our knives were strapped to our pistol belts on the opposite side of the Safariland holsters. We checked and rechecked gear until we were satisfied that it was good to go.

Opie and I made sure the other guys were ready as well. We packed extra ammo into packs for the guys to use in the trucks. The idea was to have water, ammo, and something from an MRE to wolf down when time presented itself. It was late before we finished our preparations. I looked at my watch; 12 hours or so before Opie and I were due to get into position.

The last night in the warehouse was not as hard as I expected. We had worked so hard, I was too tired to think about much of anything. It was all about the mission. I had to put the family in the back of my mind to get through the next few days. We didn't have time for men to sit around dreaming over pictures of loved ones.

The only way to get through was to just ignore everything other than the task at hand.

The morning before insertion was scheduled as a lazy day. Lieutenant Baker's team reported that all the barges had been rigged for demolition and had been successfully immobilized. He reported that there were some repair crews completely baffled as to why almost all of their barge motors had completely wigged out on them. His only worry was that the repair crews may have done damage trying to repair the broken systems. It was a risk.

The couriers were loaded down with our spare gear and their sealed orders as the last of them headed back to a rally point outside our secondary staging area. There was no word from Wytheville and it was getting too close to our operation to try and find out how things were going up there. One of the courier teams reported that the mission to bomb the Raleigh Durham airport had been a success. Nemo confirmed that the Sandy helicopter reported several explosions on the western runway and was fired upon by at least two or three green shirt air defense units. The motorcycle couriers successfully escaped to the north and reported to Rocket's team near Roxboro.

At mid-day Nemo asked, "You want any of these pictures, Huck?" He had handfuls of Intel photos taken on previous missions. I went through the stack and grabbed a few for my waterproof map case. The rest I handed back to him.

"Thanks Nemo; any word from our sub out there?"

He looked down at his hands. "None." I had never seen him so concerned. The mission was definitely taking a toll on him. "I will let you know as soon as I hear from him, though. That is, if you have not left already. He looked at his watch. "You have four hours until you and Opie cast off?"

"Yep, nothing left to do but sit and wait," I folded my hands behind my head to show that I was not concerned. Nemo knew better. We all felt the same way or we wouldn't be there.

The building was quiet and the men spoke softly among each other. We were ready. Even the men from the teams were slightly anxious. The last four hours of the day were the worst. The mind races as you sit there trying to ignore the hands of the clock ticking so slowly that you are sure that time itself has somehow been distorted. Daylight turned to twilight as Opie and I strapped on our vests and clicked our pistol belts into place. Opie and I wore our new OD green uniforms with jacket liners underneath as our only protection from the cold. Cold was a relative term. We were used to 3,000 feet above sea level where the warmest part of the day was 40 degrees. Tonight the low would be 55 according to the local weather reports.

Shady went outside to warm up a leftover car from one of the couriers. The rest of the men shook our hands as we hauled our packs onto our shoulders. Few words were spoken between us. Our goodbyes were mostly looks of quiet assuredness if there is such a thing. Only your fellow warriors could understand because so much depended on the outcome of our effort that night.

Success meant possibly years free from a pending invasion. If the Wytheville operation was a success, the green shirts would have a hard time deciding what the hell to do with us in North Carolina. We had become a fly in the ointment as it were. Better yet, the Sandys and green shirts were almost literally shooting at each other. The next 48 hours might make all the difference in the world to the free people left in our state.

Nemo stood by his office door and gave a slow salute that I returned. We had heard no feedback from the submarine in the Atlantic as I walked out of the door. If all went well at sea, maybe somebody from Nemo's teams could find us in a couple of days and tell us the good news that the operation was canceled. My hopes of that were somewhere between finding the lost city of Atlantis and marrying Bigfoot's sister.

We waited by the car for a few minutes as the stars twinkled above us. It was dark and had been for 30 minutes as we drove out of the parking lot. We used a small road that was riddled with dark houses and people milling about on the streets. We did not stop at stop-signs to smell the roses, either.

Shady finally said, "Colonel Huck, are you sure you don't want me to stand by somewhere west of here to pick you guys up after the operation?" He had been my security guard for months. I knew he was just looking out for me. Opie didn't say anything.

I responded to him by the light of the dashboard. "Kill the lights." Shady reached under the dash and flicked the switch that we put in all our vehicles. When you flicked it, all the lights went out in the car. It was a complete blackout. It didn't matter if you hit the brakes or opened the trunk, nothing lit up. We drove a small ways toward the place near where Opie and I had done our recon a couple of days before. Shady pulled over and parked the car in a lonely spot between a couple houses that looked to be deserted. Nobody was on that street and the place looked peaceful enough.

I looked over at Shady. "Your job is to watch out for Nemo. Don't let anybody get to him, Shady. You know what he has to do if it comes to it. The Sandys cannot be allowed to land that invasion force." I shook his hand as I left the car; he knew what I meant. Opie followed my movement and got out of the car right behind me. We did not linger on the edge of the street either. Once our boots hit the sidewalk, we sprinted to the cover of the nearby trees. Shady immediately pulled out and continued down the street as if he had never stopped.

Chapter 21
Battleship

Opie and I scanned the street behind us with our M4s at the ready. Opie's sniper rifle was strapped to his pack and secured from bumps and dings by a series of removable pads. I looked through my ACOG down the street to see if anyone registered our drop-off. After five minutes of listening, we only saw a single causal passerby on an adjacent street. We silently crept along the woods towards the larger tributary that eventually lead to the Cape Fear River. I wrapped my compass lanyard around my neck and took a bearing for us to track. The stars were out, which allowed me to use them as a quick reference guide in tall weeds.

We did not use the same paths from our previous recon. You never use the same route twice even if it is more convenient or comforting to recognize your surroundings. The enemy might have learned of our recons by now and might be in an ambush position just waiting for us. It had happened before to militia not following standards close enough. Each step away from the derelict neighborhood was a comfort in itself. The last thing I wanted was to run across some passerby that compromised our secrecy. This could potentially present a bad situation for us and them. You see, when you are on such a strategic mission, you have to eliminate all threats to your security. Some jerk in a boat might spill the beans on you to a local patrol out of ignorance, out of spite, or just to get a reward. What I mean by elimination is killing that person and making sure nobody will stumble across the body for a good while. It may seem harsh, but one life may make the difference between tens of thousands of us dying in the next 24 hours. When you think of it that way, it seems less horrific. I just really hoped I could avoid that scenario if possible. I just didn't want to make that decision if I could work a little harder to avoid it.

Eventually Opie and I made our way to the bank of the tributary and worked our way downstream until we reached the place where we left the stolen rowboat. Sure enough, the thing sat there under a massive shrub with the oars in the same position as we left them. With a bit more labor we managed to climb aboard and push off into the canal. This time we paddled our way for a few hundred yards north and found an easterly-flowing canal that was man-made. The grasses were not as tall as they reached from the banks. I worried that the amount of cover would be too little if a helicopter shined a light from overhead.

We paddled for the better part of an hour before we saw lights pulsing from towers in the distance. There was a major factory way out in the middle of the swamp and our canal was leading us straight to it. From the smells wafting through the air, my bet was that it was a paper mill or something just as odorous. What if there were guards on patrol and we were compromised? What if we had come too far north and did not have time to divert before daylight. Those were not happy thoughts as I rowed quietly along. As we got closer some of my fears were realized. The major portion of the plant was lit. There were chain link fences surrounding the area, but I didn't see any foot patrols yet.

Opie didn't flinch as we got closer and closer to the lights. We rowed in silence with our M4s ready to give somebody a serious jolt if we had to.

Every stroke of the oar made my nerves stand on edge. The very sound of water dripping off the wooden oar made me cringe on the inside. I felt myself not breathing and forced the air into my lungs more than once. Our canal ran the entire northern edge of the facility at least 400 yards along the northern border of the property.

As we passed along the canal, I could see a building looming in the distance. It was a maintenance shack of some sort, I hoped, and not a security outpost. The fence edged the canal banks as grass grew under the links. I looked over and the building was a short one-story structure with an aging tin roof. The whole thing must not have been more than 12 feet wide by 20 feet long.

I watched as we neared the building by the fence. I could have thrown a rock and busted out a window with ease we were so close. The lights were on inside, allowing us to see every detail of the interior. A man sat at a table reading charts. I could almost make out the logo on the paper we were so close. I wondered what he would have thought if he knew we were only feet from his door. Would he run and scream? Or, would he simply stare back at us in utter disbelief? Luckily, the brightly lit interior would keep him from seeing very far outside of the window.

About the time we finally got to the other side of the shack, a rush of water bubbled up from an underground pipe. This canal was the washout for whatever chemical this plant produced as a byproduct. The foul stench was almost overwhelming. Opie and I were pushed by the new current as we risked an increase in our paddling. In a short time, the factory faded back among the grass and was finally obscured from view. Only the tall cylindrical tanks with their pulsing red flashing warnings to low flying aircraft could be seen behind us. Once again there was nothing but darkness. The faint light of Wilmington to the east was more like a dim warning of dawn. Luckily we still had hours before the sun was due to rise.

We followed a few turns in the canal until we finally approached a larger branch of the river. Heck, this body of water I called a branch would normally qualify as a full-fledged river by itself. Opie and I guided our little row boat east along the shore. We were glad to be out of the narrow canals without any visual reference. If it were not for compasses, navigating would have been impossible.

Aerial photographs provided by Nemo showed our position to be just west of the highway 17 bridge. This was the bridge off to the northwest of our objective. We rounded a long bend in the river opposite of some docks and finally saw the bridge as it arched high over our section of the river. Lights from lampposts dotted the upper part of the bridge. It looked like every other lamp was shining down on the roadway. That was common for those days. Power was a luxury not used on trivial things like street lights.

We proceeded slowly, trying to make as little wake as possible. Nobody was in sight on the far bank. Our side of the river was covered in the thick grass because marsh land was to the south off to our right. We crept slowly towards the bridge, wondering if there were patrols watching the waterways. We knew there was likely and entire company of Sandys at the major intersection just ¾ of a mile down highway 17. I raised the M4's scope to the railing of the bridge and scanned for anyone looking towards us. Nothing, it was quiet. Why wouldn't they have some sort of sentry to keep boats out of the main river?

We passed under the bridge barely risking a deep breath. We were tense from all this sneaking. Our nerves were on edge as we pressed on to get to our final hiding place. Beyond the bridge lay the Cape Fear River another ¼ mile ahead. The lights from Wilmington shown between buildings now visible as the mouth of the tributary opened to the main portion of the river. The northern bank was littered with flat bottomed barges with cranes mounted in their centers. Some of these units were for dredging while others were rigged for lifting various machinery parts. While Opie paddled, I scanned the cranes for signs of a watch or patrol.

Then a scraping sound of metal on wood got my attention. Our boat had run over a metal cable about an inch in diameter that spanned the width of the river. We lurched forward only slightly because we were going so slowly. We came to a stop. Instantly Opie went from paddling to scanning with the M4 towards the river behind us. I scanned to the front waiting for eminent contact. Silence resumed for another 30 seconds before we concluded that nobody waited in the weeds to ambush us. Sweat poured from me as we sat there. Finally, I motioned for Opie to land the boat on the shore, which was only a few feet away. I got out and pulled the bow rope so Opie could grab the packs and chuck them onto the grassy shore. After Opie got out, we pulled the boat through the weeds until it was completely out of water. We took another five minutes to hack down grass to camouflage the boat in case we needed it in the future.

I took a compass bearing due south as Opie loaded my pack on my shoulders. I finished and helped him. We had not spoken a word out loud since we said goodbye to Shady, hours earlier. Opie was a good person to have on a team. He knew what was going on because he paid attention and watched everything that was going on. He might have been young, but he was good at his job and that is all that mattered.

I signaled for him to follow behind me at a sniper's distance. With my compass in hand, and my M4 in the other, we took off to the southeast among the grass and shrubs. It was the hardest slogging I have ever done. You could not see more than two feet in front of you. Landmarks were obscured by small trees that stood in stale water. The only thing I could think about was the alligators. In summer I would have surely been eaten alive several times over trying a stunt like this. My thoughts were completely engulfed at the promise of dozens of hideous little razor-like teeth biting into my leg from a small unseen gator. I only hoped that Nemo's information was correct and those freakin things were still dormant somewhere far away.

After an hour of tromping, the scene dramatically changed. Above the weeds a large dark object blotted the sky line and blocked the stars. Looming in the distance the dark object seemed to represent the end of the world as it stretched hundreds of feet from west to east. Reflecting light from downtown Wilmington shown on a massive array of billboards which seemed to be supported in mid-air. Behind the billboards lay BB-55, the USS North Carolina. I stopped in my tracks only feet from the water of the narrow waterway that led back to the Cape Fear River. There was only 20 yards of water from the bank to the hull of the famous battleship. The sight was breathtaking. You looked up some 25 feet or so the main deck. All the turrets were covered by the billboards. The strange Arabic figure as seen from the front was on this side of the ship. You could only just make out the smoke stacks and a few sections of the superstructure between the spaces of the billboards.

Opie caught up to me as we stood there, mesmerized at the sheer size of the thing. I motioned for us to walk a few yards to the stern portion of the ship. There, I found the rear mooring lines that lead from a concrete emplacement to a giant cleat at the main deck level. The mooring lines themselves were stranded bands of steel around two inches thick. I looked to Opie and took off my pack and withdrew a hank of 550 cord with a carabineer. I tied one end around my belt and clipped the beener around my pack.

With Opie watching over me, I slung my M4 across my back and began to Ranger crawl up the steel cable. Ranger crawl is when you climb on top of a rope instead of dangle under it like in movies. I let my left leg drape down while my right knee made a counterbalance. My right ankle provided a rear anchor as I hauled my body forward and upwards. The climb was excruciating but I finally made my way to the deck. There I was able to slide under a steel structure that had been welded onto portions of the hull. The steel beams supported the array of billboards. My arms felt like dead weights.

Opie crawled up the wire like a freakin monkey while I watched. After he made it to the deck, we both turned and hauled our packs through the brackish water and up the side of the hull. Exhausted, we sat on the wood decking inside of the billboards on the starboard side of turret #3. The North Carolina had nine of the big bore 16" cannons used for shore bombardments and fighting other battleships. These guns had shelled Iwo Jima and countless other islands in WWII as we did our island hopping campaign to free the Pacific from the Japanese. Their range was something beyond 20 miles and the shells were the weight of a 1965 mustang, or close to it. I had been on board this ship back in high school on a fieldtrip. The ship had been a museum since the sixties and tens of thousands of people visited every year to walk the decks and read the plaques.

Back before the green shirt takeover, you could tour the galley, mess halls, engine room or at least part of it, barber shop, dentist's office, chief petty officer's quarters, and a whole bunch of other things. You started right here on the starboard side of turret 3 and by the time you finished, you were one deck up and you came out under the bridge and the port side behind turret #2. Above decks, you could sit inside several of the quad 40mm guns and actually move the apparatus left and right and up and down. There were 20mm guns and the bow anchors on display above decks. A couple of the 5 inch guns were open to explore as well. You could see where hydraulic lifts brought up ammunition and the men could ram the rounds into the breach. It was a great tour back then.

Unfortunately, I was not sure what we would find on board today. A lot of museums and historic sites had been demolished when our financial system collapsed. Wilmington had been no different than other major cities. Some places had been nearly burned to the ground in some cases. But that was almost two years ago. I signaled for Opie to follow me because I wanted to see what we had to work with here. We stashed our packs underneath turret #3 and walked with our M4s towards the stern of the ship. The incredibly big barrels pointed towards downtown. In the back of my mind I had to remind myself that there was no way to hoist a one ton shell into the cannon even if I did have the necessary six

80-pound bags of powder to fire just the one shell. But it would have been fun.

The rear deck used to have two catapults for the Kingfisher seaplanes used mostly for downed pilot rescues and surface searching. The fantail of the ship had two quad-40mm gun mounts and a crane for recovering the float planes as they returned to the ship. These things I remembered from my tours years ago. In the dark of that early morning I saw that the seaplane and catapults were gone. But there in the open space were a row of tubes I did not expect. The half dozen tubes were positioned in a neat little row facing the highway 17 bridge we passed under some hour or two before. I found a couple of crates which contained a projectile that I recognized as illumination flares with parachutes. The writing on the casing looked to be Russian, but I could not be sure. This was something that I did not expect. Who would someone want to mount these here on the ship? Were they still being used or were they left behind and forgotten? I looked at the tubes and found them loaded. A cable ran from the tubes and followed around to the port side of the ship towards the bow.

Opie tapped me on the shoulder as he scanned to the south. We eased our way closer to the port side of the ship to see the two towers of the Cape Fear River Memorial Bridge way off to the southeast. My laser range finder could not pick up on either tower; they must be farther than 1,000 yards, well out of range. I looked down in front of me as I realized that the museum entrance/gift shop was fully intact. The walkway was in one piece and did not look damaged in any way. At the time, this was unexpected but was not my primary concern.

I peered to the right between billboards to see what kind of view we had of the intersection. What few trees that were there before had been removed. The intersection used to be very heavily wooded as I remembered from years prior. The recon photos did not do this intersection justice. There were bunkers and fighting positions located in two or three rows of concentric circles from the center of the intersection. The center position looked like a fortified concrete building with sand-bagged positions surrounding the walls. I risked a quick laser to the block building, 550 yards.

Hopefully nobody was using night vision that could see this wavelength of light.

Opie looked to his watch and held it up for me to see. Dawn was approaching in the next hour. According to the plans we had made over the last couple of days, Opie and I were going to hide out below deck until sometime in the afternoon. We walked from the port side quad-40 gun position under the rear of the #3 turret. I noticed the hatch was locked with a chain and masterlock. We picked up our packs and walked forward to a small housing where a door led to the decks below. I say a door because it was an actual door that had an awning mounted to the deck over a crew hatch. I pulled out my small bolt cutters and approached the door, expecting a lock. Opie lowered his rifle as I stopped and turned the knob slowly. It opened.

Opie opened the door slowly, trying to not make a sound. As we peered into the inky blackness below, a clang of metal on metal sounded from a hundred yards away. We both looked up. Opie raised his rifle and scanned the decks looming above us and forward. I did the same but saw nothing. A pelican or some other bird left its perch and flew against the sky that was not as dark as 10 minutes prior.
I looked to Opie and signaled him to proceed down the ladder. I took his pack as he made his way down into the bowels of the ship. I lowered his pack and then handed him mine. It was hard as hell to make it wearing a tactical vest and a rifle in your hands. Ship designers never anticipated armed men crawling through the hatches. Finally I made my way down the ladder closing the door behind me. The rungs of the ladder were slick with moss and leaves. That door had not been closed for a very long time in my opinion.

In the silence and darkness we were not sure of our surroundings. We could feel the steel walls without seeing them. The quiet was absolute. Our ears strained to hear...anything, but the air carried no sound. The air itself was stale and smelled of rotting insulation that covered the decades-old pipes and wiring. After a few minutes I shined my little LED map light to see around. There was graffiti spray painted on the walls and several of the tables had been destroyed by vandals. Trash, leaves, all manner of garbage, lined the floor and smells of rot filled my nostrils. I turned on my bright weapon light to the ceiling using it as a lantern. The room that was once a clean mess deck had been turned into a dank pit of despair. Opie and I blinked at the sudden light, trying to get used to it. Pipes seemed to run through every space of the ship. Valves jutted from key positions and were painted various colors according to their function. Each hatch had a brass name-plate secured above with a letter and number designation. Below the layer of filth and graffiti, you could see clean places where the paint was still fresh from the days of daily tours just a couple of years ago. It was horrible to see a ship that had been so well preserved as a museum, be subjected to ruthless vandalism this way. It was embarrassing as an American.

Finally we spoke softly for the first time in hours.

"Colonel, what was that sound from above?" Opie asked.

I looked back at him. "I don't know, maybe it was that pelican."

Opie didn't look convinced. "It sounded like metal on metal. It could have been the bird hitting a loose bracket or something, I guess. But there for a split second I thought I heard voices."

I responded, "I didn't hear voices, but those tubes were definitely added by the Sandys at some point. My guess is that they are using them to illuminate the highway."

Opie looked at me. "That intersection is the most heavily defended intersection I have ever seen. I counted four tanks on this side and who knows how many bunkers."

I said, "They designed that place to withstand a frontal assault by a major force. It would take 300 men to assault that place. By then, their artillery spotters would have turned the attackers into Swiss cheese."

We both considered that for a moment. If we had assaulted this place as we originally intended, we would have lost a lot of good people.

Opie suggested, "Maybe we should go a couple of decks down to get into a spot where we can hide out for a while. This room has definitely been *visited* by somebody."

I agreed, "Good idea. We also need to stash our packs and rifles while we search below decks. I can hardly fit the vest through the hatchways and those ladders are impossible with a rifle in your hands."

We walked forward through a double hatchway that led off to the port side of the galley. The old yellow tour signs still pointed their blue arrows leading downward to engine room #4. This area was filled with graffiti just like the other rooms. We climbed down the ladder onto the deck below and went down a hallway leading aft. There we climbed down another ladder, turned 90 degrees, and found ourselves among a room filled with pipes. This was the engine room. The sci-fi nut in me immediately thought of the Borg. The room was both massive, yet so tightly woven with piping that there was little room between equipment. I could almost imagine a Borg drone standing guard in his alcove. We climbed down more stairs until we reached the main engine floor grates. We were most likely well below the waterline of the hull. Charts on the wall indicated the contents of the pipes due to their color bands. Some were fuel, drinking water, hydraulic fluid, and a dozen other necessary liquids to keep a battleship operating.

There was little graffiti down here. There were no portholes this far down. There was no means to light the place without electricity. I doubted anyone wanted to be caught below decks without some sort of battery operated light. It might take hours to get out by feel. Heck, it might even take days.

Opie and I found a couple of different spots to hide our packs. I felt almost naked after I took off my tactical vest. The Thor and my pack were stuffed out of sight on top of a boiler. My M4 and vest were on the other side of the aisle. I took along my bolt cutters and my spare batteries from my pack which I stuffed into my pockets. Opie and I had our M9s with our pistol belts, the rest we left behind in the dark. I felt secure that our gear would not be disturbed.

We followed the tour signs by the light of our flashlights. I tried to keep my bearings, but it was nearly impossible. Every passageway must have had three alternative doorways and routes leading to hundreds of other locked hatches. Most doors had clear Lexan covers to keep tourists from touching the exhibits within. Others had wire mesh welded to keep people out of areas not on the tour. Some hatches were welded shut for safety because they led down to lower decks. Much of the ship was closed off from tours even before the power outage. We passed by several rooms full of historical exhibits. Everywhere you looked, there were pipes running along the walls or ceiling. The doctor's cabin was forced open and the contents were scattered around the floor. I guessed that some drug crazed nut job had expected to find a hit of something made back in the 40s. You had to be pretty far gone to think that.

Opie followed the tour by flashlight until we reached a long hallway that ended in a closed hatch. It was not like the others because it did not have a directional tour sign showing the route continuing up a ladder or changing directions. It simply stopped dead without any redirection. The signs read that the chief's petty officer's mess and recreation room lay ahead along with berths.

I stopped at the hatch looking frustrated. "You want to cut this one or go around?"

Opie shone his light to the right and said, "There is a door open over there." We backtracked until we found a ladder leading upward to the deck above. The ladder was blocked by a chain and a small sign from the tour days. Instead of going up, we decided to continue around towards the chief petty officer's galley. On the left side there was a circular tube leading upward through to the next deck. The brass placard read, "Z". I cut the lock, intrigued because I had never seen this on the tour before.

The inside was not like other areas because it was not cleanly painted and marked. The interior was even more stale and nasty. Wiring filled the interior as it ran along the inside of the tunnel. I shone the little light around and noticed light coming from a distant source somewhere above.

I climbed into the tube and began to climb. Opie climbed up behind me as we heard sounds echo off the steel walls. By the time Opie closed the small hatch behind him, the sounds of another hatch's latch could be heard from somewhere nearby. Neither of us moved. My heart pounded at the sudden adrenaline rush as I flicked off my light. We were not alone.

In seconds the hatch from the adjacent hallway opened briefly as two men spoke to each other in rapid Arabic. One guy flashed a flashlight briefly down the narrow dark corridor. He barely looked inside because he was distracted by a second man. One of the men hounded the other guy about something in words we did not understand. Whatever he said, he was blasting away at the guy, barely letting him get a word in. The hatch was closed back with one latch and their footsteps quickly faded into the distance.

Opie whispered, "I couldn't hear them until they freakin opened the door."

I asked with my heart beating twice its normal rate, "Who the hell are these guys?"

Opie whispered, "There's your pelicans." I grinned in the dark.

We both had our M9s drawn at the low ready just in case the men came back. Neither of us felt safe going back down the hall for a while. As we sat there, we looked around to see the source of the light from twenty feet above us. The tunnel simply led upward and downward with us in the middle. We climbed silently for several minutes, maintaining our complete silence. Three sets of rebar ladders revealed a small platform that housed a rotating turret of sorts. This was not a gun position at all. There were a couple of seats with a series of optical sights mounted in the turret. The side of the optical device passed through the exterior walls allowing some light to pass through. There was communications equipment and all sorts of wiring that led to various equipment removed decades ago. We were in the starboard side 5-inch gun director's turret. When the ship was operational, these turrets directed the fire for the 5-inch guns on this side of the ship. This was definitely not on the tour. I found a small window hatch and forced it open after years of rust and paint had locked the hinges in place. Once it opened, I looked through the hole to see that dawn had come and gone. It was daylight outside.

From my vantage point I could see the bow of the ship and about 30 degrees to the right. At that level I was above the bridge and somewhere close to the same height as the platform just above the bridge. When I looked down I could see the crosswalk leading from the bridge to the flag station where the signalmen would attach various flags to the lines. The main bridge starboard hatch was open, and I could see at least one man sitting behind several radio transmitters. The new radio equipment looked a stark contrast to the 1940s steel structure it sat upon.

I watched as the two men that were running a security sweep earlier made their way up to the bridge from somewhere off the port side of the ship. The one man was still complaining about something as the other man climbed the ladders in silence. They both disappeared into the bridge a few seconds later. I listened as an unseen voice shouted briefly in protest. It was my bet that these guys had a sergeant that had just told them to shut up. Thirty seconds later a familiar clang of metal on metal sounded from above my vantage point. I looked up to see an RPK machinegun being set into to position looking northwest towards the highway 17 bridge.

I motioned for Opie to take a look. As he switched positions with me, he pointed to the optical sighting system and motioned for me to look through it. I did so in utter amazement. I could see the whole northern portion of the Cape Fear River from here. If the turret moved, and had a hole, it would have been the greatest sniper hide of all times.

Opie and I traded spots a couple of times while we watched these guys for more than an hour, getting a feel for their number and purpose. I left the window open just in case we needed to use it again before we climbed back down the simple welded rungs. I exited the hatch where we first hid back in the Chief's galley. Opie caught up to me among the steel tables and ovens.

"Opie," I whispered. "They must be using the bridge and the decks above as a lookout for their artillery. They can just barely see over the billboards from the deck above the bridge."

Opie crouched beside me. "Yeah, I was thinking that as well. They must use this as a lookout since it is the tallest point overlooking the entire intersection. I bet from the other side you can see clear to South Carolina."

I thought for a second then asked, "How many did you count?"

Opie counted on his fingers quickly. "I made out four for sure."

"I counted the same, but I wouldn't be surprised if there was maybe one or two more," I told him. How I knew that, I didn't know. We sat there listening for a few seconds while I pondered our next move. The ship was the best place in the world for two snipers to attack the intersection. By the time they could aim and fire their tanks, we could be fifty feet away and pop up somewhere different for every shot. They would think the ship was crawling with snipers. The armored hull would not be a bad thing for us, either. Their shells would have to hit exactly on our position to get to us. Even the lightly armored gun positions had steel a half inch thick. But before we could use the ship like that, we needed to eliminate the spotter crew.

I looked at my watch, 10:00 hours, 12 hours to go before the mission start. We had time, but not a lot.

I told Opie, "Let's get back to our gear."

We opened the bottom hatch and made our way back the exact way we came. Well, mostly the way we came. The decks were completely dark even though the sun shined brightly outside. It took 20 minutes or more to travel the length of the ship even with flashlights and the tour signs. When we got back, Opie and I sat among the dull light of a single led flashlight and ate one of the MREs from our packs. The silver insulation from engine room piping reflected the light nicely. We had plenty of light. You could see down the grating some 30 feet or more below your feet. You felt like you were in a tree house inside a giant machine or something. We felt quite secure down here in the engine room because it was so secluded. The lack of graffiti meant that even the local vandals never came down this far. We took the time to relax and rest up before moving into our attack positions. We talked briefly about how we needed to eliminate this spotter crew before we could attack the intersection. We agreed that more recon was needed and the timing of our attack had to be close to 20:00. Otherwise we would risk an alarm way too soon to accomplish our mission of harassing the Sandy garrison guarding the intersection. We took our time there in the engine room if for nothing else but to blow time. We couldn't afford to be caught so many hours before the mission kickoff. The minutes ticked by slowly in the relative dark.

Opie spooned out a helping of MRE main course as he commented, "You don't want to be caught down here without a light."

"You got that right," I agreed. My MRE wasn't very tasty, but my stomach thought it was feast. "It wouldn't help to be too claustrophobic either."

Opie asked out of the blue, "Huck, why are you here?"

At first I thought it was a weird question. Then I realized something that genuinely confused Opie about me. I asked, "What do you mean? Why do I fight the green shirts and the Sandys, you mean?"

Opie stopped eating for a minute. "Not exactly; I think I know why *we all* fight them. But why are *you* here on this mission in Wilmington? Don't you have a wife and family back up in North Wilkesboro?"

I nodded my head yes and said, "This is one of those missions that if I don't make sure it comes out the right way, a lot of people will end up dying. Maybe not right away, but down the road. If the Sandys are allowed to land an invasion force, there will be no safe place to hide for any of us."

Opie kind of stared off into space a little with his eyes out of focus. "I think I want a family some day."

I asked jokingly as I sat back against a large pipe, "What, no girlfriend pining away for you back home?"

Opie turned a little red in the cheeks and laughed. "No, not really. I dated a few girls, but I haven't had much time for that in a while." He dipped his MRE spoon back in the package, thinking deeply.

We sat in silence thinking about life and what roles we were yet to play in it. It was a luxury we could not afford for long,though. We took an hour to rearrange our gear and stash the empty MRE packets so they would never be found. During that time we made our plan for the day. Our first objective was to find the port side 5-inch gun director turret like the one we used as an observation post from the starboard side. We would spend the rest of the day inside, scoping out the intersection and watching the artillery spotters. From that hide we would make our assault plan for the night as well as for the spotters. I relayed my thoughts on how we should use the entire ship as a shooting platform once we eliminated the spotters. Opie liked the idea of using the ship as our own set of monkey bars with the ability to shoot from platforms made of ½-inch steel.

We retraced our steps back up to the mess deck just forward and under turret #3. From there we found a set of chained hatches that led upward to more areas above the main deck, but were closed off to tourism. The Sandys never seemed to have used any portion of this part of the ship. I guessed they did not see it as necessary since it overlooked downtown Wilmington. I don't know what they officially called it, but the deck was above turret #3 and overlooked the quad 40mm guns. This part of the superstructure had never been on the tour in my estimation. The spaces were lit by the portholes that lined the walls. They were musty old compartments made of steel, lined with steel pipes, steel ladders, and rivets everywhere you looked. Outside, narrow walkways allowed sailors to man the guns at a moment's notice. Large square lockers painted gray once housed clips of 40mm ammunition.

We searched around until we found another set of hatches that were locked. My bolt cutters bit through more locks than I care to remember that day. I kept hiding the broken parts above piping, and any crevice large enough to hide the pieces. I didn't want to take any chances of a snap security screen that resulted in the discovery of recently unlocked doors.

We tested a set of hatches that led to the outer walkways headed forward towards the bridge. The two large smoke stacks and the 5-inch gun director's turrets obscured us from anyone in the bridge looking in our direction. I remember looking down to the water feeling like I was 50 feet up already. Then when you turned forward the smoke stacks, you had to look up at a 45 degree angle to see the top. This ship was huge.

We opened the hatch to make sure we could do so before we committed the place to memory. Some of the hatches were just too rusted to open by hand after being closed for so many years. The walkways were a series of metal grates that wound around both sides of the smoke stacks leading forward. In some cases you had to climb ladders to the deck above. In other cases you climbed down a level before traveling forward. Every level passed any number of quad 40mm gun emplacements, single 20mm guns, dual 5-inch gun turrets, or huge search lights perched 70 feet above the waterline. Eventually all the paths led to and from the main bridge.

While we overlooked turret #3, I took the time to lay out the Thor and ready it for battle. I laid out the spare ammo and magazines where I could grab them instantly. I looked at Opie.

"Go ahead and dope your scope for a 550 yard shot. Most of our targets will range from about 500 to 650 yards according to my preliminary laser findings." I double checked my drop card and made the necessary adjustment to compensate for the bullet drop during a 550 yard shot.

Opie clicked his scope and adjusted the magnification to its lowest setting. He tossed his scope cover to the side as he loaded his rifle. We grounded the sniper rifles and dropped our tactical vests nearby. We took our M4s with only the one magazine just so we could maneuver around the ship in a hurry and not be outgunned by their AK47s in a pinch. We also kept our pistol belts because close quarter battling is easier with a pistol. I stuck a fragmentation grenade in my pocket and saw Opie do the same.

We took my pack and headed down the hatches, carefully watching out for a security patrol. It was 13:00 when we left for the mid-ship 5-inch turret controller on the port side. We followed the tour route by flashlight just like we had earlier in the day. We approached the long passageway to the closed hatch just like before. This time I looked left for a hatch that would lead to our destination, but there was none. I backtracked while Opie stood guard with his M4. I checked several doors leading to offices with the typical displays from the 40s. I pulled out the bolt cutters and carefully snipped the lock and chain securing a room from tourists. The noise of the broken lock and chain dangling sent chills up my spine. Could the Sandys hear it? I grabbed the chain and stopped dead. My ears strained to hear any sign of approaching Sandy footsteps. Seconds seemed like hours as I waited. Opie kept watch with his M4 trained on the passageway, but there was nothing. I opened the gate and walked into the room that had not been used in 50 years. Machinist's tools and parts of other machinery were stacked and crammed into every space. I found a way around the shop and saw a path that led to a ladder and square hatch. I signaled Opie to follow me and he closed the mesh door behind us.

I worked the square hatch for 15 minutes before I was able to crack the red paint and lift the heavy steel. Light flooded my senses as I looked around. This deck had been on the tour and was covered in filth and graffiti. Broken display cases once held model ships and period newspapers. I climbed out and stood guard with my M4. Opie came behind me and we lowered the hatch. Everything inside was demolished. This was the main deck level that had been open to the public. I looked around thinking that this was way too open for my liking. I led Opie down to the next room where pictures of Boatswains painted the ship. Graffiti of all types lines the walls as the disgrace of the looters during the power outage was on full display.

Opie tapped my shoulder. I looked and he motioned that we should move forward. We looked for maybe three minutes, but it felt like forever. Any moment and we could have a security patrol show up and we would have to fight our way free. I was frustrated. Where is the access to the port side tube? Finally Opie waved to me. He pointed to the area directly above where we had climbed through earlier. A hatch was marked with "Z" on a brass plaque just like we saw in the Chief's galley.

I whipped out the bolt cutters, determined to make our way to our secure hiding place. Luckily the hatch opened and we were able to climb up with some effort since there was no ladder. We made our way up to the port side gun director's turret and sat in the familiar brass seats.

The interior of the turret was identical to the starboard side unit. With a bit of effort and some elbow grease, we were able to open the small window portholes on either side of the turret. Even in winter, the small room made of steel collected the sun's rays, making the air warmer that we were accustomed. I could only imagine what the WWII sailors felt as they sat in these same seats during combat tours in the South Pacific. I felt droplets of sweat drip down my back within minutes.

The optical sighting system looked almost directly south. The north side of the intersection was clearly visible over the tops of the billboards. I could see the bunkers in detail beyond rows of wire fences surrounding the perimeter of the intersection. The Sandy's fortification was everything I thought it would be. There were dozens of bunkers of various types and sizes. Some were made of sand-filled bags while others looked like concrete block structures with hardened roofs. There was nothing larger than a shrub in the whole five acres of intersection. Only short swamp grass grew between the trenches connecting the fighting positions.

Razor wire stretched in large coils underneath the cover of interlocking machine guns.

I watched as cars and trucks approached the intersection slowly. The guards stopped each vehicle between the K-rail roadblocks to inspect every box and every person. Papers were shown to prove they belonged in the city. Almost all the people I saw were from some Arab country by the looks of them. Every now and again a row of cars and trucks idled as they waited for their inspection. All the guards were armed with AK-47s as they stood by in their tan and green uniforms. I noticed that most of them wore jackets and some even had scarves; I guess a 50 degree day was cold compared to what these guys were used to.

I switched seats with Opie who was ready with his sniper data book. Since he was so good at range estimation, I handed him my laser range finder and let him sit where he could see the widest field of view. Over the next hour he recorded key landmark positions and their distances from our vantage point on the ship. Even though that distance would vary a bit as we shot from various parts of the ship, it is always good to have an idea how far your target is from you.

I turned my attention to the spotter crew manning the bridge only 60 feet away. So far, they were completely unaware of our presence. The radios were no longer visible from the port side, but I could see cables leading out of a bridge porthole. A pair of wires went upward to some antennae mounted on the deck above. The rest dangled along the port side of the ship as they ran aft. These must be the controls for the illumination rounds on the rear deck. It took me five minutes to finally figure out the bright orange cable among all the black wires. Then it dawned on me, it was a standard extension cord. Duh, there was no power generated from the ship. It must be coming from the former gift shop.

The afternoon wore on for a while like that. Opie and I drank the water with the super-Gator-aide from my pack. We also ate the last MREs, leaving only a side item or two in our pockets for later, just in case. Opie copied the range card he drew and handed me one. We reviewed the high value targets we wanted to concentrate on when the shooting started.

I gave Opie an update on the spotter crew. I could only count four at any time, but somewhere in my gut I always thought there were five. One guy always manned the RPK on the radar deck, one monitored the radios on the bridge, and one or two guys would patrol every four hours or so. But the patrols were sloppy at best. They always took the same route and haphazardly checked dark hallways as we saw before. I also noticed that they seldom carried their AK47s while on patrol. I guess it had been a long time since anyone from the 2nd battalion militia had attacked the battleship directly. From what I could remember, the Sandys had been in control of downtown Wilmington for at least a year or more. Nobody knew for sure because the militia movement in the early days was stronger further up north as we fought the green shirts. The 2nd just had too large a territory to cover Wilmington as well as everywhere else east of highway 95.

"Opie, let's spend the rest of the daylight to plan our attack on these spotters," I whispered.

Opie turned around in his seat. "I was thinking about that, Huck. How close to H-hour do you want to hit these guys?"

I looked at the digital readout of my watch. "My watch reads about 17:00, we will lose the light around 18:00 or soon after. That will give us about an hour and a half with the deck completely dark. I suggest we set a couple good-ole-boy traps for these guys."

Opie looked devilishly happy about the prospect. "Whatever we do, it has to be quiet. If they get on that radio before we get to them, they will call in reinforcements and we will be in some real crap." I liked to see him think the same way I did. You can anticipate someone if you know you think the same way as they do.

I looked out of the window and pointed to the power cable. "I bet if we cut the power to the radios, they will crap themselves. I also want to rig some of that heavy duty steel tubing they used for the billboards I saw on the port side deck."

Opie asked, "Do you think they can hear gun shots from the sections we came through earlier?"

I considered it. "If the hatches are closed, I don't see how they could. What are you thinking?"

Opie said, "What if we lure one of them down the passageways below? We put something in the hall that is white against the dark gray floor about ten feet in. When they patrol, they see it, and we pop them."

"Good, Opie. We will have to work up a counterweight for the hatch, but that won't be a problem. The hatch needs to close behind him tightly," I added.

We schemed on and on until the sun began to sink behind the far-off swamp trees to the west. The billboards cast long shadows on our side of the ship as the sun set. Opie and I watched carefully to see if the Sandys changed their routine. Once, right before dark, the man on the upper deck switched out with another guy. From time to time we watched as they roamed from position to position. For the most part they stayed in the same areas the whole time we watched them. A deck below the main deck must be where they had bunks. Sometimes during the day there would only be one guy at the radio and one at the lookout above. The others were below.

Before I could tell Opie to leave a smell wafted up to our perch.

I looked over at Opie as the light failed. "What is that smell?"

About that time light shone from an open hatch just behind the port side of turret #2. The man wore his tan uniform with a filthy apron over it as he yelled something in Arabic. Another man eased his way out of the hatch and stretched slowly. The lookout and radio man clanged their way down ladder after ladder to get to the main deck level. It must have been supper time. The lone man climbed up the vacant ladders as the other two raced below deck for their evening meal. This was our opportunity to move with as little risk as possible.

I looked at Opie, who was already standing on the rungs of our tube. "Smells like I know what end of the goat they are cooking tonight."

Opie quipped in a fake Arabic voice, "Come eat at Ali's house of goat-burgers, two for a dollar."

I choked back tears of laughter as I made my way down the tube again. With my small led light in my mouth, I worked the lower hatch and sneaked a peak around below. It was quiet and dark because the shadows from the billboards had long since draped this deck in shadow. I lowered myself until I dropped. Opie tossed my M4 down and I covered him as he lowered himself. We closed the hatch with the coolness of winter once again making our acquaintance. We had been sitting in a relative sweat box for hours. The sudden drop in temperature made our teeth chatter. The adrenaline didn't help much in that department either.

Darkness gave us a new level of boldness for moving around the ship. The billboards shielded us from view outside the ship. The lookout above was almost 75 feet above and looking the other way. We worked our way along the exterior of the ship, heading forward cautiously with our M4s pointing the way. I led while Opie followed in the cover position. My ACOG's illuminated green dot shone brilliantly against the ship's dark gray paint.

We passed several of the 5-inch turrets as the rounded turrets curved by the superstructure. There was only 18" of space, just enough for a man to pass behind as the turret swung into position. You couldn't see more than two or three feet at a time until you came around the other side. The adrenaline rush was amazing.

We searched in the dark for any sign of activity from above, but there was none. I motioned for Opie to follow as I stepped down an external ladder leading to the main deck. At the bottom, I found the hatch where the cook had stood 10 minutes prior. It was not closed and I peered through the crack. The interior was lit by a single bulb hanging over the small foyer. Beyond the foyer was a single square hatch hinged from the back allowing access the deck below. It was propped up allowing me to see down to the base of the ladder. Nobody was around; but I could hear echoes of the men below. Barely taking a deep breath lest I be heard, I opened the exterior hatch and stepped through. Opie stood by the door with his eyes wide as saucers.

The light bulb illuminated the space beyond the hatch as I looked around. The old 20mm clipping room was closed. The display of black 20mm drum magazines was in disarray from vandals by the look of things. Spray paint and broken window panes lay inside the compartment. I stepped further down the space leaving the clip room behind as Opie followed. The left side of the steel wall curved inward because we were literally on the back side of the #2 turret. A men's bathroom had a light on inside. There were sounds of someone finishing their business. I waved Opie forward so we could get out of sight. He curved around to the left and I turned right just beside the women's bathroom during the tour days. We trained our M4s back towards the hatch.

The men's bathroom door was evidently hard to open as the occupant worked the door hard to get out. With a kick he closed the door behind him in frustration. He walked to the open hatch below and yelled down, "Yahala ben hackpoo." I don't know what the hell he really said, but you get the idea.

He looked down the hatch until a voice answered, "Hackpoo to you too." Or whatever he said.

At that, the toilet man walked out to the deck and we heard his feet start up the ladder. He must be going back up to his watch. Opie and I shared glances at the close call we had just encountered. I looked around as we waited to see if anyone else was coming. There was nothing. I had led us into a really tight corner. Everything else in this compartment was closed off from the days of the tour. We had a whole battleship to use as cover and we had just backed into a corner with no exit.

Opie led us back to the hatch where we listened for the sounds of voices. We absolutely had to know how many men we were up against. At least two men talked below in an adjacent compartment somewhere fairly close. Several lights dangled from the deck above with an extension cord running overhead. There was no way we could hope to work our way down there without getting caught. I motioned for Opie to head back to the deck outside the foyer. Once he made sure the way was clear, we crouched low and made our way aft until we reached the safety of a 5" gun turret. The deck overhung the area behind the turret, allowing us free access without the worry of unfriendly eyes looking down at us from above.

Opie looked around to make sure nobody could overhear. "I count four." Then he made a questioning look like he could be wrong. I nodded my head in agreement.

I looked down at my watch and whispered, "We have about 90 minutes, let's get to work."

Work is right. We found that the tubing that lay on the port side deck was not random steel. It was the barrels of one of the 5" guns that had been cut off to leave room for the billboards. We heaved and heaved until we finally got one of them where we wanted. It took every second of the 90 minutes I figured we had to set up all our little gizmos too. It always seems too easy in the movies. Then again everything does. The hero always shoots straight without aiming, his magazine never goes empty in a scene, and he always wins the fist fight after the bullets run out. I wish life was like the movies; all I needed was a director and someone to yell 'cut'.

The last twenty minutes before I wanted to kick off the attack on the spotters, I got a revelation. Opie and I made our way aft to the open deck area behind the 16" guns. Opie looked on as I opened the metal case for the illumination rounds. Some were like mortars and others seemed to be an electric-fired type.

I whispered to Opie, "We pull the white cap off one of these barrels and we stuff as many of these mortars down the barrel as we can. We can use the C4 charge Nemo gave me in the chamber to blast these things across the river."

Opie looked at the barrels as they pointed across the Cape Fear. "That's about 450 yards to the nearest building. Do you think that will work with such a low angle on the barrel?"

I scratched my head for a minute. "I don't know, but it will make for one heck of a story if it works."

We made our way back to our packs way up on the deck thirty feet above. The climb was easier because we could use the exterior rebar rungs which allowed sailors to quickly scale upward to their gun positions. Inside we found our packs and rifles waiting for us. I unzipped my pack to retrieve the C4 charge in its own bag. Opie watched out behind us and took a knee beside me as I worked with my small led light. I took a breath to slow down after the climb. As I did so, my mind drifted off to previous engagements where I had only a few minutes before a big fight. I felt the urge to ask forgiveness for what I was about to do to my fellow man.

"Opie," I said in a whisper. "Pray with me."

Opie turned to look at me earnestly then held his hand over to me. I did not know if he was a person of faith or not, but that didn't matter. We bowed our heads and I took his hand. "Lord, please look over us tonight. We are humble soldiers fighting for the freedom to proclaim your name as Savior. Let us don the armor of your spirit and keep us from physical harm. Forgive us for the sins we commit. We make war tonight not out of hatred, but to protect others from harm. We ask these things in Jesus' name, Amen."

Opie squeezed my hand and let go. I felt a million times better knowing that I was right with the Lord and if he called me home that night, it would be okay. We made our way back down the rungs until we reached the main deck. Now we just had to load a 16" gun by hand.

Here again, it sounds easier than it was in doing. This turret had been on the tour for years and I remembered things a little differently than what I saw. The three guns of turret #3 were set up as a display to show each phase of loading a shell into the giant barrels. The left barrel had the breech open and the aluminum folding tray hinged upward as if waiting for the next shell. The middle barrel had a dummy shell standing straight up in the tray ready to be rammed home. The right barrel had several fake bags of powder being rammed behind the loaded shell by the force of a hydraulic ramrod.

I stood inside the turret among the graffiti, looking inside the displays.

Opie observed, "Do you think the billboards will get in the way? Hey, what about the crane on the stern? Won't that deflect some of the rounds?"

He was right! I ducked back outside and climbed the exterior of the turret to double check. Sure enough, the middle barrel was a no go. The crane that recovered the Kingfisher aircraft loomed in the dark. The left and right barrels were the only options. The billboards did not concern me too much, though. I figured the mortars would pass right through them if they hit at all.

Time was running short as I grabbed the bag with the explosive charge and headed back inside the turret. We chose the left gun because it looked the easiest to work. With the few remaining locks cut we had full access to the gun operator's positions. I used the fake bag of powder as wadding after I stuffed the barrel with all the spare mortar shells. I carefully placed the C4 blocks, which weighed close to 10 pounds, on the breech side of the fake powder bag. We ran the detonating wire down the barrel back outside allowing us to connect the charge to the string of mortars on the deck. Once we were satisfied, we began to close the breech. Then we tried again. We pulled and pulled the huge cylindrical breech with little movement. Finally I realized the unit was hydraulic and we used a pair of multipliers to open the control line. Fluid drained out, but it didn't help much. The weight of the thing was like that of a small truck. We finally used a board from old renovation project nearby to mechanically lift the breech using the gunner's chair as a fulcrum. Finally in place, we were ready. Sweat poured from our bodies due to the confined space and the amount of muscle we had to put into the effort, but we were finally ready.

Opie and I picked up our M4s and exited the turret, glad to be outside again. The stars were out as they twinkled in the sky. We connected the wires from our charge to the last position of the mortar rack. Our thought was that if the Sandys fired, they would start at position one and work their way to ten. We would have time if they started shooting flares to get clear of the main blast if we were right. If they started at 10, well, we might have some issues.

Once we finished with the wires, Opie said, "I'll turn this rack around so the mortars face the intersection. We will illuminate the garrison and give ourselves better light to shoot by."

I responded, "Great idea, Opie. I will head down the catwalk to the gift shop and set my grenade by the door with a tripwire." Opie nodded in agreement.

I walked slowly down the double ramp walkway to the set of glass doors that were still intact. The only other walkway was towards the port bow which used to run electricity to the forward part of the ship. This walkway had mesh rails to keep tourists from falling into the gator infested waters below.

I knelt in front of the doors thinking that anyone trying to get at us after we started our attack would try to use one of these two ramps to board the ship. The grenade was in my hand and my tripwire rolled out when the door opened. I was bowled over in a heap as the person tripped over me and fell to the ground. We both raced to gain our footing first. My M4 lay three feet away and out of reach. I grabbed at the man's face as he tried to call out. We were immediately embroiled in a wrestling fest. I was at a disadvantage because he had been higher on the ramp when we grappled. I was under his smelly armpit in a semi-headlock as I had him around the waist. My left hand punched at his face and hit him in the throat. My goal was keep him from calling out at all costs. He punched at me as we circled on the spot trying to get some measure of advantage on the other. He gasped when my last lunge caught him in the Adam's apple. All you could hear was us grunt as we fought for position. That and our boots making the wooden boards of the ramp thump in the darkness. I felt my right side lift as he tried to draw my pistol from the holster. It was no good because he evidently didn't know how to draw from a level III retention holster. Thank you, Safariland.

About that time I heard footsteps as someone else hurried down the ramp. I didn't know if it was Opie or the other Sandys coming to help their comrade. I couldn't do anything about it anyway. The sound of a thwack and the sickening crunch of bone breaking told me that Opie had arrived. My foe went limp immediately and slumped to the ground where I joined him, exhausted.

Opie crouched beside me. "Huck, you alright?" He laid his M4 down beside us as he looked at my opponent. He thrust his knife into the guy to make sure he was dead. He was. The stock of the M4 had caught the Sandy in the temple at full force. I am surprised it didn't break the stock.

"Thanks," was all I could mutter as I panted, trying to catch my breath.

Opie sat down to cover me as I got my composure. It took several minutes before I felt okay enough to go on. After that he asked, "It's about huntin time. You ready to go?"

"I'm okay," I told him. I was only slightly jittery by then. "That guy came right out of the blue. He was on me before I could do anything," I told Opie. "Did we make a big noise?"

Opie said, "No. In fact I couldn't figure out what you were doing. I thought you had hurt your hand down there because all I could see was a black blob half your normal height writhing around."

I looked down at the corpse. "Well, I told you there were five."

Opie shook his head. We made a sweep of the gift shop and determined this was the only other Sandy. Opie tied his grenade to a wire across the main hallway leading to the ship. We then turned back to the ramp where I finished putting my grenade above the doorway. On the ramp we pushed the body of the Sandy onto the watery edge of the shore. He hit with a muddy thud, but was out of sight. One down.

I held my M4 in my left hand by the forearm and racked the bolt back half way to make sure I had a round chambered. I let the bolt ride forward and locked the charging handle back in place. I pushed the forward assist to make sure it was in battery. The Berretta was checked and re-holstered. Opie looked to me and nodded that he was ready. We made our way up the ramp and boarded the North Carolina one more time, for the last time.

Our mood had changed by the time we climbed to the level just above the main deck. We were hunting our fellow man and the clock was ticking. We had thirty minutes before I figured we should start shooting to cover the divers attacking the barge crews. The time was 21:20. I wanted to get our sniper hits going perhaps ten minutes before 22:00, if we could manage it. That would give the Seals on the barges that much broader window of opportunity to complete their task.

We made our way forward until we reached the motorized whaleboat on the port side. I got behind the boat while Opie got into the position we had worked out earlier when planning the trap. We had no more than sat still for thirty seconds when the guy that regularly walked the security route, exited the forward hatch by turret #2. He jabbered on to somebody below with only the dim lights cast from the foyer within to illuminate his body. I didn't want to shoot him, because we did not have a suppressed weapon. The guy walked up the ladder and made his way to our deck and called out to the lookouts above.

The man with the machinegun on the top leaned over the side of his armor plated position and waved his hand in a dismissive way. He didn't want to be bothered by someone going on a standard security sweep. Our target walked his beat with his AK on his shoulder. My guess was that he would walk the exterior decks on this sweep which is why he carried the rifle. His older D-cell flashlight was jammed in his left pocket as he smoked casually with his right hand. He passed within 15 feet of me and all I could do was wince at the acrid smoke coming from the guy. Whew! He must have been smoking freakin camel hair or something.

Anyway, he passed slowly as I peeked from behind the boat. The guard strolled towards the ladder leading down to the main deck as I readied my rifle just in case our trap didn't work. The guard started down the steps and flicked his cigarette towards the back of the billboards which hung off the hull. The lit end spun round and round against the darkness and lightly thumped the wood until it dropped out of sight in the water.

The guard's boots clunked down every step slowly as he made his way down. When he got to the last step, his world changed forever. The final step had been unhinged by Opie and me earlier that evening. When you stepped down, the step broke free which caused a flat steel bar to transfer your weight across the deck. As the bar flexed, the heavy steel barrel cut from the 5" gun turret became unsteady and started its decent to the water 30 feet below. This old boy found out the hard way that one end of a 550 cord was tied to the barrel and the other was lassoed around his feet at the bottom of the step. In an instant, the guard was slammed to the deck and drug over the side of the hull where the mesh deck-guards had been removed during the installation of the billboards. The barrel hit the water first as it "plooped" into the water end first. The Sandy was so enthralled with the sudden jerk downward all he could do was inhale. He made a splash when he hit the water, but it was not loud. I doubted they could hear it from 75 feet above. Opie looked over the side rail and signaled that the man was underwater. All this happened in a second or two.

I joined Opie on the deck below and we worked around to the hatch on the port side of turret #2. We checked forward and aft to make sure nobody was around. It was clear. I opened the hatch slowly and scanned for Sandys. Opie went to the men's room to check as I stood guard. He signaled clear. We formed up around the square hatch leading down and peered to the deck below. The space was clear. I strapped my M4 to my back and climbed down while Opie covered me. On the deck below, I drew my Berretta because I favored a pistol in close combat. Opie closed the hatch behind him and dogged the center wheel. After he climbed down

He tapped my shoulder signaling ready. We both stuffed hearing protectors in our ears.

The steel walls were still painted a light green as they had been in the tour days. You could smell strange food being cooked between the musty walls of the historic ship. We marched around to the left beside turret #2, passing the Gunnery Office. The door was open. The bunk had been used recently and the displays from the museum days were gone. There were all sorts of personal items strewn about the place like someone was living there. Opie followed as we worked our way around the hallway to the left. A passageway turned forward with a ladder directly to our left as it rose to the next level. The sounds of a small radio crackled ahead of us. Nobody was in sight. I bet their reception was crap there below decks with tons of steel above them.

The corridor led to several officer's quarters as well as the Flag Office. All the doors had been opened by someone, but there was no sign of graffiti. I assumed the Sandys opened them at some point. It was nerve racking work to clear each space with zero noise and trying to cover your butt the entire time. The steel walls were confining to say the least. We made our way to the Flagg office as I peeked through the window of the second doorway. I just made out a figure inside when I ducked to stay out of view. I was on one side of the doorway and Opie on the other. The guy inside was sitting at a table reading a newspaper and sipping a drink with his back to the door. I signaled for Opie to sit tight while I continued the search in case there were more. He knew to pop the guy if he needed to. I gave him a thumbs-up as I continued forward and around the corner.

There I found the source of the bad smells. The Warrant Officer's recreation room and mess facility had dirty dishes piled on the old dark green tables used for dinner and ping pong. You could still see the white line painted over the center of the table where the net would have been. I continued across the room with the Berretta pointing the way. The far wall had a window where the cooks used to serve up chow. The small galley was clear, but had the distinct smell of deep-fried goat burgers heaped in crap. I worked my way through the adjacent hatch and opened it slightly until I could fit through. A man lay in one of the bunks with an old mattress and several covers. He was asleep. The room was sleeping quarters for about 16 or so men when the ship was operational. Several rows of folded up racks, four bunks high, littered the space. I counted quickly and there were five mattresses. Counting these and the Gunnery Office, there were six men on board. The only other hatch leaving the room was closed with no room for lighting. Whatever lay back there was in the dark.

With nerves shaking, I grabbed a pillow off the next bunk and pressed the barrel against it like I saw in movies. I turned my head as the man woke and fired three or four shots in rapid succession. The pillow was not that efficient as a silencer. My 9mm rounds gave sharp snaps because the 124 grain bullets were supersonic at the muzzle. I never killed anyone like that before. I hated it, but I was forced by time and practicality. Time was not on my side and that left me few choices without a second to waste.

I ran back to the passageway and knelt to the floor before peeking around the corner. Two shots from Opie's M4 echoed against the walls with mind numbing results.

I quickly jutted my head out to see. My eyes fixed on a dead man staring back at me as he lay on his stomach facing exactly in my direction. Opie stood by with smoke issuing from his rifle looking down at us. He recognized me and raised his rifle to let me rise.

Through the ringing in my ears I said, "Four down, two to go."

Opie took a deep breath looking at the man he had shot, "We heard the shots. I got him when he charged down the hallway. He didn't even see me."

I patted him as I walked by. "Good work. Thanks."

We jogged back to the square hatch leading back up to the main deck. Opie crouched behind the steps out of sight as I took out my ear plugs. I climbed the ladder with my M9 ready to take on a guard if he was alerted to our shooting. My hope was that all the portholes had been closed for winter since these guy were cold natured. If so, we had chance that the men above on the bridge, some 65 feet above, had not heard our shots below deck. Opie broke the bulb out of the socket sending down a short blue flame with the glass shattering on the floor.

I peered from the hatch, raising it far enough to point the M9's barrel through. Nobody was visible. This was the first time I was in a completely un-defendable position. Anyone could be standing right behind the hatch and blast me into oblivion like a fish in a barrel. But the shots did not come. My heart pounded as I checked every corner for signs of a hidden attacker. Opie followed me through the hatch and we made our way carefully to the main deck. We were both relieved to find the decks clear with no signs of a pending attack. We climbed the exterior ladder up to the next deck and pinned ourselves to the outer steel wall. The more you looked upward, the more areas you found to hide an entire army in the shadows.

The giant forward smoke stack looked to be 15 feet in diameter as it blotted out the few stars as it loomed into the night. Each side of the stack was guarded by the port and starboard 5-inchgun director's turrets although they were not as tall. A maze of ladders and walkways connected the various levels of the superstructure. Solid steel handrails about an inch in diameter kept you from wandering off the side and falling to the decks below. We listened intently for any sounds whatsoever from the remaining spotter crew. All we could hear were distant traffic noises from the intersection and a bird of some sort squawking in the marsh.

Opie pointed to his watch showing me we had to hurry. We had less than 10 minutes. With a deep breath he led the way to the double ladders leading upward to the deck above. I covered him as best I could and watched as he silently crept up one step at a time. That deck housed the Control In Combat, or CIC, just under the main bridge. A large, empty walkway with an outer steel wall horse-shoed around the inner spaces, protecting them from enemy fire. Nobody was inside. Our heads must have looked like bobble-head figures as we tried to point our weapon into every nook and cranny invisible in shadow. This deck led to just about every other bit of the ship. No wonder it had double ladders on both port and starboard side. We strained to see the remaining spotter crew, but to no avail. I pointed to Opie and motioned for him to go aft towards the large square steel boxes between us and the smoke stacks. These used to contain ammunition for the 20mm and 40mm guns which were located on both sides of this deck. Opie steeped up a half level and made his way around backwards as he watched for the spotters to reveal themselves. He climbed another set of steps and crouched behind the steel boxes so he was out of view from the main bridge.

In a few seconds he gave me a single finger indicating one man and pointed to the bridge. Then he pointed to the decks above and held out a single finger again. Then he pointed to me and indicated that I should go to the port side ladder and go up to the main bridge that way. I did so as quietly as possible trying not to bang anything metal on the railings. I took a deep breath and led the way with the M9 as I climbed the single ladder to the bridge level. Here, too, the exterior walkways were covered by vertical steel walls, but they only reached armpit level. We could easily see above the billboards from here. Man, that ship was tall. You felt like a bird way up there. It was amazing. You could see the whole highway 17 bridge with ease.

Opie walked across a steel-plated walkway which gave a metallic sounding wobble as it bent under his weight. I heard it and stopped dead. Opie moved off the plate and stepped under the cover of my walkway like a speedy shadow. I heard for the first time the sounds of someone else on the bridge. There were relaxed voices over the radio between short bursts of static as the users keyed their handsets. I made my way around to the port side bridge hatch which was open. This side of the ship still felt warm from all the sun we had earlier that day. I guess that's why they still had the hatch open with all those radios.

The man monitoring the radios sat in the Captain's chair with his feet on the shelf above the radios. He was busy with a PC tablet, playing games from the looks of things. A video flashed a bluish scene which reflected off the paint inside the walls of the bridge. Three AK47s sat in a rack in front of the old dials and gauges that use to be the center console with the ship's brass wheel. Without thinking I stepped inside as the sounds of the tablet were more impressive than my footsteps. The man casually acknowledged my presence by asking something in Arabic without taking his eyes off the screen. By then I had an AK in hand and gave him the hardest butt stroke to the back of the head I could muster. The metallic thwack was sickening as the man slumped into the seat. His tablet continued the video it was playing as it banged off the steel floor.

Opie appeared behind me as I finished the guy off with my knife. I won't give any more detail than that.

We paused to hear anything from the lone spotter above. Unfortunately our silence and luck had run out to an extent. The lookout from 20 feet above spoke out loud, clearly intending the man in the radio to hear him. He was not questioning the sounds, but rather making fun of the guy as if to say, "What'd you do, stub your toe?" Of course it was in Arabic and we had no way to understand or respond in kind.

Opie was great. He picked up the tablet and banged it on the porthole about five times and said out loud, "AGHH!" as if he were in total exasperation. He then flung the tablet out of the porthole and bounced it off the back of the billboards below. The tablet tumbled down until it splashed silently into the water 75 feet below.

From 20 feet above, came a series of rapid Arabic words and laugher directed at the radio man's expense. I nodded for Opie to follow as I swung open the starboard hatch and went aft to the ladder just inside the compartment behind the bridge. I found the ladder and went up without fear of my steps being heard. The guy above had no idea he was the last of his men on board. He expected to see his comrade come through the hatch any minute, complaining about the evils of Bill Gate's Microsoft software.

The deck above the bridge was just a port and starboard set of quad 40mm guns. I continued upward to the smaller radar bridge that had been a lookout post back in WWII. The hatch was closed as Opie caught up with me on the small interior landing. I undid the latch just as the guard looked backward with laughter still etched across his face. I partially caught him with the heavy hatch as Opie and I rushed him on the tiny deck. The blow from the hatch hit him in the nose and made him reel backwards to the armor plating on his heels. With both our shoulders, we slammed him against the steel and lifted him up and over in one fluid motion. The man screamed bloody murder as he fell. His body bounced off the left barrels of the quad 40mm gun turret below as he picked up speed. With a deadly thud, the last of the spotters fell onto the top of a 5-inch gun turret far below.

Opie looked down into the darkness, "That makes six."

I laughed a bit from the tension letdown. My cheek was swelling from the fight I'd had with the first guard. The U.S.S. North Carolina was completely ours.

Chapter 22
A Target Rich Environment

The ship was completely quiet. From our vantage point we could see in all directions. The swamp area between us and the highway 17 bridge was a dark mass of weeds. Darkness covered the starboard side of the ship as we looked aft towards downtown Wilmington. Electric lights from windows reflected off the waters of the Cape Fear all along the whole eastern shore. If you didn't know there was a war on, you would have thought it was just another quiet night along a peaceful mid-Atlantic coastal city. We were about to change all that.

"Opie, let's get the machinegun and set it up on the bridge below." The sound of my voice speaking so openly felt strange. It made me self-aware after what seemed like days of whispering. I grabbed a spare can of ammo as Opie grabbed the gun. We made our way back down to the bridge where Opie propped the barrel of the machinegun through one of the hatches off the port side of the bridge. The intersection was dark with only a few signs of activity.

Opie finished by closing the feed tray of the RPK and locked the bolt back; then asked, "You want me to go get the sniper rifles?

I thought for a second. "Naw, I'll go with you."

Opie nodded and we headed out of the bridge and made our way aft. Up a ladder, down a ladder, around the stack, up again, down again, it was enough to make you sick. Finally we made it back to the hide where we had the sniper rifles stowed. We raced to our gear and grounded the M4s in the dark compartment. We both donned our assault vests and strapped our M4s over our backs. The idea was to carry all our gear, because after the fight started, who knew if we could come back this way. I hoisted the Thor to port arms and told Opie, "You operate from the here to the smoke stacks. Shoot from cover at all times and remember to switch positions every two shots." You could feel the tension as Opie listened intently to my words. I continued, "I will go back to the bridge and work from there to the front smoke stack. Wait for my signal then let them have it."

Opie sat looking straight at me. "Take care, Huck." We shook hands briefly with our hands shaking slightly. I took off back down the myriad of walkways as briskly as I dared with all my gear. The fear of making noise was gone; I just didn't want to career over the edge and break my neck.

I reached the main bridge and grounded the Thor beside the RPK. My breathing was labored from the jogging up and down the middle section of the superstructure. I looked down at my watch. It was 19:51, time to get their attention. The question was, how?

I looked around the bridge, ignoring the dead body in the Captain's chair. A row of ten silver toggle switches were lined up and marked one through ten. This must have been the controls for the flares on the aft deck. Three black boxes sat on the shelf to the dead man's right. One was different than the other. Two were obviously tactical radios with their own handsets, but the other unit was different. It had a stand microphone instead of the standard military handset. There were more wires leading to a small recording device and a cable that may have been plugged into the tablet that Opie threw overboard. I traced the wires because I could follow the functionality easier than trying to decipher Russian or Arabic writing. The last box turned out to be an amplifier that blasted out the muslim call to prayers from a giant megaphone mounted off the bridge. It faced the intersection. I quickly taped the two radio handsets to the talk position and laid them facing upward.

I keyed the bullhorn's microphone amid a brief static feedback that broadcast out into the darkness. "I WOULD LIKE TO THANK ALL OUR OUT OF TOWN GUESTS FOR ATTENDING TONIGHT'S PERFORMANCE." I paused, knowing that I had gotten a whole lot of attention just then. There must have been 150 to 200 sets of ears wondering just who the heck was talking through that microphone in English. I spoke like some kind of used car salesman, knowing that my words would be translated by only a few. "THE NORTH CAROLINA MILITIA FORMALLY INVITES ALL YOU GOAT LOVING CAMEL JOCKEYS TO A GOOD OLD FASHIONED ASS WHOOPING. IF ANY OF YOU ARE MAN ENOUGH TO QUIT SNIFFING

YOUR   BUDDY'S   BUTT,   COME   OUT   AND   FIGHT!
COLONEL, HUCK OVER AND OUT!"

Yes, I know, it was pure poetry.

I reached over and clicked the toggle switch that read #10. Instantly, there was a boom as I stepped sideways to see the aft part of the ship. The left gun of turret #3 fired the two dozen or so flare mortars we had shoved down the barrel. Maybe half of them flew kind of straight while the rest danced in strange corkscrew patters all over the Cape Fear River. Bits of magnesium burned in midair giving the whole back side of the ship a luminescent quality for several seconds. It looked like the fourth of July and Chinese New Year all rolled up into one. Several of the white hot rounds impacted onto the far shore while several more blasted through windows of a seven story apartment building. Little fires formed as I watched in amazement.

I stepped back around to the bridge and inserted my earplugs with as much relaxed motion as I could muster. With the RPK's grip in hand, I ducked under the view of the portholes as I pulled the trigger and held it down. My purpose was not to hit anything, just get them shooting at us. The entire 200 round belt was expended in short order. I quickly replaced the belt waiting to hear the feedback of massive amounts of AK47 fire impact the ship's steel. There was nothing but the popping of the heated metal of the RPK's barrel as it cooled.

There was near silence. Bang, Opie's rifle sounded. Bang, he shot again. But there was no response from the intersection. I was on the starboard side of the bridge not anxious to be on the port side facing the intersection even though they were not firing at us yet.

Off in the distance, I heard a low whump created by the concussion from a large explosion. I looked north and east to see a fireball rising in the distance. The attack on the airport must have kicked off. I peeked around as I heard another bang from Opie's Remington 700. I strolled back into the bridge, determined that someone was going to shoot at me, darn it. The RPK belched another 200 rounds as I raked it back and forth to cover the whole intersection. By the time the belt finished, I got my wish. The sounds of thousands of rounds dinging off the steel plates, was like driving through a gravel pit in a Chevy. Ting, ting, pling, whirs and ricochets bounced all over the place. Tracer rounds skipped off turrets, some green streaks passed by without hitting anything. It was like being inside a fireworks display. The loudspeaker gave an audible twang as it was hit. I sat on the starboard side of the main bridge with the Thor, just waiting in complete cover.

Larger guns from the intersection joined into the fray. Distinct green tracers rang off the ship's steel. Others hit metal and took odd turns making me duck a few times as they whirred past into the marsh. It was right about then that I got the brilliant idea to make my way to the forward smoke stack. For some crazy reason I thought it would be a great place to see the intersection. The only problem was that it made me expose myself as I crossed the walkway. One ladder down I realized my mistake. A large caliber machinegun on par with the .50 cal. swept it's rounds dangerously close to me. My walkway was only six feet across as I watched two tracers zip through the billboards and pass at waist level in front of me. The rest of the rounds scattered from the lower decks on up to hit off the smoke stack 50 feet above. They were just hosing every part of the ship to get at us.

I stopped at the large square ammunition box that used to house the ammunition for the 40mm and 20mm guns on this level. The thick steel would surely stop anything short of a tank round. I flicked the Thor's bipods out and set it down on top of the 40mm magazine. The crosshairs fell between the cracks of the billboards as I noticed hundreds of small holes poking through the wood already. The scene of the intersection was dark at best. The only way I could decipher a target was by muzzle flashes.

Boom, I fired my first aimed shot of the night. The gun stopped firing immediately. I scanned for another target, boom, the round disappeared into the inky darkness of a bunker slit window. My fingers grabbed the Thor as I crouched down. It was a good thing too. A flurry of rounds impacted within 30 feet of me, sending a fresh set of sparks and bits of copper jacketed bullets in all directions.

The first tank round hit a few seconds later. It seems modern armor piercing shells would penetrate the thinner outer steel shrouds surrounding the quad 40mm gun emplacements. Fire jutted from the upper port side 40mm gun position just above the bridge. The AK fire slowed considerably in the seconds that followed. My feet barely touched the walkway as I hustled from cover and leaped up the steps back up to the main bridge deck.

The lights were out and one of the radios had been hit by a stray round that must have come through the portholes. The metal box with the toggle switches to control the mortars lay on the floor. I grabbed and coiled up as much wire as I could manage, hoping that all this risky effort was not in vain. Risking my life to get to the mortar controls only to find the wire cut by shrapnel, would be a pisser. The plug came undone as I threw the box to the decks below. AK fire was sporadic as I heard Opie's rifle report loudly in contrast to the machineguns 500+ yards away. Where was the bigger artillery? How long does it take to target a huge battleship anyway? Had I tied up their radios that much by keying the handsets? No way.

I climbed down the ladders as the relatively light AK bullets clanked away at the skin of the ship. They almost seemed puny in comparison. My feet tripped and my vest caught on the rail as I went down two or three decks trying to reach the mortar control wires. The plug lay on the port side of the deck just behind one of the forward 5" gun turrets. DAMN! A second tank shell hit the deck high above. This round must have struck somewhere just below the first as they attempted to take out the bridge. Hot bits of steel rained down from the heights above. Parts of springs, shards of steel plate, and round wheels from valves bounced off the deck around me.

A tank round hit somewhere aft as they recognized many of the shots were coming from Opie's position. Another round hit, then another. The sounds were so intriguing from the tank shells. There were two distinct events. The first was an explosive bang, but as soon as it was over, you could hear the gong-like reverberation in the ship's armor. It was like you mixed the sound of a bass drum with a cymbal, weird.

I finally managed the grab the wire and made a dash between more green streaks of the heavy machinegun fire that resumed. More tank shells hit aft as I ran to the starboard side of the ship and relative safety. Once there, I re-connected the wires and found the toggle switch marked #1. With my finger on the switch the view towards highway 17 and the bridge caught my eye. There was a lone vehicle on the apex of the bridge facing our direction. Was that the Tactical Toyota?

Through the scope, the scene was slightly obscured from thin trees blocking my view. Who else could it be? The vehicle had its lights on as it rolled down the bridge gaining speed. Should I hit the flare now or wait till they pass? What would be the most beneficial to my men if it was them? It didn't matter in the long run. The only thing I knew was that I could shoot further and more accurately with more light. The toggle switch clicked and a slight thump could be heard from the rear deck.

I raced around to where the ladder led to the main deck and raced down it. The box could only go as far as the forward 5" turret on the starboard side. It lay by the steps as I ran to get into position just under the giant barrels of the 16" guns jutting from turret #2 on the bow. The whole area between the ship and the intersection was ablaze in light. A parachute slowed the decent of the flare from hundreds of feet above giving both me and my enemy giving me enough visibility to aim properly. The Thor's bipod slid up against the armor rail only a foot tall that semi-circled in front of the turret #2. I was in the zone. Bang, Bang, Bang, Bang, four targets dropped one right after the other.

My peripheral vision saw the truck's headlights cross the double lanes and head for the old battleship memorial parking lot. The old 16" display shells were visible against the headlights of the truck as it sped 60+ miles an hour from my right to my left through the lot. The minigun of the Tactical Toyota was clear, but I had no clue where they stole one of the Sandy's flags and draped it over the hood like that. Only crazy militia would think of something like that. I cheered, "Go getem guys!"

The funny thing was the Sandy's reaction to the Toyota blasting through the parking lot. They must have thought it was one of their crews being all heroic and trying to flank us snipers on the battleship. They were surprised when the truck passed the parking lot, turned right and headed for the Cape Fear Memorial Bridge. They couldn't figure out what in the world was going on.

I put the stock firmly in my shoulder and breathed carefully. These shots had to keep their attention on me and let the Tactical Toyota do its job. Bang, Bang, Bang, three more of their ranks fell as the Thor locked its bolt open on an empty magazine. With a fresh magazine loaded, they lost more people. Some of the hits were inconclusive while others were more obvious. I watched men fall left and right. Several of the billboards were on fire by then. More had fallen off their brackets and hung sideways with more holes than you could shake a stick at. I got under cover as I loaded another magazine and took a breath to calm myself. It was like shooting those little metal targets at an old-timey carnival. So far, the Sandys had no clue I was this far forward on the bow. Almost all of the shooting was from the bridge and aft.

About the time I thought my barrels cooled down enough, I heard an air raid siren way off to the northeast among another series of thumps and rumbles coming from the airport area. Our guys sure had fired things up in this sleepy little town. The flare was descending to the ground as I heard a "BRRRRRRRRRRRP!" from somewhere about a half a mile ahead. From my vantage point I could just make out a yellow wavy string leap from the lower shrubs as it arced upward to the bridge. A moment passed and I once again heard the BRRRRRRRRP sound as if someone had pulled a giant zipper across the sky. Several more times this happened as I watched in awe of the minigun at work.

The opportunity of the resumed darkness allowed me to scamper back to my box. Two mortars sped into the air on my command this time. Back under the turret, I worked my way through my last magazines of match 7.62 ammo that I had loaded. By the time the last two illumination rounds allowed darkness to once again have its hold, the Tactical Toyota sped through our parking lot heading back out to highway 17. There were Sandy troops making their way in our direction and I could only see them as the, now dark, Toyota came under their fire. Several of the Sandy's rounds skipped off the truck's light armor. Our men fired from the windows and bed as I watched.

The Thor was allowed to fall to the deck as I transitioned to the loaded M4. I fired the entire magazine at the men approaching the parking lot area. Although it was affective, the larger flash from the M4 gave away my shooting position. Every daggon Sandy in the place must have aimed at that bow. They shot everything they had and raked the thing to bits. The 20mm deck guns were hit by tank shells, the anchor chains shrugged off hit after hit. The wooden deck boards splintered with every round.

I ran aft to the safety of the superstructure. There my M4 was reloaded with a fresh magazine of SS109 green tip and the Thor was slung across my back. I continued aft as I ran through from turret to turret along the starboard side of the ship on the main deck in relative safety. Once, I looked aft across the river to see several fires burning in a couple of the buildings where I presumed the illumination mortars had landed earlier. Fire crews seemed to stand off as the firefight on the battleship raged. Nobody wanted to get near us until it was all over.

The bow was still under fire with more shells landing towards the bridge and CIC decks. They must have figured we had camped out there or something because they kept returning to those decks. The starboard side of the ship was almost peaceful in comparison. Hey, we had 50,000 tons of steel between us and the enemy. It was great!

As I approached the aft superstructure, Opie called down to me. "Huck, up here." He leaned over a quad 40mm gun emplacement and waved to me.

I climbed up the exterior rebar rungs and made my way to him as he sat crouched in safety. My body flopped down on the debris covered deck some twenty feet off the main deck overlooking the swamp and the whole starboard side of the ship. We were both exhausted. My M4 lay beside me and the Thor was propped against the steel protecting us.

Opie handed me his water bladder. "Here, take a drink."

For the first time since the shooting began I ached for water and rest. After a few gulps, I managed to pant, "Thanks."

Opie took it back and gulped some himself. "Well, if we wanted to make a name for ourselves, we did it tonight." He smiled through his camo face paint, showing his white teeth.

I chuckled among deep breaths, "How'd you like my speech?"

"Ha!" Opie chortled. "I thought you had lost your mind there for a minute, but it worked."

"Worked?" I asked.

"Yeah, those first three shot I made were on guys standing on top of their bunkers out in the open. They were yelling and waving their hands ready to duke it out."

I couldn't believe it. "Really?"

Opie gulped some more water and handed the bladder back to me. "How much longer are we gonna stick around?"

I looked down at my watch. "It's 22:30? No way!" It couldn't have been that late. Where did all that time go? I felt like we just started this little party.

This whole time Opie and I had been sitting, our hands were busy. I had gone through my empty magazines for the Thor and reloaded four of them. Opie had burned through almost all of his ammo for his rifle. That was a feat because he was using a bolt action and I was using a semi-automatic. I gave him the rest of my spare rounds from my vest. We wolfed down the MRE side items we had saved from earlier. The idea was to keep our energy level up for the escape. Well, to tell you the truth escape seemed pretty unlikely at that point. Sooner or later the Sandys would flank us and surround the ship. I don't think Opie really ever expected us to get off that ship either.

I loaded another magazine into the Thor and slung the M4.

Opie finished and said, "Follow me; I have a good spot for you."

I followed and we made our way back up to the top of the superstructure where we could see the intersection. The Sandys had ceased their haphazard frenzy of shooting up the bow. Almost every weapon was silent. The flares had long since burned out.

I whispered, "They were just on the other side of the parking lot when the Tactical Toyota went through."

Opie asked, "Did they make it out?" referring to the Toyota.

I looked over my shoulder to see around the aft smoke stack which loomed high above me. I could see the lights of the highway 17 bridge, but there was no sign of the Tactical Toyota. That was the best thing I saw. The worst thing I saw was three large trucks disgorging men in tan uniforms by the dozen.

"Targets, three dozen or more at the bridge. They are trying to get in behind us," I announced to Opie.

He turned briefly, looked, and went back to his rifle overlooking the parking lot. "There's 650 yards to the near side of the bridge. The far side is out of range."

I clicked my rifle's elevation turret another couple of minutes and set up for a shot at the men on the bridge. My breath slowed as I scanned the bridge under the street lights for a target of maximum value. Two men stood by the middle truck. One had a radio on the hood talking into the handset. He obviously thought he was far enough away to direct others from a safe distance. Wrong!

I pulled the stock of the Thor into my shoulder, knowing that I had only one shot and I had to make it count. The trigger resisted my finger's pressure, just like it was supposed to do right before it broke at a crisp two and half pounds. Boom! The round sped to its target at 2600 feet per second. I had adjusted for a slight left to right wind blowing about 2/3s of the way to my target and held left to compensate. It worked. The Sandy captain fell against the truck as his men scrambled for cover.

Opie began to hammer the Sandys in the parking lot as they crept closer to the ships' gangplank. I helped him as we eliminated a squad of men trying to flank around to get cover behind the gift shop. I changed magazines during a lull in the shooting and yelled to Opie over the din of rounds hitting the ship, "We have about 20 minutes before things get real interesting around here." I motioned to the Sandys and the trucks littering the bridge to the north.

Just then, Opie and I froze. Something had changed unexpectedly. It was dead quiet, not a sound of anyone firing at all. We looked at each other in disbelief. The Sandys appeared to be pulling back at a dead run.

Opie said in a hushed tone, "What the heck are they doing?"

The sound of a massive shell passing through the air over our heads, announced the Sandy's plan. The 155mm shell, or Soviet equivalent, landed 20 feet from the starboard bow off the main superstructure. Mud and water flew into the air caking the ship from the main deck up to the bridge. The hull made a gong type *"thwong"* kind of a sound.

Opie looked aft. "They must have another spotter crew on a rooftop on the other side of the river."

He scanned as another shell landed on the port side of the bow, decimating the old ramp that used to pipe off sewage and supply power to the ship during the tour days. The proximity of the rounds was too close to handle for long.

Opie called out, "Targets, white building, rooftop, about 10:30."

I turned and yelled, "How far?" Another shell landed fifty yards aft on the port side and shook the whole ship.

"Opie called out, "Just under 400."

No way, I thought. It has to be further than that. Opie fired. I saw a hit and called it, "Hit! Two more targets at least up there."

Opie cycled his bolt "I'm out." Those words cut through me like a knife.

I traded positions and fired at the men calling in the artillery. They were higher than me and had the length of the rooftop to hide. I changed magazines as Opie worked his M4 back to the intersection. He steadily made shot after shot even against the dark silhouettes.

Two more of the big rounds landed. One of them hit somewhere around the forward smoke stack sending huge chunks of metal in all directions.

I tapped Opie. "Let's get below decks." I emptied my last magazine between the intersection and the troops I figured would be making their way from the highway 17 bridge. We closed the superstructure hatch behind us and started through the maze of ladders and hallways we had opened earlier. Getting through the passageways was hard even without our packs. The Thor and Opie's Remington 700 kept getting hung up because they were full length rifles. With our flashlights we hurriedly made our way deeper and deeper below the decks looking for cover. Shells continued to pound the upper levels as we felt the thunderous explosions rock the hull. The USS North Carolina was taking a worse beating than when she fought in the Pacific.

We finally sat on the familiar engine room number four grating barely able to continue. By the light of a six volt flashlight, we discussed our options.

Opie looked up at the piping after a shell hit nearby, "They have the range now."

I emptied my pockets to see what I had left. All of our 7.62 match ammo was gone. Between us, we had four full magazines of 5.56 and two grenades. Somewhere in the mass confusion I must have lost the others. Luckily we had almost all of our pistol ammo. That was pretty much it, though. We had our knives and our wits, but not much else.

Opie looked down at his father's sniper rifle. "I will be damned if they are going to get Dad's rifle. I will chuck it over the side before that happens."

I thought about what he said and realized the Thor was a goner as well. I was not about to let them parade around holding my rifle over their heads, chanting like a bunch of school girls.

I looked to Opie, "Naw, they will just fish it out of the water." I looked around taking notice of the blackness below my feet. We were still a long way from the keel. The engine was a giant room in itself. "We will pull open a grate and stuff our rifles down into the bilge where they would never find them."

Opie looked downcast, accepting my words and pointing, "Over there."

We pried open a floor grate as an artillery round shook the whole compartment. Dust fell from the deck above as we skirted around to the darkest dankest hole we could find. In the dim light I popped the Thor's takedown pin and pulled the charging handle to the rear. The bolt fell into my hands. The metal was still warm. I held it up for Opie to see. "The heart of my rifle." Opie unlocked his bolt and pressed the release in front of the trigger, releasing his bolt. We both pocketed our bolts and hesitated briefly. We each were trying to think of any other way to save our rifles, but we were out of options.

We dropped our most prized possessions into the murkiness as shells rained down on the decks above.

Chapter 23
Artificial Reef

Opie looked at his watch as we stood there in the engine room. He commented rather glumly, "The Seals should have left by now. That is, *if* they got the barges underway."

I thought about that. "I didn't hear a lot of shooting by the bridge. Maybe they got away cleanly." My optimization knob was turned to full capacity.

Opie stated, "Well then, we better start to get out of here, just in case they didn't. We only have five hours before…"

"Yeah, the big boom. It's been on my mind," I told him. "The Sandys have the south and the intersection. North is covered by a company or more in the marshes. West is no good."

Opie said, "East is downtown Wilmington and the rest of their army."

"And the river," I added suggestively.

Opie looked concerned. "It is winter, Huck. We would freeze to death."

"Better than being shot," I said as I grabbed my M4 off the old engine console.

We hustled up to the galley under turret three with the flashlight leading the way. It took several minutes because we were traveling by a single light. Our spare batteries had either been used or were lost as we maneuvered around the ship trying to dodge bullets. By the time we made it to the heavily graffitied walls of the galley, the shells had stopped pounding the superstructure above. An eerie silence fell over the ship. Smoke wafted down through the tourist entrance because the covering that held the actual door on the main deck had been removed by a shell.

I marched forward. "They will be here in a few minutes at the most now that the artillery has stopped."

Opie said, "There is another square hatch aft." He pointed the way as we managed through the piles of junk. Some of the tour displays had been shaken to the point of falling over in heaps. The place actually looked worse than before and I didn't think that possible. We ran aft until we reached the broken displays of men in the 40s pressing uniforms on the ship's laundry. We searched the deck above for the hatch franticly, wanting to get off the ship before the Sandy's assault teams got on board.

Finally we found the hatch, but no ladder leading upward. We used the old generator, a relic painted for display, sitting underneath to use as a ladder. Opie and I worked the latches with all the might we could muster to get them open. Years of paint and crud made the hatch hard to release, but it finally gave way. Well, at least partially. A lock prevented the hatch from opening all the way. Worse yet, the lock was on the outside. With great effort, we managed to cut the lock off from the inside and forced the hatch up. What should have been complete darkness was flickering yellow light bouncing off the circular steel plates protecting the two aft 40mm gun emplacements. The crane stood between them as if untouched by any of the shelling.

Opie and I climbed out of the hatch into a scene of wreckage. From the stern, we stood between the 40mm guns looking forward. Wooden deck pieces burned in piles among the remains of the billboards. Wind blew slightly from the south as smoke rolled off the ship over the marshes. The superstructure was intact from our vantage point, but a lot of the 20mm and 40mm gun emplacements had been destroyed. In contrast, the turrets that housed the giant 16" guns were unscathed. One of the smoke stacks was partially collapsed. Otherwise, what remained of the decks not on fire, was littered with mounds of debris. It was a sight I don't think I will ever forget. We stood there in awe of the destruction on one hand and the extreme toughness of that ship on the other.

Opie grabbed my shoulder and pointed. "Here they come."

We could see troops approach from the parking lot as they entered the old gift shop. Kaboom! A bright flash was followed by smoke coming from the windows. They must have triggered the grenade inside. Shots rang out from AK47s in a flurry of anger.

Opie took a life-saver ring and orange preserver off a nearby hook which he tossed to the water below. I raised my M4 to cover him and realized that the time for shooting was over. The rifle's reports would signal the enemy that we were still alive after the bombardment. Opie climbed over the rail and handed me his rifle. With a giant step, he leapt off the stern and landed into the water with a splash. I took the bolts out of the M4s and chucked them into the marsh. My last grenade rested under our M4s with the pin pulled. That was my final present for the Sandys. Then I followed Opie into the water.

Cold is when you turn on the shower and forget to let it warm up. Freezing is when you jump into the Cape Fear River in freaking winter. It was a shock to the system as I gasped for air, barely able to surface. Opie and I emptied our pockets of everything we had left in order to stay afloat. The only exceptions were our M9s and knives. Everything else found the bottom of the river without hesitation.

We paddled out into the main current on top of our little life preservers trying to keep our brains from going into hypothermic shock. You just had to keep moving and not stop for anything. But it was near impossible to put the cold behind you. We had sweated for hours inside the warmth of the turret and ran around the ship for more than an hour dodging bullets in the fight. Cold was not a problem then. The instant my body hit the water I was chilled to the bone. Every second of contact with the water made my muscles tense. Our teeth chattered by the time we were 50 yards from the ship.

Shots could be heard off and on for the next ten minutes as the Sandys retook the North Carolina; or at least what was left of her. Opie and I paddled onward. We floated with the current and kept kicking our feet just to keep the blood flowing. What we hoped to find along the river we were not sure. The water was simply our last choice for an escape. Could we go ashore and try to steal a car? Not likely, since the whole area was on alert after our attack. Wilmington residents assigned to security littered the sidewalks among streetlamps at key intersections. The bridge loomed above us. Many of the bridge's lights were out as far as I could tell from my vantage point below. The higher portions of the towers pulsed red from their low flying aircraft beacons. We could hear voices from above as rescue crews attended to men that had been on guard at their posts when the Toyota shot them up. Opie and I looked up to see if anyone was watching for us; but we didn't see anyone. We couldn't do a thing about it, but we wanted to see, none the less.

No section of the bank looked inviting, but we were getting close to the point where we had to get out of the water. Even in the low light, Opie's faced looked pale blue. I couldn't feel my hands or feet due to the numbing cold. Opie stared straight ahead and locked his arm with mine. Otherwise, we may float away and not be able to stay together.

Opie stuttered, "CCan't ffeel mmy, lu-lu-leggs, Huck."

"We're getting out, Ope" I stammered back. But we were in the middle of the channel going with the flow of the current. How we would get out of the river was quickly becoming an insurmountable challenge. We had been in the water too long already.

"P-p-paddle," I ordered weakly.

We barely made ripples in the water some two or three hundred yards south of the bridge. The western bank was fuzzy. Lights were low and a dock seemed to be in that direction. It was really dark and my vision was not what it should have been. Maybe someone could find us and drag us out was my only thought. I was getting desperate. By that time I didn't care if it was the Sandys that found us. If we were to be shot, then, well, it was better than freezing to death anyway. Opie and I paddled with all our effort and managed to get within reach of a boat as we bumped into the stern with a slight bump.

The sounds of footsteps walking towards us, was like a foggy dream somewhere in the background in the recesses of my mind. My brain was a blur, nothing made sense. My body seemed detached and numb. I didn't feel the burning pain as I had before. The hands that lifted me were strange, unknown. I recognized the sounds of dripping water and everything else seemed to float away.

I don't know how much time passed before I realized a light shone in my eyes. I was sitting upright in a small control room from the look of lights shining from various gauges. I was covered in a warm blanket. A bright light came from a small flashlight being waved in front of me from eye to eye.

A voice said, "He'll be okay. I think we got him turned around."

Another voice responded, "I'll get another blanket and put it on the manifold."

I managed to stammer, "Where?" It was all I could do to get that out.

The first voice said, "Colonel, you are on the barge. Do you remember?"

"What?" My mind was still fuzzy. "Barge?"

"I'm the Lieutenant from Nemo's team; we pulled you out of the water before we left the dock." His voice was slow and methodical as if talking to a 3rd grader. I was processing, but slowly.

"Opie?" I asked.

The Lieutenant said, "He's okay, but he is still warming up." He switched out my blanket for a fresh warm one. It was heaven against my skin. My body seemed to turn back on a little more as each minute passed. I still felt like a Popsicle, though. Pain shot through my extremities at the sudden warming. As each minute passed, I found more and more scrapes and dings where stray bullet jackets had skinned me while on board the battleship. Somewhere I must have hit my knee because it was throbbing. Time passed as I sat there, feeling each portion of my body regain feeling.

I looked left and right to see where we were. The window of the wheelhouse was barely clear enough to see through. The center of the window had been hastily wiped with a shirt sleeve from the looks of it. The bank passed slowly on either side of the Cape Fear River. I turned to see if the bridge was close enough to see, but it was not.

"Where are we?" I asked with a little more strength in my voice.

The Lieutenant steered for a second and answered, "We are about two miles south of the bridge. We will be in position in another 2.5 miles if we make it."

"*If* we make it?" I repeated his statement with question.

"Well sir, this is the last barge. We were delayed getting off the dock because some maintenance guy decided to tear apart the whole ignition system to find our sabotage."

I wondered, "Everybody else get off okay?"

The Lieutenant steered without taking his eyes off the channel, "Yeah, we are boat crew five. Everybody else left over an hour ago as far as I know."

I remembered Nemo's lecture concerning the tide. "Are we going to make it that far south with the tide?"

The Lieutenant answered academically. "The tide is going out as we speak. That will cause some problems. It will make getting there, without running aground, nearly impossible in the dark. It will make the ditch easier though."

I managed to get to my feet and walked below to the crew cabin. Another Seal looked after Opie, who lay on a small bunk. Opie was still cold. He was thinner than me and looked pale, but alive.

The Seal turned and asked me, "You guys swam all the way from the battleship to us down at the dock?"

I answered, "Yeah. We didn't have much choice."

The Seal replaced Opie's blanket with a warm one from the engine manifold and reminisced, "I remember the first swims off of Coronado back in BUDS. The sun was shining and you thought, "Hey this is going to be great down here in Southern California." Then you get in the water and find out it is like swimming in a refrigerator. They kept us cold the whole time. Instructors sweated you on the beach and froze you in the water."

Opie managed to say, "I feel a little better. Less like the c-catch-of-the-d-day." His teeth still chattered under the warm blanket.

"How close were we to full hypothermia?" I asked.

The Seal looked back over his shoulder at me. "It was time for you two to get out of the water." He left it at that and did not clarify as he padded Opie's blanket.

The barge's engine chugged us along as we steamed south into more darkness. There were almost no visible lights to show on either side of the river. The further we got from Wilmington, the darker the river got. While steering with one hand, the Lieutenant donned a pair of NVGs and requested I turn out all the cabin lights. I must admit that the darkness concerned me because I couldn't even see the bow of the barge. All the running lights had been turned off. The cargo was a mystery that simply humped in a mass well above the barge's gunwales. It was like riding a giant log ride at an amusement park. Well, sort of. This was completely in the dark with people wanting to kill you at every turn. So, maybe not exactly like an amusement park; but you get the idea.

After another hour we found ourselves trying to put on our mostly dried uniforms that had been hanging over portions of the engine. It looked like a post-apocalyptic army surplus laundry mat in there. Opie was feeling better as he sipped some re-heated coffee from a tin cup. The stuff smelled like underbelly of yack soup rather than real coffee, though. We sat there around the engine as our bodies attempted to suck in all the heat the diesel motor could provide. It was right about then when we hit the sand bar.

Instantly, the barge groaned as those of us below lurched forward trying to brace ourselves. The bow had merely scraped a shallow sand bar on the edge of the river's deepest lane. Strange sounds of gears changing speed and props sent to full reverse, made us imagine all sorts of horrors. Opie and I absolutely hated the idea we might have to get back into the water. We would have rather taken a severe beating than freeze all over again.

The Lieutenant called down to us, "You guys get top side."

Opie and I ran up the few steps with our pistol belts in hand. They were the only possessions we had left. We must have looked concerned because the Lieutenant smiled and said, "It's okay for now. But you need to stay up here in case we run aground for good. The engine might blow a gasket if the props strike or we may take on water down there. I don't want you guys to get hurt."

The prospect of getting hurt seemed almost funny after dodging bullets all night aboard the North Carolina. Luckily our barge spun around as much as a lumbering hulk could there in the channel. The river's flow pushed us further downstream as the Lieutenant steered us back into deeper water. There was no sonar on that thing. I wondered how far it was to swim to the eastern shore.

Opie looked around at the deck. "Lieutenant, what happens after we ditch? What do you want us to do?"

The Lieutenant steered for a second then said, "I was planning on putting you two in the survival raft a few hundred yards before the ditch. We will blow the charges and swim to you once the motor section goes under water. Then we all paddle to the shore and see if we can link up with the coastal patrol boat."

I asked with a lump in my throat, "Will they still be there?"

He knew what I meant. They could not have possibly stayed back and risked everyone just to wait for us.

The Lieutenant said my fears aloud. "It all depends on their extraction. If they had to fight their way ashore after they ditched, they will meet us and anyone else that was late, at the secondary pickup."

"Where is the secondary pickup?" Opie asked.

The Lieutenant hesitated. "Further downstream. We will have to float for a bit to get there."

I could see the fear in Opie's eyes; I felt the same way. We had not fully recovered from hypothermia and the idea of getting back into the water was comparable to fighting a Grizzly bear. The other Seal helped our fears when he said, "We have a pilot's inflatable life raft you guys can use."

He motioned us to the deck behind the wheelhouse. A small bag lay there among other larger duffles. The smaller bag was ripped open and the contents unfolded. The Seal cranked the knob of an air tank attached to the raft's side as it hissed air into the expanding rubber. Once inflated, the raft looked sturdy enough to hold us both, but rather small. Opie toed the remaining bag beside him. "What's in here?"

The Seal look down and unzipped the bag, "This is my dry suit. The Lieutenant and I will put these on before we ditch."

The Lieutenant spoke from the wheelhouse to his teammate, "Go ahead and pull them out. Get yours on then come and take the wheel."

"Yes, sir," the Seal responded.

Opie and I watched as they climbed into the black dry suits in near darkness without so much as a word. They had done this before and they knew their business. With an MP5 strapped to his back, the Lieutenant announced, "We should be there in the next 20 minutes. Huck, you and Opie tie whatever you want to take with you to the raft. Everything left on this boat will be underwater pretty soon."

Opie and I scrounged for anything useful. Little trinkets were wrapped up in the blankets and tied off at the end just in case we had to make camp on a remote sand bar somewhere. In the back of my mind I was dreading the approaching 04:00 deadline. Even if we succeed, Nemo might have his finger on the trigger of the nuke. He might have reports that suggest our mission had failed and was preparing to blast the ports for sure. Had our teams been completely wiped out at the airport? Had the green shirts gotten one step ahead of us and tipped off the Sandys before our attack? How many of our team that hit the airport had survived? All these doubts circled through my mind as I packed.

Opie finished the knot of his rolled blanket. "Huck, thanks for taking me on this mission." He paused then spoke again, "No matter what, we made a difference tonight."

I clapped him on the shoulder and said, "You did great out there, Opie. Your dad would be proud of you." We didn't look at each other as we wiped wetness from our cheeks.

With that, we headed back up to the deck where we lashed the blankets to the sides of the raft. The Seal lowered the raft and helped Opie down to the little boat. I followed and we made the most of what little room the small raft offered. We didn't care how small it was. We were just glad to be out of the water. With a little push, the Seal sent us on our way.

Seeing the few lights of the wheelhouse pull ahead into the darkness was ominous to say the least. You could not help but feel utterly alone. Opie and I paddled backwards to separate us from the barge. Engine noises faded to the background as the barge disappeared into the darkness. Several minutes passed with no more than a sound. Opie and I waited, almost holding our breath to hear the demolition of the barge. It was another 10 minutes before a series of blasts sounded off down the river. There were no flashes of light as we expected. But the sounds of the barge's twisting steel were clear as we looked onward. There was a hiss of water rushing and swirling somewhere ahead of us. Opie and I paddled to the eastern side of the channel as best we could tell. According to instructions, I snapped a chem-light and tied it to the bow of our raft.

We sat in the raft and drifted with the tide and listened intently. Finally, after five minutes, there were sounds of life as a swimmer pair approached our raft. The Lieutenant said, "Pocket that light. We will use it later after we get to shore." Opie put the stick in his pocket and grinned as it shone through the material of his jacket. I hoped somebody was actually waiting for us on the beach.

The Lieutenant guided us south down the channel as he and the other Seal pushed our raft from behind. Opie and I paddled to increase our speed with the current. It was another 25 minutes or so when the Lieutenant said, "Head east, this should be the channel leading to Buzzard Bay." We paddled hard to port trying to keep the raft upright. More paddling led to a calmer section of water, but I was never more lost. I could have been in Kuwait for all I knew. After an agonizing trip, the Lieutenant beached us. Opie and I grabbed our gear and pulled our raft onto the sand as the Seals provided security. We sat there for several minutes scanning the darkness for any sign of a threat. It was quiet as the constant breeze whipped around us.

The Lieutenant crouched low as he came back to where Opie and I sat by the raft. "Put that light stick in the sand over here." He pointed to a spot overlooking the ocean. He then snapped two more sticks, but they gave no visible light. They must have been infrared. He spread each one about ten feet apart so they would be visible from the crashing waves beyond the sandy beach. We waited as the waves crashed over and over with monotony. For the first time in hours, I was tired. I watched as the Seal's dark form hustled down the beach and out of sight. For several minutes he was gone in search of something or other. What, I didn't know. Finally he came back to the Lieutenant and conferred out of our earshot. The pair came by us and waved for us to follow.

We traveled a few hundred yards south along the sand bar. A few small lights shone from Bald Head Island in the distance. Maybe it was from a lighthouse, but I don't know. We came to a halt as a team of four men came out of nowhere and approached us. The Lieutenant greeted them as Opie and I tried to keep our hearts from jumping out of our chests. Luckily for us, this was our ride out. With only a few whispers, we had their inflatable zodiac in the surf with the engine speeding us out into the ocean. The little boat bounced along on top of the waves as we increased speed the further we got from shore. Between the wind, speed, and water, there was no talking at anything less than a yell. I felt like somebody had kicked me in the balls as that little boat zipped across the waves.

I finally managed, "How far are we going?"

The Lieutenant yelled back over the din. "The boat will meet us about a mile that way."

I nodded in acknowledgement. Opie hung on to the side of the Zodiac trying to keep his slight form from bouncing over the side.

After a while, the Zodiac slowed slightly as we turned. Another minute went by as a fuzzy spot ahead shined a dim green light in our direction. Several seconds passed as the ramp of a small vessel became visible. By the time I recognized the purpose of the ramp, we hit it at what felt like full speed. Our Zodiac jutted upward out of the water as our engine fell silent. Two of the Seals were already out and on the deck before I realized we had not crashed. Several hands lifted me out of the Zodiac as I looked around to see several men working to stow the boat. Before I could speak, the boat's engine's roared to life as we sped off at a rate that I did not expect. Even though this boat was pretty good size, it could move!

Opie and I were ushered forward to an angled structure above the deck where an open hatch offered us cover from the sea spray outside. The hatch closed with a clunk behind us as Opie and I looked around in dim red light surrounded by a space full of various deck gear. It was really different to be on a fully operational boat. In contrast, the North Carolina had been a mostly-empty museum for decades.

Before we could even catch our breath or say a word, a hatch from below opened. A sailor locked the hatch open and said, "Colonel, the Captain would like a word." I followed him below as the sailor ushered us forward down a narrow hallway and towards another ladder leading upward. Several of the cabin doors below led off to various compartments and storage areas. The engines must have been at full throttle because the diesel power plants were humming along as they powered the ship through the waves.

I noticed a space forward that looked like bunks. From the glimpse I got, there were at a least a few of my Mayberry team and perhaps some of the special-forces men on board. The sailor opened the hatch for me as he motioned for Opie to head forward. I noticed Opie hesitate as he instinctively resisted leaving my side. I felt the same invisible tether because we had spent so much time and effort trying to stay close enough to cover each other. I nodded for him to go and said, "Check on the guys in there." Opie nodded and walked forward while I went up the ladder.

I walked through two adjacent small compartments where I found my way to the bridge. On the wall there was a plaque that read [PC-14 *Tornado*]. Several men turned to face me as I entered. The small bridge was packed with display screens of various colors. Some showed our relative position to the coast; there were displays of engine readouts, fuel estimates, and radar screens. That little ship had more technology than the Millennium Falcon. Small chairs sat behind equipment leaving very little room to move around the bridge. There were no interior lights other than dim red ones. Everybody's face looked freakish in the red hue. The Captain stepped over and shook my hand, "Good to meet you, Colonel. Call me Captain Gerard, welcome to the Tornado."

I shook his hand, not sure what to even talk about. "Captain, how successful were we tonight?" I asked with nothing better coming to mind.

He looked to me and said plainly, "We'll see."

A sailor called out from behind a display, "Sir, we are at point alpha."

The Captain turned briefly and responded, "Turn to 110 degrees, continue full speed."

The ship lurched to port as the helm responded almost immediately. The crew stood by, unconcerned as I held tightly to the wall for support. At least the waves were better the further we got out to sea. I looked up as several LED time monitors read 03:45. Captain Gerard saw my eyes scan the display and said, "We have some of your team below. I will send out a message to brace for impact in about 10 minutes. Can you get them ready?"

I felt like a kid at somebody else's house being told to wash the dishes. "Sure, Captain."

I went below, anxious to see my men. It was all I could think about anyway. How many were left? How many had been killed?

Were any missing? Would Nemo hit the big switch in the next ten minutes? Are we far enough away to escape the blast if he did?

The forward berth was filled with racks and lockers. Men were stacked in like cord wood. Several of the camouflaged men had bloodied bandages. Equipment lined the floor and weapons were stowed in racks. Everybody looked as though they had been put through the ringer. The Tornado's crew worked on the injured as I passed by each team member. Several of the men sat up to greet me and wish me well. Oh, how I wanted to debrief each one of them and see just how injured these men were. IVs were strung on racks and lines ran to the arms of the injured. Opie was talking with several men in the corner as I announced, "It will be 04:00 in a few minutes. The Captain is going to announce for us to brace for impact in case Nemo makes a big bang. Make sure all your gear is stowed or under your racks. Look for flashlights and safety equipment just in case."

The men took the time to secure the gear and grab whatever emergency equipment was on hand. The seconds ticked by as we hurried to get squared away. Several minutes passed before Captain Gerard came over the ship's communication system, "Brace for impact!" Then a series of electronic bells rang aloud in every space of the ship.

I think we all just about crapped ourselves at the beeps. Almost everyone winced and gritted their teeth as the prospect of a nuclear explosion ravaged our imaginations. Sweaty anxious minutes passed as we waited.

0:400 came and went without a boom.

We waited and listened, but there was no thunder. By 04:20 we figured Nemo was not going to nuke Wilmington. Nobody spoke as we listened. All we did was look from man to man.

The rear hatch opened and another sailor asked, "Colonel Huck, the Captain wants to meet with you in the ready room, sir." Everyone in the compartment took a deep breath of relief.

I dropped off the rack and followed the sailor down the hallway. On the way, the engine noise subdued as the Tornado slowed considerably. The sailor opened the hatch and I walked into the small room with only six chairs and a table. Inside there was the Lieutenant from the barge, Captain Gerard, the Lieutenant in charge of the dive teams, and another man I didn't know. The last man looked to be from intelligence because he was pulling out charts and maps from shelves around the room. I shook hands with the Lieutenants glad to see them again.

The Captain started, "Thanks for coming, Colonel. It looks like we are not going to hear an explosion this morning. *A least, not right away.*"

I sure didn't like that qualification.

The Captain continued, "Jones is here representing Intelligence. He has done a preliminary assessment and has some updates on a couple of things.

I asked out of order, "What do we know about Nemo? Did he escape?"

The Captain and Jones looked bewildered at my question.

The Lieutenant from the barge added, "Nemo is the code name he used with the militia."

The Captain and Jones looked like they did not appreciate the thought of Nemo's code name. Maybe it was the Navy in them that really did not appreciate less than proper Navy decorum.

Jones answered, "We don't have any word on Nemo."

I sat back, wondering about him and the two men I had assigned to guard the weapon.

Jones summarized with the chart showing the mouth of the Cape Fear River. "Based on the reports from the Lieutenants, I think they successfully blocked the river." Both Lieutenants sat back with their arms folded as the one in charge of the dive teams added, "We got all five barges stacked in the channel just south of the MOT docks."

The Captain asked, "Are you sure you stacked the barges and blocked the center channel of the river well enough to keep out deep draught ships?"

The Lieutenant from my barge added, "When we reached the first four barges, we were running pretty deep. I didn't blow the charges until the bow actually hit the other submerged objects. When I left, I could see the edge of my wheelhouse sticking out of the water. They couldn't use that channel even if a hurricane came through. We must have 40,000 tons of ore stacked up in that channel."

Jones and the Lieutenant conferred on the exact spot where the barges blocked the river based on their dead reckoning. Further discussions revealed that all the Seals were accounted for and had made it back to the Tornado. I asked, "What about the Army and militia from the airport mission?"

The Captain looked over to me as if he were being gracious just to respond, "We haven't had time to debrief all your men yet. Several of the wounded are in the aft berth being treated by the doctor."

I was getting irritated quickly at his seemingly arrogant attitude. It was my guess that this guy was typical military and did not realize non-military were fighting right beside him.

I tried to get a handle on my emotions as I chose to try a new subject. "How about the sub? Do we know if it engaged the Sandy fleet?"

This time the Captain was surprised. "How do you know of the submarine?" He was less than pleased.

The Lieutenant from the barge answered, "Captain Nemo thought the militia may be able to provide support if they knew all the details."

Captain Gerard was clearly put out by this information and looked to Jones.

I asked again, "What do we know about the sub?"

The Captain kept looking at his papers. "We got a report some six hours ago. All we know is that the fleet was engaged about 150 miles east of here."

My mouth got me in more trouble. "We don't know much, do we Captain?"

My comments inflamed the situation somewhat. The Captain proceeded to tell me how much he and his men risked to pick us up. Then he told me a whole litany of things that sounded like a whiney brat that had been made uncomfortable by the inconvenience of the war on his career. It was a lot of crap really. I was dismissed to go look after my men soon afterwards and I got up to leave.

The Captain didn't look up as he looked at my hip. "We don't carry weapons onboard ship. You and your men need to ground your weapons in the designated lockers."

I stared down at him until he looked up to me. I said, "Yeah, right Captain." I was too mad to respond with anything else for fear of shooting him on the spot. I was not about to be disarmed by anybody and I didn't care if it was his ship or not. The looks from the Lieutenants was spectacular. They realized how much we had contributed, but would not break their chain of command to say so. Perhaps they were more professional or just too used to the Navy way to argue. They both looked like they had just witnessed a suicide.

I left and marched aft to find the men being treated by the doctor. Inside a small room were three bunks set up for serious cases. Medics attended to each bunk where a mixture of my men and SF soldiers lay. Each man had serious gunshot wounds and burns. The chief medic ushered me right back out as he explained that I needed a mask to be in there.

In the hallway the medic said, "You need to let us get to work. Those men have some pretty severe burns. Anything can get their wounds infected."

I was annoyed, but understood. "How are they?"

The medic clarified, "You mean will they live? Yes, I think I can save them. But the next 24 hours is critical. Now I have to get back in there." From behind his mask he said, "I will send word later."

I slowly made my way forward to the berth. The men sat around a pot of some sort of stew, eating as if there was no tomorrow. For all I knew there might not be. I still had no idea of our general plan or where we were heading.

Opie handed me a bowl. "Colonel, how are the men in the doctor's cabin?"

I tried to eat as I remembered the men on the cots, "They are in pretty bad shape. The medics are working on them, though."

Just sitting made me tired. It had been one heck of a night. I looked around at the faces for the first time to see who had made it. Opie, Andy, and Barney from the Mayberry squad sat on the edges of bunks. Three of Arrow's men had made it as well as whoever lay on the bunks in the doctor's cabin. I didn't even know who was in there; none of them had looked familiar.

"Who is in the doctor's cabin?" I asked Opie.

His tone was that of fear. "Floyd and two of Arrow's men. Weren't you in there?"

I simply responded, "I couldn't recognize him. He was burned too badly." I put my bowl back on the little table, unable to eat.

I looked at one of Arrow's men from the airport operation. "What happened with you guys? How did you get here?"

The man I will call Sergeant Bravo was a lean fella about six feet tall. He had brown hair and was wiry for an SF soldier in my opinion. He was strong as an ox, but was not a guy that looked like a football player like you might expect. His uniform was ripped in several places and he had blood splattered all over him.

Sergeant Bravo was bandaged in two places as he spoke, "Colonel, your guys did great. I could not have asked for more from them. We busted up that airport just about as bad as we ever hoped. I didn't expect us to get out of there, we had them so stirred up."

The room fell silent as sailors and the rest of the men within range of his voice quieted to hear.

Bravo continued, "Our truck made our way to the airport without too much trouble. We used the suppressed M4s to take out a couple of the sentries; then we clipped the fence and drove through. The Sandys had no idea we were there. I guess the other truck must have had more trouble because they were to come in from the north at the same time. But, I didn't see them until later, after the shooting began."

By now the whole compartment was on the edge of their seats waiting to hear what had happened. Some of the sailors were curious to hear from Army guys instead of their normal diet of Seal stories.

Bravo continued, "We hit the fuel tank with the AT4 to start things off. It was a good two minutes before their security realized it was a militia attack. We took those two minutes to change position and blast all the small planes on the tarmac. The gunner on the MK19 pounded the little buildings that lined the maintenance row. Fires sprouted up all over the place as we changed position again. By then there were squad cars running all over the place in every direction. One of them even passed us, thinking we were his security backup because he never gave us a second look.

The second Hummy came in from the other side and did the same to the adjacent runway. It was one of their guys that took out the helicopter. They must have used the Stinger on it because that thing blew up like a Roman candle in mid-air." Several of the sailors chuckled at Bravo's hand motions demonstrating the explosion.

I looked at the Sergeant when he paused. "Do you know what happened to the Tactical Toyota? Did you see them after they took out the bridge?"

Sergeant Bravo thought for a second. "The last I saw them they were heading *towards* the bridge. I didn't even know if they had gotten there until you just said so."

Opie quickly recounted how the Toyota snuck through the lines and blasted the guard stations along the bridge with the minigun. But none of us saw the Toyota after they left the battleship parking lot. We had no idea if they made it out or was ambushed by Sandy security forces somewhere down the road.

Sergeant Bravo took another minute to tell how the Sandys closed off the northern escape routes and blocked the humvees from leaving the airport.

Then he said something we did not expect. "Boy you guys in truck #1 really helped us out there on the northern flank there at the end. The Sandys had us pinned down just when you hit them from the road. If it weren't for you, none of us would have made it to the beach."

The other two men from Arrow's team sat there with Barney between them. All three had been from truck #1 and looked at Bravo with utter confusion.

Barney sat there and rubbed his blackened forehead thinking, "What do you mean from the road? We never got all the way up to the road."

Bravo looked incredulous, "You know, about ten minutes after you took out the helicopter. The northern side of the fence between the guard houses, come on!" He was agitated at the confused looks he was getting.

Arrow's man beside Barney looked at Barney and then at Bravo. "Dude, we never made it all the way up there. After the helicopter, we ducked between the hangers right there in all that fire on the south side. We were running from hanger to hanger after our truck got hit."

Bravo sat there, clearly remembering the firefight. "Well, whoever it was, hit the Sandys just when they were about to send us to hell. *Somebody* saved us."

I said out loud, "We had some help tonight, but I have no idea who. Opie and I were down by the battleship and never got close to the airport. Remind me to give them a medal if we ever find them." The room fell silent as we considered just who had engaged the Sandys on their own. Could it be 2nd militia that just happened along? Could it be the Toyota crew as it headed north? Bravo didn't think so, but it was a mystery we had no answers to. That was the fog of war though. You never know everything.

I asked the guys, "How did you get on the Tornado? You were supposed to head northwest after the attack."

Bravo responded, "The Navy Lieutenant told us how to meet up with extraction teams that were set up to support the dive teams in case they had to divert. Luckily for us they saw what was going on and held the boats up for us."

As for the mission to damage the airport, both trucks were destroyed. Anyone not on the boat was presumed killed or captured. As for Nemo and my men covering him, we had no clue.

Bravo commented, "You guys must have got them really pissed off down there at the battleship. After they shot up our trucks, they sent a couple of troop trucks filled with security your way. I gotta tell you Colonel; I am surprised to be talking with you. We didn't expect to ever see *you* two again."

Opie said, "I didn't expect we would ever get off the ship either. They threw everything at us but the kitchen sink."

I reviewed out loud to make sure I knew. "Me, Opie, Andy, Barney and Bravo, are okay for the most part. Floyd is in the doctor's cabin with two of Arrow's men. Everybody else, Nemo, T-Rex, Shady, all the guys from the Toyota, are either missing or we have no information on their whereabouts."

Bravo spoke up, "Otis and Howard are dead. I saw Otis get hit in the chest and Howard was in the second truck when it went up."

Opie bowed his head at the news and held his hands over his face. The news of their deaths was hard for him to take. It was hard for me too, but I did not know them as well as he did.

We were shocked to our core. The room fell silent as Andy and Barney hugged Opie. There was not a dry eye in the room. Even hard fighters like Bravo shed a tear at the grief felt by the militia. Our team deaths hit us hard.

I left the berth and walked topside. Once outside I saw the sun had come up over the horizon. The Tornado cruised along at a manageable rate with little spray coming over the bow. Two large cylindrical objects were covered in tarps and lashed to the deck. I stood with my back against the angled bulkhead as several sailors went about their work. My mind raced at the events of the last 24 hours. I had always expected to have losses on this mission, but I never expected to be standing there with salt spray hitting me on the face without a clue as to where half of my people were.

The Lieutenant from the barge walked up and leaned on the angled superstructure beside me. He had his hands in his pockets and kept looking forward to the open sea as he spoke. "The man you called Floyd just passed away."

The Tornado's engines droned on with my emotions hammering my chest. How many more would be lost? How much more could somebody take?

We sat there for several minutes looking at the dawn before I asked, "So, what are we doing now?" I motioned to the objects under the tarps on the deck.

The Lieutenant responded, "These are MK48 ADCAP torpedoes. We have the ability to lower these in the water and launch them from ships like these Cyclone class coastal boats. The MK 48 has about 20 miles of wire that allow you to steer the torpedo until you tell it to go hunt for itself. It's our last ditch effort to take out a large ship."

I surmised, "So, we are going to try a long range torpedo hit on the Sandy fleet then?" The idea seemed a little risky considering they may be on high alert from the sub attack that we hoped had taken place. But again, who knew if the sub had hit the fleet? I hated not knowing what was going on!

The Lieutenant saw my frustration and said, "The Captain knows we are only one ship, but he feels it is up to us to find out just what the Sandy fleet intends to do from here if Wilmington is all hosed up. We may end up traveling south to block Charleston in case they divert down there."

I thought for a second. "We have that kind of range?"

The Lieutenant said, "Oh yeah, this ship can do transatlantic trips if we keep under 12 knots."

Great, I thought. We could end up just about freakin anywhere. I shook my head, exasperated at the idea of ending up in another state or at the bottom of the sea. We were only one coastal patrol boat for Pete's sake. I was tired and more than a little on edge to say the least. That may have been one of the largest understatements of all times. Yet the seas spray stung my face and the engines hummed along, unaware at my utter frustration.

The Lieutenant saw my face contorted in anger and tried to assuage my emotions. "Huck, if your objective was to change the course of this war last night, you may have done it. There has been a shift of power throughout the state in the last few days. The green shirts and Sandys are all but shooting at each other. The green shirt army is bottled up there in Wytheville. And the people don't dare leave their little fortified townships while the militia owns all the rural areas. The Sandys in the state are just as frustrated because their big invasion fleet cannot use Wilmington as their intended port at all. Heck, their fleet might be wrecked for all we know. This may be the turning point in the war."

I thought about his words, then asked, "Any word from the operation in Wytheville? Are we able to pick up radio signals from up there?"

The Lieutenant pulled a stack of papers from his pocket in a clear binder and handed them to me. Without looking me in the eyes he said, "Here is all we have right now. All we know is that it's a real battle up there."

I looked at the stack of papers as the Lieutenant left me to read them alone on deck. It was my bet that it was his initial intention to find me up here alone so the Captain wouldn't know. My heart jumped double time again as I rifled through pages of partial radio intercepts. Most of it was code that I at least sort of recognized. Since we changed terms/codes for every operation, it was hard to follow the pattern exactly as units were talking to each other. Their locations were a complete mystery because they were based on pre-designated points with a reference to those points.

Names of companies were new. "Units proceeding to point Delta two miles south of junction 21. Hammerhead group, Alpha-Delta." There were more transcripts of commanders ordering supplies, personnel requests, other bits of crap that you normally get in large formations of people. Most of it was garbled and confused until I read the last page.

There were a lot of codes used, but I translated them to mean:

"Command post Charlie 13 compromised. Razorback confirmed. Send urgent 3rd batt. Intel, list of MIA as follows:

Captain Spartan: group 51
Instructor First Class: Bo
Operations Officer: FRED.........

The End

Watch for Volume Four "Border State"

Enjoy Other Fine Books from Righter Publishing Company

Thrillers, detective stories, short story collections, children's books, inspirational works, poetry collections, family histories, science fiction, romance, literary fiction, local histories, personal memoirs and self-help.

Go to www.righterbooks.com

Made in the USA
Charleston, SC
04 December 2016